White Elephant

White Elephant

A Novel

Julie Langsdorf

An Imprint of HarperCollinsPublishers

HarperCollins books may be purchased for educational, business, or sales promotional use. For information, please e-mail the Special Markets Department at SPsales@harpercollins.com.

FIRST EDITION

Designed by Renata De Oliveira

Library of Congress Cataloging-in-Publication Data

Names: Langsdorf, Julie, author.
Title: White elephant : a novel / by Julie Langsdorf.
Description: First edition. | New York, NY : Ecco, [2019]
Identifiers: LCCN 2018022061 (print) | LCCN 2018024191 (ebook)
      | ISBN 9780062857774 (ebook) | ISBN 9780062857750
      (hardcover)
Subjects: | GSAFD: Humorous fiction.
Classification: LCC PS3612.A5847 (ebook) | LCC PS3612.A5847 W48
      2019 (print) | DDC 813/.6—dc23
LC record available at https://lccn.loc.gov/2018022061

19 20 21 22 23   LSC   10 9 8 7 6 5 4 3 2 1

In memory of my father, Roger W. Langsdorf, whose smile, great laugh, and never-ending belief in me continue to guide me through the rough spots.

For my children, Ethan and Sylvie.

1

Allison Miller lay in bed in the dim light of early morning thinking about sex. It was the hammering on the new house being built next door that was responsible, the rhythmic pound, pound, pounding that ought to have chipped away at any nascent amorous thoughts instead of inspiring them. She slid her hand across the sheet, touching her husband Ted's thigh, but it was clear from the set of his mouth that sex was not in the offing this morning.

"Do you know what time it is, Al?"

The question was rhetorical. Their digital clock was of the large-numeral variety, designed for people like them, in their forties, eyes just beginning to go.

"We hardly need the alarm clock anymore, Cox is so loud," Ted said. The revving of a chain saw made him leap out of bed as if stung. He opened the window—with effort. The Millers' house was old and its parts had settled.

They'd lost the battle for the trees. Ted couldn't accept it. Nick Cox, neighbor and builder, had been given the go-ahead to cut down more trees on the property next door. The town only had jurisdiction over trees that were twenty inches in diameter or more. There were a surprising number of these junior, cut-down-able-size trees on Cox's property, a small forest that had sprung up over the years—trees not strong enough for climbing or genetically programmed to offer fruit or flowers, but still welcome for providing a little buffer of green between the Millers and the adjacent property.

Allison watched Ted with fond familiarity, the gentle curve of his rear end and the rush of red in his neck from the effort of opening the window. She waited for him to yell, to open his mouth and to really let loose. He'd threatened so many times.

She imagined Nick Cox in his jeans and hard hat, his blue eyes sparking as he yelled back. She pictured the two of them engaging in a twenty-first-century duel, fought across the yards, a battle of words over the fortress Nick was building to their left, a four-story monolith complete with battlements and a double front door that begged for attending knights in armor. It was even bigger than the faux stone castle he'd built to the right, with its many turrets and spires, where Nick, his wife, Kaye, and their two pretty blond children lived. One half-expected to see fireworks shooting into the sky above the house—if one could see the sky above from inside the Millers', which one no longer could. Allison and Ted's little house was wedged between the two, a pebble amid boulders.

In the meantime Tunlaw Place was in disarray, the air tinged with the stench of diesel. A construction truck and a dumpster were parked along the curb, along with Nick's little yellow bulldozer, which looked like a brightly painted toy.

Allison closed her eyes and stretched her arms and legs toward all four corners of the bed imagining that she—not the neighborhood—was the one at stake, she the damsel in distress, she the one for whom Ted would slay Nick Cox. Or vice versa. The winner would bed her. She was ready to make the sacrifice.

Ted stood at the window, on the verge of shouting. Allison waited, excited at the prospect. Today, it was finally going to happen. Today, blood would be spilled. She took a deep breath, filling her lungs, waiting, waiting—but Ted seemed to think better of it. He slammed the window shut and stomped off to the shower.

The alarm beeped then, an unrelenting tone that increased in volume until Allison silenced it with the flat of her palm. She set off to face the last day of August. A day that was neither summer nor fall. A day neither here nor there. A day that promised to be nothing more than betwixt and between—just like she was, Allison thought. Just like her.

JILLIAN MILLER SLOGGED HER WAY THROUGH HER CEREAL, HOPING she'd finish before her dull stomachache went full-blown. She chewed dutifully, her eyes on the leprechaun on the cereal box. She'd slipped the box into the cart on a recent trip to the supermarket. Her mother preferred organic products—brown rice, brown eggs, thin brown paper towels that dissolved in your hands.

Jillian had hoped there would be a good-luck charm inside the cereal box, but after digging around she came up with nothing more than a powdery hand and arm. No prize to put in the shoe box under her bed amid the other tokens she'd collected over the years: fortunes from fortune cookies, found pennies, rabbits' feet— until she realized they were the real feet of real rabbits. They hadn't helped so far, but you never knew when good luck might kick in.

Jillian was about to give the rest of her cereal to their dog Candy, a shaggy dachshund mix, when her mother came downstairs singing a cowboy love song. Her mother had been cast as the lead in the town production of *Annie Get Your Gun*. The thought of her skipping around in a little skirt and cowboy boots in front of everyone made Jillian want to die.

"The hammering wake you, hon?" her mother said. "It's like living in a war zone."

Jillian shrugged. Who knew if she even really slept at night? She always woke up tired, her worries buzzing around her head like the moons of Jupiter: *homework, grades, Mark Strauss, bad hair, terrorism, school shooters, racial profiling, global warming, college, police brutality, boobs, sex, death.* She hoisted up her backpack, so heavy she had to walk bent over. All the kids did. They were like overworked elves, crushed by the loads they had to carry.

"Sure I can't get you one with wheels? They have some awfully cute ones."

"Mom. Please." She shook her head, hot with embarrassment.

"Don't forget the soccer game this afternoon. Do you have your uniform and shin guards?"

"I'm not *three!*" Jillian dumped her backpack to the floor with a thud, and ran upstairs to get them. She stuffed them into her backpack and took off out the back door.

Once upon a time—last year, when she was in sixth grade—she and her best friend, Sofia, walked to school together with their matching purple backpacks. Now she was nearly thirteen and purple was a stupid color, but her parents wouldn't buy her a new one because her old one wasn't worn out. And worse even than that: Sofia had moved to Paris, leaving Jillian all alone with the idiots at the middle school. Jillian skirted the dumpster and the guy with the yellow hard hat who always greeted her with a creepy, "Good morning, young lady," and headed down the street.

She distracted herself by naming the Sears houses she could see: the Glyndon, the Hazelton. If she named all of the house models correctly on her way to school, she would have an okay day. She'd learned the names last spring, when she made a model of the town for her final social studies project. She'd stuck to the houses built before World War II. It was weird to think that in olden times you could order a house as a kit from a catalog. She imagined what would happen if you could order a house online. It would probably arrive by drone two days later, possibly crushing an evil witch or two when it landed.

It wasn't even September yet, but her school supplies had already lost their new-school-year smell. If she ran the world, she'd make it illegal to start classes before Labor Day. It was so hot. Was it hotter this year? Was it global warming? Why didn't anyone care?

The Coxes' SUV idled in the driveway next door, Mr. Cox behind the wheel, eyes on his phone. Lindy sat in the passenger seat, her blond mane glowing through the window. She looked at Jillian with no expression at all, as though Jillian were a fence post.

Jillian had had hopes at the end of fifth grade, when she learned that a girl her age was moving in next door, but it was obvious right away that she and Lindy would never be friends. Lindy liked popular girls. It was like she waved a magic wand at someone—Katie Brown, who had a pool; or Liz Godwin, who wore mascara—and suddenly they'd be best friends. They'd walk down the hall laughing loudly together and eat lunch side by side. Then, just as suddenly, the magic would wear off. Lindy would roll her eyes when anyone mentioned the girl's name. "She sleeps with a night-light," she'd say, or more famously, "She has sex fantasies about the janitor." Lindy was tall for seventh grade. There were rumors she'd been held back.

The Starlight, the Katonah. Jillian named houses while she waited for Mr. Cox to back out. The Rodessa.

Why didn't they just go? Were they secretly laughing at her? At her yellow pharmacy flip-flops? At her stupid hair? If they ran over her, her parents would probably move away so they wouldn't have to live with the memories. Then Mr. Cox would buy their house, knock it down, and build another big one on their block.

She was about to close her eyes and just make a run for it when Mr. Cox backed into the road and sped away, spraying construction dirt on her. Jillian pressed her teeth into her lower lip, the tears pricking at her eyes. The Arcadia. The Hollywood.

TED MILLER SAT AT HIS DESK AT THE FOGGY BOTTOM UNIVERSITY alumni magazine office editing an article about the championship-winning basketball team of 1962.

"Once they called him 'Hoops.' Now they call him 'Pops.' These days, you're more likely to see him at the food court than on the basketball court."

It was impossible to concentrate on a guy called Hoops or Pops when Ted's head kept filling with images of Nick Cox grinning at him through the leaves of their red maple. Ted had planted the tree for Jillian soon after she was born. He'd chosen it for the color its leaves would turn in fall, imagining the sun shining through the redness—a soft, rosy light under which his little daughter would play, followed, years later, by her own children. Ted would be the grandfather then, the old man puttering around the garden. He had been telling Jillian about that tree from the time she was little. She was bored with the story now, but Ted's brother, Terrance, still liked to hear it.

"Once they called him 'Hoops.'"

Ted skipped to the "class notes" section, where alums wrote in to brag about their lives: "Carlton and I and our seven children (You heard that right, kids—number seven appeared on the scene in February!) spent the summer in Bellagio . . ." "Win just sold his biotech firm and retired at the ripe old age of thirty-three . . ."

"Caroline, whose candidacy for governor . . ." He mangled a paper clip as he read.

Ted had never sent in a class note, not even to announce that he and fellow Foggy Bott-iam Allison Cole were engaged to be married, which was the kind of thing that gave alums heart palpitations.

Ted had only had one girlfriend before he met Allison: Margie Kastanienbaum, from Pittsburgh, a pert biology major he'd met in his Philosophy and Religion class freshman year. When he told Margie he loved her after they had sex for the first time, she laughed out loud, thus squelching his plans to give her a pre-engagement ring, to be replaced by a real diamond upon graduation.

There was no further sex for Ted the rest of freshman year. Nor sophomore or junior. He didn't really mind. Sex, in Ted's mind, was equivalent with pressure. Pressure to perform. Pressure to please. He'd grown all but indifferent to it in recent years, which was normal as you got older, he supposed. He made a better older man than a younger one, always had—opting to go home weekends to do laundry instead of attending frat parties, choosing the spot on the bunk bed with his brother instead of the sliver of a twin bed in a girl's dorm room.

Then, senior year, he moved to the group house on 39th Street and everything changed. His room was on the first floor, and Allison's directly above. She was not just the only girl in the house, but his dream girl. She was petite, with curly auburn hair, and eyes that went from green to gray to blue—sometimes during a single conversation. Allison always had time to talk, and sometimes invited Ted along when she roamed the city, taking photographs. She took in strays, from dogs, to cats, to humans, offering them all a home and warm meals, and, for the humans, symptom-tailored herbal teas when they were under the weather. She was like Wendy in *Peter Pan*. All five of the guys in the house were in love with her.

Unfortunately so was her boyfriend, Gary Holloway—why, the name alone! It sounded like the name of a used-car salesman, and he acted like one, offering what he seemed to think was a charming smile and smooth remarks, and little else by way of compensation for living in Allison's room. Gary Holloway was always there. Was he even a student? What did he do except screw Allison? Which he did a lot. The wooden floors were squeaky at the house on 39th Street, which meant Ted heard everything that happened upstairs. This was a torment the first few months— but it gave him the advantage the night Gary Holloway dumped Allison after a loud and ugly fight. Ted suffered through several hours of her unrelenting sobs before he knocked on Allison's door, opting to console his pretty housemate over getting the sleep he needed for a history test. He'd failed the test, but he'd gotten the girl. He still couldn't believe it. It was a feat worthy of his fictional brother, Thomas—a third, more confident Miller sibling whom he and his twin, Terrance, had invented as children. Thomas was the charismatic one, the success. Thomas was the brother with balls.

What would Thomas do? he and Terrance sometimes asked each other, still. He asked himself the question now.

Thomas wouldn't put up with Nick Cox's wanton destruction of Willard Park. He would have seen to it that the White Elephant was never built. At four stories, Nick Cox's latest abomination rose high above all the other houses in Willard Park, casting a shadow over the Millers' home. It was painted bright white and had been sitting on the market for months—hence the nickname, which Ted had come up with himself. It had caught on, he'd been pleased to learn, but that was the only thing about it that pleased him. Ted threw the paper clip, his mood having slipped from brown to black. It pinged off the door frame and landed with a tap on the floor. The tower bell gonged the half hour. Eleven thirty. Close enough. He took the stairs two at a time.

Ted unlocked his bicycle, donned his yellow helmet and vest, and rode through the iron campus gate, bumping down the cobblestone street. He picked up two cans of soda and a package of Oreos from the convenience store, continuing down the block to the nursing home.

Ted kept his head low as he walked by the nursing home supervisor's office—Dana had left three messages on his phone this week, none of which Ted had returned. He nodded at the gray heads in wheelchairs or standing, propped up by walkers, in the fluorescent-lit halls and common areas. It was nearly time for lunch and the steamy, overboiled string bean smell rose over the tang of ammonia.

Terrance was in the Entertainment Lounge, standing between the blue vinyl couch and the television, newsboy cap on head, mop in hand. He smiled at Ted the way Jillian used to when Ted came home from work, the way their dog, Candy, did before she lost her heart to the Coxes' German shepherd. Terrance removed an earbud from one ear. "Supertramp," he called out, his voice loud.

Terrance listened to music on his phone during work, a deal they had worked out with Dana to keep his loquaciousness under control. Terrance had received warning upon warning for hanging out in residents' rooms to chat, forgetting to mop and dust and water plants. He'd nearly lost the nursing home job last winter, when he opened an old lady's window one evening before he left work. The temperature in her room dropped to the midthirties overnight; the woman, feverish, had been rushed to the hospital in the morning.

"But she told me to," Terrance told Dana at the meeting the next day. Ted sat beside him the way their father had in similar situations at school and work for years.

"If I told you to walk into traffic, would you? Just because I told you to?" Dana said.

Terrance looked to Ted. Ted had shaken his head no. Terrance had shaken his head no, too, but he looked unconvinced.

"Check it out, Teddy." Terrance offered an earbud.

"That's okay, pal."

Terrance let the earbud dangle, keeping the other one in his ear. "It's a code orange today, Teddy. Moderately bad air. That was on the Weather Channel app, Ted. Catch!" He threw a wadded piece of paper at him. Ted threw it back. "I caught a ball at the Senators game that time, remember?"

"Sure do."

"Frank Howard was number nine. Until 1968, Ted."

"That's right."

"He was the only player ever to hit a fair ball out of Yankee Stadium."

"I thought it was a foul."

"Bobby Murcer said it was fair."

"Then it was fair."

"Pow! Remember when we played army?"

Ted smiled, thinking of long-ago summer days playing at the Willard Park creek. He and Terrance used to dig trenches and shoot stick guns, using metal dog bowls for helmets.

"We're responsible carpenters, you and me," Terrance said.

"Yep."

"Dad said."

Ted nodded. The summer they were ten, the boys and their father built a fort in their backyard, a months-long project that

consumed every long, light-filled evening. It involved lessons in
sawing and sanding and the wearing of safety goggles that slipped
down their faces as they worked. Their father had entrusted them
with the combination to the toolshed lock only when he was convinced they were "responsible carpenters," an honor that ranked
up there with "Eagle Scout" in Terrance's mind.

Their father had been an accountant for the IRS, their mother
a housewife. Ordinary people could afford Willard Park then—
teachers, government workers, hippies. That was the kind of people
Ted still wanted to live among. Normal people, who did for themselves and for others instead of hiring everything out to strangers.
People who believed in community. Soon the neighborhood would
be all power brokers who pulled into their garages at night and
drove off again in the morning. It would become a bedroom community as economically homogenous as it had been ethnically
homogenous in the 1950s.

Lucy's family had been the first black family to move to Willard Park in 1959, before Ted was born. They bought the old
Willard farmhouse and turned it into a café, naming it after their
little daughter, who would later turn it from an ordinary sandwich place into an institution. The town had welcomed the family
at a time when many Washington-area communities were still
restricted, and diversity increased at a steady pace. These days
Willard Park was a mixture of colors and nationalities, religions
and sexual orientations. That made Ted feel proud.

"What's wrong, Teddy?"

"Nothing, Terr. I'm good." Ted spread out two paper napkins
on the coffee table and handed Terrance a soda.

"Only *you* can prevent forest fires, Ted." Terrance pointed at him.

Ted pointed back. He studied his brother's mild, sweet face.
Terrance was balder than Ted and a good thirty pounds heavier. He

was like a distortion of Ted, what he would have been like if there had been complications at his own birth.

"I went on a date last night." Terrance put his hand up for a high five.

His hand was warm. "With whom?"

"A girl. She's from Free to Be Me." Free to Be Me was Terrance's social group. It met once a month for pizza or bowling.

"Good for you, pal."

Terrance closed his eyes. "Bay City Rollers," he said.

The nursing home wasn't a bad place to work. There were pots of flowers and a shaded patio. The people were kind, for the most part. And yet, Ted felt guilty. He was the son who had it all: a comfortable job, a wife and daughter, and the family home. Terrance lived in a group home with three other disabled men and spent his days cleaning up after old people. He'd worked there for twenty years—longer than Ted had ever done anything.

Routine worked for Terrance, Ted reminded himself. Terrance had practically had to be medicated after Coke changed its recipe in the 1980s, and he'd gotten so worked up when Giant closed its in-store bakery that the manager called security to remove him from the store. Ted had to walk him over to the bakery next door for a couple of mornings, until he got used to buying his morning muffin there every day instead.

Ted's dream—a small one, he knew, but a dream nonetheless—was to keep Willard Park the homey way it had been when he and Terrance were growing up, to make the town a constant his brother could count on in an ever-changing world.

"Want to see her picture?" Terrance said, eyes popping open.

"Whose?" He wiped mayonnaise off Terrance's chin.

"My girlfriend's."

"Sure. Let me see."

Terrance took out a picture that had obviously been torn from a magazine, of a model with heavily lidded eyes and sunken cheeks. "We're going to New York City. We're going to stay in a hotel and drink Gatorade."

Ted looked at Terrance. "This is from a magazine, Terr."

Terrance smiled.

"She's a supermodel. You know that, right? Not your girlfriend?"

Terrance put up his hand for another high five. "Got you that time, bro."

Ted laughed.

Terrance pointed his finger in the air a few times, then toward the ground. Disco moves. "Bee Gees," he said. "I'm John Travolta."

Ted took the offered earbud this time, singing along in a falsetto voice, his mood having turned from black, to gray, to the warm yellow of the sun.

A SOLITARY PORCH SWING: *CLICK.* A MAILBOX PAINTED TO LOOK LIKE the Cape Cod behind it: *click.* A garden gate with a welcome sign on it. The bell at the top of the town hall. The fishpond shimmering with goldfish. *Click, click, click.* The lighting was wonderful, the sky a rich autumn blue in spite of the summery heat this morning.

Allison saw the town differently when she walked with her camera—not as expanses of green or copses of trees or even houses in their entirety, but as tiny slices of the canvas that was Willard Park: the first golden leaf after summer. The autumn-toned hand-painted sign above Lucy's Café. *Click, click.* It was different shooting photos with a real camera, using lenses rather than snapping away with a phone. There was a weight to it beyond the physical; it endowed her with a sense of responsibility to herself, and to the town.

She and Ted had lived in Willard Park for nearly fourteen years, ever since the winter Ted's mother died, followed, shortly thereafter, by his father. Ted's announcement that his parents left him the house led to one of the first serious arguments of their marriage. They discussed selling it ("You're joking. Tell me you're joking, Al.") or renting it out ("to strangers?"), but sentimentality and practicality had won out in the end ("no mortgage!"). They'd let the lease on their Dupont Circle apartment lapse. The lawn-mower, the Volvo, and the baby soon followed. So much for the year backpacking around Europe, a plan Ted had agreed to only grudgingly anyway.

Allison eyed the farmers' market, snapping a shot of the wooden sign that advertised organic apples: *click;* a pyramid of homemade jams, a row of herbs in clay pots: *click, click.* She scanned a table full of brightly colored plastic toys—interlopers amid the artisan goods. Kaye Cox, toes polished in her high-heeled sandals, was handing over her credit card in exchange for a toy car. She waved when she saw Allison.

Allison smiled and waved back, then put the camera to her eye and zoomed in on a tree: *click, click, click.*

Allison wanted to like Kaye Cox. There was nothing wrong with her, really. So she was a little highlighted and made up for Willard Park—those were forgivable offenses. Allison should have stopped by to welcome them with brownies when they moved in a year and a half before, only she'd been so angry with them for building a castle on their block.

She and the other neighbors might have forgiven them the sin of bad taste with time, but as the months wore on, the Coxes contin-ued to disobey the unspoken rules of the neighborhood. They didn't compost. They had pesticides sprayed on their grass. They didn't join Friends of the Willard Park Children's Library. They didn't even recycle.

Last spring Kaye had joined the town Beautification Committee, which seemed promising, but she immediately proposed banning fruit- or vegetable-bearing plants in excess of four feet—a pointed attack on Lucy, who grew corn and sunflowers in back of the café. The Coxes were like foreign visitors who had not read up on the local customs.

Allison climbed the porch steps and opened the café's screen door. It was cooler inside the white clapboard house; the wooden floorboards were wide, the walls painted a buttery yellow. The café smelled like the lemon candles that burned on every table. Lucy stood behind the counter blending a drink, her long gray hair in dozens of braids that spread over her shoulders like lovely silvery fish. She wore a yellow LUCY's apron slung over an orange tank top.

The café was known for its lemon bars and carrot cake, milkshakes and espresso drinks. It earned a spot on *Washingtonian* magazine's "Best Of" list every year. Lucy made sure of this. When voting season came around, she asked every customer if they had voted yet and, if they hadn't, took them straight to the website to show them how. Town residents kept a mug on a hook since Lucy accompanied the distribution of paper cups with a lecture. Allison snapped a photo of the eclectic mug collection.

"I had an idea for your book," Lucy shouted over the blender when it was Allison's turn.

"Okay. Shoot."

"An aerial shot of the town."

"How would I do that?"

The whirring died. "A helicopter?"

"A little overbudget, I'm afraid."

Lucy picked up the coffee can by the register. She crossed out the word "Tips" and replaced it with the words "Helicopter Fund." She poured Allison's coffee milkshake into a glass and handed her the metal overflow cup. "Bottoms up, gal. Trees still standing?"

"Just a little chest pounding so far."

Allison stopped by the bulletin board on her way out. It was littered with flyers for babysitting and home services—one card offered "Husbands by the Hour," which gave Allison pause. Myriad items were for sale, from strollers to aquariums to training wheels. Someone was offering cooking lessons, and the town Single Parents' Club was having a barbecue. There were business cards from Nina Strauss, realtor, to Maggie Conifer, a college student offering editing services, "No job is too small!" to Monkey Mind Yoga, "Specializing in private and small group classes." People were so industrious, so entrepreneurial, so brave, putting themselves out there for the world to consider. Choose me! they seemed to cry. Choose me! She understood the feeling.

Allison found a table on the porch. She reviewed the photos she'd taken so far this morning as she sipped her shake. Not bad, if she did say so.

She would thank Jillian on the dedication page of the book. "To my lovely daughter," perhaps, or "My love and thanks to Jill . . ." Would Jillian be flattered or embarrassed by the gesture? It was Jillian's model of the town that had inspired the book Allison was working on, after all: *Willard Park: An American Dream.* That's what Allison wanted to call it, assuming the publisher approved. Once she found a publisher.

She would fill it with photos of the town interspersed with Willard Park's history and facts about the architectural styles and the oddities: the merry-go-round that used to be where the elementary school parking lot now lay, the peacocks one eccentric resident used to raise. She imagined a well-designed and informative book meant not only for residents, but for anyone who wanted evidence that idyllic towns still existed in America.

Allison was pinning a lot on this project. She wanted it to be the answer to the question "What do I want to do when I grow up?," a question that had haunted her since childhood. What was her passion? Her raison d'être?

She was determined to make her mark. She was an artist after all. She'd studied photography in college and had managed a gallery near Dupont Circle before Jillian was born. In the meantime she'd become a prostitute. Well, that's what it felt like. Allison was the photographer responsible for the nearly life-size portraits that hung on many a living room wall in Willard Park. They were traditional color photos of smiling parents and children dressed in their Sunday best—parents holding babies, children lined up staircase-style, in order of age; children in matching outfits gathered around doting parents. Oversize snapshots, in a word. They stared out at her accusingly whenever she entered one of her clients' homes, reminding her that she'd sold out.

A familiar, icy feeling swirled around her ankles and swept up her legs—the fear that she alone, of all the women she knew, had not made the transition from mother-of-a-young-child to woman-who-was-back-in-the-game. Jillian was in middle school now, for goodness' sake. Allison had run out of excuses. She often thought she should get a real job, just to stop the angst, but what was she qualified to do? Work at a photo shop? She pictured herself behind a counter at the mall alongside a pimply teenager, handing out prints. Did photo shops even exist anymore?

"Honey, honey," an image of her friend Valeria came to mind, calling her back to herself. "Better to slit your wrists."

Valeria was a Spanish teacher at the middle school, her husband, Phil, a public radio correspondent who had been assigned to cover Paris. Paris! Allison wanted to be assigned to cover Paris! She and Valeria had e-mailed each other daily since they moved in July. Well, the e-mails had been daily at first. Now it was more like once a week or so, with the occasional WhatsApp message. Valeria was busy after all—brushing up on her French, dealing with the convoluted rules at Sofia's school, trying not to incur the wrath of the landlady with the hypersensitive hearing. The only consolation for the fact that her best friend had moved away was Valeria's constant reminders that expat life was kind of a pain.

Allison poured the rest of the milkshake into her glass and drank it down to the bottom, chasing every last drop with her straw, then headed for home.

When she reached the Coxes' house, she stopped to consider it, as she often did, hoping, eventually, to convince herself it wasn't so bad. The trouble was, it was so bad. There were two Ionic columns looking fabulously out of place on the porch, two stone lions the size of ponies, towers painted gold—was it gold leaf? It was as if Nick had thumbed through a catalog of architectural features, earmarked the gaudiest, and had them stuck on his house. The inhabitants of an entire zip code could have lived in it comfortably.

One couldn't, in all honesty, accuse Nick Cox of starting the "big house" craze in Willard Park. The tearing down and building up had started long before he moved in. It was slow at first, a knock down here, an addition there, but the pace had increased with time. Now houses wrapped in shimmering Tyvek slips were a common sight. Latino gardeners spilled out of trucks in the springtime along with wheelbarrows full of mulch and trees with round, burlap bottoms. Walking mowers had given way to tractor mowers nearly as big as the modest lawns themselves. The home gardener, in kerchief and garden gloves, a pair of clippers in hand, was becoming a rare animal in Willard Park.

Allison looked past her and Ted's little house, comfortably set back on their lawn, to the house Nick was currently building, rising skyward like Jack's beanstalk. Until June a Cinderella-model

Sears home had stood there, owned for the better part of the century by Miss Theodora Frey, vegetable gardener and birder extraordinaire, now resting peacefully in her grave behind the church. Or rolling in it. Nick Cox had told her he was buying the house for his diabetic mother. Cox had completely resculpted the backyard to add another daylight level. It was nearly blinding the way the sun hit the white facade.

Nick was beside the new house, camouflaged in part by the leaves. There was something brutal about him, but it wasn't unattractive. He was so tall and fit, Kaye so petite, that Allison thought Kaye was his teenaged daughter the first time she saw them, at the town cherry blossom parade. The way they'd looked, the children dressed in cheerful pinks and greens, you'd have thought they'd descended from the trees themselves.

Good sex, Allison thought, not for the first time. *Energetic. Acrobatic, even.* It was a game she and Valeria played. Which couples had fun in bed, who wanted out of the marriage, who would split ten, fifteen years down the road.

Valeria and Phil had sex three or four times a week, down from five to six times when they first got married. Valeria had mentioned this one day, laughingly saying they'd be down to just once or twice a week by the time Sofia put them in a nursing home. Allison had laughed—just once or twice a week!—when actually that sounded like quite a lot. She and Ted had never had it more than twice a week even when they were in college. Now it was down to once or twice a month.

If that.

She frowned, thinking. When had she and Ted last had sex? She thought back over the past weeks. He didn't like to on weekdays, when he knew he'd have to be up by six thirty. He was tired on Friday nights, after work. So, a Saturday. Any recent Saturday?

She couldn't recall one. He often went to bed early, to read, then was out cold by the time she came to bed. They'd spent a week at a rental in Rehoboth earlier this month—had they had sex then? It would have been the perfect time, no work to wake up for . . . but no. She'd tried a few times, snuggling close in bed, rubbing his back, but he had just planted a big kiss on her cheek and wished her sweet dreams. July then. They must have had sex in July. Yes, she could remember the perfect storm of a Saturday night, when she raced to bed at the same time he did, not giving him time to pick up his book before she launched herself into his arms.

When was the last time he had initiated it though? She puzzled, thinking back through the summer and into the previous spring.

Nick must have felt her standing there, staring. He looked over at her and tipped his hard hat. Allison nodded at him, a waggle of electricity wiggling through her despite herself.

"Well, good morning to you, Mrs. Miller," he said.

"Mr. Cox, how do you do this fine day?"

"I do very well, thank you. Very well indeed."

She laughed; when had they started this little game of theirs, referring to each other as "mister" and "missus"?

"Be sure to leave a few standing, won't you? For the sake of photosynthesis, Mr. Cox?"

"I'll consider it, Mrs. Miller. I can assure you I will," he said, bowing a little, in a silly, courtly manner.

Then he set the chain saw on the ground, put his foot on it, and pulled the starter. He touched its blade to one of the lesser trees near the new house. Its branches swung down to the ground, as if bowing in the presence of a higher god. A few other small trees followed suit. Then, without missing a beat, Nick Cox sunk the teeth of the saw into Jillian's red maple, splitting it in two.

2

know you weren't really considering Maryland," their realtor, Nina Strauss, was saying, "but I just wanted to show you one neighborhood, if you still have the energy . . ."

Grant, sitting in the backseat of her BMW, behind his wife, Suzanne, was going to shoot himself if he had to look at another neighborhood—but it was up to Suzanne, he reminded himself. It was totally up to her.

Suzanne took a deep breath, sighed, and nodded, game. So Grant would be game too. They got on the GW Parkway and made their way up the Potomac. They had been looking at houses in Virginia for seven hours now. Seven.

"It's on the expensive side—I won't lie," Nina said. "But you won't be sorry. It's where I live. It's idyllic. I don't show it to just anyone."

Grant closed his eyes and rolled them. Hopefully Suzanne would see the next house, love it, they'd sign the contract, and that would be it. *Finito.* No more being stuck in a car with Nina Strauss. She put on such a nice face, but she wasn't nice. "Davenport-Gardner," she'd said, her expression mocking when they met this morning. "Hyphenated . . . Both of you?"

What if he were cast as Nina Strauss in a play? He'd wear a wig—a Ruth Bader Ginsberg wig, if such a thing existed. Nina's hair was black and lay flat like spray paint against her scalp and was twisted into a bun at the nape of her neck. He looked down at his lap, practicing the smile that looked too large for Nina's face. Her entire being tightened up when she smiled, not just the tendons in her neck, but practically even the skin on the backs of her hands. She looked about fifty, but he suspected she was younger.

He tapped his fitness tracker to check the time, steps, calories, and heart rate, even though he'd checked it when they got in the car. Then he tapped it again. In just a few short days he'd be starting his new job at a small law firm in Rosslyn, Virginia. He would be the low man on the totem pole, the new kid in town, a stranger. The idea made him want to go running back to his firm in Richmond, where they wore khakis and shirtsleeves when they weren't in court and he knew all the judges. He touched Suzanne's elbow for courage. She didn't reach back for him, but nor did she pull away. They were making progress.

He'd made some bad decisions in his life—he'd be the first to admit it—but he'd made some good ones too. Becoming a lawyer had been a good choice. A more responsible choice than becoming an actor. As a child Grant had reenacted entire sitcoms for his mother while she cooked dinner. Those pockets of time before his father got home from the family hardware store were among the sweetest of Grant's childhood.

A slight, pleasant vibration in his pocket. Grant fished out his phone to find a text from Marie. Going for coffee. The usual for you?☺ It was weird to think she was still working at Fitzpatrick, Oppler and Moore, while he was up here, about to start from scratch. Marie, a childhood friend, hadn't even planned on going to college, much less law school, but he'd inspired her. "I figured if you could do it, I could, General," she'd told him after she aced the LSAT. He'd put in a good word for her after she'd taken the bar, and the firm hired her, just like that. They thought they would spend their careers the way they'd spent their childhoods, side by side.

Have a double espresso for me—spiked with vodka, he started to write, then reconsidered, and just sent back an emoji of a yellow cat with a fat blue tear dripping from its eye.

"Hi, honey bunch," Suzanne said, her voice loud, and for a moment Grant felt buoyant—but she was talking to her phone, not to him. "How are you doing? Is Grammy making dinner?"

Grammy, Suzanne's mother, was taking care of their son, Adam, while they house-hunted. She lived around the corner from their house outside Richmond, close enough to look after Adam every day. Strangers—well, older strangers—sometimes mistook Grammy for Adam's mother, a compliment Grammy laughingly mentioned every time it occurred. Grant always wolf-whistled in support, but Suzanne just uttered a taut, "So you've told us, Mom."

Grammy had offered to move to the D.C. area to help out with Adam, but Suzanne turned her down. Grant pointed out that they'd miss having a babysitter on call, but no amount of lobbying on Grammy's part could convince Suzanne otherwise.

"Addy wants to talk to you," Suzanne said, handing her phone back to Grant.

Grant's heart took wing. "Hiya, buddy!"

Adam retold the story Grammy had just read to him in minute detail, and recounted the moves of the Scrabble game they'd played. Scrabble. The kid was five! Grant listened, happy, simultaneously admiring the back of Suzanne's head: her long neck, her long silky hair. He loved all of Suzanne's long-ness—her long feet, her long thighs and calves too. So what if she was taller than him? It was just by an inch, easily overcome if he wore shoes with a very slight lift and she wore flats. Suzanne Gardner was a catch: student government president, president of the Young Entrepreneurs' Club, a woman who had gotten a full academic ride to college and attended a prominent business school. She was a gifted athlete to boot. He used to get winded climbing the stairs before he started running with her. Suzanne was the best thing that had ever happened to him. Everyone said so.

Adam begged him to make the noise, so Grant obliged, making a raspberry with his lips. Adam laughed and laughed. He loved it when Grant put his lips to Adam's belly, their nightly ritual, but this was the best he could do from afar. Suzanne gave him a sidelong glance, her expression pained.

If Suzanne was the best thing that had ever happened to him—and she was, she totally was—Adam was the best thing he'd ever had a hand in creating. True, Adam felt more like Suzanne's creation than his own, but he'd decidedly played a significant role. Adam looked like Grant, like a mini, skinny, Grant, but his brain was Suzanne's. Grant's sisters had that brilliance too. Grant wasn't stupid—he'd done well in the classes that had interested him, and got surprisingly high scores on his college and law school exams—but he didn't have that razor sharpness. And he made mistakes.

Adam loved him though. Grant taught him show tunes and talked to him in cartoon voices. They wrestled like puppies and stirred their ice cream into soup. Adam tended toward serious, like Suzanne—which made making him laugh all the more fun. Soon—as soon as Suzanne gave him the go-ahead—he was going to introduce Adam to the old sitcoms—shows from his childhood and even further back, from the dawn of the television era. It was an education of sorts. Not as fancy as learning to play the piano or learning French, but an education in popular culture, and valuable in its own right. Suzanne thought exposing Adam to screens of any kind was like exposing him to a virus—a harmful, if not fatal, one. Grant went along in the interest of marital peace. Maybe she was right. Who knew? Adam was certainly just about perfect so far. And just-about-perfect Adam adored him. It was a heady, precious feeling to be adored by a child. One day he would no doubt realize that Grant didn't shimmer the way he and Suzanne did, but that day was a long way off. Maybe ten years. Five or six at least. Grant wiped the spittle off the phone and handed it back to Suzanne.

They turned off the highway and onto a wide road that was thick with traffic in both directions. Nina tuned the radio to a classical station.

"Music to distract us from the fact that D.C. is a commuter's nightmare . . . ?" Grant murmured.

Nina smiled as though she wanted to sink her fangs into his flesh. "So tell me about your little boy."

"He just graduated from preschool cum laude," Grant said.

Nina stifled a laugh. Had she? Was it a laugh or was she just clearing her throat? Suzanne creased her brow at him. They had a non-bragging pact.

He couldn't abide by it though. How could he? "Gifted," Grant said.

"Gifted!" Nina said. That time it was definitely a laugh. "Does he like soccer?"

Neither he nor Suzanne responded. In this department, they knew, they had neglected Adam to the point of possible abuse. They had never enrolled him in a soccer-for-toddlers skills course, had never exposed him to any ball sports—much less one that forbade the use of one's hands. Soon there would be no catching up.

"Willard Park's seventh-grade team is the only coed middle school team in the county. My son, Mark, is on it. Not only that," she said, making them wait for the clincher: "I think they're playing today."

She turned down a shady street with well-spaced Victorians lined up on either side. Grant could practically feel the car swell with her pride. There were sidewalks, a park with a playground, and a soccer field full of children in jerseys and shin guards. Parents sat along the sidelines on a vast field. They passed what looked like a church with a TOWN HALL sign below a stained-glass window, and parked near an old house that, upon further examination, turned out to be part café and part post office.

"Welcome home," Nina said, sliding her elegant car to a stop.

JILLIAN SAT AT THE SIDE OF THE SOCCER FIELD PULLING BLADES OF grass out of the ground one by one. If she slid a blade up by its root without breaking it, that was good luck, and if she did three of them in a row, Willard Park would win the game, she told herself, knowing it wasn't true. There were two minutes left and the other team was killing them. Jillian had been sitting on the sidelines since the start of the game, unlike Lindy Cox, who'd been playing the whole time. Jillian's mom wasn't missing anything by not being there. Where was she? She came to every game, even the away games. *Car accident, sleeping pills, heart attack.*

Mark Strauss, the hottest boy in Willard Park, was goalie. He was a terrible goalie, but the real goalie had stomach flu or something. Mark's hair, cinnamon colored, hung down into his face. He flipped his head back so he could see. Jillian tried to catch his eye but he was studying the tops of his cleats.

The other mothers were there—a couple of dads, too, but mostly moms. Chandra Sharma's mom was there, as were both of Simon Washington's dads. Mrs. Santos had brought all three of Luis's little sisters, who were watching the game as intently as if the seventh-graders were professional soccer players. Lindy's mom was on a big, striped blanket, her hair yellow in the sunlight; Lindy's brother, Jakey, drinking sodas and eating chips, beside her. Jillian's stomach growled. Her mom always brought a boring snack like apples and peanut butter, but it was better than nothing. *Hostage situation, alien abduction.*

Lindy raced down the field with the ball neatly tucked between her feet, her hair flying out behind her like birthday party streamers.

Trip, Jillian thought, but Lindy kept right on going. What did Lindy have against her? Did she stink or something? Sofia was the only one who would have told her, and she was an ocean away.

Mark's mother, in her usual black suit, walked over to the field with two strangers. There must be a house for sale—she never came to games. *Look up,* Jillian told Mark through ESP. She'd read a book about it, and it was real. A tall boy on the other team had stolen the ball from Lindy and had sent it toward the goal. *Look out!*

She watched Mark the way she'd watched the film of President Kennedy's assassination in her English class last fall, with a dark sense of inevitability. Her teacher had shown it to mark the anniversary of Kennedy's death. The kids thought it was cool—gross, but cool—but the parents went crazy when they heard about it. They bombarded the school with angry calls and letters about the inappropriateness of it until the teacher resigned. It was too bad because he'd been one of the nice ones.

Mark yawned up at the trees. Meanwhile Lindy took off after the ball, her teeth bared. She threw herself between the ball and the goal and tried to block it. The blade of grass in Jillian's hand broke. A cheer went up from the other team just as the whistle blew.

"IT STARTED OUT AS A STREETCAR SUBURB AT THE TURN OF THE LAST century," Nina narrated when they were back in the car again, the home team having lost rather spectacularly. Suzanne took it all in. She wasn't sorry she'd agreed to one final stop for the day. Not sorry at all.

Nina was talking about nuts. The streets were named after them. The street they were on, Almond Avenue, was clearly the showcase street, wide, with old, well-maintained houses where trees grew tall and swings hung from high branches. They passed a Victorian with a wraparound porch, where two little girls sat on a swing, a dog at their feet. Suzanne imagined the girls away, replacing them with herself and Adam. Then she put the girls back again. What could they possibly find in their price range here? Everything was so much more expensive around Washington. She'd known it was going to be bad, but not this bad.

Nina rolled down the window. "Hi, Madeline. Your puppy is getting so big, Jordan!" The girls looked at her as if they had never seen her before. If things were better between her and Grant, Suzanne would have caught skeptical eyes with him—but they weren't good. Not good at all.

"Peanut, Hazelnut—you name a nut, we've got it. We've even got a Brazil Nut Street. Willard Park is very multiculturally oriented."

"Multicultural is good," Grant said, possibly just to show that he was awake.

"It was quite progressive in the sixties. One of the houses was a commune even, but most of those folks are gone now, retired or . . ." She stopped herself. What had she kept herself from saying? Dead?

Nina slowed down as they drove by a series of little older

houses, many with porches, most somewhat run down. "These are our Sears houses. Aren't they just darling?"

They were darling. They were small—quite small—but darling. Could they buy a very small, somewhat dilapidated house in a perfect neighborhood? Would it be like buying a lesser property in Monopoly? Baltic Avenue wasn't worth much, but it got you on the board.

Nina sped up as they drove by the ranches and split-levels, as if she wanted to drive right through them. "It was really only after World War Two that the town began to grow in earnest. We're up to nearly thirteen hundred residents these days."

They passed what looked like a one-room schoolhouse, which turned out to be a children's library, and a bandstand decorated with red, white, and blue bunting. "It's so Norman Rockwell," Suzanne said.

"Right?" said Nina.

Grant said, "Yeah. A little eerie. Remember the *Twilight Zone* episode . . . ?"

Nina jumped in, telling them about the cherry blossom beautification program. She waved to a little boy examining the sidewalk with a magnifying glass, then slowed down to let them admire the wooden train, big enough for kids to climb on. "Willard Park is a place for the imagination."

"That little fountain," Suzanne said. "Can people picnic there?"

"It's a favorite spot."

"Mmmm," Suzanne purred. She didn't even know she could purr.

"We have a snowman-building contest after the first snowfall. All the kids go home with a ribbon. There's a children's bicycle parade on Labor Day, a town pride day in July, caroling in December . . ." Nina sped up, racing by a street that had potential.

"Let's go down there," Suzanne said.

Nina coughed and shook her head. "Well, there's some con-struction . . ."

"That's okay."

"Tunlaw it is," Nina said, turning right.

"Tunlaw," Grant said. "How is Tunlaw a nut?"

"Good point! I never thought about that. Is it a nut?"

A man biked past, a bright yellow bicycle helmet on his head and a reflective safety vest over his shirt. "Hi, Ted," Nina called out the window. "Ted and Allison live—" Nina began, but Suzanne had seen the apocalypse.

They were all silent as they drove by this property, with its looming white house.

It was oddly bright surrounding the house, the sky vaster seem-ing, like the skies out west. It took Suzanne a minute to understand what was wrong. It was more than just the size of the house, it was that the trees were gone, their freshly sawn stumps left behind like amputated limbs. A woman with curly auburn hair sat on the curb in front of the yard, legs crossed, as if she were meditating.

"Did a tornado . . . ?" Suzanne said.

Nina's smile tightened, her eyes a little wild as, apparently, she considered how to respond—but a man's scream interrupted her. It was a lingering scream, a scream of obvious anguish. The man with the yellow bike helmet tumbled off his bike and onto the lawn.

"Is he hurt? Can you stop the car?" Grant said.

Nina stopped, but it was a slow stop.

The meditating woman sprang up, embracing the fallen biker. Grant wheeled the bike out of the road. "You all right? Need a hand?"

Nina motioned for him to get back in the car. "His mother died," she whispered when he got back in. "They just got word."

"How sad," Suzanne said.

"Sad," Nina said, bowing her head. "Very, very sad . . . but she was old."

Nina pressed the automatic lock, sealing them in. "Off we go! To your dream house. I think it's just around the corner," she said, speeding away from the scene of the crime.

3

Nick Cox sat on the couch in the media room, images from the television flickering in the dark. He thumbed through the channels with the remote. He had the biggest flat-screen TV on the market—not just HD, but ultra HD. It was like a movie theater. Better than a movie theater, really, because of the leather couch and the surround sound, and the absence of popcorn-eating, candy-wrapper-crumpling, soda-spilling strangers. He and Kaye usually spent their evenings here after she put Jakey to bed, but she got the yawns around ten. The leather was cold without her.

Rex, their German shepherd, nestled beside him, licking Nick's hand constantly and thoroughly, dedicated to the cause. Ordinarily Nick did not care for dogs that licked, but Rex was one of a kind. He liked watching TV as much as Nick did— especially when dogs were on: he would wag and bark. He wasn't much of a watchdog. He was more likely to lick a stranger's hand than bite it. He slept in their bed, on Nick's side, which made it hard to get in a comfortable position, but what was he going to do? Put him in the garage?

Officially the dog was Kaye's. She'd asked for a puppy for her birthday. Nick hadn't wanted one—the last thing he needed was a yard full of dog crap—but Kaye looked so disappointed when he gave her the tennis bracelet. "I need him for security," she said, eyeing the Millers' house. "That brother gives me the willies. He stares."

"He's all right," Nick said.

"I'm lonely, too, with the kids in school all day." She said it in her baby voice, and he, feeling a little turned on, gave in.

She probably was lonely. She'd had a bunch of girlfriends when they lived back in Beaufort. There was always some woman or other sitting on the couch or poolside when he got home from work, sometimes a whole squad of them, sitting around, laughing. Northern women seemed to be afraid of getting caught enjoying themselves. Kaye had tried to make inroads in Willard Park last spring, hosting one of those toy parties, but it had been a flop. She still had a closet full of plastic buckets and stacking toys no one wanted.

"They're jealous of us, huh, Nick?" Kaye said. "For having nice stuff?"

Nick said they must be, but in fact he didn't think they were. Up here people seemed to think it was classier to live in a crumbling old house than a new one. Who knew why? If Willard Park was all about families, as it claimed to be, they should have seen that his house was family oriented, with its multiple family rooms and hot tub. Those little houses made everyone want to go outside instead of staying in. What good was a house that made you want to leave it?

Kaye wanted to move back to South Carolina, but no one was exactly begging him to build down there anymore. So he'd violated a few building codes. He hadn't killed anyone, for God's sake, but he was persona non grata anyway.

They were going to throw a party in a few weeks—Nick's idea—to give Kaye something fun to think about. He was inviting a bunch of business contacts so he could write the whole thing off.

Rex jumped off the couch and barked in the direction of the Millers' house, where Ted Miller sat on the porch in the dark. Rex had been at it all night. It was a different bark, an edgier bark, from the one he used for the Millers' funny-looking little dog; it was a bark that said, "I'm no pussycat."

Ted had been out there since early evening. Nick could just make out the shape of him by the moonlight, hunched over in his chair. "Quiet, Rex," he said, but Rex whined to be let out.

"All right," Nick opened the door, then went out himself. It was still hot out even though it was nearly eleven. He threw a tennis ball into the yard and Rex ran off to get it.

"Evening," Nick called to Ted. It would have been weird not to say anything: the guy was sitting there staring at him. But Ted just glared back. He was creepier than the brother, if you asked Nick. Nick threw the ball a couple more times, but he felt kind of stupid doing it with this guy watching him. Nick whistled for Rex and headed back toward the house.

Nick turned to face Ted before he opened the door. "They were my trees."

"One was mine."

"I just cut down the half on my land." It was a vertical cut. He'd meant it as a joke, really, a slice off the side, a little showing off for Allison—Mrs. Miller, he thought with a private smile—only the saw had moved so fast.

"We planted it for Jillian." Ted shook his head disapprovingly, looking just like Nick's father when Nick showed him his report card. *This is the best you could do?* Nick went back inside, Rex at his heels.

"Good dog. Good puppy!" he said, rubbing Rex's back vigorously when they were safely ensconced on the couch again. Rex wagged his tail and smiled.

He didn't know they'd planted it for their kid. Christ. How could he have known that? He'd just wanted to clear the property, give the place a little more light, maybe entice a buyer. The house was going to be a stunner—indoor pool, sauna, you name it: anything the new owner wanted. He was leaving it unfinished so the buyer could customize—or so he told people. The truth was, he didn't have the money to complete it.

The place was coming in way over budget. If he didn't sell it soon, the bank would come after him. His other properties in town would be next, a couple of tear-downs he'd snatched up at good prices.

He'd been an idiot to buy the excavator. It was just a mini excavator, but that didn't make it cheap. The trouble was, he'd fallen in love with it. It was little and round and clean and yellow. How could any red-blooded male resist? He thought it would pay for itself, but now it was just another chain around his neck.

The whole thing had seemed like such a no-brainer a couple years back: buy up the crummy old houses in Willard Park, which no one who could afford the land would possibly want to live in—or so he thought—and build new houses, fresh houses, houses with modern amenities like central air. Some of the little shacks in town still had window units, for God's sake! He imagined great rooms instead of splintery porches, home gyms where paneled rec rooms now moldered.

His vision went further. He pictured an expanded shopping district, a real business zone complete with cafés and boutiques and a promenade by the creek. A thriving Willard Park downtown would bring in income so the town could show those monthly movies in a real movie theater instead of on a screen in the town hall basement. They could hand out trophies to the little kids on the soccer team instead of ribbons, and have the potlucks catered.

Didn't Ted and Lucy and the other old granola heads see? He wanted what they wanted: a comfortable, livable town near the city, somewhere beautiful, somewhere safe. But it was never going to happen if his houses didn't sell. He threw the remote. It bumped off the front of a speaker and landed on the floor with a clatter. He was stuck watching an aging blonde with big teeth trying to sell a diamond necklace.

He felt an urge to apologize to Ted for killing his kid's tree. He tried to think of what to say. "Hey, dude, I'm sorry for cutting . . ." "You know, pal, I didn't intend . . ." Words were so fraught. Anything that might be construed as an admission might bring on a lawsuit—he'd been there before. So was it better to say nothing? To just feel like crap? He smacked his hand on the couch in frustration, startling Rex. "Hey, bud. I'm sorry." Nick scratched the dog's chin, right where he liked it, making Rex close his eyes and lean his face into Nick's hand. He heard feet on the stairs. "Hey, Lindy-ba-bindy." His fellow night owl.

"You missed my game."

"I'm sorry, Chicken Little."

"You never come. You go to all of Jakey's games."

"Not true," Nick said, though it wouldn't do any good. She still hadn't forgiven them for knocking her off her single-child throne.

"I scored both our points."

"You're pretty good for a girl." He smiled, shielding his face, ready to be pummeled with a pillow.

She pinched his arm instead.

"Ouch," he said.

"Don't be a baby."

"I'm going to get one of those necklaces for Mom." He nodded toward the screen.

"That's crap, Daddy. Can't you tell?"

"Get the remote, will you, Lin?"

"You get it."

"Come on. I'm an old man."

"Don't say you're old, Daddy." She nestled next to him on the side Rex wasn't occupying, resting her head on his arm.

The clock ticked its way into the next day as they stared at the changing images, their skin flickering blue, the specter of Ted Miller fading like a miasma into the night sky.

4

The new family was moving into a Carlin model Sears home circa 1918, a sweet two-bedroom bungalow with a porch and a second-floor balcony. Allison, at her desk in her attic office, studied the catalog page on her computer. In the drawing, the house—which originally sold for $1,172—was perfection itself, with two hanging plants on the porch and well-tended flowers lining the curving path. Now, a hundred years later, it admittedly needed some work, but it was still a precious little home.

Their own house, built in 1910, was so old that Sears hadn't even started naming the models yet. It was similarly small, tiny even, for a family of three, with just two bedrooms. A previous owner had turned the attic into a somewhat usable space, but there was still barely room for her desk and a futon; it was too cold in winter and too hot in summer. But Allison didn't mind. A sense of home and community: that was what mattered—not whether you had a second bathroom. She and Ted were in agreement about that.

Allison printed a copy of the Carlin catalog page. She planned to take it to the new family this morning along with a write-up of the history of Willard Park and a loaf of Lucy's banana bread—a little welcome kit. She started humming "You Can't Get a Man with a Gun," one of the few *Annie Get Your Gun* numbers they could choreograph without a leading man. Valeria's husband, Phil, usually played the male lead, with Valeria as the leading lady, but with the two of them living in Paris, the town theater company threatened to fall apart. The director, Rainier, who had moved to Willard Park from Austria a few years ago, talked about hiring an actor to play Frank. Allison laughed the first time he mentioned the idea, but it was starting to seem like the best option. Allison had to wonder why she was even doing the show this year.

She opened the little window above her desk and looked down on Ted, sitting in the yard beside the forlorn little maple with his bagel and coffee. There was little hope for the maple's survival according to the tree guy, but Ted still sat beside it the way he had sat at Terrance's bedside when Terrance had pneumonia that time.

She called down to him, "Hey."

Ted lifted his hand in a halfhearted wave.

The seedling sat on a little stump, nearby. She and Jillian had bought it with the hope that he would transfer his affections, but the tiny maple sat in its pot, unplanted. "Plant the new one," she urged.

He shrugged.

Allison had been upset about the tree, too, but it had been four weeks since its demise. Time to move on already. She suspected he was depressed, which might explain why they hadn't had sex for so long. She'd been monitoring the situation closely for the past month, after her somewhat shocking realization that they had not made love since midsummer. She Googled "How to jazz up your marriage" and, after eliminating some of the more absurd suggestions—"Come to bed in high heels" and "Greet him at the door naked with a rose between your teeth"—had come up with a viable list.

She'd executed her attack over the subsequent weeks, starting with wine with dinner, which he'd declined, reminding her it was a "school night." A sexy text a few days later had been ignored; when she asked him about it, he blushed and said he thought Siri had bungled her words. A tongue in the ear the following weekend led to a giggling fit. Last night she slipped her hand under the covers to give him a surprise hand job, but his penis lay on his leg like an overcooked asparagus, unresponsive, after which she burst into tears.

"What's wrong?" he said, as if he had been in the other room during the failed hand job.

"We haven't had sex for over two months."

He laughed. "That's not true."

"Yes it is."

"You're keeping track?"

"I started to. Yes."

"Great," he said, his tone a little bitter.

She rolled onto her back, not sure if she wanted to scream or pummel him. Weren't men supposed to want sex all the time? What was wrong with him? Or, more frighteningly, what was wrong with her? "Are you still attracted to me?"

"Yes. Of course I am."

"Not 'of course.' I can't even remember the last time you kissed me."

He leaned over and kissed her forehead.

"Not like that." She leaned in to kiss him properly, but it was like kissing a paper plate.

He patted her hair. "It's just, I'm not feeling it."

"'Not feeling it.' Terrific."

"It's not a permanent condition or anything."

"Can we talk about it?"

"There's nothing to talk about. It'll pass," he said, and he turned his back toward her.

They'd fallen asleep that way.

She opened the slide show of the photos she had for her book so far, hoping for the energetic boost the project usually gave her, but the pictures looked ordinary this morning—the shot of the town hall, washed out; the mailbox shaped like a cow, blurry. Even Lucy's scarecrow sagged. Discouraged, she exited the file and opened her e-mail. Oh good, one from valeria@wanadoo.fr. She hadn't heard from her in over a week. She smiled, readying herself for the laugh that Valeria never failed to provide.

"Just back from Venice. Opera, gondola ride, bought a gorgeous glass sculpture in Murano. Reservations for Christmas in Barcelona—*estoy tan feliz*!"

Allison wanted to ask what she should do about their sad sex life, but not wanting to bring down the mood, instead wrote, "Wow! You go!" and enthused about Italy and Spain. She preferred Valeria's e-mails about petty civil servants and nasty shopkeepers, to be honest. *Bad friend,* she chided herself. *Bad, bad friend.* She ran her fingers over the keys, making them clatter like hail, then closed the lid of her laptop, escaping. The sight of Ted in the yard was enough to make her snap. "Plant it already!"

He looked up, surprised.

"I'm sorry. It's just . . ." Just what? "Resume your vigil."

"It's not a vigil, Allison."

"What*ever*," she said, sounding just like Jillian in a mood.

She made her way down the narrow stairs. Jillian was downstairs on the couch, reading, Candy lying on the rug beside her, belly up. "Want to take a walk, Jillie?"

"Nnnn." Jillian turned a page.

"We could stop by Lucy's for a snack." The ultimate treat, the jump-up-and-down "Thank you, Mama!" thrill of Jillian's child-hood.

Jillian looked at her, a studiously patient expression on her face—one that Allison recognized, having doled it out herself so often. "I'm reading."

Allison, who wanted a hug, but would have settled for a smile, nodded. She finally understood why some people had a second set of children when their first were nearly grown. She grabbed Candy's leash and made kissing sounds. Candy rolled onto her feet and followed her out the door.

"Good dog! Yes you are!" She rubbed Candy's muzzle until the dog whipped her entire backside back and forth with joy. Allison bent down to hug her. Candy—flea bitten, collarless—had followed Jillian home from school a few years before. Neglected hamsters and scrawny cats, too, had found a home with the Millers over the years. Allison was a soft touch; it was just her nature.

Nina Strauss sped by in her BMW, a car so heavy and luxurious it seemed not to notice Willard Park's many speed bumps. She had places to go, people to see, her driving said. Nina had moved to town not long after Allison and Ted did, when both she and Allison were pregnant. Allison had thought their simultaneous pregnancies might inspire a friendship, but Nina worked day and night. Rumor had it that she'd suffered through her early labor pains at the conference table at the realty office, loath to leave in the middle of a closing, and had driven herself to the hospital as soon as the signatures were secured.

Candy was on high alert as they approached the Coxes', her tail and nose high. Rex ran up and down in a straight line parallel to the sidewalk, as far as the invisible fence would allow. He leaped in the air, a jagged, maniacal look on his face when he saw Candy. Candy darted onto the lawn. The dogs tumbled over and under each other, bared their teeth, and bit at each other's furry legs and jaws. Then Rex started to hump Candy. Vacant, not dissatisfied, looks clouded both dogs' eyes.

Kaye, sitting on the porch with a magazine, shook a manicured finger. "No, no, Rexie!" she called to no noticeable effect.

"Maybe you should get him neutered," Allison said.

"Nick's kind of sensitive about that . . . Hey, Nicky!" she called.

Nick came out and whistled with two fingers in his mouth. Rex ran over and lay at his feet like an odalisque. "You've got to woo them, fella. Don't you know?" He flashed a smile.

Kaye gave him a girly smack on the chest. He grabbed her wrist and pretended he was going to twist her arm. Allison, feeling as though she'd just climbed in between them in bed, yanked Candy's leash and walked on, her face hot.

Oh! It was all Valeria's fault. She'd found a way to fight back at the ennui, escaping to Europe, leaving Allison behind to circle the streets of suburbia with a husband who was more passionate about a tree than he was about his wife.

SUZANNE FELT LIKE A TRAFFIC COP IN THE MIDDLE OF A BUSY INTERsection, pointing and waving the movers to the different rooms of the new house. Living room. Dining room. Two bedrooms. Unfinished basement. The bathroom. That was it. She was more like Snow White than a traffic cop, come to think of it, in her tiny cottage with her two resident fairy-tale dwarves—one of whom was jogging down to the hardware store to make copies of the house key. Why did he need to do it now, in the middle of moving day?

The dwarfier of the dwarves appeared in an inside-out striped Polo shirt and plaid shorts. "I counted seventy-three boxes, Mommy, and the man with the mustache is named Juan and you spell it with a *J,* and he's from Guadalajara, and that's spelled with a *G,* and he doesn't have a green card but he wants one. Can I make him one, Mommy? A green card? I'm hungry. Let's get sushi." Adam bounced up and down on the balls of his feet, a pixie with unbrushed, curly hair.

Suzanne handed him a dollar from her purse. "After lunch we're going to go to Lucy's, just you and me. What do you think you can buy with that? Do you think it's enough for a cookie?"

He shoved the money into his pocket like a man stowing his wallet. "I'm going to save it for when Grammy comes."

Suzanne kneeled so they could be eye to eye. "Grammy's not coming."

"Yes she is."

"To *visit*. Grammy will *visit*."

"Grammy will live with us. She'll sleep next to me. We planned it, Mommy."

For a moment Suzanne let herself imagine her mother moving in, sleeping next to Adam, as the two had covertly plotted, 24/7: *I think you deserve a puppy, too, but Mommy's the boss;* and *I always think it's best if the mother doesn't work, if it's not a* necessity, *but maybe I'm old fashioned!* and *It's a wonder he doesn't come down with pneumonia wearing those thin pajamas, but you're the mother, you know best.* Point, aim, fire, repeat; her mother was a sharpshooter who pretended she'd never handled a rifle.

"Mommy," Adam said, no doubt alarmed by the expression on Suzanne's face.

She gave him another dollar. "Would you like a milkshake? A little bird told me Lucy makes great milkshakes."

"I want a tall skim half-caf latte and a hazelnut biscotti!"

Suzanne gathered him up in her arms. "I'm going to eat you up."

"Mommy! I'm not food."

She did, in fact, want to eat him up. She wanted to hold him so tight their hearts beat in time. They'd never bonded properly. Because she hadn't breastfed? She'd tried, but it had been a fiasco that resulted in tears and screaming on both their parts. Her mother was the one he called for in the night. "Did you see your room? They set up your racing-car bed."

Adam sat on the floor with a book that looked like it weighed as much as he did. He was the one who had figured out that Tunlaw was walnut backward. Tunlaw Place. "Shouldn't it be Tunlaw Ecalp, Mommy?"

The local elementary school seemed well prepared to deal with gifted children, but there was a downside. They only offered half-day kindergarten. She was supposed to have all-day kindergarten by now. She'd waited five years for all-day kindergarten, five years to stop relying on her mother for child care—her mother, who had worked full time when Suzanne was growing up, who, thanks to some nifty stock options, now had all the time in the world to sing and play hide-and-seek with her grandson. While Suzanne worked. Not that she minded working; she loved working. But she wanted both: to be a success in her work and to be the one her son adored. It didn't seem like too much to ask. Half-day kindergarten? By the time she dropped him off at school and got the breakfast dishes done it would be time to pick him up again. She vetoed Grant's suggestion he go to aftercare, having done time in it herself for so many years, and a sitter was out of the question: Adam would just transfer his affections from her mother to the sitter, leaving Suzanne in the cold again.

Things were not happening as planned. Half-day kindergarten was the first misfortune. The second was running: she was supposed to have made her best time ever in the New York City Marathon last November, not blow out her knee, reducing herself to a hobbling jogger. Misfortune number three: Grant was supposed to have made partner at his firm in Richmond. They were going to move to the countryside after that, buy an old house and refurbish it. She'd had one all picked out.

And on top of all that, the maraschino cherry on the tippy top of her problem sundae, was another potential possible maybe fourth problem. The evidence was not all in. Her breasts were tender, which might just mean that her period was on its way. She was late, but being late was not unusual. Maybe it was the flu—easy to get when you were run down from moving. How could she be pregnant? She and Grant had only had sex a couple of times since The Incident. Her disappointment in him had been keen. It still was. She thought he'd changed.

Suzanne needed a vacation. The camping trip on Chincoteague in August had been anything but relaxing: Grant and Suzanne had barely been on speaking terms. They'd spent the week fending off mosquitoes, ticks, and sunburns. Then there were the deer—great lingering herds of them, which were pastoral when they were off in the meadow, but downright spooky when they clustered around the picnic table staring like orphaned children.

Adam looked up at her from the kitchen floor. "My head hurts, Mommy."

"Mine, too, sweet pea. Moving is hard work." She had an urge to sit down with him, to cuddle him in her lap and finger his curls, but there was so much to do.

A mover stopped in the front hallway with a box. "This isn't labeled."

"Of course it is," Suzanne said. It wasn't. "Put it in the master bedroom."

"Isn't one," the mover said.

"Excuse me?"

"There isn't a master bedroom."

"The bedroom to the immediate right at the top of the stairs."
It *was* bigger.

"Mommy! What's this word?" Adam pointed to a page in his
book.

"This light was already cracked, right?" A mover held a tiny
Tiffany-style table lamp aloft like a torch.

The lamp from her childhood night table. Her father told her
he'd be home from his business trip before the bulb burned out,
but that bulb and another burned out before she understood that
he wasn't coming back. Suzanne kept it as a physical reminder of
the way life could let you down.

"This chair go upstairs?"

"What?" Suzanne stood, her focus lost. She tried to remember
what they owned and why, energy seeping from her like air from a
punctured tire.

"Mommy! A stranger!"

A woman stood on the porch with a long squat dog with a
fluffy feather of a tail. Someone collecting for a charity? Something
green, Suzanne guessed—Save the Seals or the Humane Society.
The woman had curly, untamed hair and wore an Indian-print top
paired with dangling, arty earrings. She had unusual blue eyes. No,
green. She looked familiar. "Can you come back another time?"

"I just wanted to welcome you to the neighborhood." She held
out an envelope and a foil loaf pan.

Suzanne accepted the offerings, standing awkwardly on the
threshold of what she hoped would, one day, feel like home.

GRANT JOGGED AROUND THE GREEN, PAST THE CAFÉ AND THE TOWN
hall and the soccer field, where a tai chi class had gathered near
the goal, the students' movements eerily slow, like plants moving

underwater. He ran past the tennis courts and the children's library and down a side street. He timed a loop, imagining how familiar it would become after running it every day. He would come to know every tree and every dog, every mailbox and every streetlight.

He sprinted over the creek to Willard Park's little shopping area, where the market and the hardware store, Mitchell's Variety, and a few other stores were lined up, awaiting customers.

He tapped his fitness tracker, eager to see his heart rate, and nodded, pleased. His pulse was famously slow, unlike his wife's— Suzanne's heart raced. He bought a bottle of water at the market— more gourmet shop than deli with its foreign chocolates and extensive wine selection—and stretched his Achilles tendons on the curb before heading around the gold SUV that was parked out front with its hazard lights on, and into the hardware store.

All he needed was a whiff of the store to feel calmer—rubber and machine oil, insecticides and fresh-cut lumber. The comfort of the familiar had driven him here this morning, not the urgent need for spare keys. He just had to get away, forget about everything. The pressure was extreme. A move and a new job? Who could do both of those things at the same time and stay sane? A young guy in a red vest and a nametag greeted him. Grant shook the fellow's hand. It was like reaching out to his former self.

Grant had grown up in his father's hardware store, graduating from playing on the wood floor behind the counter, to runner (Can you get this young lady a can of WD-40, son? Can you show this gentleman where we cut glass?), to advising and ringing up customers. He'd been proud when his father had given him the green vest all of the Main Street Hardware employees got to wear, but not so proud that he wanted to make the store his life. His father had been caustic when Grant told him he did not want to take over upon his father's retirement. "Then who in God's name am I doing this for?" his father had said, smacking his hand into a row of clay pots. Grant picked up the shards, keeping an ingratiating smile on his face for the customers.

He strolled down each row now, familiarizing himself with the layout. Garden gloves and trash cans, cleaning solvents and mousetraps. He caressed door hinges and ran his hand over a row of air filters. He wasn't the owner's son here, but a stranger. It was a funny feeling.

He'd known anonymity for such short bursts in his life. His first weeks at the university—well, not really, since so many of his friends from high school went there. In law school—but it was only an hour from home, easy to go back for the weekend. At Fitzpatrick, Oppler and Moore—but that wasn't right, either, since many of the law firm's clients were neighbors or customers at the store. Then, of course, Marie got hired, and it was like being in school all over again. It was impossible to be anonymous when you settled down where you grew up. While some people found it claustrophobic, incestuous even, he loved the feeling of being known, the pride he felt in being the first Davenport to attend graduate school.

Until he started dating Suzanne, he and his old gang got together on the weekends to hang out: grab a few beers, maybe listen to a local band and hit up Denny's for breakfast in the wee hours. Marie was part of that group, the only girl. She was fun, with her knack for impressions and spontaneous tap dancing. She had aspired to be the next Shirley Temple as a child, took classes for years. Grant had taken them for a while, too, just enough to fake being Fred Astaire to her Ginger Rogers at the senior year talent show—which they'd won. Some of his high school pals still called him Fred.

He'd been stupid to get high with her during lunch last spring.

He hardly ever smoked anymore, and never during the workday. Marie was the one who'd brought the joint to the state park, where they sometimes took subs they picked up from Capri's—but she'd been smart enough to take the afternoon off. He, on the other hand, had gone to a deposition. The senior partner had told him to find another job before he fired him.

Suzanne, predictably, had gone bananas. Did he have any idea what he was risking? Any idea at all? She accused him of reverting to his old ways, his old slacker ways, with his old slacker friends—which was simply not true. She hadn't known him in college, when weed was both his intramural and his varsity sport. She was way overreacting. Not only was medical marijuana legal in many states, recreational marijuana was legal, too, he reminded her.

"Alcohol is legal, too, but you can't get drunk on the job, Grant. You never grew up, and you never will."

"Yes I did," he said, his hackles up the way they used to get when his sisters teased him. "I can change."

"Swear then," she said, holding up the photo of Adam on his first birthday, chocolate frosting smeared all over his face.

"I swear," he said, his hand on the frame. "Never to smoke weed again."

"I'll divorce you if you do," she said, eyes pinpricks. "I will."

And she would. Ridiculous as it might be, she would do it.

Thus he hadn't lit up in four months. He'd thought about it, sure, but only because he still had some weed. If he were smart he would just open the Baggie and flush the contents down the toilet, but he liked knowing it was there, just in case, like potassium iodide pills in case of a nuclear attack.

Had he been asking to be fired? It was a question Suzanne had put to him, and he wondered sometimes. He'd fallen into being a lawyer the way he'd fallen into pretty much everything in life. His high school guidance counselor suggested law as an alternative to acting—careers that were not without their similarities. The important difference was that his father didn't smash clay pots when he suggested he might go to law school.

Grant thought being a lawyer would be an easy job for a bright-enough guy, but in truth you had to work long hours. And lives were often on the line. People could—and did—lose their shirts because of him. Clients went to jail. Sometimes he wished he'd been disbarred instead of told to start job hunting. Then he could have started over.

He admired the garden rakes, each more ergonomically designed than the last, and noted the high stacks of brown leaf bags. Electric drills and screwdrivers took up an entire section. The gas grills were off to the side—real behemoths. Big red SALE signs dangled from their lids.

Grant opened one and stuck his head halfway inside. He made an expression of mock terror, took a selfie, and sent it to the gang: Dave, Pete, and Marie.

A couple of men stood around the larger grills communing silently. One of them, a guy maybe ten years older than Grant, in good shape, opened and closed the lid of a big charcoal grill called the Smokin' Joe. "It looks like it's talking," he said.

Grant smiled, unsure if the guy was talking to him.

"'Feed me.' That's what it's saying." The man did a poor attempt at ventriloquism. "'Feed me.'"

Grant laughed. "It's the Tin Man. 'Oil can.'"

"Think it's too much grill?"

"I don't work here," Grant said.

"I just wondered if you thought it was too much grill."

Grant considered. It was like a coffin in both size and shape. "You could cook a lot of burgers in there."

"Or a whole cow, right? Hey, Chip," he called to one of the red-vested employees. "Put this on my account."

"Okie dokes. We've got them in back."

"I want this one." The man tipped the grill sideways. "Lend me a hand?"

"Um. Sure." Grant helped wheel the grill to the SUV out front.

They attempted to heft the grill into the back a few times, but it was awkward. "On the count of three," the man said, but it landed on its side with a clatter. They checked for dents, then tried again, this time with success.

"Cocks," the man said, offering Grant a hand to shake.

"Excuse me?"

"Nick Cox. I live over on Tunlaw. You're the new people, right?"

"That's us. I mean, me. Yep."

"We're having a party in a couple weeks. Stop by. We'll put that grill to good use."

Grant watched him drive off. He'd made a friend of sorts, a thought that cheered him. He went back in the hardware store and, spontaneously, bought the same grill. He felt oddly as though the man—Cox—were performing ventriloquism on him. The grill they owned was fine. Small, gas powered, but fine. He offered his credit card. "Davenport-Gardner," he said, giving the clerk their new address, for delivery.

FROM HIS SPOT IN THE YARD, NEAR THE LITTLE STUMP OF WHAT HAD been Jillian's red maple, Ted could see all the chores he ought to have been doing—cleaning the gutters, trimming the bushes, seeding the grass. But he didn't get up. He sat on the ground, legs crossed. It must nearly be noon, judging by the sun's angle and the hollowness of his stomach, he thought, when Jillian came out into the yard with a plate. "For me?" he said, seeing the sandwich and brightening.

"No." She took a bite. Turkey, lettuce, and tomato. Or was it that Tofurky stuff that Allison liked? Ted looked at Jillian the way Candy did, with sad, pleading eyes. Jillian rolled her eyes and gave him half.

They ate in silence. Companionable silence, Ted thought, but Jillian furrowed her brow when she finally spoke.

"Are you okay, Dad?"

"Sure, hon. Why wouldn't I be?"

"Because . . . it's weird to sit in the yard so much?"

"Not so much. When I have time, that's all. I think out here." It wasn't as if he was missing work to sit in the yard. It was just weekends. Maybe the occasional evening. When the weather was good, that was all.

"It's just, I mean, it's weird."

"Nothing to worry about, Jill. Promise."

"It's just a tree, right?"

"Of course. You're right. And I'm fine. You don't have to worry about me."

She nodded, the clouds leaving her face. "Can I have some money then? For poster board? I mean, if you're all right . . ."

"Sure," he said, and he grabbed a twenty from his wallet, to show how fine he was.

She gave him a big smile, then, as a bonus, a very brief and awkward hug. It nearly made him want to give her another twenty.

Candy came over after Jillian left, as though they were taking shifts, keeping an eye on him. He and the dog sat side by side, soaking up the sun. Allison appeared with two mugs of coffee not long after.

"Just what I needed."

She took a breath as if she was going to say something, then closed her mouth again and sipped her coffee. Then she did it again.

"What?" He steeled himself for an attack.

"Don't take this the wrong way, but I think I know how you can overcome your tree obsession," she said.

"It's not an obsession."

"Well, it's something. An extreme preoccupation, whatever. I just have a thought about that and, well, our other problem."

"We don't have another problem."

She frowned, the three lines in her brow gathering, and her eyes went from blue to gray. "We have a problem," she said, her voice low.

He looked away from her, avoiding further eye contact.

"Just, I was thinking, maybe some therapy."

"I don't need therapy. For Pete's sake, Al. Everyone goes through lulls. Everything's fine."

"It's not fine for me."

He stood up.

"What?" she said.

"I'm going to go get some stamps."

"Good!" she said, as if he were a patient making progress.

He went from the backyard to the front. She was making a big deal out of nothing. Sex slowed down at their age—that was totally normal. He'd want to again. And of course he was upset about the trees. Who wouldn't be? He'd thought he'd be counseling Terrance through the crisis, and Allison was suggesting therapy for him!

Terrance hadn't even noticed Cox's deforestation, truth be known. When Ted pointed it out when Terrance came for Tuesday-night tacos, his brother nodded and said, "Looks like the trees got a buzz cut. Get it, Teddy? Like a buzz saw?"

Terrance could be so reasonable sometimes. More reasonable than him or Allison. More reasonable than that idiotic Dana at the nursing home, whose most recent call Ted had accidentally answered. She told Ted she was suspending Terrance for a day for heating a patient's coffee in the staff microwave.

"For heating coffee?" he'd said.

"For heating coffee."

"Was it cold?"

"That's not the point."

"Did the patient get burned?"

Again, not the point. So what was the point? Ted had to bite his tongue to keep from asking. Suspending Terrance for heating coffee would only ensure that he would not heat coffee in the future, not that he wouldn't heat soup or add ice to a lukewarm drink.

Poor Terrance. He was forever trying to do nice things only to have them backfire. Like the time when they were kids, when he stole a cookie from the school cafeteria because Ted was hungry, only to be caught with a fist full of crumbs; or the day he gave Ted his dry shoes when Ted's got wet in the creek, and came down with a bad cold.

Did Terrance ever get homesick for their old room with the bunk beds? For the wallpaper with the nautical theme and the fishnet their mother had pinned up between the bunks? Ted never asked, and Terrance never said. Jillian slept in that room now. It was painted lavender with white trim. "Who's been sleeping in my bed?" Terrance liked to say when he saw Jillian. Jillian, who had adored Uncle Terry when she was little, now just smiled, tolerant. Ted and Allison slept in his parents' bed, which still made him feel a little funny.

He decided to go the long way, to stay out of the scrutinizing gaze of his wife and daughter for that much longer, and wound up in front of the new people's house. The fellow was mowing the lawn—an odd thing to do on moving day, but an encouraging one.

The man's handshake was so firm it hurt. Ted couldn't hear his name over the roar of the mower; it wasn't till the fellow turned the mower off that he got it: Grant Davenport-Gardner.

"I use a manual mower. Beats buying gas all the time," Ted said.

"I suppose a lot of people have lawn services," Grant said.

Ted nodded. "Especially the people with the new houses, who don't have much lawn to cut."

Grant laughed. Did that mean he was on Ted's side on the big-house issue? Ted tested him. "Some of these houses are unbelievable. Like hotels."

"You said it."

They stood there for a while, nodding at each other. Ted offered Grant a wave instead of his hand when he left. There. That was something to tell Allison and Jillian about.

Nick Cox owed them a new tree, Ted thought as he continued his route to the post office. Not just a seedling, but a full-size tree. He should have just offered it outright—any decent person would have—but he hadn't. Ted had imagined confronting him many times: "Look here, Cox. You owe me a new tree." What would Cox say? "Don't you have anything more important to think about, Miller?" He could just hear him.

Ted wanted his neighborhood to be at rest again. He wanted someone to pound the gavel and tell Nick Cox, "That's enough now." He wanted a father figure to break up the fight.

So far no such person had appeared. Instead, there had been committees and committees in charge of those committees, all created to try to figure out what to do about the changing face of Willard Park. Meanwhile the older houses fell like dominoes.

Back at the house, he set the stamps on the kitchen table, at Allison's place, where she would be sure to see them. Then he went back out to the yard. To think.

5

Allison and Ted's long-debated decision to have their dinner party on the back porch on this Indian-summer night would have been the right one if the Coxes hadn't decided to throw a party as well. The Coxes were having a luau for goodness' sake, complete with tiki torches and leis, a shindig so over the top it was a parody of itself.

"Cultural appropriation," Jillian said, disapproving.

The Conways were at the Coxes', and the Fensterheims, the mayor, and a wealth of other town residents, along with a whole crew of people Allison had never seen before. Nina wore a dress that was either black or a deep blue—it was hard to tell in the dark. It was sexy, with its fitted skirt and open back, sexier than Kaye's grass skirt and bikini top. It was so warm out she didn't even look cold. Nick wore a Hawaiian shirt. Allison caught glimpses of him twirling Kaye to the Beach Boys. She forced herself to pay attention to her own guests. She, Ted, Suzanne, and Grant sat around the table, the remains of their apple pie on their plates.

Ted frowned at the goings-on next door as though they were a personal affront. He put so much energy into hating Nick. Maybe all of his energy. Nothing had changed in the sex department. It made her feel lonely. She nudged him, to remind him to be social.

"You're a lawyer, I hear?" Ted said, not taking his eyes off the Coxes' party.

"Hm?" Grant's attention seemed to be with the kids on the Coxes' couch, watching a movie on the enormous screen. His body jerked every time something exploded.

Suzanne watched Adam appear and disappear in the floodlight as Jillian pushed him on the swing—the centerpiece of Allison and Ted's yard. It hung from the forty-foot-high branch of a tulip poplar tree, and when you sat on it, you felt as though you were flying.

Suzanne's expression was complicated. Yearning, perhaps. She'd barely eaten any chili and had hardly touched the wine. It was a pinot noir that Allison and Ted liked, but they were no connoisseurs. Maybe they should have splurged on something better. Or offered white. The ice cream slouched on Suzanne's untouched apple pie. Allison kept an ear out for the kettle, on for tea.

"She usually disappears into her room when little kids come over," Allison said, nodding toward Jillian.

"What?" Suzanne said.

The music was loud. It made Allison think of driving in convertibles on open highways, of sun and sand—things that had nothing to do with her own youth, in upstate New York. She raised her voice. "The kids seem to be hitting it off."

"Adam wanted to bring his atlas, but I said no. He's always surprised when no one wants to sit around and memorize foreign countries with him."

"He reads?"

"Since he was four."

"Bright kid."

"Four is pretty typical," Suzanne said.

Was it? Jillian had learned to read at six. Had kids changed that much since Jillian was little, or was it the moms? It was stressful being a mother these days, increasingly so. Mothers who chose to stay at home were so well educated—and so ashamed about not earning a paycheck—that they put every ounce of their abundant energy into mothering, determined to get results.

She would take Suzanne under her wing, Allison decided. They already ran into each other all the time—at the post office, at the supermarket, on the green. She'd asked them to dinner one afternoon last week, when Adam was climbing on the town train and Suzanne was sitting on a bench looking despondent.

Allison would ask her if she wanted to go to yoga at the town hall next week. Maybe they would stop by Lucy's afterward for coffee. And of course Suzanne and Grant would come to the Halloween festival at the end of the month.

There was something serendipitous about Suzanne's arriving so soon after Valeria's departure, as if she'd been selected especially for Allison, to fill the empty space in her friendships. Allison imagined a different kind of a relationship with Suzanne, one more mentor/mentee; Suzanne would see her as a role model. Allison imagined a phone call in the not-too-distant future. "Will you watch Adam for a while? I just need a little 'me' time," to which she would answer, "Sure, hon. Let me just finish up some work on the book here, and I'll be right over." Suzanne would envy her her intellectual life, as well as the free time that came with having an older child. "Your time will come," Allison would assure her.

". . . near the river and all the restaurants—you can't beat it," Grant said, nodding at Ted until Ted nodded along with him, agreeing that Rosslyn sounded like the ideal place to work. She imagined

Grant in court, nodding at a jury until its members nodded back, agreeing that his client could not have committed the murder.

Grant was grasping the back of his neck with interwoven fingers, making his elbows jut out in a diamond shape behind his head. It was impossible to avoid looking at the defined muscles in his arms. The shirt he was wearing—a snug polo style with short sleeves—only added to the effect. Was it some sort of alpha-male posturing? Ted was softer, his arms more like Allison's, his face round, in contrast to Grant's strong jaw. He and Suzanne were so tall and angular, she and Ted so much smaller and rounder; it was as if they were different species. She thought of the early species of humans, some tiny, some big. Or dogs. Dogs were like that too.

"We were very sorry to hear about your loss," Suzanne said to Ted.

"My loss . . . ?" Ted said.

"Your mother," Suzanne said.

"We heard she died," Grant said.

"She . . . did."

"Well, we're very sorry. Was it expected?"

"Not entirely." Ted looked to Allison for help.

Allison heard the kettle, so she went inside, leaving the odd conversation on the porch to puzzle itself out. What was that about? Bringing up a death that had happened so many years ago?

Allison thought of all of the changes that had happened in those years: Jillian's birth and her advancement to preteen status, her and Ted's descents into middle age. Allison's favorite aunt had died during that time—young, only sixty-one—and her father had had his heart attack, which led to her parents' move to assisted living. Time was rolling on and gathering speed.

Allison was setting the teapot and cups on a tray when Adam shuffled into the kitchen.

"My head hurts," he told Allison, his voice world weary.

"I know just the thing." She got a silk scarf from the front closet and wrapped it around his forehead, a technique she'd learned at yoga, and gave him an oatmeal cookie. He thanked her with a big smile. If only she could still satisfy her own needs so easily. She put a few of the cookies on a plate. Maybe she could tempt Suzanne with those.

"On what show?" Ted was saying. He said it loud, over the music, but the music ended in the middle of his words, leaving him shouting into the night. For a moment Allison experienced the evening she'd intended to have, with cardigans and candles, the sound of Ella Fitzgerald instead of Elvis Presley.

"*Law and Order,*" Grant said.

"We never watched it."

"*Law and Order?*"

"We don't watch much TV."

"We love TV," Grant said.

"*You* love TV," Suzanne said.

"*I* love TV. She's right. She's more sophisticated than me. There's no use arguing it."

Suzanne's nod was small, nearly imperceptible.

Jillian—listening, always listening—called from the swing, "Tell them we need a smart TV."

"You don't have a smart TV?" Grant said.

"We don't *want* a smart TV," Allison said.

"*You* don't want a smart TV," Jillian said. "Dad and I do. Right, Dad?"

"Not me," Ted said, hands up in surrender.

"You could stream those shows from the old days. The ones you always talk about," Jillian said.

"*Leave It to Beaver,*" Ted said, sheepish. "*I Love Lucy.*"

"Dude," Grant said, nodding his approval.

Jillian pushed Adam on the swing, back and forth, back and forth, the motion mesmerizing Allison, who'd had two glasses of wine. Big ones. They made wineglasses so big these days. Like cups of coffee. Like cars. Like houses. The Coxes were playing the Eagles now. How was it that she couldn't remember if she'd fed the dog that morning, but she could remember every word to "Hotel California"? She poured milk in her tea until it was the exact shade she liked, not too milky, not too tea-y.

She ought to dye her hair for *Annie Get Your Gun,* she thought, noticing that Suzanne had no gray hair at all. Well, she didn't either in her thirties. Not that she had so many now, but no one would mistake her for a young girl. Annie Oakley was supposed to be, what—seventeen? It was absurd casting a woman in her forties in the role. They'd postponed rehearsals for the duration, till they found a Frank. Maybe the show would never go up. All the better for her dignity, she supposed.

Elvis was singing "Love Me Tender." Couples held one another. She looked around for Nick, but couldn't find him in the dark. He must be playing host somewhere. Filling glasses. Piling plates with pineapple and poi. She felt bad for wondering. She grabbed Ted's hand and kissed his knuckles. He squeezed her hand in return.

She felt bad, too, for turning Terrance away this evening. He'd stopped by earlier, as he often did, looking for company. She and Ted had discussed letting him stay for dinner, but in the end they agreed it would change the dynamic. "Come back tomorrow night, okay, Terrance?" she'd said, as kindly as she could, but she still felt mean. Little had she known that in marrying Ted, she'd be marrying his brother as well.

"Squirts for Squirts," Suzanne said when Allison tuned back into the conversation.

"What's that?" Allison said.

"Suzanne's new business," Grant said. "She's an entrepreneur."

"Nonviolent water toys: spitting tigers and spouting whales. You know. Not every mother wants her kid shooting an AK-47, even if it's just filled with water. I'm hoping to have a plastic animal in every kid's hand in this country by summer," Suzanne said.

Allison made a plosive sound, which she hoped sounded like the laugh of a mother who could appreciate not wanting kids to have weapons, even toy ones. She held fast to her fragile ego as Suzanne told the story of her entrepreneurial life, starting with Pop!, a flavored popcorn business that she'd nearly sold for a tremendous profit, but then the cupcake craze came along, and sales dried up. She'd invested what money was left into Sweet Dreams, a line of custom-made beds so famous and ubiquitous that Jillian had one—the *Harriet the Spy* bed, which had hidden drawers that opened with a secret code, and came with extra spy notebooks and a recipe for tomato sandwiches.

Grant rattled off a list of the beds—the Wright Brothers' plane bed that came with flying goggles and a flight notebook, the princess canopy bed with its jeweled-crown headboard and matching tiara, the pink teapot-shaped *Alice in Wonderland* bed, the queen-size cruise ship bed with lifeboats for the kids, the crib that looked like a Victorian birdcage. "We were headed toward early retirement till Nighty Night Beds came along and teamed up with Target. The legal fees just about ate us up."

Allison felt her face burn. The idea that Suzanne would look up to her! She hadn't actually said aloud, "Your time will come," had she? She sat back and waited for the inevitable question, *And what do you do, Allison?*

"Suzanne likes setting up businesses, getting them running, and setting them free," Grant said. "Once she learns to set them free a little sooner, we'll be golden."

There was a *whomp* under the table. Grant's eyes bulged as he leaned over and grabbed his shin.

Allison waited for Suzanne to apologize—who kicked their husband?—but she started talking about marketing without missing a beat. Allison smiled. She was right. Grant deserved it.

Sinatra was singing "My Way" in the Coxes' backyard. Kaye's face was nestled against Nick's chest as they danced, his hand on her ass in its grass skirt. Allison stood. "How about an after-dinner drink. Does anyone want an after-dinner drink?" She never had an after-dinner drink. Did they even own any after-dinner drinks?

Grant started singing along. His voice was smooth and rich, unexpected.

Suzanne shook her head at Grant, eyes wide, a silent but plaintive plea to stop.

"No singing at the table," Ted joked. Only Allison could tell it wasn't a joke.

"Wow," Allison said, sitting again. "You don't happen to act, too, do you?"

Grant rattled off the theatrical roles he'd played as if he'd been waiting for the chance to roll out his résumé: Sid in *The Pajama Game,* Sky in *Guys and Dolls,* Curly in *Oklahoma!* He got a dreamy look in his eye. "Chicks and ducks," he sang. He winked and held out his arm, gesturing to an imaginary surrey with a fringe on top.

Suzanne laid a restraining hand on his arm.

"You're really good," Allison said. "He's really good. You sound the part. And God knows you look like a Frank. Doesn't he, Ted? Isn't he a ringer for Frank?"

"Sure," Ted said, turning his spoon over in his hand. "I guess."

"I'm going to call Rainier and get him an audition," Allison said. "You'll do it, won't you, Grant? Try out to be Frank in the town production of *Annie Get Your Gun?*"

"He's the lead, isn't he?" Grant said.

"He and yours truly." Allison swung an imaginary lasso.

"You can't call him now, Al. It's late," Ted said.

"Are you kidding? I'd call him at three in the morning with this news." And she went inside to find her phone, Grant following close behind, practicing his scales.

IT OCCURRED TO SUZANNE THAT GRANT MIGHT BE HIGH. SHE DIDN'T have any concrete evidence—belting out show tunes at dinner wasn't exactly aberrant behavior for Grant, but there was something vague about him. He was paying more attention to the party next door than to the party he'd been invited to.

Then again, Ted seemed more interested in the other party too. His expression swung from easy smiles at the guests dancing on the grass, to frowns of annoyance and back again. He used his thick eyebrows to great effect, raising them and lowering them, like a mime. The Millers' casual clothes—untucked shirt and Birkenstocks for him, a woven blue shawl over a T-shirt and harem pants for her—made Suzanne feel fussy in her pressed slacks and blouse.

Until tonight she hadn't pieced together that Allison, the familiar-looking woman with the curly hair she kept running into, was the woman they'd seen comforting the biker in the yellow helmet near the tree stumps the day they were house hunting. It all made sense now.

"Can you believe they'd do this tonight? We haven't had people over for three months, and they have to have a party tonight," Ted said. The two of them were alone now, the thespians off making phone calls.

"What can you do?" Suzanne said. She sipped her tea, wishing she could down her wine instead. It lingered, jewel-like in its stemmed glass. She hated what a saint you had to be when you were pregnant. When you were maybe pregnant. Maybe, probably. All of life's sins taken away at once. She'd eaten a few bites of vegetarian chili just so she wouldn't seem rude, but the smell alone gave her heartburn. What she really wanted was spinach. She didn't ordinarily care for spinach, but these days she wanted it all the time, raw or steamed, puréed or sautéed. She would take a pregnancy test soon. This week, maybe, although she preferred not having confirmation. It was better to think she might still be in control of her body. To be in control of her life.

Maybe then she could gain control of her businesses and turn a profit she could keep, something she could grow into a fortune all her own. She felt a little bad for kicking Grant. Not awful—why would he embarrass her in front of the Millers? But he was right. So far she'd always sold her companies too late. If she'd been a little more savvy she would have had quite a little nest egg by now.

"Ready to be a stage widow?" Ted said.

"He might not get the part."

"Oh, he'll get the part."

"It'll be good for us. Get him out of the house." She zipped her lips with her first finger and thumb. "I didn't say that."

He laughed, which made Suzanne smile. She couldn't help enjoying the thought of silent evenings: Adam in bed, the house all hers. A play would be a positive distraction for Grant. And it would keep him from running so much, an idea that pleased her. Her feelings toward his running were admittedly schizophrenic. She didn't want him to stop. She just didn't want him to be better than she was.

Theater was a good hobby, an interest they didn't share. Grant was a ham. His sisters told terrible stories accompanied by hysterical laughter about his childhood, when he dressed in a bow tie, slicked back his hair, and sang for their parents' guests.

Their first date had been an odd one. She hadn't even known it was a date. Grant gave Suzanne a ticket to a community theater production of *Mame,* in which he was playing Patrick. She sat alone in the front pew at the church. The usher grinned at her a lot. "You're as pretty as Grant said you were." As pretty? He was her lawyer, not her lover.

At the time she was working for a tobacco company, which was against her principles, but they were the ones who made the best offer when she graduated from Kellogg, and as earning a good living was among her goals, she accepted the job.

In those days she had been one of only a handful of women who held positions higher than assistant at the company, and it was quickly made clear that she was never going to be one of the boys. The men talked over her in meetings, claimed her ideas as their own, and when they bothered to ask her to join them for drinks or lunch, "kidded" about which one of them she was going to sleep with. When, after many such incidents, she indicated, finally, that she was tired of being harassed, they accused her of not being able to take a joke. She suspected she earned less than they did, but if they ever talked about their salaries, it must have been during their frequent golf outings—to which she was never invited, even though she had taken golf lessons for that very purpose. She wanted out nearly as soon as she got in, and thus she worked on building her own business—Pop!—nights and weekends, preparing for the day when she earned enough money with her own ingenuity that she didn't have to put up with their sexist palaver.

She'd met Grant when the owner of Pop—no exclamation mark—a small, Wichita-based company, threatened to sue her. The man claimed that her popcorn business threatened his business selling custom-designed items—T-shirts, baseball caps, and the like—for fathers and grandfathers (Pop Pop was a subsidiary).

Grant solved the problem with a well-crafted letter on his firm's letterhead.

Maybe if he'd been a little less handsome she would have had the good sense to keep the relationship strictly business, but he was cute and affable. She wasn't meeting anyone except the jerks at the office, so why not? He was so different from her other boyfriends. She'd had two: Geoffrey, a fellow athlete and merit scholar, whom she'd dated from the day they met in AP English junior year of high school until they graduated from UVA, and Daniel, a brilliant fellow Kellogg student whom she'd been with from the first day of graduate school until they accepted jobs in different cities. He'd wanted them to stay together, to have a long-distance relationship, but she said no. It seemed silly to her. So inefficient.

After she and Grant started dating, she got him to take up running and join a gym, and to stop partying with his old high school friends, who'd graduated but hadn't moved on. She showed him how to style his hair with gel instead of a blow dryer, and went with him to buy a wardrobe that was more Brooks Brothers and less JCPenney. He was her Eliza Doolittle. All signs pointed to his continuing to develop as the years went by, gradually shedding his second-rate ways entirely.

Had she been a little smarter, she would have instituted a probation period. Then she would have seen that he would only get so far before he stopped short, but she'd met him toward the end of the window of years when—according to the Life Plan she had created as a college freshman—it was time to get married. Thus what should have been just a poorly chosen boyfriend at most, became not only her husband but the man who fathered her child—something that was not on her Life Plan at all, but had penciled itself in of its own accord when her back was turned. She was glad that it had, of course; Adam was her dream child, so smart and determined. He reminded her of herself when she was young, but with all the advantages of a two-parent home.

She still had hopes that Grant would get his life back on track now that they had moved. His job in Rosslyn had potential, and he might meet new, more ambitious friends if he was in the play. Then he could finally let his old friends go. He was still quite involved with them, texting or calling one or another of them incessantly. How many times a day did he look at his phone and burst out laughing? There was Dave, the insurance agent with the poly-blend shirts and the goatee; Pete, the smarmy restaurant manager who was always giving her the eye; and chubby little box-jawed Marie. She was in love with him, obviously, but Suzanne had seen pictures of Grant's continuous string of girlfriends in high school and college, all tall and pretty. Marie would have had to come to terms with the fact that they would never be more than friends years ago.

"I like your house," Suzanne said, returning to the present. It was like a fairy-tale cottage, small and cozy and full of books.

"I grew up here," Ted said.

"I grew up in an apartment," Suzanne said.

"I always thought elevators were exciting when I was a kid."

"Ours broke a lot."

Adam climbed up the porch steps and plunked himself down on Suzanne's lap.

"Hi, little fellow."

"Can Grammy come this weekend?"

She fingered the scarf on his head. Silk. "Are you playing pirate?"

"Allison put it on me. For my headache. Can Grammy come, Mommy?"

"You have a headache?"

Jillian jumped up the steps and grabbed a cookie from the plate. She was a wholesome-looking kid with freckles and straight brown hair, a human Peppermint Patty. Suzanne searched for the resemblance to her parents. Perhaps a bit more of Ted. Eyebrows that she would eventually want to pluck. Ted's wide, expressive mouth. Straight hair in contrast to Allison's curly. Jillian twisted her arms around one another, like a pretzel, then unwrapped them and twisted them the other way. "Come back out, Adam. It's boring."

Adam broke free from Suzanne's embrace, assaulting Grant when he and Allison returned. "Daddy, push me!" Soon the men were on the lawn, pushing the kids on the swing, Adam on Jillian's lap. Adam laughed, his scarf waving behind him like a young Amelia Earhart.

"What's wrong?" Allison asked Suzanne.

"Things aren't going as planned," Suzanne said.

"What things?"

"My life. My life is not going according to plan."

Allison laughed. Her cheeks were high and round, like ripe peaches, making it look as though her eyes were closed when she smiled. "Does it ever?"

Yes! Suzanne wanted to say. *It does! It must!* "I'm screwed."

"Why?"

"Half-day kindergarten. Three measly hours—which basically means I'm a full-time mom. I have a business to attend to. I can't spend my days making cookies." Allison's eyelid ticked, just enough for Suzanne to realize she'd insulted her. "I mean—"

"I'm a photographer," Allison said, a beat too quickly.

"Oh! Should I have heard of you?"

"I don't know. Should I have heard of *you?*"

They caught eyes, then both of them looked away at the same time, into the yard, where Grant was pushing the kids up to the heavens.

"Hold on tight," Suzanne said, wanting to tiptoe back through the conversation, to the moment before she put her foot in her mouth. No wonder she didn't have any friends.

"How about first grade? He's so bright. Have you thought about him skipping a grade?" Allison said.

"They don't recommend it."

"Who are they?"

"You know. *Them.*" She moved her arm around in the air. "The ones who write the books and articles."

"Are 'they' going to pay the psych bills when you go crazy from a surfeit of cookie baking?" She smiled, forgiving Suzanne her gaffe.

Suzanne smiled back. She allowed herself a fantasy: Adam at school every day till three, getting so much intellectual stimulation he'd nap all afternoon, letting her work. "Hm."

"Mmm," Allison echoed. "Listen to that."

"What?"

"Silence. Do you hear that? The silence between the songs. It's like the white space on the page."

Suzanne wasn't sure what she meant, but it sounded nice. The white space. Was it about seeing positives where there were negatives? Or vice versa? She took a cookie from the tray. "I like your shawl," she said, fingering the fringe.

"I made it. I have a loom."

"You made it? All I make are appointments."

Allison laughed.

"What made you think my mother died?" Ted was asking Grant when they came back to the table.

"Nina Strauss told us. When we saw you in the road the day we were house hunting," Grant said.

"Nina!" Ted and Allison said, as one. "You can't trust Nina."

"My mother died before Jillian was born . . . ," Ted said.

Grant and Suzanne looked at each other, Suzanne wondering what else Nina had lied about.

"That was the day Nick Cox cut down the trees," Ted said, his voice low, nearly biblical in tone.

"Oh!" Allison said. "Don't bring up the trees!"

They all were silent for several seconds, as though giving the trees the moment of respect they were due.

"Have you met Nick Cox?" Ted said.

"No," Suzanne said.

"He cut down the tree we planted for Jillian. It wasn't even on his property. I should sue him. You're a lawyer. Do you think I should sue him?" Ted asked Grant.

"Ted's obsessed with that tree," Allison said.

"I'm not obsessed," Ted said.

"Does this Cox have a gold SUV?" Grant said.

"The only one in town."

"I think he's the guy I met at the hardware store. Buying a grill."

"Someone delivered a grill to our house by mistake the other day," Suzanne said. Grant looked up sharply, then down again.

"That's the Coxes' house," Allison said, pointing next door.

"That house and the one over there. The White Elephant. Rumor has it that it's going to have a racquetball court," Ted said.

"How about that, Grant?" Suzanne said. It was a joke between them. He refused to play after Suzanne beat him a couple of times when they were dating.

"The new house he's building?" Ted said. "It's so close to our house, you can nearly touch it. I stood on the edge of the yard and reached out a broom handle. I got within inches."

"You did?" Grant said.

"It's getting out of control. There has to be some way of getting those fat cats out of here. Get the town to reconsider letting them build these huge things," Ted said.

"Do the other neighbors feel the way you do?"

"Most of them. No question. What's in it for them?"

"Higher property values, I'd guess," Grant said.

"I think it'll lower them. People move to Willard Park to get away from all that," Ted said.

"Yeah?"

"You want to live in a big house, move to Potomac."

Grant seemed to make a mental note.

"It used to be nice out there. Horse country. Now it's just mansion after mansion." He shook his head. "That's where Willard Park is headed, I'm afraid."

"Draw up a petition. If you have enough interest, you might be able to get a building moratorium. Other towns have done it."

Ted beamed at him, an expression not unlike Adam's on the swing.

"Look at your son," Allison said.

"When's the last time you had that much fun?" Ted said.

"Probably when—" Grant began.

Suzanne cut him off. "It was a rhetorical question."

"My head still hurts," Adam called when he saw the adults watching him.

Grant went out to the yard, and gave him a big push, edging him up to the second floor. Adam shrieked.

"Grant! He just said his head hurts," Suzanne said.

Grant slowed the swing down awkwardly. Adam sat down on the ground and howled. It was time for them to go home. She couldn't be the only one who felt it.

Grant offered to give Adam a piggyback ride home, but he wanted Mommy to do it. "I wish I could, pumpkin," she said, and Adam hit her leg. She briefly considered hitting him back.

They smiled and thanked and pledged to do it again, soon, at Suzanne and Grant's, once they got it fixed up, oh you'll have it to your liking in no time, looking forward to it, good luck, good night, good night, they called to one another. Good night. Good night. Suzanne, Grant, and Adam walked down the path to the sidewalk, past the Coxes' party—still going strong—and down the street, toward home.

6

A bunch of grapes was in the lead. It seemed unlikely, with all those purple balloons wiggling to and fro, but there she was, a girl of maybe ten, outrunning the bewigged pop stars and the superheroes in their padded chests and capes. The kids' Halloween fun run was a quarter mile long, around the green a couple of times; the adults' race was three miles through the neighborhood. Grant was warming up for it, jogging in place in his jodhpurs. He snugged the string of his cowboy hat tight against his chin, hoping the flapping wouldn't slow him down.

The cast of *Annie Get Your Gun* had been given cowboy clothes to wear, things Allison found at Mitchell's Variety: a little advance publicity for the play, of which Grant was now an official cast member. It was lucky Mitchell's didn't carry cowboy boots. You couldn't run in cowboy boots. He held his phone out, made a wry smile, and snapped a selfie, messaging it to the gang. Their message thread was a comfort—like carrying his best friends around in his pocket.

Adam, dressed as a vampire, sat on the curb, fake blood painted by the corner of his mouth, white plastic fangs in hand.

"You should've run it, buddy," Grant said. "You could have

won in the five and unders. Being five would have given you a huge edge."

Adam tore open a bag of miniature pretzels, tossed to him by a clown on an oversize tricycle.

"Jillian's going to babysit you while I run if Mommy's not back." Grant pointed to a table on the other end of the soccer field, where Jillian and another girl handed out water in cone-shaped paper cups to kids in the race. The girls wore the black T-shirt adorned with the white outline of a ghost that many of the older kids wore.

A note in the town newsletter laid out the times of the races and the costume parade, during which the Willard Park fire truck would make a special appearance. In the afternoon the kids were invited to trick or treat at the local shops. The day would be capped off with a potluck, followed by ghost stories and music on the green after dark.

Residents were reminded that the town council supported the healthy Halloween initiative sponsored by the town Halloween Fun Committee. They offered a list of suggested alternatives to candy such as carrot packs, stickers, and pencils. What a bummer. Grant liked those little candy bars. He had looked forward to stuffing them in his suit jacket pocket to nosh on during stressful moments at work, of which there had been none too few in the weeks since he started. He anticipated more of them. Extended hours of them. "Can I have a pretzel?" he said, and Adam gave him one.

A faint buzz in his pocket. A text back from Marie: Giddy up, cowboy! R u seriously running in that? Haha. Then one from Dave that said simply, Dude.

The Beast was walking toward him. A small, matching blond boy accompanied him, a tiny groomsman. The Beast costume was clearly a rental: a purple velvet jacket and black boots, furry arms and horns. His beastly hair cascaded down his back.

"You missed my party," the Beast said, his voice muffled through the mask. He extended a paw.

Grant shook it. "Cox? Is that you in there?"

Nick Cox took off his mask and held it in his arms like the head of John the Baptist. "I cooked bison on the grill. Did you ever eat bison? I have this idea about tasting every mammal on Earth before I die."

"Humans?" Grant said.

"Why didn't you come?"

"Never got an invitation, I guess."

"You kidding me? I invited you personally."

They introduced their sons, who looked about the same age. Adam extended his hand as Suzanne had trained him to do; Nick's son looked at it as though he were handing him a fish. "Did you see the tree?" Nick said.

"The tree?"

"My neighbor, the tree." He pointed to Ted Miller, standing on the café porch. Branches were stuck to Ted's sombrero and his arms and legs were covered with leaves. He wore a green sandwich board, the front of which said DON'T STUMP ME OUT!

"I guess you heard about the petition," Nick said.

"I heard something . . ."

"It says 'Let's run Nick Cox out of town.'"

"It does?"

"Might as well. 'The Petition for Peace,' Miller's calling it. He wants a moratorium on building houses in Willard Park." Nick lifted the edge of his lip in a snarl. "This town . . . It's crazy, all the regulations here. What a joke! No sugar. No playground slides at too extreme an angle. Twenty miles per hour speed limit. No fun, in a word. What's the point of living like a bunch of nuns?"

Grant tapped his fitness tracker, tap, tap, tap. "Hm?"

"If I want to live in a nice house, don't I have a right?" Nick said.

"Why not?" Grant would have preferred Nick's house—either one—to the dolls' house they'd bought. He didn't find it charming to have a bathroom so small you could hardly stand up straight in the shower, or a kitchen with a refrigerator that wasn't much bigger than the one in his college dorm room. Suzanne was so taken with the town that she didn't seem to care, but to him it felt like a demotion from their four-bedroom Colonial.

Adam pulled on Grant's sleeve. He had to go to the bathroom. "*Now.*"

"Where?"

"Home," Adam said.

"No time. My race is starting soon."

"Lucy's. She has lemon soap."

Father and son walked toward the café. Adam was slow despite his supposed urgency. Grant hoisted him onto his back. "Did you eat breakfast? Maybe that's why you don't feel good."

"I had a spinach-avocado smoothie," Adam said, indignant.

A spray-painted sheet hung from the porch roof: SIGN THE PETITION FOR PEACE AND GET A FREE CIDER!

An overweight version of Ted, dressed as a baseball player, stood beside the real Ted on the porch. "Free cider!" the faux Ted called. "Get your free cider!"

Grant shook hands as Adam tore into the café.

"Do you want to sign this?" Ted's brother said. He flapped a laminated information sheet in front of Grant.

Grant smiled. "Looks pretty professional."

"I got fifteen signatures in the past hour," Ted said. "Some people are probably doing it for the cider—that was Lucy's idea—but it doesn't matter. The point is to get the town council to consider the moratorium. Thanks for your help, by the way."

Grant confirmed that Nick was out of hearing distance. "No problem."

He eyed the races. The older kids' run was over now. Allison was taking pictures—not of the kids, but of the parents, taking photos with their phones. All the kids got blue ribbons.

"I tell them the catch is, if we don't do something, we're going to end up with wall-to-wall houses. It's Halloween. Scaring is allowed," Ted said, chuckling at his own joke. "How are you enjoying *Annie Get Your Gun* rehearsals? Rumor has it you're a real pro."

Grant shook his head, modest. "I'm no pro."

"I didn't mean you were actually a pro."

"I was nearly a pro."

"Really?"

"My mother took me to L.A. when I was ten. I nearly got on a kids' TV show. Sort of like *The Mickey Mouse Club*."

"We used to watch that." Ted nudged his brother. "Remember, Terr? Remember *The Mickey Mouse Club*?"

"We had mouse ears. We went to Disney World," the brother said.

"It wasn't *The Mickey Mouse Club*, but that kind of thing. A kids' variety show. I nearly got on."

"Wow," the brothers said.

Grant felt both pride and shame surrounding that audition. Pride that he'd gotten that close to television fame. Shame over the blue earrings. The young actress who had led the pack of children through the auditions asked him to keep them safe while she taught them a dance number. He didn't even remember that they were in his pocket until he and his mother were on the flight home the next day, long after the crying jag and the banana split that was meant to console him for not making the final cut.

He still had those earrings, wrapped in white tissue and secured with a purple rubber band. He should have gotten rid of them years ago—given them away, thrown them away even, but he couldn't somehow. They were another mark against him, like the weed in the plastic Baggie in his closet: another piece of evidence that showed him, if not the world, that he wasn't really cut out to be a lawyer. Not scrupulous enough. Not law-abiding enough.

Ted handed Grant the clipboard with the Petition for Peace on it. "Sign away."

Grant twirled the pen in his fingers like a miniature baton. He understood Ted's point of view, but he also understood Cox's. That was the trouble. He agreed with both of them. He looked over at the people gathering for the fun run, neighbors dressed as movie stars and political candidates. Where was Suzanne? She'd left for the grocery store ages ago. "Looks like the race is about to start . . ." He handed the petition, unsigned, back to Ted.

JILLIAN PICKED UP THE PAPER CUPS THE KIDS IN THE FUN RUN HAD thrown on the ground. She was earning student-service-learning hours, volunteer hours required to graduate from middle school. She and Sofia used to do their hours together, tallying them up in a "do-good" notebook they'd planned to keep adding to till they graduated from high school. It must have been someone's idea of a joke to assign Lindy Cox to the same job. Lindy stared at her like Jillian was a maid who'd been hired to help out at a party. Every now and then Lindy would shake her head, a mystified expression on her face.

Did she think Jillian looked stupid in her T-shirt? It was the one that had won the annual T-shirt design contest. Mark Strauss had designed it this year, which was cool because a girl usually won. Come to think of it, Lindy was wearing the same shirt, so that couldn't be it. Was it her pimples? Jillian had woken up with a red pimple on her nose. She should have dressed up as Rudolph the Red-Nosed Reindeer. "What?" Jillian finally said, unable to stand Lindy's scrutiny.

Lindy pointed to a crumpled cup by the tree. "You missed one."

Jillian snatched it up, then felt stupid and wanted to throw it down again, but that would be stupid too.

"Why are you picking them up, anyway? No one said we had to," Lindy said.

"Haven't you ever heard of global warming?"

"Paper cups don't cause global warming."

"Someone has to pick them up."

"Glad it's not me," Lindy said.

Grant jogged over. He was pulling vampire-Adam by the hand.

"All set to watch my little man here?" Grant jogged in place.

Jillian felt a little seasick watching him bounce up and down. "Sure." She took Adam's hand. "See you later, Mr. Davenport-Gardner."

"Call me Grant. 'Mister' makes me feel too much like a grown-up. Ha! It makes me feel like my dad!"

"Okay . . ." What was he, if not a grown-up?

It was unclear what to call adults. Some, like teachers, insisted on mister and missus. Or miz. Then others were all about their first names, as if they wanted to be your friend. Sometimes it was easier to call them nothing at all.

"Where are your fangs, kid?" Lindy said.

He opened his other hand to reveal them. They looked sort of orthodontic. "Do they hurt?" Jillian said.

"Who are you?" Lindy asked.

"A vampire," Adam said.

"I mean, what's your name?"

"Adam Davenport-Gardner," Adam said.

"You're going to learn to spell that when you're what, thirty?"

"I know how to spell!" Adam said.

"They're the new people," Jillian said.

"Tell your mom I babysit," Lindy said.

"I'm his sitter," Jillian said.

"I'm nicer," Lindy told Adam.

"No she's not. She's mean," Jillian blurted out.

Lindy laughed. It wasn't a mean laugh. More of a surprised one. "Want some candy? At my house, we're giving out candy. All the candy you can eat. Tunlaw, 2201. Halloween night. Be there."

"Okay," Adam said.

"Don't eat pretzels," Lindy said. "They make your teeth rot."

Someone blew a whistle and the adult runners were off. Mr. Morton, as Superman, and Mr. Li, as a long-haired rock star in sunglasses, led the pack, along with the *Annie Get Your Gun* director, who wore an Indian headdress. Lucy was a blue-haired witch and Mrs. Rosenberg, the French teacher, wore a chef's hat and apron.

Mr. Davenport-Gardner—Grant—started at the back of the pack, then bounded out in front. He pointed at Adam, Lindy, and Jillian with imaginary pistols. The only thing worse than imagining her mom pretending to be in love with an unknown person in the town play was knowing who the person was.

Her parents weren't running in the race, which was a relief. Her mom was on Lucy's porch taking pictures in a too-short denim skirt and cowboy hat. Jillian had to look away. "My friend designed this shirt," she said, showing her shirt to Adam.

"Oh, your *friend*," Lindy said.

"He is my friend."

"Then why don't you say hello to him? Hey, Mark!"

"Shut up!" Where was he? Could he hear them? Jillian looked around, but Lindy was laughing.

"I'm kidding. God. You don't have to freak out. He's over at his mom's table, handing out magnets. He's hot, huh?"

Jillian studied Lindy, not sure if she was making fun of her. "He's, like, the best goalie, right?" She felt mean serving him up that way. Mark was nice in addition to being insanely cute. He was interested in things other than sports and boogers, like art and animals.

"He sucks, but he's hot. How well do you know him?"

"We went to preschool together."

"He's in my math class."

Jillian nodded; she knew. Mark was in Seventh-Grade Math, which was really remedial math. The grade-level classes were for the kids with learning issues, and the so-called gifted classes were for everyone else. It was either done so the kids who needed help wouldn't feel bad, or so the other kids would feel like they were brilliant, but everyone knew it was fake.

Jillian picked up more cups. Lindy even tossed a few in the box. They held out waters when the runners came past them, but only a few people took them—probably just to be nice. It wasn't hot. Jillian looked for Adam, but he was gone. "Hey, Adam!" She looked around, frantic. "Where is he?"

"Hey!" Lindy called. "Get back here, kid, or no candy!"

"I'm here," he whispered from under the table.

Jillian squatted. "What are you doing there?"

"It's quiet," he said.

"Quiet?" Lindy squatted too. "You're looking for quiet at a Halloween thing?"

"I have a headache," Adam said.

SUZANNE DODGED A COUPLE OF HIP-HIGH FAIRIES AS SHE WALKED across the green toward Lucy's. She needed her latte. She had a headache that shot right across the bow, a headache that only caffeine would cure. The baby—if there was indeed a baby—would survive a little caffeine. She'd just come from the grocery store, where she'd bought a home pregnancy test. It sat in the trunk of the car, cowering between the milk and the bread.

Nearly everyone in town was dressed up, adults and children alike. Suzanne looked around for a familiar face. If she was lucky, she wouldn't run into the elementary school principal, a slight, brittle woman who had been rabidly opposed to skipping Adam to first grade. As stubborn as the principal was, Suzanne was worse. Or better. She'd gotten Adam settled into his new grade on the first day of school, before the morning math block began. Now she had six and a half hours a day to work. Six and a half glorious hours.

Allison was near the café, taking a photo of a shaggy-haired boy holding up a black T-shirt. Nina Strauss, dressed as either a cat or a raccoon, kept trying to dab gel in his hair; the boy leaned away from her gelatinous hands.

"Okay, Nina. Thanks," Allison said. "Let's try again."

The problem was clear. The boy kept flipping back his hair every time Allison tried to snap a photo.

Nina leaned in with the gel again. "It's for the newspaper, honey."

"Mom! No one cares about a T-shirt contest," the boy said.

"Yes they do," Nina said, nodding at Allison, then at Suzanne when she saw her. "Don't they, Suzanne? Ask Suzanne. Isn't winning a contest a fabulous résumé padder?"

"It is, actually," Suzanne said.

"Don't you want to be in the newspaper?" Nina said.

"Newspapers kill trees," Mark said.

"Don't bring up trees where Ted can hear you," Allison said.

"You must get more light now, though . . . ?" Nina said.

"I suppose. But now we have to look at that awful house."

"Let's hope he doesn't start a trend. The trees make this town. Honestly. They're half its charm. Take down the trees and I'm going to need to find a new place to hang my shingle."

Allison turned her camera to Mark and got her shot. "Hurray! You're dismissed," she said, and the boy ran off, away from Nina, who went in the other direction, glistening hands aloft.

"Grant was in the fun run. Did you see him?" Allison said. "He won. Not that winning is the point in a fun run . . ."

"Fun run. Isn't that an oxymoron?" Suzanne said. Yes, she was a runner, but no, she didn't have "fun" doing it. Runner's high was made up, as far as she could tell.

"Touché."

"I just bought a hundred dollars' worth of school supplies," Suzanne said as they climbed the steps to Lucy's. "Are they nuts? Six different colored notebooks. A three-inch-thick binder. Ten mechanical pencils. Colored pencils. A protractor and compass. A rolling knapsack—this is first grade we're talking about. You didn't tell me about the principal."

"She's new this year . . ."

"He had to bring toiletries too. Antibacterial soap and paper towels. What kind of doomsday scenario do they have in mind?"

"In my day first-graders were issued a thick red pencil," Ted said. He was on the porch with a clipboard.

"Nice costume," Suzanne said. "All we have to do is plant you."

Ted bowed as much as his sandwich board would allow. "Where's your costume?"

Suzanne looked down at her slacks and blouse, her cashmere pullover. "I'm a stressed-out mother. Aren't I convincing?"

Ted gave her the petition. "All we want to do is get the town council to discuss the idea. That's all you're doing by signing. Saying you support that. We just want to keep houses like Nick Cox's out in the exurbs, where they belong."

"He has a nice new house," said an alternate, heavier version of Ted dressed in a baseball shirt and cap.

"I didn't know there were two of you," Suzanne said, receiving an introduction. "Baseball fan?"

Terrance nodded. "And Ted likes trees. Allison likes cowboy stuff, right, Allison?"

"Sort of . . . ," Allison said.

"What do you like?" Terrance asked Suzanne.

Suzanne could feel her smile cracking, aging. "I like . . . ," she said. What did she like? It was an interesting question. To win? Did that count? "I like coffee. I'm going to get one."

She went into the café, where she meant to become a regular. She studied the menu above the counter in search of a size larger than large.

Lucy, with blue hair and blackened teeth, was serving up a Halloween menu of hot and cold Jack-o'-Lantern Juice and Ghostly White Hot Chocolate. There were candy apples, and, in addition to the ordinary bars and cookies, frosted cookies shaped like witches and ghosts—some for humans and others for dogs. A big jug full of candy corn sat on the counter beside a small sign: GUESS HOW MANY AND WIN A LUCY'S T-SHIRT! Lucy could teach her a thing or two about marketing, Suzanne thought.

Beauty sat at a table in the corner with a little boy. Blond hair, yellow gown—she complemented Lucy's color scheme perfectly. Kaye Cox. They'd met a few weeks ago, when Kaye stopped by with a bright pink plate full of fudge.

Suzanne, in the midst of unpacking that afternoon, nearly had invited her inside, but the overeagerness of Kaye's smile made her hold her at bay. Suzanne set the fudge on the kitchen counter after Kaye left, cut a square, and went back to unpacking the pots and pans. The fudge was cloyingly sweet, but it called to her all day long nonetheless, drawing her close with its siren song. She'd eaten four pieces before she dumped the whole thing, neon plate and all, into the trash. In another life, she would have gone for a long, hard run, to burn it all off—but how could she with a bum knee and Adam to watch? She wanted her mother. She really did. She nearly called her, but in the end refrained, afraid "Grammy" would pack the car and drive up, to her rescue. *I always said it was too much running, but who listens to the old lady? What does she know?*

Suzanne thought about Kaye's plate now, cracked in a landfill somewhere. What if she asked Grant or Adam how they liked the fudge? Or asked for her plate back? Suzanne turned around, intending to walk out of the café, meaning to spend the next thirty years avoiding Kaye Cox.

"Susie!" Kaye called.

"Suzanne," Suzanne said, smiling as wide as she could manage. "I'm just getting a coffee. A big one, I think."

Kaye nodded, knowingly. "I feel you."

"Can I get you anything?"

"Oh gosh, no! This is Jakey. Have you met Jakey?"

Jakey was eating a cookie as big as his head, crumbs falling onto his plate.

"Hi, Jakey!" Suzanne said. "Thanks for the fudge, by the way. It was really good."

"My mother's recipe. Hey, your husband won the fun run." Kaye shimmied, which felt weirdly inappropriate.

Suzanne decided to use her joke again. "Fun run. Sounds like an oxymoron."

Kaye laughed a little loud and long. Did she know what an oxymoron was? They said you couldn't judge a book by its cover. But sometimes you actually could.

Kaye patted the empty chair beside her when Suzanne came back with her latte. "Come sit with us!" she said.

"I have to . . ." What did she have to? "See how the champion is doing!"

"Rain check?" Kaye said.

"Absolutely."

"How about my house Monday morning?"

Suzanne was unprepared. Monday, Monday. "I have to take Adam to the doctor." It was true. He had been feeling under the weather for weeks.

"Tuesday?"

"I'm going to yoga." Yoga! What made her say "yoga"? What was the point of yoga? You couldn't win at yoga.

"How about after class?"

Suzanne, out of ideas, nodded. Half an hour. She could spend half an hour with Little Mary Sunshine. Maybe it would be good for her, actually, to spend time with a smiling person, even if the smile seemed slightly desperate.

She walked out into the October sun, taking in the smell of her coffee. She waited for the ahhhh, the sensual, lift-me-off-my-feet feeling the smell always gave her, but her stomach tightened. She breathed out through her nose, emptying it of previous notions, and sniffed again. Again, it smelled off. Damn it. She didn't need the stupid pregnancy test. She offered her latte to Allison, sitting on the café steps, reviewing her pictures on her camera.

Allison smiled. "How did you know?"

7

T ed and Allison sat on beach chairs on the grass in front of Lucy's listening to old Mr. Fitzwilliams play the fiddle while Mrs. Fitzwilliams sang "If I Had a Hammer." The moon was bright enough to light the green, casting flickering moon shadows of the older residents and children dancing on the grass. The Halloween festival was drawing to a close, the bowls and platters from the potluck down to their last bites; the fire truck, upon which the children had climbed, back at the firehouse.

When Ted was a child, there had been a parade starting at the elementary school for the mothers on Halloween, during which the children showed off their costumes, most of them homemade. In those days kids dressed as gypsies and ghosts, hobos, witches, and ballerinas with cardigans over their sparkling tutus. At twilight they knocked on doors holding a bag for candy in one hand and a small orange cardboard box in the other: "Trick or treat for UNICEF," they would cry, and receive candy along with coins they gave to their classroom teachers the next day. What ever happened to those little boxes? They were such a simple way to remind children to think of others.

These days Halloween went on all day and into the night, dinner on the green followed by music and two cauldrons of cider, one spiked, provided by Lucy. This was a change, but not a bad one; even Ted could see that.

The Fitzwilliams started playing "The Fox Went Out on a Chilly Night" and Allison clapped along. Ted was not a clapper. He didn't have a good sense of rhythm, and the idea of being off beat embarrassed him. It was the same reason he wouldn't dance. Allison couldn't understand why he wouldn't dance with her. She didn't understand the deep feeling of humiliation he felt that he moved so gracelessly, so out of time. She was disappointed in him these days. She'd wanted to have sex the other night, so he pretended to be interested—but it was clear pretty quickly that he wasn't all that interested after all. She'd asked him if he'd be open to trying something new. "Sure . . . ," he said, not at all sure.

"How about porn?" she'd said, as casually as if she were suggesting they order a pizza.

"Porn?"

"Can't hurt," she said with a laugh.

He was glad to see that she appeared to be new to it. She typed a few words into her laptop, and then a few others, until they came up with a website that seemed to specialize in this sort of thing. It was shocking, really, what you could find with a few quick taps of your finger. The offerings were like items in a candy machine—so many choices, each more decadent than the last. Who wanted to watch someone do that? Or that!

"How about this one," Allison said, but then she looked at Ted's face, and her own face closed down. She shut the computer, turning the room dark. He could hear her set it on her night table.

"Well, good night," he'd said, and they'd gone to sleep on the far reaches of the mattress.

His mother used to say that he and Terrance marched to the beat of a different drummer. Another boy might have felt embarrassed to be compared to his disabled brother, but Ted agreed with her. He was never a teenager the way he was supposed to be, had never rebelled against what he already realized was the good life. As a boy he assumed that the four of them—he and Terrance and their parents—would spend their lives together in their house. Well, the five of them, he thought, smiling as he thought of his and Terrance's imaginary brother, Thomas.

"You okay?" Allison said.

Ted nodded. "Yep."

Thomas would approve of the petition, he thought—but he wouldn't settle for the number of signatures Ted had garnered today. Thomas would get everyone in town to sign it. Starting tomorrow Ted would go door-to-door and ask his neighbors directly to support the preservation of their town. He would embody Thomas.

Terrance approached with a cup of cider. He gave it to Ted, then sat on the grass beside him. "It's not spiky," he said.

Ted sipped. No. He wouldn't have minded a spiked one, but oh well. "Thanks, pal."

Terrance still had his baseball outfit on. Ted had dispensed with his uncomfortable tree costume at Jillian's behest, but Allison was wearing her cowgirl outfit by design—she got up now, joining Grant at the microphone.

"And now, little lady, if you'll kindly step up to the parapet, I'll give you a lesson in marksmanship," Grant said. He pretended to shoot a bird out of the sky and catch it.

"You couldn't give me a lesson in long-distance spittin'!" Allison said, hands on hips, and she began singing: "Anything you can do . . ."

Jillian, sitting nearby, was clearly wishing she was anywhere else, but the truth was, they weren't bad. Their choreography still needed a little work, but Allison could carry a tune, and Grant had stage presence. When they finished, a trio of boys with guitars from the high school Spanish club performed "Guantanamera," which inspired a whole new crop of dancers to join in. Allison held out a hand to Terrance. "Want to dance?"

Terrance, too, was a lousy dancer, but he didn't care. He did a few disco moves, then some Irish dance steps, with a little Mexican hat dance thrown in. Meanwhile Allison danced fluidly, smiling and laughing. The Cox boy danced with Kaye. Grant danced alone, while Suzanne and Adam sat on a blanket, both looking like they'd rather be home, sleeping.

Terrance tipped his head and body from side to side, making Ted think of the *Peanuts* characters dancing on *A Charlie Brown Christmas*. When the song ended, Allison kissed the top of his hand, and he kissed hers. Then he gave her a big bear hug, which made her laugh.

Ted offered some cider to Terrance, who was still tipping his head to the side. He was hot from dancing, his face moist looking. "The trees look funny," he said.

"Funny how?"

"Like they want to take a nap."

Ted looked where Terrance was looking, at the little copse of woods near the playground—he was right. Something did look off. Ted headed over to investigate, and Terrance followed. It was quieter there, and darker, the moonlight straining to make its way through the leaves.

Most of the trees looked fine, but others, no. The moon shadows were sideways, and indeed the trees themselves were sideways, their trunks bent or snapped clean. Not the big ones; the big ones looked all right. It was the small trees, saplings—just a handful of them. Two of them just leaned over toward the earth, but two others were uprooted, their trunks on the ground like fallen soldiers.

"Odd," Ted said.

Terrance tugged the less broken trees upright, but they sagged again. He looked at Ted. "Don't cry, Teddy. It's okay."

"I'm not crying."

Terrance frowned. "Okay," he said in the tone of someone who has been told the world is flat when he knows it is round.

"Cox," Ted said, shaking his head.

"What's that?" Terrance said.

"Our neighbor. He did this."

"He did?"

"Yes." Ted sighed.

Terrance sighed too. "Cox," he said.

8

Lindy's kitchen smelled good—like butter and cheese and all the things you were supposed to eat "in moderation." Lindy's mom was making a grilled cheese sandwich.

"Hi, girls." Lindy's mom smiled over her shoulder as though Jillian walked through their door every day. In fact it was the first time Jillian had ever stepped inside the Coxes' house. Lindy had been saying hi to her in the halls for the past couple of days, ever since the Halloween festival. Then, today, she'd come up to Jillian when Jillian was opening her locker at the end of the school day and said, "D'yawannacomeoverandworkonthesocialstudiesthing?"

Jillian had to take the sentence apart—slowing down the words, peeling off the southern accent—to understand her. Lindy wanted her to come over? She felt flattered for a few seconds, until she remembered that they were the only people in third-period social studies signed up to make a model of a Greek temple for the Ancient Greece unit. "I can't today," she said.

"Why?"

"I . . . have Recycling Club," she said, but that wasn't the only reason. The main reason was that her dad would kill her if she went to the Coxes'.

Someone was cutting down little trees around town. Her father was convinced it was Lindy's dad.

"Recycling Club? That's a thing?" Lindy laughed. "That's so lame. Recycling Club," she said again, inspiring a new round of laughter in herself.

It was lame. Jillian couldn't deny it. All they did was talk about the different kinds of plastics that could be recycled and make posters urging kids to use the recycling bins in the cafeteria.

"Skip it. You can skip it once, right? Next time you could pick up a bunch more cups or something."

In the end, Jillian had agreed. The environment wasn't going to get that much worse if she skipped one day of Recycling Club. Her parents didn't have to know.

Lindy kicked her shoes into the mud room by the kitchen. One bounced off the back wall and landed on the dryer. The other just missed the window. Jillian set hers side by side on the mat by the door. The dog came over to sniff the insides.

"Off!" Lindy said, her face up close to his. "Watch out or he'll hump you."

Jillian stood still, ready to push the dog down, but he just sniffed her ankle. He tipped his head sideways when she scratched his chin.

"Soooooo?" Lindy's mom slid the grilled cheese sandwich onto a Barbie-pink plate.

"He said, 'Hi,'" Lindy said.

"That's good!"

"I said hi first. My mom is pimping me," Lindy said. "She's trying to get Mark to like me. Jillian likes him, too, Mom."

"I do not!" Jillian said. She leaned back on her stool at the

Coxes' counter, in case her mom happened to be looking out the window.

"Boys!" Lindy's mom said.

"Yeah boys. Boy oh boy oh boys," Lindy said.

"Do you want some grilled cheese, Jillian?"

"I'm okay." She did. Badly.

"Share with her, Lin."

Lindy tore off a bite-size corner of her sandwich.

Her mother watched them chew. "So! What are you girls up to today?"

"We're supposed to make a model of a Greek temple," Lindy said.

"We should go on a cruise in Greece sometime. Would you like that, Lin?"

"I guess."

"I got us some new jeans." Her mom darted for the row of shopping bags by the door. She held up a pair of jeans in each hand. One pair was marginally bigger. They came with a glittery pink belt.

"Mom. No," Lindy said, covering her eyes with her hand.

"And . . ." She pulled out two white T-shirts with sequined flowers on them.

"No. Just . . . no." Lindy grabbed a bag of cookies and set off up the stairs.

Jillian put the plate in the sink. "Thank you, Mrs. Cox."

"Oh, please! Call me Kaye."

"Okay Kaye," Jillian said, then felt embarrassed. Did she understand she meant okay Kaye and not okk, which was just dumb? She could call Lindy's mom by her first name. It suited her. But Lindy's dad was definitely Mr. Cox.

Jillian ran her fingers over the sequined petals on one of the shirts. "They're pretty," she said, wanting to make up for Lindy's rudeness.

"You think?"

"I like them. The jeans too."

Kaye smiled. "Why, thank you. Sometimes I just don't know with Lin, you know? It's hard to tell."

Jillian nodded, not sure what she was agreeing with, but just the fact of her nodding, agreeing with Kaye that she had a point, whatever it was, seemed to draw some of the worry out of Kaye's face.

"Did you get enough to eat?"

"Yes, thanks."

"'Cause if you're hungry . . ."

"I ate a big lunch."

"Did you? Do you buy or bring?"

"Bring. The food at school isn't good for you, my mom says."

"Your mom is smart."

"She's writing a book," Jillian said. "Well, taking pictures and all."

"That's neat."

"It's about Willard Park. About the houses and stuff."

"Nick could help her. My husband? He's, well, you know, a house builder?" She said it as though she wasn't sure.

"Are you coming or what?" Lindy yelled from upstairs.

Jillian had the urge to ask Kaye to come along, to help them make the Greek temple. She was pretty sure she would jump at the chance—but Lindy might not like it. "See you," Jillian said, grabbing her backpack.

"Have fun!" Kaye said, her smile jumbo size.

Jillian made her way across the marble floor, up the curved staircase. She felt like Maria arriving at the von Trapps' in *The*

Sound of Music. The chandelier was on even though it was the middle of the day.

Lindy wasn't in the first room, an all-white room like a hotel room with a bathroom that was about the size of Jillian's whole bedroom, and a sitting room with a fireplace; nor in the next, which had bunk beds and walls painted like outer space, with rockets and planets.

Jillian found her flopped onto a big bed in a huge room painted spring green. It was crammed full of stuff—a website's worth: a bright blue couch piled with flowered pillows, a computer, a television, a couple of soccer balls, a box of stuffed animals, an iPad, a purple bean bag chair, a pink chandelier, model horses, heaps of inside-out pants and shirts, and a high shelf full of smiling American Girl dolls. Jillian counted ten of them. Ten! Molly, and Felicity, and Samantha, and Kit among them. Jillian only had Elizabeth, the Colonial doll.

"What are you looking at?" Lindy said.

"Nothing."

"My dad's going to let me drive soon," Lindy said.

"But you're too young . . ."

"Once we were at the beach and he made a bonfire and the fire department came . . ." She got a funny smile on her face. "That's what *she* said," she said. "Get it?"

Jillian smiled, not getting it.

"Our TV is like five feet wide."

"That's really big."

"That's what *she* said," Lindy said.

"Who?" Jillian said.

Lindy scoffed. Maybe she had ADD. A lot of kids at her school did—so many that it was a regular cafeteria conversation: what kind of meds they took, how much. It made Jillian think of conversations she'd overheard between her grandmother and her bridge-playing friends about arthritis and cholesterol medications.

"How old are you?" Lindy said.

"I'll be thirteen in January," Jillian said.

"I'll be fourteen in July."

"Oh." Rumor about being held back confirmed.

"Sit down." Lindy shoved the bag of cookies she'd taken from the kitchen at her.

Jillian perched on the edge of the bed, ate one, her hand under her chin.

"Why are you doing that?" Lindy said.

"So I won't make crumbs."

Lindy raised her eyebrows, as though crumbs were something Jillian had just invented. Lindy tore a piece of paper out of her notebook and made a dot in the middle of it with a pencil. "Know what that is?"

"No."

"A Greek pimple."

"What?"

"Pimple. Temple. Get it?"

Jillian laughed even though it wasn't funny.

Lindy crumpled up the paper and tossed it in the air. "My dad'll do it for us. Well, he'll get someone to."

"What?"

"Make the temple. He's a builder. Look! Rubber pencil!" Lindy said. She held her pencil between her thumb and forefinger and shook it up and down.

"Weird!"

They shook their pencils, Lindy showing her just how to hold it, loosely, between her thumb and forefinger, to make it look rubbery.

"Look at me! I'm rubber too," Lindy said, and she started to shake her body back and forth. Her lips and cheeks did look rubbery, as though she weren't quite human. "Try it!"

Jillian hesitated, afraid Lindy would stop shaking the moment she started, and laugh at her, but Lindy kept at it. Jillian joined her. They shook, laughing, until Lindy eventually did stop short. Jillian did too.

"So Mark's hot, huh," Lindy said.

"He's got a nice smile."

"And nice pecs."

"Lindy!" "Pecs" sounded dirty.

"What-y?"

"It sounds . . ."

"Pecs not pecker! Did you think I meant *pecker*? Oh my God! You have a dirty mind."

"No . . ." Sofia would know what it meant. Jillian felt a sudden longing for her.

"Want to explore the new house my dad's building?"

"Are we allowed?"

"Why not?"

"Isn't it dangerous? Like, nails and boards and stuff?"

"I go there all the time. I have a fort."

"How?"

"How? I just walk in. I have a key," she said, sly. "I stole it. Come on! Let's go!"

"Not right now . . . ," Jillian said, meaning *not ever*.

"Chicken." Lindy started playing a Chipmunks song on her phone. The Chipmunks sang Christmas carols in high-pitched voices. Lindy sang along. Jillian watched her until Lindy pinched her and made her join in. Jillian could get sick of the Chipmunks pretty fast, but not Lindy, it seemed. They all kept singing and singing.

Suddenly she turned the music off. "Okay, now," Lindy said.
"Now what?"

"Now we're going to the fort." She got a key out of her night table
and slid open the window above it. Then she dug out a contraption
made of metal and rope from under her bed. She hooked the two
metal arms over the windowsill, and unfurled a rope ladder toward
the ground.

"Your parents let you have a rope ladder?"

"In case of fire, duh." She climbed out the window and down
the ladder. She landed on the ground with a thump. "Your turn!"

Jillian wasn't sure what to do. She could just leave. That was an
option. She could just walk downstairs and out the front door and
go home. That would be that. Safe and sound. No friendship with
Lindy—but that seemed like a long shot anyway.

"You coming, Miller?" Lindy called up.

Miller. No one had ever called her that. It sounded kind of
cool. Kind of tough.

A girl named "Miller" could climb out windows and sneak into
houses. Maybe.

"Hurry up," Lindy called.

Jillian climbed onto the table, her heart beating hard. Lindy
was down on the side lawn. She smiled up at Jillian, making Jillian
feel like she'd passed a test. She took a deep breath and climbed out
the window. The rope waggled back and forth, but it felt strong.
She climbed down, rung by rung, her heart loud in her ears. By the
time she reached the ground, Lindy was running around the back
of Jillian's house and over to the White Elephant.

"... AND CINDERELLA FORGAVE HER STEPSISTERS—" KAYE READ. JAKEY
was edging toward the lip of the couch. "But it's not over yet,
buddy."

"I know what's gonna happen," Jakey said.

"Well, o—"

Jakey burst off the couch, racing up the stairs. Kaye sighed, closing the book of fairy tales.

She sat alone on the couch, eyeing the furniture, all Baker, all upholstered in white velvet: the $8,000 sofa, the $4,000 lounge chair and matching $5,000 chaise. The dining room table, visible through the arched doorway, had cost $11,000 and the ten chairs $2,000 each. The chandelier was nearly $9,000; it was made of glass from Venice. The painting of the rosy nude over the couch—$6,000, chosen by their decorator—picked up the pink of the stones around the fireplace. But what good was it all when you didn't have any friends to envy it? Down in Beaufort, they were the popular family; here, they were nobodies. Why? She wasn't doing anything differently that she could tell.

Not that she could complain! She was lucky and she knew it. To have all this stuff? God was looking out for her, no doubt. She'd grown up this side of poor, on a little South Carolina sea island where the tourists never came anymore. You couldn't blame them. The beaches were worn away and the government had never cleaned up the old dye plant, where the old-timers used to work, Kaye's father included. When Kaye was small the tap water still ran sweet, but since then they'd declared the water unsafe to drink. Residents had to get fresh water from the town hall in jugs. Her father had left her their little house on Sea Breeze Court when he died, two years ago. It wasn't much, but it was hers. Everything else they owned seemed like Nick's. He earned the money, after all.

Feeling nostalgic, she unlocked her phone and opened her Facebook app. There were Darla and Maureen clinking champagne glasses at Tara's. There Amber, Kitty, and Bonnie after manicures.

Tina and Lila and their kids at the beach showing off their tans. Kaye "liked" each photo, thinking, *Don't like. Don't like. Don't like.*

She'd had a hope that the new neighbor, Suzanne, would start coming by with her little boy for playdates, but Suzanne had practically had an allergic reaction when she came over last Tuesday. She'd gasped—actually gasped—when she saw their television, and Kaye could tell it wasn't in awe, the way Grant had when she gave him a tour. He'd said "Wow" about a hundred times, and "You gotta be kidding me!" He counted the bathrooms out loud and they had to go around the house a second time for confirmation: yep, there were six of them. He seemed super nice, but Suzanne was a little stuck up, frankly.

"How many video-game systems does Jakey have?" she'd said, eyeing the game cabinet with something like fear.

"Oh, you know boys!" Kaye had said. Who knew how many systems he had? Did people count things like that? Suzanne left after a scant half hour, never having touched the fudge or the coffee Kaye had put out.

Maybe Kaye had laughed too much. Or chattered more than her fair share. She couldn't help that she was a happy person. She'd always been a happy person, cheering up friends, cheering up her father, keeping busy, busy, busy. She and her girlfriends had practically run Lindy's old school, organizing talent night, the spring fair, field day—you name it. Up here, the women did things differently. Multicultural night at Willard Park Elementary? How were you supposed to contribute when you didn't have a culture? "Do you think I'm not serious enough for her?" she'd asked Nick, who'd said, "Let it go, babe," as if Suzanne were a fish too small to keep.

With no kids or husband to see to, no housekeeper to chat with—she and Carmen always ate lunch together, which was sort of like having a paid friend—no piles to clear or online shopping to do, Kaye was free for the moment. Free to indulge in the pastime she'd meant to keep as just that—a little something to do while the kids were occupied. Now that Jakey was in first grade she couldn't keep him home from school just for company anymore. She'd just do it for an hour, to get it out of her system.

She wandered down the basement steps, slipping past the wine cellar, past the lounge and the gym to her room. It was her own room. She'd begged for it when Nick was allotting purposes for the rooms in the house.

"Promise never to go in," she'd told him, her finger to her smiling lips, her eyelashes batting.

"Why would I?" he'd said.

He wasn't even curious about what she did in there. He wasn't curious about her, period. Did he consider her a trophy wife? She was only a few years younger than he was, but she looked better than a lot of women her age. A little hair color and a lot of hours with a personal trainer went a long way. Well, if she was a trophy wife, he was a trophy husband. He would always be a trophy husband since the trophy aspect of husbands had to do with cash value, but what was going to happen to her? At thirty-nine, her chrome was starting to lose its shine.

She opened the door, then went around the room turning on the light boxes that hung at intervals on the wall. Each was topped with a mammogram film. Some were of single breasts, but most were a pair, two films side by side, like globes of the world with land masses and seas. They were painted in a rainbow of colors, and she'd named them: *Red Sky at Night, Orange Storm, Sea Change.*

Something was wrong with her, to want to paint breasts. She felt that deep within her in a clammy, embarrassed way, but she couldn't help herself. It was like an addiction. Worse than shopping.

She ought to have stuck with watercolors of sailboats and

sunsets, like her mother used to make. She and Kaye used to sit side by side in beach chairs with their palettes and easels when Kaye was little. Kaye was the one who emptied the dirty water in the sea and brought back fresh cups to dip their brushes in. Her mother was really talented. Kaye had a few of her paintings framed in the guest bathroom even though the decorator disapproved. That was a normal pastime, something you could tell people you did. But this . . .

She'd had the inspiration during a mammogram several years before. The doctor had shown her the films on a light screen, her right breast and her left. "Such frequent screenings are overkill at your age," she told Kaye, who was thirty then. Kaye, lost for a moment in the symmetry of her own breasts, had snapped to. "I'll get them every month if I choose," she said. Her mother's breast cancer had been fast and virulent, leaving Kaye motherless at eight.

She'd painted dozens of films since then. A technician at the radiologist's had given several hundred to her, as many as she wanted, when the office moved from film to digital images. They didn't care what happened to them as long as the patients' identities were stripped off. What was she going to do with them all? Keep painting them, she supposed. Maybe one day she would find she'd had enough of breasts and she would be able to move on to something normal, like fruit.

Kaye locked the door. She got out her paints and turned on a "nature sounds" playlist. The first song was a recording of ocean waves; she chose a breast with a vast white patch that looked like a desert island, and she started to paint.

9

Jillian's father stabbed a tiny potato and held his fork up like a king holding his scepter. "I got four signatures last night," he said.

Jillian and her mother made encouraging sounds. They talked about the petition every night at dinner.

"And guess what?" he said.

"Four trees were down?" her mother said.

"A maple sapling. Down by the creek." From his expression, you'd have thought he'd run over a dog.

"That's how many by the creek, eleven?" her mother said.

"Easiest place not to get caught. He's such a coward."

"We don't know it's him," her mother said, cutting her salmon.

"The town ought to hire a dick to follow him."

She and her mother both looked up.

"A dick?" Jillian said.

"It's a term for a detective," her father said.

Jillian nodded. It was a term for something else too. She lined her string beans up in a row. They looked like the planks of a raft. Or the posts of a picket fence. That was it. A fence. She slipped them under the table one by one, to Candy's waiting mouth. Candy kept sniffing her leg. She probably smelled Rex. It was lucky her parents' sense of smell wasn't as good as the dog's.

Her mother looked at Jillian's plate. "Not hungry, Jill?"

"I had a late snack," she said. Lindy had candy bars stashed in the White Elephant fort, Twixes and peanut butter cups among them, Jillian's favorites. She and Lindy had been going up there every afternoon all week. That was what she did after school now. She didn't go to clubs. To heck with clubs. The fort was a wonderland with lemon candles from Lucy's ("Did you steal them?" "I *bor-rowed* them."), a big beach towel, throw pillows, and sugar. There was a Ouija board and Gypsy Witch tarot cards, which they used to learn their fates. "Does Mark Strauss love me?" they asked the Ouija board. Y-E-S the board said, and it didn't feel like Lindy was pushing it. Lindy kept it all in a box she stashed in the rafters, transforming the room from construction site to magic fort in a few short minutes.

"Did you like those new rice cakes?" Jillian's mother said.

"What?"

"The ones I packed. They're a new kind."

"Mm-hm," Jillian said.

"Club went late today, didn't it?"

"I didn't go," Jillian said, not thinking.

"What?" Her parents paused midbite to look at her.

"I mean, I went . . ." They told her they wanted her to be honest with them, but they didn't. Not if it was to say something they didn't want to hear. "Late. I went late because I wanted to finish my English homework first. We picked up trash by the creek."

"I hope you wore gloves," her mother said.

Her parents resumed eating, order restored to their world.

The conversation shifted away from her to *Annie Get Your Gun*. It was a relief. And a letdown. Was that all they cared about? If she wore gloves? What about *her*? Her parents had no idea she loved Mark Strauss. They didn't care.

"Grant and I are working on 'Anything You Can Do' tonight," her mother said.

Her father took a sip of his milk.

"He's terrific. Picks up the dance numbers so quickly. Knows everyone's lines. I swear he could do a one-man show. Did you hear he nearly was on a children's television show?"

"Yes," her father said. He started clearing plates.

"He's got a beautiful voice. No real training."

"Are you finished?" her father said. Her mother handed him her plate.

"Come on, Ted. Suzanne signed it, and most of our other friends. You can't have everything."

"But he was the one who suggested the damn thing!" her father said.

"I like them."

"I like her well enough, but him . . ."

"She's pregnant," her mother said.

"Good for her."

"I wasn't supposed to tell anyone yet. Don't say anything," she told Jillian.

Jillian shook her head. Why would she? Who cared?

"They're going to have to put an addition on the house," her mother said.

Her father threw a fork in the sink. It landed with a clatter. "Are they going to tear it down? Is that what this is about?"

"She just wants to add a room or two."

They were quiet as they washed up, her father probably thinking about making time stand still, her mother about the wonderfulness of Grant. *I'm friends with Lindy Cox,* Jillian screamed. In her head.

Her father grabbed an armful of signs from the hall closet. They were signs protesting the big houses—as if a sign would do any good. He had asked her to draw the picture like he thought she'd be excited to do it. At first she'd said no—more specifically, *No chance, Dad*—but he looked so sad that she agreed to, as long as he didn't make her sign it.

It was a drawing of three little square houses, each with two windows that looked like big, sad eyes and a frowning door, alongside a huge house that towered above them all, with an expressionless door and squinty window eyes. That house had a red *X* drawn through it. He gave one to anyone who would sign the petition. A lot of the lawns in town had them up now, and it made Jillian feel secretly proud when she saw them.

"I'm off to get more signatures. Want to come, Jillian?"

"Homework," Jillian said.

"Rehearsal should be over by ten," her mother said, kissing the top of Jillian's head.

Jillian laid her books across the kitchen table, still slightly moist from the sponge. She didn't have much homework, a half hour maybe. Unless she did the Greek temple project. But Lindy had assured her that that would be taken care of. How weird was that? She wanted to watch TV, but their TV sucked too much to bother. She sighed and settled into her homework, looking up now and then to see the changing images on the Coxes' TV next door, a vivid reminder of all she didn't have.

SUZANNE ROLLED FROM SIDE TO SIDE LIKE A ROTISSERIE CHICKEN, UN-able to stop thinking about Adam, unable to get away from Grant.

They slept in a double bed now, a so-called full, but all it filled was the room. Their king-size bed was too big, a fact they'd discovered when the movers tried to get the mattress into the room on moving day. Grant was always touching her now, accidentally, if not on purpose. His foot would graze hers, which would remind him that he wanted to have sex, which meant he was constantly pulling at the waistband of her pajama pants. "Hey, hot mama," he whispered now, nuzzling her neck.

"I am not your mama!" she snapped.

"Whoa, there! I meant it carnally, not maternally." He started rubbing her shoulders. She softened a little, silently forgiving him for yet another cowboy exclamation.

"Adam's doctor today called me Mom, the nurse—they all do, the whole staff, like I'm Old Mother Hubbard. I hate that."

"What's the prognosis?" he said, working his thumbs into the hollows just below the base of her skull, where tension had calcified nearly to bone.

"She thinks it might be a sinus infection. She put him on anti-biotics. Do sinus infections cause headaches? He's had a headache for a month, Grant."

A better mother would have taken him to the doctor right away. Or just a more hovering one? Her hesitancy wasn't out of a lack of love or compassion, she told herself; it was optimism. She had a surfeit of it: She wasn't pregnant, it was heartburn. Her son wasn't sick, he was just getting accustomed to the new school. Her father hadn't left, he was just on a very long business trip.

Her mind began to peek into the dark and terrifying alleys the Internet seduced her into when she'd Googled "headaches" this afternoon, something she had not allowed herself to do until today—*carbon monoxide poisoning, blood clot, aneurysm, brain tumor—*

"He'll start to get better now. He just needed the right medication," Grant said, drawing her back again.

"He will, won't he? He's a healthy five-year-old."

"That's right. And the smartest one I've ever known."

"He is!" She laughed, her relief exploding into the room.

Grant's reassurances allowed her to believe that everything would be okay. He did this for her. He had always done this for her. Brought her back from the brink. It made no sense, really. He knew no more than she did—less, he usually knew less—but his voice was steady and soothing and it allowed her to breathe again.

Neither of them mentioned Adam's parent-teacher conference, which they had attended before the doctor's appointment. *He interrupts other children. He cries easily. He looks out the window instead of at the board.* This, too, was surely the result of the headaches.

When she walked Adam home from school after the conference, they passed three little trees that had been cut low on their slim trunks, not all the way through, but half to three-quarters, like a slash to their Achilles tendons. They leaned together, holding one another up, reminiscent of three children crying, which had inspired Adam to cry too.

Who was damaging them? The residents of Willard Park were hot with curiosity and concern. She, along with everyone else in town, had received a poem about trees in her e-mail inbox today. It was the second time this week. This one had been by Robert Frost, the first by Thoreau. Who was sending them? The address was mysterious: wptreepoet@gmail.com. It might be a town employee or a member of the town council—someone with access to the resident e-mail list. It was probably Ted Miller, who was, well, preoccupied was one way of putting it. Apparently that was all he and Allison talked about anymore.

Ted thought Nick Cox was to blame, but what did he have to gain from damaging the trees that weren't on his property? If she were to hazard a guess, she'd pick the little gang of teenagers in town, the ones too young to drive, who tromped around in hiking boots and leather jackets laughing loudly and pushing one another. Or maybe Nina Strauss, trying to drum up a little interest in Willard Park before the weather turned cold. She was just loony enough to think any publicity was good publicity. Or maybe it was Grant, turning to petty vandalism now that he couldn't smoke weed anymore. God. She hoped it wasn't Grant.

"What's your theory on the trees?" she said.

"What trees?" Grant said, which was confirmation enough. He worked his fingers into the steel beams that were Suzanne's shoulders.

"That feels great. Can we just do this? You rubbing my back?"

"Sure, hon. Roll on your belly and I'll give you a real massage."

She tensed, the work he had done so far undone in a single instant. "I can't."

Adam appeared at their bedroom door like a benevolent ghost, saving her—for the moment—from having to tell Grant.

"I can't sleep!" he screamed.

"Hold on there, partner. It's okay. I'll sit with you." Grant climbed out of bed.

"I want Mommy!" Adam cried, so Suzanne, feeling victorious despite herself, took him back to his room. She lay down beside him and rubbed his back, much as Grant had rubbed hers. She took in the smell of him, the sweet smells of the soap from his bath and little-boy sleep. After a while, Adam fell asleep, his thumb in his mouth; she was nearly asleep herself, but she made herself get up. She had to tell him.

He, too, was asleep by the time she returned.

She tapped him on the shoulder. He didn't budge. She squeezed his upper arm gently. "Grant?"

He murmured a little.

"I'm pregnant," she said, sotto voce. *Okay*, done.

She started breathing more deeply now. She imagined herself as a big balloon, inflating, deflating. She was on her way to becoming a big balloon, that was for sure.

"You're what?" Grant said, his voice quite alert for someone who had just been asleep.

"Pregnant."

"Pregnant?"

"Yes."

He didn't say anything.

"You're upset," she said.

"No! No! It's great!"

"I thought you'd be glad," she said. "You're the one who wanted a big family."

"I did," he said. "I mean, I am. I do!"

He kissed her cheek, embraced her. But she'd heard that initial internal groan.

"I do. I mean, of course I do. Suze, you're a great mother."

"I can't get any work done as it is, Grant."

"Hire a sitter. It's worth it."

"He wants me."

"Get your mom to come up."

Did he have to bring up her mother? Her mother wanted to come for Thanksgiving, but Suzanne told her the house wasn't ready for visitors. Actually, Suzanne had shouted into the phone, "Not now, Mom!" She'd meant to call back to apologize, but hadn't.

It wasn't her mother's fault, she reminded herself. Why was it she couldn't manage to forgive her? And for what? Her father was the one who had abandoned them.

For years, she'd thought he'd left because she was a disappointing daughter. The inner child in her still thought so—a psychologist had explained this to her—but the outer adult could see it was ridiculous: fathers didn't throw over their families because their daughters failed their ice-skating tests. Still, it was hard for her to rule out a correlation. The night before he left, when he came to kiss her good night, she'd told him she'd fallen while doing a backward swizzle. "That's all right, champ," he'd said. "You'll get it next time." But there hadn't been a next time. She'd given up ice skating. Given up the clean white skates and the promise of sequined dresses, the glides and twirls that felt like flying. She'd never flown again.

She lay awake for a long time, tolerating Grant's arm around her, imprisoning her. She felt him drop off to sleep, his weight sinking into hers.

"You'll never leave us, right?"

"What?" he said, waking. "No."

She had made him swear to it before she agreed to marry him, and she needed to hear it periodically. Neither she nor their potential children were going to go through what she and her mother went through. That was part of why she wanted to be a success. Needed to be a success. If ever she were alone, she had to be able to support her child—her children—without subjecting them to humiliating compromises.

"You love me," she said, after long minutes.

He had drifted off again; this time the sleep was deeper.

"Right?" she whispered, into his ear.

"Mm-hm," he said, turning over. In an instant he was snoring, leaving her to lie awake, wondering whether he had heard her.

10

NOVEMBER 24

They were fat with food, full of it, drunk with it, nearly asleep from it. Thanksgiving was like that, which was part of what made it Ted's favorite holiday. It was the one day when everyone's job was to overeat, to take a deep breath and make room for seconds. That was really all that was expected of you. And cooking, of course, but Ted liked to cook. He made all of his mother's old recipes, from sweet potatoes with marshmallows, to cornbread stuffing, to pumpkin pie with butter pecan ice cream. He preferred pumpkin pie with whipped cream, but tradition was tradition. Terrance made the cranberry sauce; he loved to watch the cranberries boil and pop.

Around four o'clock Allison's parents called, full of the details about the dinner at the assisted living home: Four turkeys. Five kinds of pie. Three kinds of potatoes. It was like the Twelve Days of Christmas. They used to come down for both of the major holidays, but they seemed to prefer Thanksgiving at Brighton Manor, which was both hurtful to Allison and easier at the same time. After the annual Miller family Boggle tournament—a game Terrance could play as well as the rest of them—they were free to do as they pleased. Allison stretched out on the sofa with her script, and Jillian disappeared back into her room. Ted got his coat on. Terrance did too.

"Tree watch?" Allison said.

"Vandalism doesn't take a holiday," Ted said.

"Isn't that an Agatha Christie book?" Her tone was testy. She missed sex, she'd told him the night before. He had nodded, sympathetic. She was both trying to be patient, and, on occasion, making an effort to engage him in what had once been a normal marital activity. He ought, at least, to try to do his part, he thought uncomfortably.

"Ready with my flashlight," Terrance said, turning on the flashlight on his phone.

Outside it was cold enough to see your breath. It felt late, but it wasn't. Thanksgiving was like that too. Seven felt like eleven.

"I forgot my gloves," Terrance said.

"Just keep your hands in your pockets," Ted said.

He, on the other hand, needed his hands to take notes in his vandalism notebook. The police were always polite when he called in the day's damage—three more trees cut down; another tree toilet-papered; graffiti on a mailbox; stickers on the stop signs that said, beneath the word STOP, "clinging to the past"—but they had only come out a few times at the very beginning to have him file a report. Sometimes a police car drove through town at night, but what good did that do? Ted had suggested to the mayor that a volunteer force of residents take shifts monitoring the town since it was really too big a job for him alone, but she refused to add it to the November meeting agenda. Alternatively, he'd suggested a hotline for residents to call in anonymous tips, but this had not met with her approval either.

It was Lucy who had, inadvertently, provided a platform for

town residents to help when she asked residents to take a vote: Were they for the moratorium or against it? She took everything off the bulletin board and set out two bowls full of thumbtacks: blue meant "for," and red "against." At the end of the month she would tally which side had the most tacks, and declare a winner.

It was clear there was cheating from the get-go—someone (Ted had a guess) stuck all of the red thumbtacks in the board before the end of the first day—so you could say it was a failure, but Ted thought it was a success because people started using the tacks for their intended purpose: to attach notes to the board: *Small fire along the creek, teenagers in attendance; Mindy and Juan Sanchez have retained an architect; Bob Wilson took an electric hedge trimmer to his azaleas November 11; Kenny Adisa spotted taking a late-night walk.*

Ted had some concerns Lucy would take down the board: it made the town into a little bit of a police state. But wasn't a police state what they needed right now? You had to go early and often if you wanted to see the dirt before the accused took it down: *Melanie Frank said her black walnut trees are "not worth the trouble"; Ana Lopez cheats on her taxes; Antoine Beignet has a second family in Toledo.* Some of the notes had nothing to do with the matter at hand.

The semiweekly quotes and poems from wptreepoet@gmail .com were another step in the right direction. Some people thought Ted was sending them, which flattered him—it was a good idea. He couldn't think who it might actually be. A woman, he guessed. Most men didn't care for poetry. Well, he did, but he wasn't most men. The most recent poem was Joyce Kilmer's famous "Trees." Allison had read it aloud at breakfast yesterday. "It's all about sex," she'd said, inspiring both Ted and Jillian to cry "Mom!" in dismay.

Still the question hung in the air in Willard Park: who was cutting down the trees? And the answer hung there, too, just out of reach for lack of concrete evidence.

Over thirty lawns in town sported the sign Jillian had made. Ted was proud of that. He'd had to replace several of them after they were damaged—some by weather, others by intent—but that was to be expected. He checked to make sure theirs was intact, then headed toward the Coxes'. Lights were on in every room. This seemed like a sort of vandalism in its own right: a crime against the planet. Nothing new for Cox and co.

In the front yard, there was something new though: Cox had posted a sign of his own, one that depicted houses of different sizes and styles, all with smiling doors. The words "Living in Harmony" were written across the bottom. While Jillian's sign looked like it had been made by a twelve-year-old—as it had been—Cox's looked professionally rendered; it sported red and blue ink instead of just black.

"Look at that, Terr! Do you believe it?"

"Living in Harmony," Terrance read, sounding out the words. "That's nice."

"No. It's not. He doesn't mean it. It's aggressive."

"Oh," Terrance said.

"He's trying to say that people who don't want to allow big houses in town are the ones causing the trouble."

"But, Ted . . . harmony means together."

The police would react in the same way, if he were to call it in. *Let me get this straight: you're protesting a sign that says, "Living in Harmony"?*

Typical Nick Cox! He could make an attack look like an olive branch.

They saw more of Cox's signs as they walked. He wondered if Cox had even asked the neighbors for permission or just hammered them into the ground while they were basking in their post-turkey haze. He used two wooden posts instead of one, which made them sturdier.

The neighborhood was littered with signs now. It not only took away from Ted's message, but made a messy time of year look even messier. Leaves were stuck to the road after last night's rain, clogging sewer entrances. On the lawns that had not yet been raked, they clung together, turning into a mucky brew. The neighborhood was a study in opposites: lawns with leaves, lawns without; houses lit and full with people, houses dark and deserted; lawns with pro-moratorium signs, lawns with anti. The roads were particularly quiet. When, every now and then, a car did drive by, it was jarring.

"You're quiet tonight," Ted said to Terrance.

"It's peaceful at night, Ted."

"You're right."

"I like it at night."

"Me too."

"When we were little we were scared of the dark," Terrance said. "We used to sleep with four night-lights. Remember, Ted? Now they have glow-in-the-dark stars, but they didn't have that then, Ted, did they? Does Jillian have a night-light or does she have stars? I think she has stars. Do you think they have night-lights in space, Ted? Or do the Martians just have stars?"

Ted was sorry he'd said anything. And not. Terrance's chatter was a comfort. He'd known it all his life.

He caught the sound of something squeaking, an irregular metallic sound accompanied by a rattling and clunking. What in the world? "Hear that?" Ted said.

"Yes," Terrance said.

"Is it a bike?" Ted said, though it didn't quite sound like a bike. "A little weird to be out biking in the cold at night."

"It's not normal," Terrance said.

"Not really. No."

"But what is normal?" Terrance said. He could sometimes be quite philosophical.

The sign on Cathie and Jim Buchanan's lawn had been knocked over and was torn, graffiti written in black marker across the front: *Move with the times or move away!* Ted picked up the pieces and put them in the garbage bag he'd brought, and made note.

The squeak and clatter were coming closer, but there was no light to accompany them. There was also the sound of footsteps— running and jumping feet, as well as more sober walking feet.

"Halt! Who goes there?" Terrance said, shining the flashlight behind them. He moved it through the air till he landed on a woman pulling a child's wagon. Nina Strauss.

"Oh, for God's sake," Nina said, covering her eyes.

Terrance waved athletically, as though he were flagging down a rescue boat. The light from the flashlight bounced off the tree branches and the road.

"Why it's the Brothers Miller," Nina said.

"The Miller brothers," Terrance said. "Miller comes first."

She handed them each a jar of apple butter with a sticker of her face affixed to the side.

"Are you the Apple Butter Fairy?" Terrance said.

"No," she said, but she sort of was. She gave jars to the neighbors every year.

"It's kind of you," Terrance said.

"Hardly," Nina said. "It's business."

The sound of running and jumping explained itself then, too, as her son, Mark, jumped down from a tree. Leaves fell with him, like rain.

"Say hello, Mark," Nina said.

"Hi," Mark said. He shook his shaggy hair out of his eyes and gave a little wave to Terrance, which was sweet, as if he could see that Terrance was a kindred spirit. Then he ran on, scrambling up another tree.

"Did you spend the holiday with relatives?" Ted said.

"Yes," Nina said. "My son."

He'd never felt sorry for Nina before, but he did now, a little. Two people was small for a Thanksgiving gathering. They'd be eating leftover turkey till July. He nearly suggested she join them next year, but he caught himself just in time.

"It's a little hard to sell houses when the town looks like the outside of a polling station," she said.

"No one buys this time of year anyway, right?"

"Not this year, they won't."

"Not long till the hearing," Ted said.

Nina harrumphed. She rolled down a walkway toward the Chatterjees' house, and Ted and Terrance continued down the street.

Terrance was the one who spotted the maple lying on the Lamberts' lawn as if it were sunbathing. He shined the flashlight on it, making the shadows deep on the grass. This tree was a little bigger than the usual, a few years older, its trunk and limbs a little thicker. Cox seemed to be upping his game. "This is a big tree. Why would someone . . . ?"

"They can plant another one. Right?" Terrance's voice reflected the upset he'd heard in Ted's. "Trees grow. Right?"

"Of course, but. Well, yes. You're right. Trees grow."

"Trees grow. That's the thing about trees. So it's not so bad, Ted."

"I guess . . ."

"That's the thing about trees," Terrance repeated, self-soothing. "People don't grow back, but trees do."

"That's right," Ted said. When their parents died Terrance had had hopes of resurrection. "Time to go off-road."

They cut into the woods, down along the creek, where it was easy to destroy trees undetected. Everything looked all right down here tonight, the only fallen trees ones Ted had already taken note of. They were headed in the direction of the old tire swing, where kids used to spend summer days back when Ted and Terrance were boys. Ted took a path away from the water, and Terrance followed.

Shame was strange. It didn't wear off over time the way other emotions did. Hate calmed down with time, and passionate love did, too, both of them settling into something softer, something easier to bear. But shame . . . All he had to do was think of that day and he felt it roaring right back up through him, steaming through his chest and settling in his head, where it stayed, throbbing.

That day, the summer they were eleven, it was even hotter and more humid than usual. Ted and Terrance had gone to collect tadpoles. They had jars to catch them with the creek water. They walked along the water's edge, shorts rolled up high, until they came to where the kids were taking turns on the swing. Ted turned around to avoid the big group—he'd learned to steer his brother away from packs of kids—but as they started to head back, one of the older boys asked if they wanted a ride on the swing.

Ted stopped, trying to decide if the boy was teasing or meant it.

"Who wants to go first?" the older boy called.

He sounded friendly. A ride on the swing would be fun. "Okay," Ted said.

Terrance shook his head at Ted. "No, Teddy."

But Ted wanted to swing. He wouldn't even have to wait in

line. One time. He just wanted to do it once. "It's okay, Terry," he said.

"It's dangerous. Dad said about ropes and frays."

"It's okay, Terry. I'll be okay," Ted said. One time on the tire swing. That was it. One wild swing and splash. He was a little afraid, sure, but he wanted to. Needed to. He started to wade toward the other kids.

Then Terrance started to cry. He splashed toward Ted and grabbed his arm.

"Listen to the retard," someone said, and some of the kids snickered.

A feeling welled up in Ted, one that had been inside him, but, for the most part, dormant till then. A kind of rage. It was rage. It wasn't fair. Why couldn't he just be like everyone else? Why did he have to take care of his brother? His stupid brother? "I'm going to," he said, peeling Terrance's fingers off, conscious that the other kids were watching him. "Go home, *retard*."

Terrance's face went slack, his expression that of someone who had been grievously betrayed. As indeed he had been. He ran up into the woods. And Ted took a joyless ride on the swing.

He'd searched the woods for Terrance for hours afterward, finally finding him in their bedroom, lining up dominoes. He'd set up a long row of them. Ted apologized, tears in his eyes, and Terrance, who usually said, "It's okay, Teddy," said nothing. He frowned, concentrating, and placed another domino in the row. Ted sat down beside him, tears running down his face. "I'm sorry, Terry. I'm so sorry." Terrance put his hand on Ted's. "It's okay, Teddy. You didn't mean to." Then he asked Ted to tap the final domino and they watched them fall one by one, rippling around the room until they all lay down flat.

The thing was that he had meant to. He had known that his

words would hurt his twin and he had said them anyway. It was something that Terrance, who had never had an unkind thought in his life, would not have been able to fathom. Ted had regretted those words for the better part of his life.

"Do you ever get scared in the woods?" Terrance said.

"Not when I'm with you," Ted said.

"Should we sing a song?"

"You can sing. Go ahead."

"'The Teddy Bear's Picnic,'" he said. "Remember that? Mom used to sing that. Sometimes she would sing the Terrance Bears, but that's just made up, right, Ted?"

"I guess it's all made up," Ted said.

"If you go out in the woods tonight," Terrance sang. "Join in, Ted."

"No, I'll just listen."

"Why? Sing, Ted."

What the heck, Ted thought. So they sang as they walked, never minding if someone could hear them—if there was anyone, it was only Cox on a vandalizing spree. And if he was out there, let him hear them sing. Let him know what he was missing. Let him see what love looked like.

11

Suzanne adjusted her legs to redistribute Adam's weight. He sat on her lap at the kitchen table in his yellow-and-blue-striped pajamas and a red cap Grammy had knitted, his fingers like vines around Suzanne's neck. She fought back tears of frustration. She was a failure. Adam was wilting away, and it was her fault.

She'd been fielding calls from the school regularly since the parent-teacher conference. *Adam says he's feeling poorly. Adam crumpled up his math test and threw it at another child. Adam refused to participate in recess.* The final straw came a few days ago, when Adam unleashed a string of curse words so foul the teacher wouldn't even repeat what he'd said. She told him he could come back when he could behave himself. He claimed he still couldn't.

Maybe he was stressed out. Maybe the principal had been right. He wasn't ready for first grade. Suzanne had been wrong to insist.

A good mother would have found a cure for Adam by now. A good mother wouldn't want to leave him at school, headaches or no, and get back to her nascent squirt-gun business.

"You used to love school, Ad," she said.

"The teacher gets mad at me."

"Because you misbehave."

"I suffer from debilitating headaches, Mommy."

Debilitating? Where did he learn a word like that? Then again, where had he learned the curse words that had gotten him suspended?

Grant thought it might be Tourette's. Blurting out swear words. Grant had had a case involving Tourette's once. If it was Tourette's, they could sue the county for discrimination, Grant said. Neither of them would ever have to work again. That was the way Grant looked at things.

Adam thumped his forehead against Suzanne's chest. "My ankles hurt. I need more medicine."

The joint pain was new. Ankles. Knees. Wrists. Suzanne swung from being afraid that the pediatrician was missing something serious, if not fatal, to believing her when she said that pediatric headaches were more common than people thought. When Suzanne took Adam back with the news that the sinus medication wasn't working, the doctor gave her a scrip for a refill and said, "Hang in there, Mom."

Something about the wording, something about the casualness, the near cavalierness of her remark, lit a flame inside Suzanne. She stood up from the molded orange plastic chair, bumping her head into the clown mobile that hung from the ceiling tiles, and slammed her palm against the desk. She demanded testing! Immediately! The doctor—rational, unruffled—assured her they would begin tests if the second round of antibiotics was unproductive.

For better or worse, the second round, too, was useless. Suzanne had since taken Adam to a phlebotomist who had had to stick him twice to find a good vein, trauma that even a dinosaur Band-Aid could not assuage. The good news was that the standard workup had not shown anything out of the ordinary. It didn't mean they were out of the woods, but it seemed positive. The bad news was that he still had headaches. A visit to the neurologist was the next stop, but the doctor, a woman of national renown, was booked solid for the next several weeks.

The baby was coming at a terrible time, in the midst of what might be deemed a family collapse. Suzanne wasn't working—how could she, with Adam on her lap? And Grant was vague these days. He was present physically during dinner, but he was like a Stepford Wife, smiling and nodding even when it wasn't appropriate to smile or nod.

Adam had a full-on tantrum at the grocery store today.

I got a flat tire and had to wait an hour for AAA.

Smile, smile. Nod, nod.

After rehearsal, he went straight to the TV instead of coming to bed. She could hear him laughing through the floorboards as she tried to sleep. She'd thought it was hard to sleep when he was in the same too-small bed with her, but his not being in the bed was even worse. He would take a shower right before going to sleep—he knew she was especially sensitive to smells when she was pregnant—but the noise woke her when she finally had managed to drop off.

The house plans. The house plans were her only hope. Her life raft in her ocean of despair. She eyed the ideas for the addition, spread across the kitchen table, bleaching in the sunlight. Two bedrooms simply didn't work for a family of four. She shifted in the kitchen chair, trying to lean closer to the plans without disturbing Adam, resting his cheek against her shoulder.

Initially, they'd planned merely to add a ground-floor master bedroom and bath, but Grant thought that as long as they were adding an extra room on the first floor they ought to add another room onto the second floor—an office slash guest bedroom. They'd add a walk-in closet. They could throw in another bathroom upstairs as well, thereupon turning a miniature house into a small one.

Glass bricks, Suzanne thought, inspired. Yes. They could build the exterior wall of the master bath with glass bricks, to bring in light. She reached over Adam's shoulder for the pencil to sketch in the idea.

"Mommy, don't."

Then, at the side door, a welcome sight: Allison with a paper cup in each hand and a white paper bag between her teeth. She looked like a dog with a bone in her mouth. She set everything on the counter. "You should have seen the look Lucy gave me, asking for paper cups. But how else was I going to bring them over?"

Suzanne, who was not a hugger, wanted to hug her.

"Oh my gosh, the bulletin board," Allison said. "Did you know little Petey Smith isn't toilet trained and that Phillis Ray is addicted to Ambien? And Jay Gatsby killed a man."

"What?"

"It's crazy. She'll be lucky if she doesn't get sued." She lured Adam off Suzanne's lap and sat him down at his little wooden table with the lemon bar she'd brought him.

"Can I watch a movie?" Adam said, testing the waters.

Suzanne set him up at the TV with a nature program. The camera panned a great forest. The trees were aflame with autumn colors, golden, brown, red.

"There were rumors she might take it down, but she just put it on the porch. It's been great for business. She's even changed up the menu. That's Lucy for you! Started offering Deforestation Decaf, Leave 'Em Standing Lattes, and white-frosted gingerbread cookies shaped like houses. She added a drink size too: now you can get small, medium, large, and White Elephant."

"Genius."

"There was even a reporter there! No kidding! She was interviewing Nina. The woman kept trying to get her to talk about the trees, but Nina kept telling her how Willard Park is such a great place to live. I hope she finishes up in time for the shoot."

"Shoot?"

"I'm doing her holiday card in a little while. Want to come?"

"No."

"Promises to be entertaining."

"I'll pass. How was yoga?" Suzanne said.

"Great. You should come sometime. I keep telling you. It's great for stress."

Suzanne rolled her eyes. "It's boring. Yoga's boring."

"May God smite you," Allison said.

"I think he already has."

"That bad? How are the house plans coming?" Allison opened one of the books she'd left Suzanne from the library, books with titles like *The Not So Big House,* and *Creating the Not So Big House,* and *Inside the Not So Big House.*

"Can I have some sparkling water, Mommy?"

"I'll get it," Allison said.

"I'd like a slice of lemon, too, please," Adam said.

"Jillian can come babysit anytime, you know. She's sweet with him," Suzanne said.

"I haven't seen a lot of her recently. She's wall-to-wall after-school clubs these days." Allison set Adam up with his water, broke an oatmeal cookie in two, kept half for herself and handed the other half to Suzanne.

"Clubs sound good," Suzanne said, chewing.

"I guess. She's been such a loner since her friend Sofia moved away. I guess they keep her busy though, right?"

"Gives you the whole day to yourself."

"I have plenty to do. It's not like I sit around and eat bonbons."

"I know."

"She's cagey these days. Won't talk about where she's been. Her grades are down."

"She's nearly thirteen, right? Sounds pretty normal to me."

Adam eyed them darkly. "I can't hear about the conifers."

Allison nodded at Adam, her finger to her lip. "Have you considered allergies?" she whispered.

"What?"

"Maybe his headaches are from allergies. Maybe you just need to get the dairy out of his diet or something. I know a good allergist."

Suzanne brightened. She loved Allison: Allison, who brought lemon bars. Allison, who came up with ailments that had a cure. "You're an angel. Give me that tea." Suzanne cradled her cup in her hands, feeling warm, feeling safe, feeling cared for.

AGAINST ALL ODDS, ALLISON AND SUZANNE'S FRIENDSHIP WAS GOING just the way Allison had imagined it, with Allison the one Suzanne could rely on when things were bleak. Allison felt like a character in a fairy tale whose wish had been granted.

And, perhaps more amazingly, a second wish had been granted, something she'd just about given up on. Ted had surprised her the night before, presenting her with a small prescription bottle from the pharmacy while they were brushing their teeth. Toothpaste foam frothed from both of their mouths as she studied it, but it made no sense. A prescription for sildenafil? What was sildenafil? She looked at him, puzzled, and spat into the sink.

"Isn't that what you wanted?" he said, spitting in turn.

"What is it?"

He'd gotten a prescription for Viagra after Thanksgiving.

Sildenafil was generic Viagra. Viagra was expensive, he explained, but the generic stuff was cheap. They could have sex every night if she wanted. It was that cheap.

Allison "whooped" her delight, which drew an "Are you all right?" from Jillian, across the hall, in the kitchen.

They had decided to wait till tonight to try it. Anticipation about the evening would make it all the more exciting, Allison suggested—she was now quite well versed in these things—and Ted had agreed to take it after dinner the next night. Tonight.

This was good news. This was awesome news. And didn't wishes come in threes? Her career was the next area that needed sprinkling with fairy dust. She looked skyward, waiting for the silvery dust to fall, turning her into a photographic sensation.

In the meantime, she was back to doing Christmas cards. She'd done a photo shoot with Lucy and her staff for Lucy's one-page eco calendar yesterday, and now it was time for Nina Strauss's session. Suzanne had agreed to come after all, and, together, they got Adam into his coat with the promise that he could watch the nature program over there. Allison pointed out Valeria's house as they passed it.

"The one who's in Europe . . . ?"

"Betraying me by having a life. She's cheating on me with the city of Paris." She mimed putting a knife to her heart, and twisting.

"You hear about all these people having affairs, but who are they, really? Do you know any of them?" Suzanne said, out of the blue.

Allison was caught short. Had she betrayed herself in some way, giving room for Suzanne to intuit that she had a teeny-tiny, off-limits crush on Nick Cox? Or was it a more pointed question? In fact, Allison wondered about Grant sometimes. He texted a lot when they took breaks at rehearsal. She didn't think it was with Suzanne.

Whoever texted him made him laugh, sometimes made him help-less with laughter.

Allison hadn't mentioned Grant's texting to Suzanne. She'd considered it, but it seemed petty, gossipy. On the other hand, what if he and Suzanne were having marital problems? What if one day Suzanne said, *I think he's seeing someone,* and Allison were to say, *He sure does text a lot at rehearsal.* Allison would come out looking like a bad friend. She would wonder what else Allison might be hiding. Then again, Allison might bring up the texting without prompting, and Suzanne would tell her to back off. *If I'd wanted your advice, I would have asked for it.* Maybe she should put a note on Lucy's bulletin board. That would give Suzanne a heads-up at least.

"What?" Suzanne said, eyeing her strangely.

She had a bad habit of acting out imagined conversations on her face. "Nothing."

They parked at Nina's split-level, pulling out Adam, lights, and cameras. Nina opened the front door before Allison had the chance to ring the doorbell.

Tonight, she thought with an excited shiver.

"This will have to be quick," Nina said, letting them in.

Nina was wearing black, the wrong color for a holiday card. The wrong color for her, period, since it gave her skin a greenish tint, but what was Allison, a color consultant? That sounded like something Kaye Cox might do. Invite people over for a party to tell them they should stick to fall colors, or spring, depending on their complex-ions. She would sell them the appropriate makeup to match.

Allison reprimanded herself. She'd promised not to pick on Kaye after the toy party last spring.

She'd been embarrassed for Kaye, who had sent out an invita-tion featuring a drawing of a red bucket, a poem inside with lines that ended in exclamation marks. Allison and Valeria had begged off, as must have every woman in town. Allison still had a painful image of seeing Kaye through the window, alone with the refreshments and the demonstration toys, an image so excruciating that she'd gone next door and bought a dump truck and a couple of board books, and ate a sickly sweet piece of fudge. Kaye had practically made out with her from gratitude.

"Can we get set up? I thought the couch might be good." Nina ushered them into the living room. The couch was the green of money.

"Don't you own a more cheerful suit?" Suzanne said.

"Like what? A Santa suit? Get real," Nina said.

"I don't know. Mauve. Blue. Anything but black," Suzanne said. "Right, Allison? For a Christmas card?"

"She's right."

Nina flared her nostrils. "I guess I have blue." She and her pumps clicked down the hallway.

Allison set up the lights, making use of the mirrors Nina had on the walls instead of art. Was it done with the intention of making the house look bigger, or out of sheer narcissism? She had a few low-nap area rugs. Her chairs were upright and she had roller blinds that snapped up tight, no curtains to soften things.

Adam whined for his nature program. "You *said*," he said, which was true. They had said. Suzanne turned on the TV. She tried channel after channel, but they all seemed to be airing talk shows.

"Turn on a game. Mark has tons of them," Nina said, reappearing in her blue suit, which was just a shade up from black.

"I'm against them," Suzanne said.

"A little gaming won't kill him." Nina fiddled with the controls for a while. Nothing. Then she unplugged a cable and plugged it in again. Finally Adam pushed a button on the remote control. Cartoon sword fighters appeared on the television screen accompanied by heroic music. The women cheered. Adam pushed more buttons, but the sword fighters remained poised, ready for battle, yet unable to fight. Adam lay on the rug, facedown.

"Let's get going. I have to get to yoga." Nina sat on the couch.

"Not you too," Suzanne said.

"Hot yoga. Not the religious kind, are you kidding me?" Nina rested her elbow on the armrest, held up her chin and turned on her smile for the camera. "It's intense. Relaxing in spite of itself, if you know what I mean. You'd love it."

"Suzanne's not a yoga girl."

"She'd like Bikram."

"No, she wouldn't," Allison said.

"She would. You sell a house to someone, you learn a thing or two about them."

"It's not *her,*" Allison said.

Suzanne laughed. "I'm right here, folks."

"Want to come?" Nina said.

"Stop moving, Nina." Allison zoomed in on Nina's teeth, on her too-big smile, on the bleached hairs above her lips. She focused on her mascara, crumbling around her eyes. She could make her look horrible if she wanted to, but that wasn't what she was being paid for. She zoomed out, into safer terrain.

"Seriously," Nina said. "It's like doing yoga in a tin shack on the beach. You sweat. Do you ever."

"Doesn't sound like a sport for a pregnant woman," Suzanne said.

"So don't do it when you're pregnant."

"Too late," Suzanne said.

"You're not!"

"See my bump?" She turned sideways, revealing a faint bump.

"Mine's bigger," Allison said, pressing her shirt against her pooch. No one laughed. Valeria would have laughed.

"Congratulations," Nina cooed.

"I used to be a runner," Suzanne said.

"Me too—till I broke my ankle. I tripped over a curb in the Marine Corps Marathon."

"I blew out my knee in New York!" Suzanne said.

They clutched hands like long-lost sisters.

"Let's get going here!" Allison snapped. Suzanne and Nina looked at her. "Sorry, I mean. Well, we want to get you to yoga, don't we, Nina?"

Allison clicked away, wanting to end the photo session quickly, wanting to go backward in time, so she could say it all again without the edge. What was the matter with her? She reviewed the photos on the camera. Nina looked frighteningly similar every time, as though she were made of wax. "It's a wrap," Allison said.

"So, are you coming?" Nina said, rising from the couch.

"To Bikram?" Allison said with a scornful laugh.

"We can still make it." Nina's eyes were on Suzanne. Of course she meant Suzanne.

"I can't," Suzanne said.

"Just sit on a mat and check it out. It'll be like taking a sauna. A sauna won't hurt."

"I've got Adam."

"Can't he go to school?" Nina said. "Most children do."

"He's not feeling well."

"What about Allison? You're not doing anything, are you, Allison? Allison can watch him."

"Wow. Could you?" Suzanne said.

Allison nearly said no—but Suzanne, who'd looked so glum all morning, suddenly looked happy. "I suppose . . ."

"You're a gem," Suzanne said.

"Not at all," Allison said reflexively. What a sucker she was. Sucker, sucker, sucker. Then she remembered that giving Suzanne time for herself had been one of her mentoring dreams. She packed Adam back in the car, and took him home.

Adam stopped to study something invisible on the walkway to her house. "Come on, sweetie," she said.

"That's a termite," he said.

"Hopefully an ant."

"No. It doesn't have a pinched waist."

"I better call the exterminator then."

"Don't kill it!"

It was going to be a long afternoon. But then the evening would arrive. *Tonight!*

Candy wagged through the window as Allison climbed the porch steps. "Candy's excited to see you."

Adam caught up to Allison. "I like you," he said.

"You do?" She stopped turning the key in the lock, and looked at him, wanting to hear more. It was pathetic, but right now, validation from anyone would suffice.

"You remind me of my grammy."

"Oh. Your grammy."

"She's my best person yet." He put his hand in hers. It felt as soft and warm as a fresh bun.

ALLISON LAY ON THE BED IN A LACY, CREAM-COLORED TEDDY. SHE'D bought it at the mall this afternoon after Suzanne picked up Adam, in honor of what was about to occur. It had been the most discreet of the silky little outfits she had tried on, all of which seemed to be more lacy panels and wildly plunging necklines than actual fabric. Unfortunately it had a thong, which she simply did not understand. Why was it necessary for women to wear thongs? Why did men like this? The salesgirl waved away her concerns. "First-world problems," she said, and rang up the purchase.

Allison lit a candle while Ted washed up, then lay back down again. Her breasts oozed out on either side of her getup, giving her a flattened look. So she moved onto her side, propped on one elbow. Her breasts slid down to the side as a pair, seeking the comfort of the mattress. By the time Ted came out, teeth brushed and flossed, she was on her side, one arm under her head, the other under her breasts, holding them together in a way that made her look like she had more cleavage than she actually did, which had been quite an art to arrange.

Ted brought the bright light of the bathroom in with him. He wore striped pajamas with long pants and a top that buttoned up the front. The kind of pajamas her father wore. Maybe Suzanne should start a men's lingerie company. Teddies for men. That might do well with women who had lost enthusiasm. Although there couldn't be thongs. She shook off the thought.

He blew out the candle.

"That was for effect," she said.

"Oh." He turned on the bedside lamp, singeing her eyes and exposing all of her puckers and sags. She turned it off, and, after a few failed attempts with the matches, they were back in business.

It was very early. Not yet eight. That would have raised an eyebrow with Jillian. *Why are you guys going to bed so early? Are you sick?* But she was conveniently out, at the Conservation Carnival at the middle school, after which a friend's mother would drop her off.

Ted had taken the sildenafil just after Jillian's ride arrived, while he and Allison were doing the dishes. He'd poured himself a glass of water, opened the bottle, and popped four in his mouth. Then, for good measure, he took a fifth.

They looked at his crotch as if his penis might start rising there and then, erect and mighty, ready for service. But, well, it didn't work that way, Allison had learned from the Internet. It still would need encouragement before it reported for duty.

Ted studied the medication vial. "Shoot."

"What?"

"I think I took it too early."

"Too early?"

"It only takes a half hour to an hour to start to work. It can last a long time, up to five hours, though, so we could wait."

Nope. Allison wasn't going to take any chances. She turned off the water, leaving the dishes unwashed, took his hand, and led him to the bedroom.

"No need for those," she said after he'd gotten under the covers, and she proceeded to undress him, unbuttoning his pajama shirt and easing his arms out of the sleeves, inching his pants down his legs with slow and sexy precision. The faux Viagra seemed to work quite well, she was pleased to see. Soon he was lying on his back, his penis at attention, holding the sheet up like a tent.

"'Let's go on with the show!'" she cried, quoting a line from *Annie Get Your Gun* with a laugh. She felt so happy. He cared after all. She'd begun to wonder.

"Why are you laughing?" he said.

"It looks like a circus tent."

"Don't laugh."

"I'm not laughing at you. It's just funny. It's a funny image."

He looked at the circus-tent sheet. "Why do I have to do this?"

"What?"

"Take medication. Why does what you want become what we do?"

She, who had been about to move down under the covers, taking matters to the next level, sat up. "What are you talking about?"

"Why do I have to take pills? Why can't we just wait till I'm into it again?"

"We're going to have a fight? Now?"

"All right, if you want to. Yes."

"Don't you care what I need in our marriage?"

"Don't you care what *I* need?"

Poof. All of the excitement, all of the anticipation and planning, strategizing and executing fled toward the ceiling and the gaps in the windows, through the attic, out the roof and into the heavens. Gone. That fast. They'd gotten so close. She lay down, eyes closed. "So you don't want to make love with me."

"Well, *part* of me does, I guess," he said angrily, pointing toward the unflagging pole holding up the sheet.

She laughed.

"It's not funny!"

"Okay," she said, but it was.

"Let's just have sex, Allison." Irritation saturated his voice.

"I don't want to if you're going to be like that."

"You don't *want* to?"

"Why would I want to have sex with someone who feels like it's a job?"

"I said I'd do it."

"But you're doing it against your will."

"Let's just get it over with."

"Over with? Really, Ted? Forget it."

"Really? We can forget it? Because that's what I want."

"Yep. Forget it," she said, and she rolled away from him, throwing off her ridiculous teddy and putting on her flannel nightgown.

Before long Ted was asleep beside her. She couldn't resist a peek before blowing out the candle. As suspected, his erection remained high and lofty, waving a flag for no one.

12

When Nick Cox, comfortable in a leather armchair, swilled his glass of wine, Grant, sitting in the matching chair opposite, swilled his. When Nick Cox shut his eyes and sniffed his wine, Grant sniffed too. When Nick Cox unfolded the preliminary plans for the addition to Grant and Suzanne's house, Grant interlaced his fingers behind his head and eyed the mural on the wall.

They were in Nick's basement, in the lounge adjacent to the wine cellar. Grant had stopped by for a "quick sec" after this evening's *Annie Get Your Gun* rehearsal, to see what Nick thought of the plans. He was a builder after all.

The mural was fantastic. You really got the feeling you were somewhere in Italy, with all those grapevines and blue sky, that villa off in the distance. He shut his eyes and basked, imagining himself on a sunny patio, not far from the olive trees.

Nick's house was like an American villa. It had everything—a gym with an amazing sound system, an endless pool, carpeting so thick you could lose golf balls in it. Everything was padded. Everything was shiny and enormous. Grant wanted to leap onto the sectional leather sofa in the media room like a kid jumping into a pile of leaves. He wanted to sack out with the remote control in his hand, surfing through channel after channel on their huge TV. Everything was top of the line, new, new, new, from the shimmering kitchen counters to the conference-table-size dining room table. Two dishwashers in the kitchen! A three-car garage with heating and air-conditioning! The Coxes' house was otherworldly. Truly. Like another world from his and Suzanne's little house, where Adam had pounding headaches and Suzanne was climbing the walls.

And now a baby. A baby!

He'd responded to the news with unrestrained joy. What choice did he have? You couldn't say *not now* to your pregnant wife. He had to act assured, under control, the dad guy. He had to behave the same way at work, to leave his employers in no doubt that they had chosen wisely when they hired him.

Things weren't going well on the new job. He was distracted, struggling to force himself to work the long hours a Washington law firm expected. There was just so much pressure on him these days. Even *Annie Get Your Gun,* which should have been a release, was a stressor. He felt terrible if he missed a line or sang a bad note at rehearsal. He didn't like to let anyone down.

Grant thought of his little cache of weed with something like love. He took it out to look at it sometimes. He unzipped the top of the Baggie and breathed it in, fished through it with his fingers in search of buds, like a forty-niner in search of gold nuggets. Nothing illegal about touching and smelling marijuana, if you ignored the fact that possession in Maryland was illegal without a medical marijuana license.

He thought about getting a license now that he lived in a state that allowed it. If he had it on doctor's orders, Suzanne couldn't object to it anymore. It would be like having a snack when you were hungry, water when you were thirsty, cough syrup when you were coughing—nothing anyone could find fault with. All that stood between him and that humming sense of peace was a piece of paper.

He wouldn't smoke again till he had that document, he told himself. Not anymore—because, well, he had been smoking a little. A very little. Just on the way back from rehearsals. It wasn't like he was in the habit. Okay, he was in the habit, but he was just having a couple of hits a night. He had to conserve it since he didn't know who to buy it from up here. He was mildly stoned right now, but what was the harm in that?

Honestly, what was so bad about weed? He'd never figured that out. As long as you weren't out-of-your-head stoned behind the wheel, who cared? It was no worse than alcohol. It probably made more sense to make alcohol illegal since people often got angry when they were drunk. People who were stoned usually just mellowed out.

All Grant really wanted was to relax a little. Suzanne acted like relaxation itself was a felony. She would kick him out if she knew he was smoking—she'd already made that clear. So he was careful. He went to bed after her, scrubbing himself down like a victim of nuclear fallout and rinsing with mouthwash in addition to brushing. Suzanne was a real bloodhound when she was pregnant. She could sniff out souring milk days before the expiration date, not to mention meat that was on the verge.

His phone pinged. Maybe it's a sympathetic pregnancy, Marie texted, continuing a conversation they'd been having about Adam's headaches.

Maybe.

Remember how fat I got when my sister was pregnant? She wrote. I'm still fat. She lost it all, the bitch, but me, I'm still paying for that brat.

He wrote Hahaha.

He liked the fact that all she needed was a laugh, not reassurance that she wasn't fat—though she wasn't. Since when did a little meat on the bones mean someone was fat?

The two of them had dated for a while, after college. Not really dated. More like friends with benefits. They used to get together when they were stoned or bored, make out, sometimes more. It went on intermittently for years, in between girlfriends. Marie always said they'd get married someday. He'd apologized to her over drinks after he and Suzanne got engaged. "I didn't mean I'd be your first wife," she'd said dryly.

Grant took another sip of wine. Nick had a special refrigerator filled with bottles.

"Nice, very nice," Nick said.

Grant nodded. "On the dry side." He had a fifty percent chance of being right.

"I meant the house plans," Nick said. "They're nice, but they could be a hell of a lot nicer. Can I talk to you man-to-man?"

"Of course."

"That house of yours is a tear-down. But you knew that when you bought it."

Grant nodded tentatively. A fixer-upper, he thought they were called.

"What's keeping you from gutting it and building something really gorgeous, something worthy of you and your beautiful family?"

Grant imagined transporting Nick's house onto his lawn. He envisioned helicopters carrying it the way storks carried babies.

Then he came to with a sigh. "Might not be possible. We'll see what they decide after the public hearing."

"Yeah, what a joke, right? A moratorium will never pass. It's not even legal." Nick drained his glass.

"I don't know about that . . ."

"It's legal? You're shitting me."

Grant nodded.

"What would it mean?" Nick's voice crept up the register. "Crackdowns? Retroactive fines? Or worse? Are they going to make people tear down houses they decide don't 'fit in'?" He made air quotes. "It's discrimination, that's what. Discrimination against the successful."

"My guess is what's been approved, stays approved."

"A 'Petition for Peace.' What a load of crap. You didn't sign, did you?"

"Not me," Grant said.

"I ought to start a petition of my own."

"A Petition for War?"

Nick laughed. "I like you, Davenport."

"Davenport-Gardner."

"Yeah. Whatever." He clapped Grant on the shoulder.

Grant felt himself blush, more pleased than he would have liked to admit.

Nick grabbed another bottle of wine by its neck, like a chicken, tore off the foil with his teeth, and poured fresh glasses for them both.

ALLISON, BACK FROM REHEARSAL, SAT AT THE DINING ROOM TABLE with a cup of mint tea. It had been a good day after all, two Christmas card photo shoots and another afternoon of babysitting. Adam was fine company. She'd sung songs from *Annie Get Your Gun* to him while he lay on the couch, eyes closed. "Brava," he'd cried whenever she finished a number, and "Encore."

Ted, sitting opposite Allison, frowned over the enlarged map of the town spread across the table in front of him. Jillian sat at the head, math book and notebook open. "Domestic Life in Willard Park," Allison thought, snapping an imaginary picture.

Ted had come home from work with flowers yesterday. He'd given her a kiss on the cheek as well.

"What's wrong with Dad?" Jillian had said, worried by these uncharacteristic gestures, so they'd waited till bedtime to talk, side by side in their flannel pajamas in the dark.

He loved her. There was no doubt about that, he said. She closed her eyes, waiting for the "but," which soon followed: He just needed a little break from intimacy for now. Not forever, he assured her, just for a little while. How long was a little while? she asked him, but he didn't have an answer. "It'll happen though. Then I'll get right back on the horse!" he said, then, hearing how it sounded, amended, "I mean, back in the saddle." Which was no better.

She wasn't sure how to answer, and so she hadn't. It wasn't a question anyway. What would a refusal to accept his personal moratorium mean? Divorce? Who divorced someone for a tempo-rary suspension in marital relations? Soon the stress of the town would be a thing of the past, and then they could revive that aspect of their lives, she told herself, wanting to believe it. They had fallen asleep nestled like spoons. It wasn't sex, but it was something. But it wasn't sex.

She reviewed the choreography for "Doin' What Comes Natur'lly" in her head. She and the three kids in the show had been taught the steps during rehearsal tonight. The song was a corny one, no doubt considered risqué when the show opened on Broad-way in the mid-1940s. "I feel a little silly, singing it. My country accent is supposed to be over the top," she said in an over-the-top country accent.

Ted made a noise that seemed to indicate that he was listening, but Allison suspected he hadn't heard a word. He had marked the spots on the map where the trees had been damaged around town, a total of twenty-three now. Granted, most of them were the size of brooms, but they were still trees.

Who was doing it? She made a list of possibilities. Nick, okay, he was definitely a suspect, having cut down so many trees on his properties; but there were a lot of other possibilities, people who were just fed up with things and needed a release. There was a lot to be fed up with these days. The idea that someone would want to exert control over something, even something as weird as the trees, was not unreasonable. Could it be Lucy? Could the bulletin board and the trees and everything else be part of a scheme to drum up business for the café? Maybe she wanted to expand it. Turn it into a chain. Or maybe it was that crazy new principal at the elementary school. Or Ted himself. Maybe he was trying to frame Nick. The idea was ridiculous—but he was probably at least WP Tree Poet. She'd liked the Khalil Gibran quotation the town had woken up to today, *Life without love is like a tree without blossoms or fruit.*

"What?" Ted said, feeling her eyes on him.

"Looking for patterns, Monsieur Poirot?"

He turned the map sideways and squinted. "Don't seem to be any."

He was absolutely obsessed. Was she wrong to ask him about them? Did that make her an enabler?

Not that trees were his only obsession. He was obsessed about the moratorium hearing too. He'd collected more than enough signatures, a personal victory. He worked on his testimony in bed at night, often reading it aloud to Allison, whose job it was to make sure it didn't go over three minutes. He seemed to think his nightly changes were radical, but Allison usually couldn't tell the difference between one version and the next. She'd be able to recite it from memory by the time the hearing rolled around next week. He was even making a slide show to accompany it, not a PowerPoint, but with actual old Kodak slides.

Jillian nodded her head up and down like a bobblehead on a car dashboard. It was a wonder she could concentrate on what she was writing, her head was moving so much.

"How can you concentrate on your schoolwork with music playing?" she said, but Jillian didn't hear her.

Ted put on his glasses, which he only wore when he was tired. They made him look older. They'd been a couple for more than half their lives. No wonder their sex life had died. Life was changing, evolving, for better or for worse. Soon they'd be old. Jillian would have to take care of them before long. She was glad she and Jillian were so close. Or were they close? She couldn't remember the last time they had had more than a two-sentence conversation.

"What are you listening to, Jill?" she said, wondering, literally, what was going on in her daughter's head.

Jillian sang aloud. "What?" she said, when she caught Allison looking at her. She pulled out an earbud, looking cross.

"You were singing."

"I was not!" she yelled.

"I'm going to take a walk," Allison said in her best faux-chipper voice. "Join me?"

"Math sucks," Jillian said.

Allison weighed her options. If she ignored the bad language, it might encourage Jillian to open up to her. But in the end, Allison couldn't resist suggesting an alternative. "Math stinks," she said.

Jillian rolled her eyes and stopped up her ears again.

"Candy could use a walk," Ted said.

"Not tonight." Allison had the right to go alone. Ted never took Candy on his nightly walks. He came home with mud on his shoes. He claimed just to be taking inventory of damaged trees and property, but Allison suspected he had visions of catching Nick in the act, and turning him in, vigilante-style. It reminded her of when Jillian and Sofia used to wander the neighborhood in raincoats and sunglasses, pretending to be spies.

And, too, you couldn't take photos when you had a dog along. That was what Allison was going to do tonight. She grabbed her coat, camera, and tripod and walked into the glow of the night.

December was a miracle in Willard Park. Every house was decorated with tiny white lights no matter the religion of the resident, a town tradition. It looked like a toy town, despite the contrasting house sizes. The lights were officially lit on the first Sunday evening in December, a ceremony that included caroling and deep cauldrons of hot chocolate. The town tree, a Douglas fir planted on the green years ago so they wouldn't have to sacrifice a new one each year, stood nearly twenty-five feet tall. Schoolchildren made the ornaments—religion neutral, so as not to offend.

Usually neighbors on ladders decorated the town tree, but this year Nick and Kaye, as cochairs of the decorating committee, had hired a company to do the job courtesy of Cox Design and Build. A woman in a suit and dangerously high heels had stood below, directing, clipboard in hand. The result was worthy of a magazine. There were so many lights, kids could play by the glow of them after dark, which, while excessive, was also kind of fun.

Allison appraised the house decorations as she walked around the block, judging them privately since the town no longer offered prizes, a practice that ended a few years before, when someone unstrung most of the lights on what would certainly have been the winning house. The Garcias had electric candles in the windows and icicle lights dripping from the eaves, like the witch's house in "Hansel and Gretel." *Nice,* Allison thought. The Conways had opted for blinking lights around the window frames. A family of mechanical deer grazed on the lawn. *A little tacky.*

Nick and Kaye had put up colored lights their first December in Willard Park, prompting the town council to draft a letter informing them that colored lights were against town regulations. This year their house was outlined with white lights like a drawing in a coloring book—a streamlined and effective look. The same woman who had coordinated the decorating on the green had supervised the work. It went against the spirit of the thing to hire out, but Allison had to admit that the house looked magical. *The winner.*

Allison set up her tripod on the sidewalk, lowering the legs so she could take the shot from the ground up, to make it look like a looming fairy-tale castle. If she angled it right, she could make the stone lions by the front door look life-size. She was about to screw the camera onto the tripod when Rex came around from the back of the house, barking.

"Hush, Rex."

He barked again, but it was more of a come-pat-me bark than an I'm-going-to-eat-you-up bark. Allison crept up the path and sat on the top step, hoping to mollify him. Rex sniffed her hands and legs, his tail wagging. He emitted excited yelps periodically and licked her face.

Nick opened the front door. "Rex!" he yelled. Then he saw Allison.

"Hi." If she acted normal, maybe it wouldn't seem weird that she was sitting on his steps. "He's a good watchdog."

"Can I help you, Mrs. Miller?"

"I was hoping to take some pictures of your lights, Mr. Cox. They're stunning." The praise felt like a betrayal, but there it was. She'd said it.

Nick came out on the porch, the storm door easing closed behind him. "I suppose Ted's home preparing for the hearing?"

"I'll just be going . . ."

"No. Stay." He sat beside her. He was barefoot, in jeans and a dark button-down shirt—not enough clothes for a winter's night. His feet were unexpectedly long and narrow. Practically hairless. Allison's face grew hot with embarrassment, which was silly. They were only feet.

"Is it for your book?" he said.

"What?"

"The photos. Are they for your book?"

"How do you know about my book?"

"Kaye told me."

"How does Kaye know?"

"Lindy told her," he said. It was descending into the absurd. "Mind if I see them?"

She had a creeping sensation he would erase all of the pictures on her camera as revenge against Ted. Well, most of them were backed up. She slipped the camera strap over her head and gave it to him.

He thumbed through the shots, making positive sounds. He smelled like wine. Allison felt a little like they were on a date. Teenagers sitting on the front porch after an evening at the movies.

"These are really good," Nick said.

"You sound surprised, Mr. Cox."

"We should collaborate, Mrs. Miller."

"Collaborate!" She laughed.

"Printing costs have got to be astronomical."

"A publisher would deal with that."

"You got one in mind?"

"I've got a few ideas . . ."

"It'd make a great coffee-table book."

"It's a history book," she said, arching. "You and I could never 'collaborate.' We'd have completely different ideas. It's all a matter of taste."

He smiled. "Taste? You think? What do you suppose my book would look like?"

"You really want to know?"

"Absolutely."

"A real estate book, like that glossy 'Superior Properties' booklet we get in the mail all the time. My guess is you'd focus on freshly minted mansions, complete with prices."

"As opposed to the recycled newsprint you have in mind, the profits designated for the 'Save the Ferret' fund." He leaned away from her, smiling, as though he expected her to hit him, which was exactly what she felt like doing: not in the way siblings were said to do—out for blood—but in a playful, giggling, go-down-groping sort of way.

"I'd better go."

"I'll bet we could work out a compromise. I could pay the up-front costs. I'm kind of a regular at the bank."

"What would be in it for you?"

"Done well, it could put Willard Park on the map."

"It is on the map. It's a town."

He laughed. "On the *map* on the map. I've got some ideas for this burg." He went on to tell her about the business district he envisioned, complete with restaurants and fancy shops. He talked with his hands, framing his ideas in the air in front of both of them. "I'm a dreamer, I guess."

"It's not so bad to dream," she said, again feeling like a traitor. His dream ran in direct contrast to Ted's.

The front door opened behind them. Grant leaned outside. Allison jumped up. "Frank!" she said.

"Why it's Annie Oakley!" He turned his fingers into guns and shot at her. His eyelids looked heavy, as though they wanted to seal shut.

"I was just going," she said.

"This gal can sing. Did you know she could sing?" Grant said.

Nick raised his eyebrows. "I'll bet she can."

Allison's face went hot. "I'd better go."

"Have a glass of wine with us. We saved you some cab," Nick said.

"We're talking about the hearing. Might interest you," Grant said.

"Nothing could interest me less," she blurted out. "I mean . . . I didn't say that. Good night, gentlemen." Her photo session could wait.

Nick laughed. "Good night then, Allison."

"Lasso you later," Grant said.

"Yee-haw." Allison gathered her camera and tripod and headed across her lawn, toward home.

The Christmas lights on their house went out as she stepped onto their front porch. They were on a timer, set to go off at ten thirty, but the serendipity of the timing made it feel like a judgment. She glanced back to see whether Nick had gone back inside. He hadn't. He was watching her from his porch, his feet bare upon the wood.

13

DECEMBER 14

If Suzanne heard "Jingle Bell Rock" one more time, she was going to take one of the guys who was selling tiny remote-controlled airplanes throughout the shopping mall and throw him and his little Styrofoam planes down the escalator. Four months into the pregnancy, she was supposed to be beyond the nausea, but the lights and the noise, the sugary stench emanating from the stores, the pomposity of Santa's crystal palace in the atrium, and Santa himself, who had winked at her lasciviously as she walked by, all had a weakening effect.

She ought to be relishing this, she reminded herself. Allison had offered to watch Adam again today so Suzanne could go to her ultrasound appointment and her obstetric appointment—a gynecological double date that culminated in a shopping mall nightcap. A terrible combination, but arguably better than sitting in a sauna watching Nina Strauss sweat her way through hot yoga. Who knew if she would get another chance to Christmas shop? *Enjoy, enjoy!* she commanded herself, marching into Nordstrom's boys' department. She chose three size 6 polo-style shirts in yellow, red, and blue; a little white dress shirt and tie; a blue pullover vest and a pack of socks, then went up to the men's department, where she bought the same for Grant in men's large.

She fought a yearning to slip over to the baby department to buy something tiny and soft for the baby. She didn't want to jinx the pregnancy. She wanted this child. She hadn't realized how much until she went in for her ultrasound. She'd been nervous driving to the appointment. What if something was wrong with the baby?

Suzanne, lying on her back beside the ultrasound monitor, needing desperately to pee, had held her breath as she saw the image of the baby appear. The baby—a girl!—was perfect. She was so tiny and delicate, with her miniature forehead and nose.

Suzanne's abdomen suddenly felt heavy. She sat in an armchair by a fern in a brass pot, an area reserved for bored husbands, and listened to the holiday pianist play "Silent Night."

Dr. Fielding, the obstetrician Allison had recommended, was concerned about Suzanne's cervix. He'd mentioned it twice now, once a few weeks ago, and again today. He'd had the technician who did the sonogram check its length.

"It's a little short," Dr. Fielding said. "I'm keeping an eye on you."

"My cervix is fine," she said to the white ceiling. She was wearing a blue paper gown, feet in cold metal stirrups, a hard position from which to be authoritative. "It never gave me a moment's trouble during my last pregnancy."

Dr. Fielding peeled off his gloves and helped her up to a seated position. He had a warm smile, long eyelashes, big brown eyes. He was too good looking, really, to be an obstetrician. She and Allison often discussed his cuteness, how disconcerting it was to be attracted to your obstetrician. Not unpleasant, just disconcerting. They theorized about his sex life. Was sex with his wife more like work than fun for him? Just another vagina after a day of vaginas? Allison was the one who brought it up. She was more deviant than she looked.

Adam's size at birth—nearly nine pounds—and his eagerness to leave the womb had weakened her cervix, Dr. Fielding explained. She might need a cerclage to carry the baby to term. The word "cerclage" sounded French and lovely, like something you might find at a patisserie, or an aperitif. It sounded much less terrifying than "stitching up your vagina to keep the baby in."

"An incompetent cervix is manageable," Dr. Fielding said. "Not that I'm calling it that at this point."

"Incompetent." The word stung.

Three girls walked through the juniors' department, laughing. Two of them, blondes, were dressed nearly identically in miniskirts without tights, ankle boots, and thin fitted jackets. A brunette in a practical-looking red parka and clogs was between them. Suzanne flashed forward to her own daughter, several years from now, out shopping with friends. One of the blondes wasn't a girl, Suzanne saw now, but a woman: Kaye Cox; the other was her daughter, Lindy. The brunette was Jillian Miller.

Suzanne nearly called out a hello, but Jillian disappeared behind a rack of blouses before she had the chance. Suzanne thought about going over to her, but it sounded tiring. And she would have to talk to Kaye. She picked up her shopping bags instead, and slipped out of the store.

JILLIAN PULLED A SHIRT OFF THE RACK AND HELD IT UP, AS IF CONSIDering it. What in the world was Adam's mom doing here? Had her mom sent her to spy on her? Would there be a note on the bulletin board the next day? *Jillian went to the mall without her mother's permission.*

"That is so ugly," Lindy said, tugging on a sleeve.

"I know, right?" Jillian said. It was ugly, an odd mixture of pink and olive green with kimono-style sleeves. She looked over the top of the hanger to see if Suzanne had seen her, but she was leaving. Phew. Jillian put the shirt back on the rack, pretending to consider another equally ugly shirt, giving Suzanne time to disappear before they continued to their destination.

After school today Lindy had decided Jillian needed new clothes. Her clothes were crap. She needed to work on her brand. She'd grabbed Jillian by the arm and pulled her downstairs, to the kitchen, where Kaye sat thumbing through a catalog. "We are going to the mall right now, Mom. We have work to do!"

Kaye seemed as eager as Lindy. "What fun!" Jakey was on a playdate, so it was perfect. "Just perfect."

"You're just dropping us off," Lindy said.

Kaye's expression slid from happy to sad, like a pair of emojis. "I'll just walk in with you. I have a little shopping of my own to do."

Jillian wished Kaye would stand up for herself, but who was she to talk? She was just as afraid of Lindy as Kaye was—not to mention her fear of her own parents. A not-afraid person would have told her mother she was going to the mall, but that would have meant admitting she was friends with Lindy, something Jillian wasn't prepared to do. She'd been sneaking over to the Coxes' house every day after school for over a month now, always afraid her mom would see her going in the front door, or running around back to Lindy's fort in the White Elephant. And what if her mom ran into one of the teachers who ran the after-school clubs? She would be sent to her room forever.

Jillian, confirming that the coast was clear, followed Lindy and Kaye toward the escalator. Was the stress of sneaking around worth the thrill of being at the mall with Lindy? Jillian wasn't so sure. It wasn't as if she could actually buy anything. She'd spent all of her allowance on Christmas presents for her parents and Candy. Lindy, on the other hand, had her own credit card. Talk about cool.

There were a lot of cool things about Lindy Cox. A lot of creepy things, but enough cool things to offset them. Having brand-name clothes and your own bathroom was cool. So was having a mom who kept up with the fashion trends and liked the same music you did.

Spying on neighbors with binoculars fell in the creepy category. Dancing in your bra and panties to YouTube videos also was creepy, or what Jillian's grandmother would have called "unwholesome." Then there was the fort, which was the best place ever. Jillian always felt as though she was going to fall through one of the planks or step on a nail and get tetanus, but it was worth it. The other day they'd had a séance and brought back the ghost of Lindy's grandfather. They both had felt his presence in the room.

Lindy called Jillian her BFF, her best friend forever. "Am I yours?" she would ask, and Jillian would, reluctantly, say yes. Was it possible to have two BFFs? One in France and one in Maryland? For a while Jillian had been suspicious about why Lindy was being so nice to her, but over time she'd started to ease into the novel concept that Lindy liked her for her. It was flattering to have been chosen—and exhausting at the same time.

Lindy was unpredictable. For a while, she would be nice, fixing Jillian's hair so it would look cooler, or giving her a makeover, then, all of a sudden she'd blow up, and go up to her room and lock Jillian out. Like the other day after Jillian mentioned, in front of Kaye, that she usually got straight As. Lindy screamed like a tea kettle, then left Jillian and Kaye alone in the kitchen, where she and Kaye talked about horoscopes and drank diet soda till Lindy dragged Jillian upstairs.

There was no chance Jillian was going to get straight As this semester. She might even fail social studies. Mrs. Baxter, the social studies teacher, called Lindy and Jillian in over lunch one day

to ask them whether they had made the Greek temple by themselves. It was obvious that they hadn't. It was built of measured,
stained, and sanded dowels and sheets of plywood spray-painted
to look like stone. It looked like it should be in a museum. The
man who made house models for Lindy's dad's company had built
it—but that didn't keep Lindy from swearing that they'd done
it by themselves. She described cutting the wood at her father's
workbench and sanding with squares of sandpaper. Mrs. Baxter
had said she was going to call their parents to verify the story, but
she hadn't so far. Maybe Jillian should turn herself in before they
were found out; she could leave an anonymous note on Lucy's
bulletin board: *Jillian and Lindy did not make the Greek temple.*

"Ta-da!" Lindy said. They were standing in front of a store Jillian
had never been in before. Of course she hadn't. It was a store for
teenagers, and she was only twelve. When she went shopping with
her mother, they went to the Girls 7–16 section of the department
store, where identical clothes of assorted sizes hung on plastic hangers in tightly packed rows. The music was soft, classical, or an instru-
mental version of a song that had been popular a few years before.

But this was something different. This seemed to be not just
a place where teenagers shopped but where they lived. There were
hammocks and record players, tables with stacks of shirts with
shoes below, as though the teenagers had just kicked them off on
their way over to the big pillows and scented candles. Bras in Easter egg colors hung on the wall like art, and dresses relaxed on
wooden hangers in small but tasteful groups. The music was loud
and peppered with words kids got in trouble for saying. Everyone
was older, and wore denim and black and impractical shoes, and
looked as if they had left their lives with their parents behind for
something much, much better.

Lindy moved to the music as they walked through the store,

smiling at Jillian, and Jillian tried to smile back. Lindy pointed to short dresses and shorter skirts, outfits that looked too small for a grown person but too revealing for a child. "You'd look so cute in this," she said, picking up a tube top. Jillian imagined coming down to breakfast in a shirt that looked like a sock with the foot cut off.

Lindy started pulling T-shirts out of folded piles. She looked at them, then tossed them aside. Jillian tried to fold them again, but Lindy unfolded them faster than she could neaten them up. She handed Jillian a heap of sweaters and leggings and dragged her toward the changing room.

The girls stood back-to-back as they peeled off their clothes and tried on the new ones. Jillian found a price tag on a light blue sweater that Lindy had picked for her. Nearly sixty dollars! "I don't have any money," she whispered.

"I do."

"I can't take your money."

"Why not? If I give it to you? It's a Christmas present. Merry Christmas."

"It's too much." She'd gotten Lindy a pack of three lip glosses for Christmas—one strawberry, one grape, and one lime.

"It's fine."

Jillian frowned, struggling with what to do.

"Jill. My parents are loaded. Do you want it or not?"

Jillian wanted it. "That's so nice of you."

They waited in line to pay alongside wooden bins filled with vegetable-scented face masks, glass vials of flowery perfume, and lipsticks in shades from pink to black—treats as tempting as the candy in the checkout aisle at the supermarket. Was it okay to draw on the back of your hand with a lipstick? To paint a stripe of nail polish on the side of the bin to see what the color looked like? Jillian put caps back on as Lindy tossed the treasures back.

When they finally got to the register, Lindy stuck the credit card in the reader as if it was nothing, handing Jillian the bag with the sweater in it. Jillian would have to throw out the bag, of course, which felt wasteful since it was made of fabric instead of paper. Maybe she could wear the sweater home. Maybe her mom would think it was just an old one, though she doubted it. Her mother knew what Jillian owned better than she did. "I don't have any sweaters," Jillian might yell on her way out the door on a chilly day, and her mother would rattle off all of the sweaters she owned, going back to third grade.

"That was so generous of you, Lindy. My present is a lot smaller."

Lindy took her hand, which was so cute. Anyone who saw them would know that Lindy was her friend. She must be a little special to have a friend as cool as Lindy. They stopped in front of the Piercing Pagoda.

"Today's your lucky day," Lindy sang.

Jillian laughed.

"Which pair do you want? You have to get gold or your ears will get infected or something gross."

"Oh, I'm not. I can't."

"You can't?"

"My mom says—"

"Are you going to let your mommy tell you what to do your whole life, Jilly Billy? What a sad life that would be." Lindy called the woman behind the counter over. The woman wore a white lab coat, as if she were a doctor. "She'd like to have her ears pierced," Lindy said.

The woman looked at Jillian. "Is that right?"

All of the advice she'd ever gotten about peer pressure wafted out of Jillian's head, leaving her powerless. She nodded yes.

"You're going to need your mom's consent."

"She's sixteen. She just turned it," Lindy said, but the woman shook her head no.

So Lindy texted her mom, who came over from another part of the mall laden with shopping bags. She winked as she signed the form giving permission for "her daughter" to have her ears pierced. Jillian smiled back, hoping Kaye would understand it was the smile of a girl being held hostage, but she didn't. What was going to happen to her when people started pressuring her to drink or do drugs? She'd become an addict, out on the street with a bottle in a paper bag all because she couldn't say no.

She held both Kaye's and Lindy's hands as the woman came at her with the big gun. They all promised it wouldn't hurt, but it did. She yelped and her eyes welled, and then they did it on the other side. Lindy sent her mother off again and dragged Jillian to the food court.

They sat at a metal table with pink milkshakes, the smells of hamburgers and cinnamon buns floating around them, fear seizing Jillian's body. She was so going to be in trouble. Hanging out at the White Elephant, skipping after-school activities, and going to the mall without permission suddenly looked like minor offenses— jaywalking—compared to the crime she'd just committed. Her parents were going to kill her—she, who had never done anything worse than reading under the covers with a flashlight, until this fall. It wouldn't matter to them that it was Lindy's fault. She felt her ears throb, pulsing reminders that she was bad.

"Check this out." Lindy tore the end of the paper wrapper off one of the extra straws she'd taken from the smoothie counter. She put the straw in her mouth and blew the paper at a little girl a few tables over. The girl touched the side of her head and looked around, not sure what hit her. Lindy laughed out loud.

What if the needle wasn't clean? What if she got a staph infection? What if she got AIDS? If her parents didn't kill her, a disease would.

"I got my ears pierced when I was four. I wouldn't leave the mall till my mom got it done for me. Then I ran all over the place showing everyone," Lindy said. She aimed a straw wrapper at a boy about their age. "I'm glad you did it. It's like we're sisters now."

"They're never going to trust me again," Jillian said.

"Trust is for losers." Lindy sent another wrapper straight into the air. "Here, I got you something. A present for being so brave." Lindy took a little vial of perfume out of her purse.

"That's so nice." Jillian uncapped it and sniffed.

"Crap!" Lindy cried. "It's him!"

She grabbed Jillian's cheeks and turned her head to the right, to show her Mark, sitting alone between Cinnabon and the Panda Café. His binder was open on his table and he was tapping his phone like crazy, obviously playing a game. Jillian's ears began to ache.

"Go say hello to him," Lindy said.

"No!"

"Why not?"

"Let's just go find your mom, Lin. It's getting late."

"But he's your friend."

"I know . . ."

Lindy narrowed her eyes. "He is, isn't he?"

She nodded.

"So, you don't want to say hello to a friend?"

"Not right now . . ."

"Why?"

"I just . . . He looks busy."

"You made out like you and he were best friends and now you won't even go talk to him?"

"Not *best* friends."

"You're such a liar." Lindy looked disproportionately disappointed.

"What?" Jillian said, realization raining down on her.

That was it. She ought to have guessed. How stupid was she? It wasn't her Lindy was interested in: it was Mark. Lindy had become friends with her to get to Mark.

"Come on." Lindy grabbed Jillian's wrist. Jillian didn't dare say no. Lindy might freak out, abandon her at the mall. What would she do if that happened? Call an Uber? Her mom had gotten her the app in case of an emergency. What kind of emergency? Was this an emergency?

"Hey," Mark said when they were standing next to him. He looked up from his game for an instant before looking back down again.

"So what're you up to, Mark?" Lindy said, smiling to show her professionally whitened teeth.

"Homework. While my mom gets Christmas stuff," he said, and Lindy laughed.

"Homework? Liar. Hey, Jillian just got her ears pierced."

He nodded, his eyes still on his game.

"Doesn't she look good?" Lindy pinched his arm as if they were friends. "She wasn't supposed to. Boohoo, huh?"

He tapped on the screen wildly for a few seconds, then looked up, smiling. "I won!"

"See her ears?" Lindy said.

He looked up. "What?"

"My parents are going to kill me," Jillian said.

"I've done things my mom would kill me for, but so far so good," he said.

"Like what?" Lindy said.

He shrugged. "What she doesn't know won't hurt her, if you know what I mean. They might even help."

"I don't know what you mean," Jillian said, but Mark had started a new game.

"I'm bad too," Lindy said, nodding.

"Yeah?" he said, not looking up.

He liked Lindy. That was obvious. Boys liked girls who were daring and blond. Jillian might as well go now. Lindy had gotten what she wanted from Jillian. She no longer needed her. Jillian took the perfume out of her bag and sniffed it again.

"Can I see it?" Lindy said, putting out her hand. She sprayed perfume on Mark's arm.

"Hey!" he said.

Lindy sprayed Mark's neck. He grabbed it and sprayed her throat.

Jillian watched her new perfume evaporate in the air. When had Lindy bought it? she wondered, watching them play.

Lindy's phone rang. "What, Mom," she said, her voice suddenly bored and irritated.

Mark gave the perfume back to Jillian. "Sorry." Their fingers touched in the transaction.

"I don't mind." She didn't. Not the wasting of the perfume. Certainly not the touching of the fingers.

When *had* Lindy bought it? Not when she bought the sweater. Jillian had been with her. She rolled the bottle back and forth between her palms. It had a pleasing weight to it.

"My mom says to meet her at Starbucks in five," Lindy said. "You smell good, Mark."

He sniffed his arm. "I kind of do."

Lindy grabbed his phone and swiped through his recent calls. "Mom work, Mom cell, school . . . blah, blah. How about your dad? Don't you have a dad?"

"Lindy!" Jillian cried.

"My mom's a black widow spider. She ate my dad after he impregnated her," Mark said.

Lindy laughed and started tapping on his phone.

"Don't." He reached for it, but she held it away.

Her phone chirped. "Oh, a text telling me you think I'm hot? How sweet, Mark."

"When did you even buy this?" Jillian said, holding the perfume aloft.

Lindy rolled her eyes. "We better go. Bye, Marko. In Italy, they'd call you Marko."

"*O solo mio,*" he said, returning to his game.

"Well," Jillian said when she and Lindy were on the escalator. "When did you?"

"What?" Lindy sounded annoyed.

"Buy the perfume."

"When you were trying on stuff, duh."

"You were with me."

"Not every minute, God," Lindy said.

Jillian thought about it. "Yes you were."

"Oh my God! I was just trying to be nice! If you don't want it, throw it out!"

Jillian stepped off the escalator in silence, looking out for the mall guards who were going to arrest them both for shoplifting. Jillian had used the perfume, and it was in her bag. Wasn't that nearly as bad as stealing it herself? She was sweating under her coat.

Jillian Miller is not sixteen.

Jillian Miller is a shoplifter.

Jillian Miller is not as good friends with Mark Strauss as she pretends to be.

Kaye, in line at Starbucks, waved to them. "Coffee before we go, girls?"

"Yeah!" Lindy said.

Coffee, too, was off limits until she was older.

"Jillian?" Kaye called. "Frappuccino? Peppermint Mocha?"

Jillian stood frozen at the precipice; then Lindy came along and gave her a push.

NICK REGRETTED NOT GRABBING A WARMER COAT THE MINUTE REX pulled him out the door into the yard. He might have turned around and gone back, but Rex was raring to go, tail up, full speed ahead—and really, was there anything more beautiful than a dog who was finally, finally being given his walk? He couldn't deny him his moment, not for another moment. The afternoon dog walk had become a regular gig for Nick these past weeks, ever since the financially imposed hiatus on work on the White Elephant. When had he started calling it that? It seemed like a bad sign.

He walked down Tunlaw, past the old houses he still imagined into gold, and over to the green. He'd walk Rex around, maybe let him run leash-less—a forbidden and punishable offense—then go over to the elementary school to pick up Jakey. Jakey would be glad to see him—or maybe he wouldn't. He usually just said, "Where's Mommy?" and pulled out his phone so he could play games as they walked home. So much for bonding time; he was basically just there to make sure his son didn't walk into cars.

He stuck the hand not holding the leash in his pocket. A hot drink. That was what he needed, he thought, spying Lucy's. Kaye swore by it, but to him a café in an old house was on the bed-and-breakfast spectrum: more folksy and intimate than he wanted from a business transaction; he'd choose Starbucks and a Westin any day. Still, a cold day was a cold day, and it was the only place to eat in town.

By now the bulletin board, which he'd heard about—everyone in Willard Park had heard about the bulletin board—was outside behind Lucy's. She'd apparently replaced the small one on the porch with a big one and nailed it to a couple of two-by-fours. She'd also brought some tables and patio heaters out back. The tables were all full, and a number of other people were standing by the board, studying it. No one said hello to him as he passed by; a few people glared. Was there something about him up there? He wouldn't dignify it by stopping to look. He went around front and up the porch steps. The three tables up there were all empty, with neither heater to warm nor bulletin board to titillate.

Nick tied Rex to the railing. He patted Rex's head. "Good boy." Nick didn't like to leave him outside alone, but it was the law, a discriminatory one, he thought—why were dogs less deserving of the respite of a café than humans? "You're a good, good boy," he said and turned toward the café door without a backward glance, not wanting to see Rex's mournful eyes and low, sad tail. Inside it was warm and there was music, something Dylan-like but not Dylan; it wasn't loud enough to cover up Rex's cries for help.

"Cold day," Nick said to Lucy when he made it to the front of the line.

She looked at him as though he had just walked into her house without knocking.

WTF? Wasn't he being a good neighbor, supporting a local business by coming here? Try as he might, he didn't get this town. He stifled an urge to give her the finger and walk back out, and instead ordered the biggest hot chocolate on the menu—a White Elephant–size Mexican, because it was pricier, not to mention spicier—along with a lemon poppy seed muffin, lemon bars for the kids, and a beautiful frosted dog biscuit shaped like a house. Kill 'em with kindness—wasn't that a thing?

"Do you have a mug?" Lucy said.

"A mug?"

"A mug." She flicked a finger at the mugs on hooks, maybe a hundred of them, of varying shapes and sizes.

The answer was no. No, he didn't have a mug. Was he supposed to bring it with him? In his experience, cafés provided not only food and drink, but *dishes*. That was kind of the point, he thought. "No. Can I buy one? Do you sell them?"

"Do you think you can buy everything, Cox? That everything is for sale?" Lucy snapped. The kid washing dishes snickered.

Nick was nine years old, the teacher shaking her head at him. *Didn't you read the book, Nicholas? Or can't you read?* The other kids laughing. He had read it. He had sat down with it every day after school that week. It was just that the letters flipped and flopped on the page. *B*s were *D*s. *O*s were *E*s or *C*s. They squeezed together and drifted apart; they gave him a headache instead of a story.

"I'll take a paper cup then. Don't tell me you don't have paper? That you're a paper-free café?" he said, aware that he was only making things worse—but what was he supposed to do? If he didn't have a mug and she wouldn't sell him a mug, what did she want him to do? Hold out his cupped hands?

Lucy filled a cup with the hot chocolate and pushed it toward him. He didn't dare ask for a lid.

Back on the porch, Nick untied Rex, who was grateful, beyond grateful—then, beyond even that when Nick gave him his fancy biscuit. He ate it in one enormous bite. "Know how much that thing set me back? Five fifty. Five fuckin' fifty."

Why not talk to the dog? No one wanted to talk to him, that was for sure. Nor he to them. Nor he to them.

He scratched the sweet spot under Rex's chin. Rex's eyelashes fluttered and he leaned into Nick's leg, sinking into a pool at his feet, as if Nick's scratching were a drug that he craved, that only Nick could provide—which made him feel maybe as good as Rex did. "Good boy. Good puppy."

He breathed in the lemony smell of his muffin, then took a bite. It was possibly the best muffin he'd ever tasted. This irritated him. He wanted to hate it, just like the town hated him. Why did everyone blame him for everything? Why was his lawn sign bad and Ted Miller's good? Why were all the editorials in the crappy little town newsletter against him? Why did everyone assume he was behind every lousy thing that went wrong in Willard Park? Why, why, why?

He took another bite of muffin, chewing slowly, isolating the ingredients on his tongue: the tang of the lemon zest, the minuscule snap of the poppy seeds. It was very moist, but not oily.

One day, when he was old and there wasn't a lot else he could do, he would take up baking. It would be his retirement hobby. He baked on occasion already: he was the one who made the family birthday cakes. Chocolate with chocolate frosting for Jakey, chocolate soufflé cake for Lindy, and, for Kaye, yellow with raspberry jam between the layers and chocolate icing. Nick enjoyed adjusting the recipes, adding a little almond extract, coffee instead of water, orange zest instead of orange juice—things like that. He decorated with fresh raspberries or even edible flowers. Who knew you could eat flowers? It was like being a chemist. He'd only recently shared his plan with Kaye, late one night in the hot tub. She'd loved the idea.

"You could open a bakery! Call it . . . what? What should we call it? 'Park Row Bakers' or 'Mr. Willard's Bakeshop,' or maybe after the kids, 'Lindy's,' but no, Jakey would—"

"No," he said—apparently too abruptly or something, because she clammed up and her eyes filled with tears.

"I just mean. It's not meant to be a business. It's just for me," he said and, because a tear was running down her cheek, "Just for us. Just you and me."

She sniffed and smiled a tiny smile. He always managed to hurt her feelings. Was it because she'd lost her mother so young? She was like a skinless bunny.

"It's just for fun, I guess. Haven't you ever wanted to do something just for the satisfaction, Kaye? Just to experiment?"

She sighed, like she was about to say something, then she laughed—as if it was a crazy notion, as if the idea of an older Nick baking was weak, ridiculous. Which hurt his feelings. Which he did not tell her, of course, but instead got out of the hot tub and into his robe. They'd gone to bed without making love, which was nearly unprecedented after they'd been in the hot tub.

He took another bite. Did he detect yogurt or sour cream? There was a tang that went beyond the citrus. He closed his eyes to better parse out the flavors.

Rex stood. His tail snapped against Nick's leg as he wagged it. He started barking in that mournful way that could mean only one thing. Nick opened his eyes.

And he was right. There was Rex's other true love, his canine paramour: the squatty little Miller dog, her lush tail swaying back and forth. Allison held the end of her red leash in one hand, and in her other, the hand of a little boy. Davenport's kid.

"Well, Mr. Cox. Fancy meeting you."

"Frau Miller," he said. Frau? *Frau.* He tried to snatch the word out of the air, suck it back into his mouth, but it was gone, released, ridiculous.

What made him act like a kid with a crush around this woman? She wore shoes more suited to a hobbit than a human; her coat was as puffy as a marshmallow; and her hat, made of thick knitted wool and adorned with two red pompoms, was so primitive it looked like maybe her kid made it. Maybe the treeless Jillian. He guessed Allison woke up looking pretty similar to how she looked right now: curls this way and that, eyes a little sleepy, lips just a shade up from the color of her face. Kaye was maybe her exact opposite: she woke up plain, as if her eyes and lips were something she kept in the bathroom, which she kind of did. She emerged after about an hour looking like a model, her eyes big and her lips full, her ponytail replaced by liquid gold. He might not have believed it was the same person if he hadn't witnessed it so many times over the years. Sometimes he envied women the way they could create themselves anew each day; but Allison Miller chose not to do all that, which he kind of admired. He was drawn to something else about her, too, a power she herself probably had no idea she had: if she accepted him, the rest of the town would follow suit.

"Do you know my friend Adam here?"

Adam reached out to shake hands. His grip was surprisingly strong for a little kid. "Can I buy you two a drink?" Nick said, pulling Rex off Candy.

"Yes," Adam said. "Ginger tea can help constrict the blood vessels when you have a headache, so I'd like that."

Nick looked at Allison. She offered a faint shrug and lift of the eyebrows, indicating that this was likely true.

"All right. A ginger tea it is. Young lady?" *Young lady.* Was there no end to it?

"Nothing for me, thanks."

"A coffee? A coffee from your coauthor. Your colleague."

She laughed. "Okay, an espresso. If you can expense it."

"I can expense anything," he said, again not happy with his words. She already thought of him as a braggart. He started to tie Rex up to the railing.

"Don't worry—we can take him," Allison said. "Right, Adam?"

Adam, now seated in a chair, head resting on his arm, didn't lift his head to speak.

"You sure? He can be a bully."

"Candy would be thrilled."

Nick untied Rex and Rex ran under his arm toward Candy; he wound around Allison, then Candy wound around Nick. Then the dogs wound again, to get closer to each other, which meant Nick and Allison were knotted together along with the dogs. He didn't find many occasions to laugh these days, but this made him laugh. "It's like Twister," he said.

"Right hand blue, left foot red," she said, and suddenly they were face-to-face, so close that he could smell her breath. She smelled like coffee. Had she already had coffee?

"What are you smiling about?" They were so close now that all she had to do was whisper.

"Just smiling." He saw that she had a little bit of chocolate at the corner of her lip. Just a tiny melted bit. "Have you been eating chocolate?"

"Are you stalking me?"

He pointed to the corner of her mouth. She stuck out the tip of her tongue and reached it around to the edge of her lip. She worked her tongue into the crease. He felt himself heating up.

"Did I get it?"

"Almost. May I?" He touched her lip with his thumb, wiping away the rest of it.

She was blushing. But not unwinding the leashes. He wasn't unwinding either, but the dogs were starting to tumble, which threatened to knock them down. He took her right hand in his and Rex's leash in his left, and unwound the leashes, freeing them from each other. His hand was still in hers though. They both saw, then let go.

"So, coffee!" he said.

"Right! And ginger tea!"

He gave Allison Rex's leash, then he braved Lucy again, feeling fortified.

Lucy all but rolled her eyes at the sight of him. "Again?"

He ordered.

"And two paper cups, I presume." She shook her head in disapproval as she spoke.

"The espresso is for Allison Miller," he said. "Does she have a mug?"

Lucy's expression softened an infinitesimal degree. "She has a little espresso cup too. And the tea? Paper?"

"For the Davenport kid."

"Davenport-Gardner?" She pulled a red fire-truck mug off the hook and ran Nick's credit card. She seemed a little disappointed he wasn't getting more paper cups.

"The muffin . . . ," he said.

"What about it?" she challenged.

"Delicious. Maybe the best I've ever tasted," he said, hoping to maybe, possibly, draw a smile out of her, to maybe, just maybe, begin to make a little headway in this tightly closed community.

She shook her head, eyes half rolled, handing him back his credit card. "Kiss ass."

JILLIAN'S FATHER GOT OFF HIS BIKE IN FRONT OF THE HOUSE JUST AS Jillian got out of the Coxes' car in the driveway. It was like a dance, it was so synchronized. Her door opening at the same moment he dismounted. His vest and yellow helmet shone under the street-light. She could feel his stunned eyes on her.

If she'd been thinking straight, she would have told Kaye just to let her out in the garage and would have snuck home around back, but she was buzzing. She'd gone for the Frappuccino at the Starbucks as they left the mall, a twenty-four-ounce caffein-ated frozen coffee-flavored milkshake with whipped cream and a straw and a rounded lid. It was a shock for a girl who had just had a pink shake in the food court and was not used to an all-sugar diet. Her heart beat so quickly she thought she was going to throw up.

Jillian said goodbye to Lindy and closed the car door. She didn't even thank Kaye for driving. "Hi, Dad." She walked up the path, her eyes on her feet.

"Jill?" he said.

"Yep," she confirmed. *Jillian Miller is a sneak. Jillian Miller is a fraud.* She climbed the porch steps, hoping for a few final sweet moments with her mother before the game was up.

Her mother was sitting on the living room couch with her arms crossed over her chest, her expression stony. Jillian froze, trying to decide whether it would be better to go back outside, to her father, or to continue toward her mother. She was like a murderer in a house surrounded by the police.

"Hi, Mom," Jillian said, wondering which scenario had come to pass. Had Mrs. Baxter called about the Greek temple? Had a teacher reported her absence from the after-school clubs? Had her mother, too, seen her get out of the Coxes' car?

"I did some babysitting today," her mother said.

"You did?"

"Adam. Suzanne came by not long ago to get him, in fact. She said she saw you at Nordstrom."

"Oh . . ." Jillian closed her eyes and held her wrists together in front of her, awaiting the handcuffs.

14

Now. This is your entrance," Allison whispered to Grant from behind their makeshift backstage, gritting her teeth so she wouldn't inadvertently scream.

"Me? Not yet. Do I?" Grant said, questioning and answering himself for so long that he missed his entrance entirely.

"Cut!" Rainier, the director, called. "Cut, fucking cut!"

They were rehearsing in the town hall basement instead of in the elementary school all-purpose room, leaving the school open for the public hearing that was to start in half an hour. The town hall was usually a spacious venue for town meetings, but tonight residents were going to testify about the proposed building moratorium. A standing-room-only crowd was expected.

Meanwhile, *Annie Get Your Gun* was in danger of collapse. Troubles had haunted them from the start. To begin with, so few people had auditioned that Rainier had cast everyone who showed up, even the parents who'd just brought their kids to try out. Some cast members could sing, some could dance, and some could act, but virtually none could do all three. Buffalo Bill kept calling for line cues; Lucy, who was playing Dolly Tate, sounded as though she was developing vocal cord nodules—"like poor Julie Andrews," she kept pointing out, though that was where any similarity between the two ended. She'd left rehearsal early tonight to set up a dessert table at the hearing, abandoning them midscene.

Then there was Grant, who was having trouble remembering his blocking and the words to his songs. Sometimes something mysterious struck him as hilarious and he couldn't stop laughing. What had happened to him? He'd been terrific, memorizing his lines and everyone else's before the cast was required to be off book, but recently he'd been coming to rehearsals looking as though he was half asleep, and maybe he was. He had a lot on his mind, with a son having undiagnosed headaches and a baby on the way. Not to mention the addition they were planning to put on the house. Well, an addition had been the original plan, but now Grant wanted to knock down the whole house and build anew. He and Suzanne were locked in battle over it.

A good Frank was nearly as important as a good Annie. Was she a good Annie? Valeria would have been better. What should they do? Allison wrote desperate e-mails to Valeria, but Valeria seemed to have no advice to pass along from her perch in Paris. She was too busy sprinting off to the Louvre and the Pont Neuf.

All of these things were happening, and Allison did her very best to care about them, her very, very best, but in fact there was just one thing on her mind. It had started last week, when she ran into Nick at Lucy's. When he had touched her lip. She'd had to work very hard not to lick his thumb. But she hadn't. That was the point. She hadn't done that. So if someone at the café saw them together, someone inside or around back, there would have been absolutely nothing to report.

She and Nick were collaborating—on the book. That was all. His interest in it had given her new energy. In the past few days they'd run into each other more than usual. She'd stood with him once in his yard while Rex and Candy tussled over a tennis ball, and they'd had coffee again at Lucy's. Nothing remotely as line-crossing had happened. Giving her a bite of his brownie was not in the same category. They talked about photography and architecture, paper quality and text-to-photo ratios until he left to pick up his son.

Then this afternoon . . . well. She still hadn't let herself fully process what happened this afternoon. She'd found him parked a block away from the café. He rolled down the window. "I'm going to take you on a tour," he said.

It felt mildly illicit to be getting in his car, but she did it anyway—first having a quick glance around to see if anyone was watching. She sank down low in the passenger seat. It was warm in the car and it smelled like aftershave, a smell she didn't ordinarily like.

"Sears Modern Homes are cute, I'll give you that, but they sure ain't modern," he drawled, cutting off a car as he took a right onto Wisconsin Avenue. "Don't get me wrong. I'm all about preserving what's best about the town."

"So you're not a complete monster," she said.

"Mostly, but not complete."

It felt safe now to relax a little. They were out of her zone, where people might look at them and wonder. She settled back into the seat, which had excellent lumbar support and a seat warmer.

Nick argued that there were certain houses in Willard Park that could be torn down to the betterment of the town. "They're ugly, right?" She had to agree. The sixties and seventies had been unfortunate years architecturally.

He slowed down as they approached Winterset, a community not unlike Willard Park, where tear-downs on quarter-acre lots sold for a million plus. People were replacing the older houses with bigger versions. "All of the benefits, none of the decay, none of the outmoded wiring, no tiny closets and miniature bathrooms," Nick said.

They walked around, Nick pointing out big porches and gabled roofs, Allison nodding. He had a point.

"They're nice houses," he said.

"They're like Sears houses on steroids."

"So you agree with me."

She laughed. "I guess."

"I knew you were my kind of gal," he said, which she found embarrassingly flattering. His kind of gal. What was his kind of gal? How could Kaye and she both be his kind of gal? How could a comment both feel sexist and sexy at once?

He put his hand on her lower back and he steered her down another street. Well, it was mostly on her lower back. His fingers extended a little below that, touching the top of her ass. Did he realize he was touching her ass? Her coat was long, so he might just think he was touching her back. Which, in itself, was somewhat intimate. She thought he would take his hand off once they'd gone around the corner, but he didn't. Nor did she make any moves to remove it for him. It felt kind of nice to be touched by a man, even if it was accidental.

"Let's get coffee," he said after they'd had their fill of the neighborhood, and they drove to the drive-through Starbucks near Winterset. Pumpkin lattes and pumpkin bread in hand, they parked in back, the only car there on this cold day. He put the car in park and left the engine running. They drank in silence for a while, the windows starting to fog up, the warmth in the car meeting the cold outside.

"Pumpkin lattes are better than crack," he said.

"Have you ever tried crack?"

"No. You?"

She laughed and took the pumpkin bread out of the bag. "In my perfect world, pumpkin would be in season all year long."

"I'd like to live in that world," he said. He was looking at her.

She broke the slice in half, and gave him his.

"I don't know why they put pepitas on it. Walnuts and pumpkin are like peanut butter and jelly. The perfect combo," she said.

He smiled, then leaned toward her, over the console where their pumpkin lattes sat, and kissed her.

She pulled back, looking at him with surprise. Nick Cox had just kissed her. And she wanted to kiss him back. There was no part of her that didn't. Okay, there was a very small part, but it was microscopic, nearly undetectable. She couldn't remember the last time she had partaken of a good, juicy kiss. It was high time. And was it so wrong? If her husband was on a sexual sabbatical? She looked out the windows, and, once she'd confirmed that the glass was sufficiently steamed up for no one to see in, she kissed him. After all, a kiss was just a kiss.

Kissing a man told you a lot about his lovemaking style, she'd found in her not-all-that-extensive dating life in college. Nick kissed her like he wanted to eat her face, and she kissed back the same way, resisting an urge to bite. His hands were in her hair, on her neck, pressing against her throat just a little bit, just enough to heighten the sensations in other parts of her body, then a hand slipped under her coat and onto her right breast and gave her nipple a squeeze.

"Ouch," she yelped through her kissing lips. And, shocked into realizing what exactly it was they were doing, she pulled away.

Nick, too, seemed a little surprised. He leaned back into the driver's seat and ran a hand over his hair. He looked at her, and she looked back, both of their expressions a little scandalized. "Well!" he said.

"Well!"

"Some coffee break!"

"No wonder Starbucks is so popular!"

They both started laughing.

"I better get you home."

He put the car in gear. Her entire body was humming. It felt nearly audible, it was so strong. She felt like a human tuning fork. Did he?

"Look," she said as they drove back down Wisconsin Avenue. "Why don't you just drop me off at the dry cleaners." No need for the neighbors to see them returning together.

"The dry cleaners?"

"Yeah. Just. Yes."

So he pulled up to the dry cleaners and she opened the door, looking back at him.

He leaned over and gave her a light goodbye kiss. The kind a husband would give a wife. The kind a lover would give a beloved. But they weren't either of these things. She relived that moment now, a less complex thing to relive than their harried make-out session. A warm, soft kiss.

It was bad, what they did, no doubt. Poor Ted would be so hurt if he knew. Even if they were living more like siblings than lovers right now, there were still those pesky vows. But it wasn't a terrible thing, was it? Well, a little terrible, but also a little wonderful. When was the last time her body had lit up that way? It was like being on a diet, she thought. A diet in which someone handed her a bowl of chocolate mousse, and she'd had a small taste. A taste was not the end of the world.

"Allison. Hello, Earth to Allison," Rainier was waving at her, trying to get her attention.

"What? Sorry," Allison said, her face heating up as if Rainier might have heard her thoughts.

"We're going to try the shooting scene one last time," Rainier said, but Grant's phone rang. He went outside to take it.

Rainier's clipboard bounced off the doorway, missing Grant by a few inches. "Go home. All of you. Better yet, go to the hearing. It might be the only chance you get to perform this year."

Allison put her character shoes and script in her bag.

"I'm going to cancel this show. I swear," Rainier said.

"It's not a bad idea," Allison said.

"You too?"

"We suck, Rainier." She suddenly understood why Jillian favored the word. It was more satisfying than "stinks." More to the point.

Rainier laughed. "Ready to testify?"

"Ted's representing us."

"Ted? You're the actor in the family."

"He'll do fine. He's been practicing."

"Practicing. Where does that get you?" he said, casting a cold eye at the actors. Allison gave him a hug.

Her mood lifted the minute she walked amid the lit-up houses outside. Most of the townspeople seemed to be coming out, the adults walking toward the school en masse, the younger teenagers heading off to various houses to babysit. She ran into Jillian at the intersection of Walnut and Tunlaw.

"Where's your coat, honey?" Allison tried to kiss her, but Jillian dodged her.

"It's not cold."

"It's winter."

"I'm *fine*."

"What's the matter?"

"Why do you always think something is the matter!" She skulked off, toward the Davenport-Gardners' house.

Jillian had been irritable since last week, when she came home with pierced ears. Allison went over and over it, trying to figure out how she and Ted could have handled it better. As far as she could tell, they had been model parents, listening without interruption to Jillian's story about her secret friendship with Lindy and their clandestine trip to the shopping mall.

Allison had been disturbed by Jillian's lack of candor, but it seemed designed to protect her and Ted rather than offend. It didn't seem worth punishing her for. All in all Jillian was a good kid. Even good kids messed up sometimes. Ted was less forgiving. He looked at Jillian with such a hurt expression that Jillian burst into tears. Soon Allison was consoling both of them.

The ear piercing was a disappointment for Allison, who had pictured going to a nice jewelry store to get them pierced on Jillian's sixteenth birthday. She'd imagined helping pick out earrings that Jillian would treasure, earrings in which she might walk down the aisle one day. Instead, Jillian's experience had been tawdry. A mall kiosk. Cubic zirconium baubles. Apparently Kaye had given her consent, which was a serious lapse in judgment.

But who was Allison to judge Kaye? She'd kissed the woman's husband! What kind of person was she?

She spotted Ted and Terrance near Peanut Place. Their gaits were identical. She felt terrible, seeing Ted. Poor Ted. "Yoo-hoo," Allison called.

Terrance gave her a bear hug.

"Ted's going to say my name at the show," Terrance said.

"It's not a show, Terr. It's a hearing," Ted explained. Allison could hear in his voice that it wasn't the first time he'd said this.

"He's going to talk about brothers and stuff. About the old days," Terrance said.

"You can wave if you want to, to let the audience know who you are," Ted said.

"I'm going to wave at the show," Terrance said.

Ted sighed. Allison moved in between them, linking arms with them like Dorothy in *The Wizard of Oz*. She kissed Ted's cheek, cold from the night air. "New hat?" she said, touching Terrance's Smokey the Bear ranger's hat. "Going to put out a few fires?" She smiled at Ted, but Ted didn't smile back. She kissed Ted again. "You'll be fine. Everyone's on your side."

THE ALL-PURPOSE ROOM WAS SO CROWDED THAT THE WINDOWS HAD steamed, blurring the white lights on the houses outside. People scrambled for seats like kids playing musical chairs. The high school cheerleaders, enlisted to help, escorted newcomers to the back, while the elementary school chorus stood on the steps of the stage, singing about Santa, dreidels, and Kwanzaa in turn.

Nina Strauss, legs crossed and mouth firm, sat in the second row, phone in hand like a weapon. Two seats beside her were vacant, saved with a spread-out coat. People kept pointing to the seats to see if they were available, but Nina shook her head no. Allison waved to Lucy, who was handing out coffee and enormous white frosted cookies shaped like elephants to anyone who could edge close enough to her card table. Joan, the yoga teacher, gave out bright orange flyers that read: IMPROVE YOUR SEX LIFE WITH TANTRIC YOGA!

Soon the chorus members were marched off, replaced by the mayor, a woman so tiny that only her glasses and tight curls were visible above the lectern. "Nice to see so many of you . . ." The mic squeaked and cried, as if to protest all of the heated words that soon would be spoken into it. ". . . probably won't get to fifty, but we've given them out in the hopes that . . ."

Numbers had been handed out to the first people who signed up to testify. Everyone else had been invited to submit comments in writing. Speeches would be timed. A yellow light would blink a warning when they had thirty seconds left, and a red light would turn on when the time was up.

Bad sex, Allison thought, considering the mayor. *No, good.* The mayor was funny looking, it was true, but her husband, whose shirt pocket always had a smear of blue ink at the bottom, was just as odd. They both wore Keds with their suits. *Kinky sex,* she suddenly thought, surprising herself, but yes, it seemed right.

Sex was on her mind these days, no doubt. More than ever. She had to make sure she never got in a car alone with Nick again. Maybe she had to make plans never to talk to him again, never to be in a contained space alone with him ever again. If they had done as much as they did in two minutes, what might happen if they spent ten minutes together? A lot. The answer was a lot. She would avoid him. Forget collaborating on the book. She couldn't allow herself to be tempted. The next time she saw him, she would look away.

Suzanne squeezed in the gym door. She appeared to be pinned to the wall, the room was so packed. Allison waved to her, to show her she'd saved a seat, but the room was too crowded for her to make her way over. She made an apologetic face at Allison and sat in one of the two seats near Nina.

The mayor spoke to the residents seated on the side of the stage who held the first five numbers. "Please state your name and address and speak clearly into the mic. Number one?"

"I'm Edna Stant, and I live at 3405 Pecan Place. I've lived there for forty-two years."

Mrs. Stant lamented the lost trees and her formerly dry, now frequently flooded basement: the result, she'd been told by three experts, of construction runoff. "My house is constantly in shadow because of the new house."

She was followed by Lucy in a cowboy hat. Lucy signaled to a high school kid sitting at the upright piano, who started in with a little intro. Allison recognized it immediately. The *Annie Get Your Gun* song "I Got the Sun in the Morning and the Moon at Night" became "I Got No Sun in the Morning and No Moon at Night." Lucy couldn't sing well—it was all the more evident when she was doing a solo—but she received an abundance of laughter and applause nonetheless. "Really, people," she said afterward. "Isn't this planet in enough trouble?"

The next several speakers supported the moratorium, including many who had added on to their houses already, but then a rash of anti-moratorium folks came forward. Allison's assurance that a moratorium would be a shoo-in was suddenly called into question. She thought of election night 2016: that ghastly realization that things were going the other way. Ted would curl up and die if the moratorium was voted down. After speaker number fourteen—a newcomer with two bedrooms, one and a half baths, and four kids—a murmur filtered through the crowd.

The door by the stage, which had been locked when Allison tried it, had opened and there was Nick Cox, sleek in a long leather coat. People moved aside to let him pass. His boots squeaked on the linoleum floor.

Allison felt her heart catch. Was it her heart? Maybe it was another more netherly organ. She wasn't in love. But she was in lust all right. It was good she was in the middle of the row or she might have gotten up and hurled herself at him.

"What?" Ted said, frowning at her.

"Nothing," Allison whispered hotly.

"Sssssssss," someone hissed, prompting the mayor to come forward.

"Let me just remind everyone that we're all neighbors here," she said.

GRANT WAS HIGH. HE HAD BEEN HIGH AT REHEARSAL, AND NOW HE was more high, having lit up behind the town hall after Rainier told them to go home. He was careful to find a dark spot well amid the trees. You had to be careful in Willard Park these days. Everyone was spying on everyone else, desperate to find a juicy tidbit for Lucy's bulletin board. If only they could figure out who the tree cutter was. He felt like all of it would stop then, the graffiti and the spying, all of the crazy nonsense. The tree cutter was the head honcho.

His plan had been to go by the house to get Suzanne and go to the meeting, but being high had inspired him to go the long way so he could admire the lights on the houses. Everyone else was headed in the opposite direction, toward the school. Soon the town was deserted, save for him—and, as he saw when he looked on the Coxes' porch, the beautiful Kaye Cox. She was sitting on an outdoor sofa, like a fairy princess in her wonderland of white lights.

"Where's your prince?" he called from the sidewalk.

"At the meeting," she said.

"Aren't you going?"

"Nope."

"Why?" He came up the walkway to the porch and sat beside her. She smelled like cotton candy.

"Because I don't get it. Does that sound stupid to say? Because maybe I'm stupid. That's what I'm starting to think. I mean, who gives a Sam Hill about how big the houses are? Do you care? Do you think I'm stupid for thinking it's all stupid?"

"I kind of think it's stupid too."

"Well, high five!" she said, but she didn't make the accompanying hand gesture.

"Do you smoke?" he said.

"Cigarettes? I quit."

"Weed, actually."

"Oh! No. I mean, not for years. Nick's more of a drinker, you know? But, hey, you go on ahead."

So he did, and as he held the smoke in his lungs, letting the weed work its magic, she took the pipe and inhaled. They both held their breath, then let out a cloud of smoke at the same time.

"I like the smell," she said. "It makes me think of high school."

"I'll bet you were the homecoming queen."

She clapped her hands. "I was!"

"I thought so."

"And my boyfriend was homecoming king. That was the best time of my life. Is that bad to say? The worst years were when I was eight till high school, then high school was the best."

"You didn't like being a kid?"

"My mom died."

"I'm sorry."

"She was a great mom. I'm not a great mom. I'm a bad mom. If I was a good mom Jakey would be able to have a conversation with people and Lindy wouldn't be so snotty. They didn't used to be this bad."

"What did she die of?"

"Breast cancer. Nobody told me she was going to die, not even when she was in the hospital. She'd been in before, so I didn't think it was a big deal, but one day I came home from school and Daddy was sitting in the living room and he said, 'Mommy died.' I didn't get to say goodbye."

"That's awful."

"He was just trying to protect me. That's all. He didn't like to see me sad." The tears in her eyes caught the shine of the Christmas lights.

"I liked my high school years the best too."

"See?"

"See what?"

"I don't know!" She laughed, and he did too. "Why is everyone so mean here?"

"I don't know. They are."

"Right? My friends at home would not believe how things are, if they were to see. They would not believe it. I mean, I was the girl there. The one. My college girlfriends were my sisters, so I didn't feel it so much, not having a mom. That doesn't change once you graduate. Sorority sisters are your sisters forever. Or they're supposed to be." Sadness crept into her face, but it disappeared when she started talking again. "Our house was the center of everything, kids running in and out all the time. All my sisters hanging out. We had a whole refrigerator of sparkling wine and snacks—that's how fun it was. Everyone was always welcome and they knew it, right? We had a big outdoor pool and a bunch of lounge chairs. It's hard to see them all on Facebook having fun without me. I guess I had an idea it wouldn't be as much fun without me there, but, well, it looks like it is."

He nodded.

"Did you see the tree poem today?" She pulled out her phone, then read aloud: *A tree is known by its fruit; a man by his deeds. A good deed is never lost; he who sows courtesy reaps friendship, and he who plants kindness gathers love.*

"That's pretty deep."

"But is it true? So far, courtesy hasn't reaped diddly-squat as far as I can tell." She took another hit. "What am I doing wrong?"

He shrugged. Then he took another hit too.

"Why did I ever stop smoking pot? That was a mistake," she said.

He laughed. "Luckily it can be remedied. For a while, at least. I'm going to need to buy more eventually. Know any high school kids we could buy some off?"

Her expression went serious. "No. You mean, this might be it? It's like Cinderella? Magic for one night?"

"Might as well enjoy it, right?" He held out the pipe.

"I better stop. Jakey's asleep inside. And well gosh, if Lindy comes out and sees me . . ."

"Gotcha," he put the pipe down. "I better go to the meeting. I told Suzanne I would."

"Why doesn't she like me?"

"She likes you."

"No. I can tell. Nobody does. Nobody likes any of us. Not me, or Nick or Lindy or Jakey."

"I like you."

"You do?" She smiled. She was like a little child, just wanting to be liked.

"Yeah. I think you're fun."

"I am! I am fun!" she said, and she grabbed the pipe and took another hit. She held the smoke in her lungs for a long time, a dreamy smile on her face.

JILLIAN PUT AWAY THE BOOKS AND STUFFED ANIMALS, TAKEN OUT TO soothe Adam, but which only seemed to make him crankier. She washed the almond milk out of his cup and put it on the dish rack. He'd spent the half hour before his bedtime lying on the floor with his knitted cap pulled down over his ears. Now he was in bed, thanks to a chocolate bribe. He'd been such a cutie the first few times she sat for him—but now!

She opened the cabinet above the stove, grabbing a handful of popcorn and popping it in her mouth. Cheese flavored. Yum. She took three gingersnaps and some low-fat barbecue potato chips. "Why didn't you eat any snacks, Jillian?" Suzanne would ask when they got home. Little did she know. Lindy was the one who had taught her how to raid the kitchen so stealthily. They team-babysat last time. It was more fun to babysit with a friend. Other people's houses were a little creepy when you were alone.

Lindy wasn't coming tonight though. She'd asked Jillian if she was going to babysit during the hearing, and Jillian had said no. It was a white lie, and white lies, while not great, were not terrible. The truth was, she didn't want Lindy to come. She didn't want to be friends with Lindy anymore. She thought Lindy would ditch her now that she'd gotten to know Mark, but it turned out Jillian was the one who'd had enough of their "friendship." Lindy was a thief, and a sneak, and mean, and no amount of coolness could offset that, not really.

Jillian swung the refrigerator door back and forth, turning the light on and off. She scooped some chocolate powder in a glass and poured milk over it, stirring until the milk became a muddy brown. The straws were under the sink. Was sneaking food this way stealing? She thought about it, and decided that no, it wasn't. Suzanne had told her to eat, and she was just making a game of it.

She checked to make sure all the doors were locked, then heaved her backpack onto the kitchen table. Her phone buzzed.

A text from Lindy. Im bored. Jillian ignored it. She had a lot of catching up to do after slacking off on schoolwork for so long. She opened her math book. There was a funny ticking sound. She sat up straight, on the alert, until she realized it was just the heat.

Math used to be easy. She and Sofia used to do their homework right away after school. They'd even joined the Math Club. It sounded nerdy, but it had been fun. They'd competed to see who could finish problems the fastest. She started the first problem.

Something was tapping on the window. *Branches,* she told herself. She made bubbles in her chocolate milk. It covered the sound. She could see herself in the black reflection of the kitchen window, so she closed the blinds.

More scratching or whatever it was. Or maybe knocking. On the door? She hummed so she wouldn't have to hear. Then she stopped, realizing the song she was humming was from *Annie Get Your Gun.* She thought about Mark and his amazing hair. They said hi in the halls now, and yesterday, they'd had an actual conversation after English—that was the good thing to come out of the day at the mall. She went over their conversation in her head. "Did you start your essay?" "Yeah. Did you?" "Yeah." She'd been trying to think of something good to say, something funny and relationship sealing when Lindy appeared and messed up everything.

"Mmm," Lindy said. "You smell good, Marko." Mark and Jillian exchanged looks.

That was the thing about ending her friendship with Lindy. Lindy couldn't know Jillian was doing it or she would make her pay. She would turn the whole school against her. She had to be sneaky. It was sort of like stealing snacks. She told Lindy she couldn't come over to her house anymore because her parents forbade it, even though they hadn't. Why hadn't they? They hadn't punished her at all for getting her ears pierced either, which made Jillian mad. Weren't they supposed to set limits or something? It wasn't fair to make Jillian do all the work.

She kind of missed Kaye. Kaye understood about kids and school and stuff, unlike Jillian's mother, who always came up with some cheerful, eye-roll-inducing piece of advice when Jillian confided in her: "Tell her you don't like it when they gang up on you." "Tell her you're free to make your own choices." It was enough to make Jillian want to shake her.

Jillian's phone rang. She didn't recognize the number, so she didn't pick up. Unknown numbers were nearly always fake calls, about some mortgage she didn't have or a special interest rate she'd qualified for. Had she somehow accidentally gotten on the list of grown-ups? How? She was only in seventh grade. The call went to voice mail, then, within seconds, her phone started ringing again, another call from the same number. What if it was Grant? Jillian only had Mrs. Davenport-Gardner's number in her contacts. If she didn't pick up, they'd think she was a bad babysitter and they'd never hire her again. They might even tell other people she was a bad babysitter, and she'd never get work in Willard Park again, which would be a shame because she was on the cusp of some very good income-earning years.

"Hello?" Jillian said.

There was silence on the other end of the line.

"Hello?" Jillian waited for as long as she could stand it, then she hung up.

She opened the refrigerator and tore off a cheese stick from the pack, separating it from its mates. She liked this type, which peeled off in strips. She was supposed to make a Greek dish for the social studies party, scheduled to take place at two forty-five on Friday, the last day before break. A fifteen-minute party. Big deal.

What was Greek? Baklava. Feta cheese. Pizza. Was pizza Greek? She wouldn't panic about the phone call. Nope!

The phone rang again.

"Hello?"

Someone breathed hard on the other end, as if he'd just been running.

Jillian hung up again. She shoved the rest of the cheese stick in her mouth. It rang again. Maybe it was the hospital. Maybe it was the police. "Hello?" she said through cheese.

"I'm calling from upstairs. I've already killed the boy."

Lindy. She hadn't even disguised her voice. Jillian laughed helplessly, her relief nearly making her cry. "Whose phone are you using?"

"My Dad's. Open the door, Jillster."

"Where are you?"

"At the Davenport-Gardner people's front door. Why'd you say you weren't babysitting?"

"I wasn't sure . . ."

"Let me in."

Jillian, defeated, hung up the phone.

THE SAME REASONS IN SUPPORT OF THE MORATORIUM CAME UP AGAIN and again: tree canopy, soil permeability, privacy, height, noise, proportion, diversity, architectural integrity—it went on and on. Those against were concerned about their rights. "I've always wanted a breakfast nook and a Florida room," a bent woman with an oxygen tank said.

Suzanne wanted to rip the mic out of her hand. *First of all, the moratorium would expire in six months. Second of all, additions that don't extend the footprint more than five hundred feet would be exempted. And third, if you've lived this long without a Florida room, you sure as hell don't need one now.*

Was the council going to let old biddies like this one determine the future of Willard Park? The moratorium had to pass. Passage would work in Suzanne's favor, and more than just as it pertained to the town's appearance. Grant would agree to a small addition rather than wait for the new rules on reconstruction—rules that would, no doubt, be stringent. He'd turned against their house in the past few weeks, calling it a dump. A tear-down. They deserved better, he said.

In the meantime, Suzanne had put a call in to the contractor who had done Nina's screened porch. Well, at least she was doing something! She had to have the feeling she was moving forward on something! God knew, everything else was at a standstill. Squirts for Squirts was hardly more than a name at this point, and summer was just half a year away.

She caught a whiff of cigarette or, perhaps, pot smoke. Crowds were the worst. She could smell everyone's bad habits: smoking, drinking, infrequent bathing. She tried to close her nose, but the smell of weed seeped in nonetheless.

Was the smoke coming off Grant? Instead of stopping by the house to get her, he'd come in late and had barreled over people's legs to sit next to her, like a clumsy puppy. She frowned at him. He looked back at her, his eyelids heavy, and smiled. She closed her eyes. It could not be Grant. She would not allow it to be Grant. She had enough to worry about without its being Grant.

Adam had been out of school with headaches for ages now—three weeks? Four? She'd lost track. Suzanne called the neurologist and the allergist daily, sometimes twice, to see whether there were any cancellations. No matter. They were finally edging up on the actual appointments.

Then there was the baby. At her appointment this morning, Dr. Fielding recommended she schedule the cerclage. Suzanne argued against it. She was so busy! Was it even necessary? Couldn't it wait?

"Maybe I haven't been clear about the danger here," he'd said.

She shook her head. She didn't want to hear about the danger.

"Where's your husband on all of this?"

"He doesn't have an opinion." How could he? She hadn't told him there was a problem.

Dr. Fielding put his hand on her arm. "You don't want to lose this baby, Suzanne."

"No," she had admitted, her voice small.

"It's my property. Why shouldn't I be allowed to do what I want with it?" Nick Cox, number twenty-two, argued.

How had he gotten a number? He'd arrived after people started testifying, long after all of the numbers had been handed out—and yet, there he was up at the lectern.

"A man's home is his castle," Nick said.

"Get off it, Cox!" Suzanne cried.

"You're out of order," the mayor said.

"A man's and a *woman's* home," Nick Cox said, winking. At whom? Suzanne scanned the crowd. Allison was smiling back at him. Beaming. Was she beaming? Not possible. It must be a smile of disdain, but it bore a close kinship to a beam.

"A *family's* home. It's a matter of personal freedom. That's my point," Nick went on.

Freedom. There was something she lacked. Was anyone free, she thought, looking around the room at her neighbors. Edna Stant, with her short right leg—was she free? That fellow Jack, with his blind mother? Ted Miller with his disabled twin? It was an interesting question.

She put her hands on her belly, wishing she could simply will the baby to stay put till she reached term. She felt like howling.

There were some things you couldn't simply will to be. Most things, come to think of it.

The baby fluttered within her. Suzanne imagined her bouncing and floating like a baby mermaid, a gummy smile on her perfect face. Adam, her merman brother, was at home, swimming in his sleep. Suzanne had the urge to dash home and slip into his little racing-car bed with him. She imagined closing her eyes and sleeping side by side with her two babies. In and out, they would all breathe together, in and out.

AS TED MADE HIS WAY UP THE CENTER AISLE TO THE STAGE, COX MADE his way back down. They bumped shoulders as they passed each other. Well, Cox bumped into him. Was it an accidental bump . . . or a shove? A shoulder shove? His shoulders were big, but were they so big that they had to slam into Ted? Ted nearly pushed back, but then thought about how it would look—likely no one had registered Cox's shoulder shove, but everyone would see Ted stick out his hand and push. Shaken, but dignity intact, Ted reached the lectern in time to see Cox leave through the back door, letting in a gasp of cold air. How had the bastard gotten to testify before him? Had he bought the slot?

Ted looked at Allison for reassurance, but she was looking at the door Cox had just exited. She turned back around and looked at Ted; she looked a little shaken herself. She'd probably seen the shove. She smiled and gave Ted a thumbs-up. "You got this," she mouthed. He turned on the slide projector and the first image appeared on the screen: a shot of the Willard farmhouse circa 1900 with Mr. Willard standing on the porch in a white suit, a straw hat on his head. Someone turned out the lights, and Ted brought the picture into focus.

"Once upon a time . . . ," Ted said. The timer started, the green light glowing, reminding him he had only three minutes to make his case.

He told the story of Willard Park, about the original farm and the plans for a community of twenty "stately homes in a countrified setting" Mr. Willard had proposed to build in 1890. Ted brought to life the soda fountain and the trolley tracks, the chickens the Willard family used to keep, and old Willard Pond—where kids sailed toy boats in summer and skated in winter. He told them the story of his parents, who'd bought one of the second generation of homes. There they were in front of the house, young again.

"Mom and Dad!" Terrance called.

Ted smiled gently at Terrance, giving him a wink to remind him that he was just supposed to listen.

There was Mr. Victor, who ran the general store; there Mr. Willard's daughter in the 1970s—an old woman by then; there were the peacocks, feathers spread.

"Remember we played tickle with the feathers, Ted?"

Ted shook his head at Terrance, and showed a series of photos of children playing, at the fountain, on the green, on the playground over the years.

"We used to play marbles!"

Ted closed his eyes. All of the work he'd done. All of the effort selecting just the right slides, just the right words—just the right everything—and now Terrance was spoiling it.

"Down by the creek," Ted started, showing a slide of a young couple picnicking, circa 1920.

"We played army," Terrance called.

"Terrance," Ted said, his voice firm.

Terrance stood and waved his hat above the crowd. He clambered over legs until he got to the aisle, and took a bow. People laughed and clapped good-naturedly.

He joined Ted at the lectern. "Not now, Terr," he said, a whisper that got caught in the mic and amplified. A few people laughed. Ted swallowed. He could still regain control of the room.

"Children have been sledding on the hill by Wythe Manor—" Ted projected a slide of the sledding hill at the turn of the last century.

Terrance reached for the microphone. Ted moved it away from his hand, but Terrance reached for it again, smiling.

Ted felt a bubbling within, a simmer that threatened to boil. "You need to sit down, Terr," he whispered, again a little too close to the mic. Someone yelled, "Let him talk!"

Ted scanned the room for the heckler, giving Terrance his chance. He grabbed the mic and breathed on it, filling the room with Darth Vader–like breath. "Hi."

Ted tried to pull the mic from him—the timer was blinking yellow now—but Terrance held on fast, grinning, as if they were playing a game.

Ted felt reason take wing. Fury, the furies, flew into his head, and seeped out, through his eyes, through his ears. *Go home,* he wanted to say. *Go home, retard.*

No sooner had the words formed in his head than he released his grasp on the mic and took a giant step back.

"Hi," Terrance said again, louder.

"Hi," some of the audience members called back.

Ted moved to the other side of the lectern. He was sweating. What was wrong with him? Was he losing his mind?

Terrance clicked the button on the projector, and no slide came up, just the bright yellow light from the bulb; then he clicked again and a slide of Ted and Terrance appeared: they were rolling down Willard Hill in summer, hair cut into crew cuts.

"We used to roll so much we got dizzy!" he said. He clicked

to the next screen, a shot of the houses on their street. "We used to go to your house and you gave us cookies." Terrance pointed at Adela Lambert. "And we shoveled your snow when you were sick that time." He nodded to Martin Thorp, who was in negotiations with a developer.

The light turned red, but Terrance went on, holding tight to the mic while the mayor "eh-hemmed" a couple of times, then grabbed for it repeatedly, without success.

"You were my teacher and you helped me. And you," he pointed at Jeff Tyler, the hardware store manager. "You teased me."

Jeff smiled, uncomfortably.

"I don't remember a lot of things. Dana gets mad at me about that. But I remember my mom and my dad and my brother and my home. I always remember my home." He presented the microphone to the mayor and saluted. He gave Ted a hug, then he stepped off the stage and walked down the center aisle, toward the back door, just as Cox had done.

People stood, clapping. Some were even wiping their eyes, Nina Strauss among them.

Ted clapped so hard his hands hurt, tears in his own eyes. "Ladies and gentlemen: my brother."

"LOOK AT THIS UNDERWEAR!" IT WAS BIG AND SAGGY, THE KIND OF thing an old granny would wear. Lindy waved it overhead like a flag.

Pregnancy underwear? How awful. Jillian snatched it out of Lindy's hands. What if Grant and Suzanne came home now? Raiding the kitchen was one thing, but snooping through Suzanne's bureau? "Please stop."

Lindy pulled out little soaps and shampoos from hotels and tiny plastic bags of replacement buttons, a pocketknife—"Think they're into weird sex or what?"

"Lindy, stop!"

"Okay. No problem." Lindy closed Suzanne's drawers—finally—then, with a wild laugh, she opened one of Grant's. His boxers and socks were all mixed together, along with some white briefs, the opposite of Suzanne's orderly collection. "Tighty whities!" She threw them like snowballs. Jillian felt like one of the kids in *The Cat in the Hat*.

Lindy fished little bits of paper out of the back of his drawer. Receipts for meals. A wad of tissue paper held closed by an old purple rubber band. A big color photo of a woman with big boobs and porny panties sitting on a red couch—not Suzanne.

Jillian and Lindy both screamed. Jillian attempted to stuff the picture back in the drawer, but Lindy was faster. She grabbed the photo and held it tight in both hands.

"Put it back, Lin."

"No way. I'm keeping it." Lindy laughed.

Jillian felt sick. She grabbed for the picture, but Lindy just held it out of her reach. Jillian got hold of it, tearing off a corner in her attempt to get it back. "Look what you did, Lin!" she cried.

"Me? You tore it. Now calm yourself. Let's go raid the fridge." Lindy folded the picture and stuck it in her pocket, turning off the light as she left the room.

LATER, WHEN ALLISON TRIED TO PIECE IT TOGETHER, SHE COULDN'T remember the order in which it happened, or even what exactly happened. Admittedly, she'd been a little distracted since Nick left the meeting, but she wasn't the only one who was confused. Some people remembered a child coming to the school, opening the door and yelling. Others said that there was no child, but that sounds between moans and screams—sounds more suitable to Halloween than a December night—alerted them to the problem.

It came in the middle of speaker number forty's testimony. Everyone agreed on that. Ned Lehrer had just broken down in tears about the state of his retirement fund. That would have been a dramatic enough moment, but people forgot about the crying in the tumult that followed.

Most of the crowd stood simultaneously, their chairs scraping against the linoleum. There was pushing and panic as they squeezed out into the night. Someone opened the emergency exit, which set off an alarm, driving out anyone who considered waiting at the school until the hubbub had died down.

The lights on the houses guided them to the green, daylight at night. The murmuring got louder as they got closer. "What a shame," people said, and "What kind of jerk would . . . ?"

The tree was lying on its side, all twenty-five feet of it, sawn off at the base and left for dead. Its lights were still on, thousands of tiny white lights twinkling throughout its branches, though some had broken in the fall. Whoever had done it had taken care not to damage the electrical cord. Some ornaments had clung to the branches; others were strewn about the ground.

"Cox," Ted said, a look of devastation on his face. Allison, feeling guilty, held him close. She thought of *How the Grinch Stole Christmas!*, the Whos in Whoville, joining hands and singing, swaying back and forth, determined not to let the Grinch win the day.

"Let's start some carols going," Allison said, inspired.

"Are you nuts?" Ted said.

And together, they walked home.

15

DECEMBER 25

Five days. It had been five long, long days since their kiss, five days of the schizophrenia of the angel on her shoulder saying, *Never again. Never again,* and the devil countering with *When? When?* She felt like a machine whose switch had just been turned on after more than forty years of dormancy, a machine whose sole purpose was to suck face with Nick Cox. Possibly more. The machine that she was might be designed for a whole lot more than that. But it would, of course, never be permitted to function as intended. Their kiss would remain an isolated event, a secret she would take to her grave. She flicked the devil off her shoulder, enjoying a few minutes of respite before he climbed back on again.

It was for the best that they didn't run into each other—obviously it was for the best—but it was still awful. It actually wasn't that they never saw each other. They did, but just glimpses—through the windows of their respective houses, in line at the liquor store, at the town holiday lantern festival with their kids and spouses; it was arguably worse to have him dangled so close than not to see him at all.

Today, Christmas Day, had been lovely, she reminded herself. Ted had been delighted with his gifts from Allison: new socks, a blue cashmere cardigan, and a book—the perfect book: *The Hidden Life of Trees*. He'd read aloud from it throughout the day, telling her and Terrance—Jillian had spent most of the day in her room—all about the friendships and the hibernation of the trees, the social networking and the love. Tree love. Ted and Terrance had gone in on a gift card to Trader Joe's for Allison, which was— well, they knew she liked Trader Joe's, so it was thoughtful on some level. Allison's parents opted to spend Christmas at Brighton Manor, the first time they'd spent both Thanksgiving and Christmas there. Allison had offered to drive up on the twenty-third, after school let out, but her parents discouraged her. The traffic. The weather. She, Ted, and Jillian could come up in spring. They could attend the Easter party, when they served spiral ham.

Didn't her parents want to see her? It felt like a rejection of her as a daughter, yet another rejection after being rejected as a wife and mother. Teens were supposed to reject you; that was their job. But it was still a lot of rejecting all at once. No wonder she was so preoccupied with Nick. He was the only person she knew who actually seemed to want her.

Their paths would cross again. It was inevitable. Maybe when Jillian went back to school next week. She imagined running into him on the porch of Lucy's one cold afternoon, tapping the rims of their coffee cups together as they toasted what might have been. Or maybe he would have forgotten about it. What kiss? He kissed women all the time. That was a more likely scenario.

After dinner Allison left Ted and Terrance playing their annual Christmas-night checkers tournament, and walked Candy to the green. She meant to honor the carcass of the fallen Christmas tree before it was sawn up and carted off—and lo and behold, a

Christmas miracle: there were Nick and Rex, apparently doing the same thing. The tree lay like a fallen dinosaur, construction paper and cranberry garlands its funeral shroud. Was Nick responsible for its demise? Had he come back to the scene of the crime, as criminals were said to do? She didn't think so. But she didn't want to ask either. Who was it, if not him? It was just so heartless. It was depressing to think someone so heartless lived among them. She didn't want to think about that. Not right now. There he was. Him!

Candy and Rex barked and cried out their delight. They leaped and pulled, drawing their owners side by side.

"Well, hello, Mr. Cox," Allison said, hoping he didn't hear the quiver in her voice.

"Mrs. Miller." He nodded, and his bedroom eyes and white teeth caught the light of the streetlamp. "I was thinking I might die if I didn't see you again soon."

And there, alone together on a cold, dark Christmas night, their lips met and their bodies glommed to each other, their kiss more passionate and wild than even their episode in the parking lot might have predicted, a kiss that rapidly became more than a kiss: his hand that wasn't holding the leash yanking down the zipper of her coat, then diving under her sweater, her free hand leaping for buttons and zippers in turn, his teeth biting her lips, her teeth biting back. They were a head-on collision on the highway, an accident too late for brakes.

Allison was the first to surface. She looked around the green desperately. Anyone might see them! Anyone might report the sighting on Lucy's bulletin board! "We need to stop," she whispered, starting up again.

"We need to go," Nick said. He grabbed her hand, and led her and the dogs off the green and down the street. Allison let herself be led, the pompoms on her hat bouncing as she ran, Candy and

Rex running, too, the cold air feeling colder for their speed, her hand warm in his. Where had her gloves gone? Who cared? Where were they going? They were just running. Like children. Running away.

They stopped in front of the Sawyers' old house. It was dark and the moon was reflected in the windows.

She opened her mouth to ask why they were there, but she started kissing him before the words could come out. It was like the French fairy tale, the one in which frogs or toads came out of the girl's mouth when she spoke. Except in her case, it was kisses: hungry, libidinous kisses.

He laughed, gently separating his mouth from hers. "Hold on, doll!"

Doll. Again. Sexist and so fucking sexy. *Doll.*

He pulled a set of keys out of his pocket and opened the front door.

"What are we doing here?"

"You'll see." He let the dogs off their leashes and into the house, then leaned over—she thought to kiss her again—but he scooped her up in his arms, like a groom carrying a bride over the threshold. She laughed, her arms around his neck. Were they crazy? Were they so crazy they were breaking into houses?

He carried her up the small flight of stairs and into a bedroom. She'd never been farther than the Sawyers' powder room. What was he thinking? What was she thinking? She wasn't thinking. She didn't want to think. He set her down and lay his long black coat on the floor. Then they suctioned to each other again, shedding clothes, shedding all sense, easing their way down to the ground.

16

Suzanne didn't mean to destroy the house. She didn't wake up on the first day of the new year thinking, *Today I will wreck my house*. In fact, she woke up thinking about spinach. She rolled out of bed at first light, turned up the thermostat, and ate cold, cooked spinach at the kitchen counter, straight from its BPA-free plastic container.

Allergies were to blame for Adam's headaches. That was it, plain and simple, she told herself, her teeth sinking into the squeaky leaves. It was the thought that had kept her up the better part of the night. What else could be causing the headaches?

The neurologist had spent nearly an hour with Adam the day before Christmas, taking a family history, taking a history of his symptoms, making him walk a straight line and touch his finger to his nose, tapping his knee, giving him lists of items to remember in order, and quizzing him on the number of fingers she held up as if Adam were a circus poodle. She wrote up orders for a slew of tests and suggested Suzanne keep a headache diary.

"For me or for him?" she asked the doctor, who laughed, but it had been a serious question.

They'd spent the day after Christmas in doctors' offices as well. Grammy, who had been in town for the holidays, had wanted to come to the appointments with them, but the idea made Suzanne want to jump out a window. She gave her mother a guidebook and a Metro card and told her not to come back till five o'clock. But her mother didn't go downtown at all. Instead, she stayed home, wiping down the ceiling fans (*You can't imagine the dirt! I wish I'd taken a picture!*) and cleaning out the pantry, throwing out the spices that had lost their pungency. This only added to the fury Suzanne felt at her for giving Adam a video-game console, in complete and utter defiance of her instructions.

Adam's CT scan, thankfully, had shown nothing abnormal. The MRI, too, though it had been a terrible morning watching a terrified Adam sit strapped like an astronaut to an oversize machine that took pictures of slices of his brain. She wanted to unbuckle him, to spirit him out of the office and keep on running. Instead, she'd waited until the technician gave them the all clear, then took him back to the blood lab for additional testing by the sadistic phlebotomist. The results wouldn't be back until later this week. Suzanne was convinced that they, like the tests the pediatrician ordered, would show nothing. It was the allergy tests that held the answers.

She'd spent last night on the Internet doing research. She missed the annual dropping of the mirrored disco ball in front of Lucy's at midnight, an event Grant attended alone. He'd gone over to the Coxes' afterward for champagne, returning blurry eyed and horny around two in the morning. Suzanne rebuffed him. She had work to do. There were so many allergies to consider: dust mites, dander, cockroaches, chemicals, pollen, peanuts, ragweed, eggs, soy, wheat, nuts, mold—and those were just the most common ones.

Mold seemed the most likely culprit. Toxic black mold, perhaps, an allergen that was well covered online. An old house like this must be full of mold. That would explain why Adam's symptoms had come on so soon after they moved to Willard Park. That explained the fuggy, weedy smell that she sometimes caught a whiff of: it wasn't weed, it was mold.

Suzanne, fortified by her spinach this first morning of the new year, walked through the living room, past the Christmas tree, out the kitchen door, and down to the basement, turning on lights and sniffing for mold as she went. The basement smelled a little suspicious, she thought, tucking her nose into the crawl space and around the water heater. She sniffed her way upstairs, past a snoring Grant and into the bathroom. She studied the sink and the grout between the tiles, then pushed back the shower curtain. The caulk that sealed the border between the wall tile and the shower floor was darker than it ought to have been. She scratched at it and came up with a ridge of dark crud under her fingernail. She stood, her hand trembling. "Grant!"

She plopped herself on his side of the bed where he lay, facedown. She tapped his shoulder until he turned his head sideways and opened his eyes, presenting her dirty fingernail to him the way a cat might drop a dead bird at its owner's feet. "Mold," she said. "It's mold."

"Mm," Grant said, turning his face to the pillow again.

"Mold. It's an allergen."

"From the bathroom?" he said.

"Yes."

"It's probably mildew. Mildew in a bathroom is normal." He pulled the covers over his head.

She pulled them down. "It's black mold. Toxic black mold."

"So let's sue," he said.

"Is that all you ever think about?"

He thought for several seconds. "Not all . . ."

"What about Adam's health?"

"Is it real? Toxic black mold? I mean, didn't someone just invent it a couple of years ago to scare people?"

"It's real." Suzanne filled him in on her research: Black mold could be deadly. Black mold caused asthma and pulmonary bleeding. Black mold caused permanent cognitive damage. Black mold destroyed houses. It was so invasive, so pervasive, that bleach solutions didn't kill it, nor did removing drywall. One family in New Orleans she'd read about moved back home after the waters from Hurricane Katrina had receded, only to come down with unexplained respiratory symptoms that left them barely able to breathe. The cause?

"Let me guess," Grant said.

"Explain our new roof. Why would someone put a new roof on a house just before they sold it if there were no water issues?"

"Old roof . . . ?"

"Explain the brown stains on the dining room ceiling."

Toxic black mold arose from hidden leaks. Its spores lurked behind the drywall. There was only one way to find out if their house had fallen prey to the scourge: look behind the walls. But how?

And so Suzanne put in a call to Nick Cox, who came over dressed from head to toe in protective gear, a crowbar in his hand.

TED SAT ON THE CURB ACROSS THE STREET FROM THE DAVENPORT-Gardners', his hands jammed into the pockets of his down jacket, his legs splayed in the blocked-off road. He watched Nick's yellow bulldozer standing at the ready, engine running, gnashing its teeth, ready to tear the boards off Grant and Suzanne's house at Nick's command. The bulldozer wasn't much bigger than the Coxes' SUV. A Volvo, oddly enough, just like his and Allison's wagon.

Jillian sat beside Ted, more engaged than he'd seen her since her Disney princess phase. "Wow," she said between bites of bagel and smoked salmon from their abandoned New Year's brunch. Ted had run out of the house empty-handed after seeing the bulldozer roll down the street. His stomach was growling, but he didn't want to leave for fear things would get worse in his absence. The bulldozer might have at the house, removing chunks, leaving it as airy as a hunk of Swiss cheese. They had been dragging out big hunks of drywall already, as if they were planning to hollow it out first. "Can I have a bite of your bagel?" he asked Jillian.

"A small one," she said.

Ted took a nibble.

"Oh, Dad! You nearly ate the whole thing!" She wrenched back the bagel and walked away.

A sound like a jackhammer came from within the house. White clouds puffed through the open windows, dust settling onto the grass.

Allison, sitting on Ted's other side, held her camera up to take a picture, then lowered it without taking a shot, an action she'd repeated several times since they'd arrived. "It was the best example of a Sears house in Willard Park," she eulogized.

"It's still standing, Al," Ted said.

"Not for much longer. Damn him!"

Ted put his arm around her, but she pulled away, not wanting to be held in her moment of grief. "Yes. Damn him," he agreed.

The Thorps, who'd just arrived with beach chairs and Bloody Marys, waved to Ted and Allison. They settled down between the Conways and Mrs. Olden. Ted was reminded of the spectators at the Battle of Gettysburg, who came out for a pleasant afternoon of picnicking.

Nick Cox was willfully and wantonly defying Willard Park's

newly passed moratorium. You couldn't hack away at your house on a whim! It required applications and permits, all of which Ted had shouted to the demolition crew, only to be shouldered back behind the yellow tape that rimmed the property.

He called every county department remotely associated with building construction and destruction, but all he got were voice recordings wishing him a happy new year and advising him to call back during business hours. The emergency number appeared to be disconnected. Finally, he called 911. The operator promised to send someone right over. That had been nearly an hour ago. Meanwhile, Willard Park town council members pecked about like geese, waving official-looking papers.

Suzanne and Grant sat on their couch on the front lawn alongside a heap of furniture. Suzanne sat bolt upright, like an engaged student, the opposite of Grant, who was wrapped in an afghan, possibly sleeping. Adam, on the frozen grass at their feet, was the happiest Ted had ever seen him. What better fun for a kid than to watch a bulldozer pull up at your house, prepared to, perhaps, eat it? It occurred to Ted that Suzanne and Grant might be doing it for Adam's amusement, like the king in one of the fairy tales Jillian used to like, who was willing to do anything to make his youngest daughter laugh.

He didn't blame Grant and Suzanne—Nick Cox had clearly been the instigator. He was obviously the force behind the felled Christmas tree as well, though no eyewitnesses had come forward. All anyone knew was that the lights on the tree had been off for about a half hour during the public hearing, presumably while the tree cutter sawed at the base in the dark.

Cox had arrived at the moratorium hearing late and left early, giving him plenty of time to cut down the tree. Or maybe one of his minions had done it while he testified. Nothing seemed to be happening at the White Elephant these days, though houses already under construction before the moratorium were grandfathered. Rumor had it that Cox had run out of money, a thought that made warm feelings rise up in Ted. He pictured Nick being evicted from his grand house, couches and televisions piled on the curb, a scene not unlike the one before him.

The destruction of the holiday tree was just one of a series of recent outrages in town. Muddy rocks had been left in mailboxes, and recycling bins had been upturned on lawns. So many signs had been ripped up that the town had issued an order to remove them all; and the little trees were still being cut down, ripped out of the ground, pushed over, left for dead. They were up to thirty-one now.

Meanwhile, Cox pretended to be on the side of justice. He'd joined the Moratorium Implementation Committee, the very committee Ted was on, and he made a big year-end contribution to the playground fund, sticking a red, white, and blue COX DESIGN AND BUILD sign in the ground lest anyone forget who owned it.

Ted called Terrance two or three times a day to check on him. "You doin' all right, bro?" he would say, and Terrance would say, bravely, that he was fine.

What would Terrance do when he found out the Davenport-Gardners' house had been decimated? It might put him over the edge. He might go to bed and decide not to get up for work in the morning, which would mean a sure and sudden end to the nursing home job. Ted had a terrible image of his brother spending all day, every day, watching television, his self-confidence sinking into the sofa cushions.

Adela Lambert's granddaughter stopped at the curb in front of Ted, a plate of sugar cookies in hand. "Two for a dollar," she yelled above the sound of the destruction.

Ted felt his pockets. No wallet. He laughed. "Can I get a couple on credit?"

The girl shook her head at him sadly, then walked on.

THE CROWDS HAD DISSIPATED BY THE TIME ALLISON FOUND NICK alone that afternoon. He was sitting in the now-silent bulldozer, gazing at Suzanne and Grant's house. The sun was setting rather gloriously, as if it understood that it was witnessing the end of something.

Nick saw her approach and smiled, flirtatious. "Hey, beautiful."

She leaned into the cab. He closed his eyes, readying for a kiss.

"Fraud!" she cried. And she pushed his shoulder.

He opened his eyes and laughed. "Happy new year to you too."

"You tricked me."

"They had mold."

So he said, but who knew if that was even true? Suzanne had pulled her aside during the early, giddy part of the day, to tell her about the bathroom caulk and the black streaks under the kitchen sink. Suzanne, in CEO mode, told Cox to tear down walls "and keep on tearing" until he found the mother lode.

"You said—and I quote—'I'm all about preserving what's best about the town,'" Allison said.

"I am," Nick said.

"It was an original Sears Modern Home."

"Modern for what . . . 1920?" He looked disappointed. "I thought you got it."

"Got what? What are you talking about?" Allison said.

"That old houses are obsolete. You agreed with me."

"I agreed that the arts and crafts houses in Winterset were nice."

He nodded. "And you agreed that some houses in Willard Park weren't worth keeping."

"I didn't mean everything built before 1980 should be bull-dozed!"

"It's not a bulldozer, Mrs. Miller. It's a compact excavator."

Allison wasn't playing. "Let me rephrase that: I didn't mean we should *compact-excavate* everything built before 1980."

"God you're sexy when you're mad."

"Be quiet," she said. Were people watching them? Were they going to report that they'd had a heated conversation and come up with damning theories? "And I'm not," she protested. She wasn't sexy. She was cold, and her nose was probably bright red, and she was mad.

He smiled again. God, that smile. "What is up with your eyes?"

"Nothing . . . They're just eyes."

"They were green a minute ago."

She blushed, gently waving his words away.

"You are a witch. You've bewitched me."

She pushed at his shoulder again, but not as hard. "Don't try to butter me up."

"Ooooh," he said. "That sounds fun."

"Don't." She tried to refuel her anger, to ready it to lob back at him. He was a monster. He was ruining their town. What was wrong with Allison to be sleeping with him? She was sleeping with him now. They'd slept together twice, both times at the Sawyers' when she was allegedly walking the dog.

"There they go again," he said, gazing into her eyes. "Now they're blue. How do you do that?"

It was all she could do not to tear off his clothes and sit on his lap right in the middle of the Davenport-Gardners' lawn, peering eyes be damned. Had she flipped her lid? "I hate you!" she said, stepping out of hands and face reach. "I hate you, I hate you, I hate you!"

"Ten o'clock?" he said.

"No!" she said, then, remembering how good it had felt, how otherworldly after so many months without intimacy, cried, "Yes! God damn you!"

He laughed and pointed his little compact excavator toward home.

She was a horrible person. There was no way around it. Cheating on poor Ted! She rarely thought of him without the adjective "poor" these days. It wasn't a good adjective to associate with your husband. Your poor husband.

On the other hand, Ted didn't want to have sex anymore, and that was kind of a marital right. She'd suffered through more than five months of sexual drought before succumbing. Five months was a long time. And Ted had given her no indication about when that might let up. She might agree to an indefinite hiatus if he let her have sex with Nick to fulfill that need.

But he wasn't going to agree to that. Of course not. Especially not with Nick. Not that a friend would be better. Who would agree to that kind of marriage? Well, some people would, she'd learned. Some people were polyamorous, which had sounded like a dangerous idea when she first heard about it, but now sounded like a pretty great option. Would Ted agree to be polyamorous? It wouldn't even be polyamory, actually. It would be monogamy. Just not with him.

But what about Kaye? Poor Ted was one thing, but what about poor Kaye? She made herself picture Nick's wife, his pretty, well-meaning wife. It was something she really hadn't done in a serious way until now. In what way did Kaye deserve to have her marriage destroyed by Allison? Or their children? What right did Allison have to potentially destroy Lindy and Jakey's family? And for what? It wasn't as if she and Nick were going to make a life together.

Allison made a decision. She would not meet up with him again tonight. She would not meet him ever again. She was done with it. Done hurting her husband, done hurting Kaye and the children. How had she let herself become a potential homewrecker—with a man who actually wrecked homes? She sent Nick a text, a cryptic one, in case someone in the family picked up his phone before he did. Cannot make meeting tonight. All collaborations off. Then she blocked his number.

It was a relief to know it was over, she thought as she walked home, that she would not behave in a morally reprehensible manner anymore, would not get caught in any wayward acts. She nearly had been caught. The other night when she was going to meet Nick, Ted came out to do a little more sleuthing even though he'd been out once that night. He joined her and Candy on the sidewalk walking toward the Sawyers'. Thank goodness she hadn't caught up to Nick, who was half a block ahead. When Ted saw Nick, he insisted they follow him. So they trailed him past the Sawyers' and around the green. Then Nick walked across the middle of the green, and they did too. After that he went back and forth in front of the closed market three times—as did they—then made his way home, where he waved to them both from his walkway.

"We saved a few trees tonight," Ted said, clearly pleased—but then they saw this wasn't the case at all. Their little dogwood, which they'd planted in front of the living room window a year or two back, had been attacked in their absence. A few of the branches were broken, and dry leaves lay scattered at its feet.

"How the heck . . . ?" Ted said.

"So it's not him!" Allison said.

"Of course it's him."

"How can it be? We were just following him."

"One of his people then . . . ," Ted said.

He wouldn't let it go.

Allison headed up the path to their door, prepared to find not only Jillian and Ted, but the Davenport-Gardner family, whom she had invited for dinner since their house was uninhabitable. *Good-bye, Nick Cox,* she thought. *Goodbye, and good luck.*

NINE O'CLOCK AND ALL WAS WELL. WELL, IT WASN'T PERFECT. ALLISON and Ted and the Davenport-Gardners sat in the living room after dinner, listening to Grant try to explain the house situation to Suzanne's mother over the phone. Suzanne's mother had, it seemed, bankrolled the house.

His voice was eerily calm, which lent an aura of surrealism to the situation. Everything about this first day of the new year was surrealistic, when you came down to it. Allison had just ended her affair with Nick—she'd had an affair. She wasn't the type to have an affair—and their neighbors had destroyed their house and were homeless. It was a lot for one day.

"I'm not sure where we're staying," Grant told his mother-in-law.

It was a question that had been simmering in Allison's mind.

"With *you?*" Grant said, his eyes on Suzanne.

Suzanne shook her head. "We can't go to Richmond. You have a job."

He put his palm over the speaker. "She wants Adam to come."

"No way." Suzanne shot Allison a desperate glance, but Allison looked down at her hands, dry from the winter weather. She was staying out of this one.

It wasn't clear what Suzanne had against her mother. She was clearly devoted to Adam, reading aloud to him at every opportunity during her short holiday visit, giving him a haircut, and orchestrating Christmas dinner—each gesture of which inspired

Suzanne to phone Allison, to vent. "She's underfoot. Doesn't she realize?"

The worst offense seemed to be her Christmas gift to Suzanne: an appointment for a ninety-minute massage at a spa in Georgetown, which she insisted Suzanne have before she went back to Richmond. While Suzanne was at the appointment, her mother not only wiped down every single one of Adam's toys and cleaned the oven, but got Adam out of the pajamas and cap he'd worn for weeks and into some fresh clothes. Then she walked him to the playground, where she pushed him on the swings. He'd come home rosy cheeked. Suzanne had been apoplectic. "Wasn't that going too far? He's sick!" Suzanne asked her, a question to which Allison hadn't responded. It might be good for him to stay with his grandmother for a while.

Allison surveyed the room, full of family and friends, the way a home should be. She snapped an imaginary picture, which she dubbed "New Year's Night." She took care to Photoshop the expressions: in reality Suzanne's eyes were fierce, like that of a she wolf protecting her young; Grant's mouth was frozen in an odd smile; Ted's lips were pursed like a drawstring bag. By the time Allison was finished, they all looked beatific.

She turned her expression into something serene as well, because if her outsides reflected her insides at all, her expression was probably that of a madwoman.

Jillian and Adam barreled down the hallway and into the room, bursting into the imagined photo. Adam jumped into the rocking chair and Jillian sat on top of him, making him scream with laughter.

"What are we going to do?" Suzanne said.

There was really only one thing to do. Allison was the root cause of the demolition, after all. She was the one who had suggested to

Suzanne that allergies might be causing Adam's headaches. If she and Ted didn't put them up, who would? "Why don't you stay with us?"

"That's too much," Suzanne said. "We can't."

"Why not? You could sleep in my office." Allison let herself look at Ted, who looked as though he'd just swallowed a hard-boiled egg, whole. "Tonight at least. Of course! Where else would you go?"

"A hotel," Ted muttered.

"We can pull out the futon in the office," Allison chirped.

"Maybe just for tonight," Suzanne said, looking at Grant. His eyes were closed. She nudged him.

"What?" he said, startled.

"They're letting us stay here tonight."

He extended an arm toward Ted for a fist bump.

Ted hesitated, then reluctantly bumped back.

Allison went upstairs with bed linens, trailed by Jillian, who sat on the floor while Allison unfurled the bed and put on the fitted sheet.

"I can't believe you didn't ask me," Jillian said.

"Ask you? Since when do we ask your permission to have house-guests?"

"Adam is not going to sleep in my room, Mom."

Allison pulled the sheet taut and smoothed it with her hand. It was ten fifteen now. Nick might think something was wrong. Maybe he would be worried that something had happened to her. Maybe he would be angry.

"Is he, Mom?"

"Is who what?"

"Mom! Is Adam going to sleep in my room?"

"No, of course not."

"He's going to mess up my stuff."

"Go get ready for bed."

"I'm nearly thirteen!" she yelled.

"Jillian," she warned in a voice that would have chastened her daughter in the past, but Jillian shot back a venomous "What?"

Something clattered against the window. It sounded like hail. They both looked toward the sound, but it was quiet again. The window was unbroken, the curtain undisturbed. "A little sleet," Allison said, knowing exactly what it was. Her heart sped up at the thought. *Stop it,* she told it.

Jillian would imagine the sound into robbers or vandals. She'd been a fearful child, forever climbing into their bed, for safety. Allison felt a little sad, knowing Jillian would never cuddle between them in bed again. She let the top sheet billow over the mattress and float down with a sigh.

The sound came again. Allison went to the window and pushed the curtain aside. There he was in his long coat and boots, grinning up at her. God, he was bold. And sexy. And very, very tempting.

"What is it?" Jillian said.

Allison looked at him for a long moment; then she let go of the curtain.

"Well? Should I be scared?" Jillian said.

"No, honey. There's nothing to be afraid of," Allison said, shaking the pillows into their cases. She pulled up the blanket and gave Jillian a hug, a hug that said *It's over,* a hug that said *I'm back.*

"Mom," Jillian said, arching away from her. "Don't."

17

There was only a little snow, just enough to cover the grass, but Rex was outside leaping around in it. He looked surprised every time he came up with a white nose. Kaye watched him through the window. She and the dog were the only ones in the family who even cared about the snow. The kids had gone upstairs after dinner, Jakey to play video games and Lindy to do homework. Why couldn't the kids be more fun? Like Adam and Jillian, out making snowballs in the dark. Every now and then Grant would appear in the Millers' yard and the kids would ambush him.

She waved to Grant through the window and he waved back. He was nice. He was the only one of them who was. She'd only exchanged a couple of words with him since their night on the porch, saying "Hiiiiii" in a way that he would know she meant "high." Maybe if she could find a way to buy some weed they could hang out again.

Jillian ran by with snowballs in her hands; Kaye waved, but Jillian wouldn't even look at her. It made her sad that the kids had taken sides in this whole housing-war thing. Meanwhile, Ted shoveled the driveway.

Suzanne and Grant had been living with the Millers for ten days now. Ten days in that teeny little house! It didn't seem like it could fit all six of them. Seven of them, if you counted Ted's brother, who was there most of the time. There he was now, looking out the window at her. He waved. Kaye closed the blinds.

Kaye couldn't stop spying on them. They made pancakes together on Sunday morning, and stayed up late playing board games and cards. It was like a Christmas special on TV.

They seemed to be the only ones in town having a good time these days. Things had gotten so ugly. Anonymous notes and toilet-papered trees were becoming a daily thing. Even the playground had scars. Someone had scrawled "Fuck the tree huggers" in shiny blue spray paint down the slide. Pro-moratorium neighbors crossed to the other side of the street when they saw her or Nick coming, and she didn't even want to think about the nasty letters in the town newsletter this week. People acted like Nick just woke up one morning, went over to Suzanne and Grant's, and said, "Hey, let's rip up your house!" Maybe he'd been a little overenthusiastic, but that poor little Adam had such bad headaches.

When Kaye was growing up, her father used to say: never let the sun set on your anger. Wouldn't he be disappointed? The sun had set on the anger in Willard Park for so many nights now. Kaye was good at bringing people together. She'd gotten an award for being the friendliest girl in her class at Live Oak High: Sweetest Senior, they called it; she still had the little bottle of perfume they gave as a prize. Maybe that was God's plan for her. To bring the town back together. She might as well start with the Millers.

"Okay, you-all," she called upstairs. "Let's get out there and do some shoveling."

No one responded. She went to Jakey's room and turned off the TV.

"Hey!" he cried.

"Come shovel," she said. "You can wear your new jacket! Don't you want to get out in the snow?" She knocked on Lindy's door. When no one answered, she opened it. "Come—" she started, but Lindy wasn't there. Hadn't she come up to do homework? Wasn't that why she couldn't help with the dishes? She'd probably snuck off to watch TV somewhere. "I'm warning you, Lindy," she called, closing the window by her bed. An open window in winter. For goodness' sake.

Kaye went down to the mud room for her winter things. She loved winter things, puffy coats and fuzzy gloves, things she'd only seen in movies when she was growing up. She put on a down coat as light and airy as a meringue.

Everything felt crisp and new outside, like a fresh start. The snow sparkled in the light of the streetlight. She started shoveling in front of the garage, pushing the snow to the sides. It was a thin layer and dry, so it wasn't hard to do. She liked it, in fact. It felt good to do physical work. Ted was down at the bottom of his driveway, scraping where it had turned icy. She tried to think of something to say. "Hope the plow doesn't push it all back again," she said.

"What?"

"The snowplow. You know how they block driveways some-times?"

Ted stopped shoveling. "Is that a threat?"

"No! It's just—you've done such a nice job, is all. I hope they're considerate. That's what I mean." She smiled hugely, to show she came in peace.

Maybe she should ask him for shoveling advice. Men liked to be asked for advice. They would go back and forth exchanging pleasantries for a while, and then she'd ask everyone over for cocoa and cookies. That would be the beginning of the end of all the anger. The garage door hummed open, and there was Nick.

"Someone to help me. Hurray," Kaye said. "I was starting to feel like the little red hen. Remember? From the story?"

"Who?" Nick rummaged around in the garage.

"I've got the shovels out here," she called. "You know, the little red hen. 'Who will help me mill the wheat . . . then I shall do it myself.' Remember?"

A motor started up, and Nick pushed the snowblower onto the driveway.

"No need for the big guns. There's only like an inch here," she called, but he started blowing snow from the driveway onto the lawn.

Ted stopped shoveling. "Hey," he called out.

Nick kept blowing snow.

"That's really loud," Ted yelled, his gloved hands cupped around his mouth.

Nick kept blowing.

"Cox!"

"What?" Nick turned toward the Millers', spraying snow on the part of the driveway Ted had already cleared.

"Cut it out," Ted called.

Kaye reached for the snowblower's handle; Nick steered away from her. He walked across the lawn, spraying snow as he went. The Millers' driveway was turning white again.

Ted picked up a clump of snow and threw it at Nick. It hit his neck.

"Why you . . . ," Nick said, blowing snow right at Ted.

"Don't!" Kaye yelled.

Jillian and Adam had stopped packing snowballs. Ted threw another snowball at Nick.

"Don't, Daddy!" Jillian said.

Nick picked up a handful of snow and rubbed it in Ted's face. Ted grabbed him by the neck. Kaye shouted for them to stop. Jillian ran inside, yelling for her mother. Meanwhile, the snowblower's motor screamed for attention. When Allison came out, the men let go of each other and looked at the ground, like kids caught in the act.

"Unbelievable," Allison said.

Ted and the kids followed Allison inside, leaving Nick and Kaye in the dark.

"For goodness' sake!" Kaye yelled. She stomped off to the back deck, and paced, expecting Nick to come over and apologize. When he didn't, she took the cover off the hot tub—which was not an easy job even though she worked out. She threw her clothes into the yard—coat, scarf, gloves, shirt, bra. They lay scattered in the snow, dark against light. When Nick appeared, she threw her jeans and panties at him. "What is the matter with you, Nick?"

"With me?"

"Yes, you. All I wanted to do was to make peace, and you have to go and ruin it."

"I'm not the one who choked me."

"You started it," she yelled, shivering, as he walked across the deck, toward the house. "Don't you walk away from me," she called, but he already had.

Kaye, rattled, slipped into the hot tub. The hot water prickled against her butt and the backs of her legs. Wasn't there fighting enough without him having to start a brawl? People had been mad at him plenty over the years and it had never bothered him before.

Maybe it was about money. She knew he was upset that the White Elephant hadn't sold, but it would eventually. In spring, probably. Then he could pay back his loans or what all. The ban on building would end in a couple of months, and he could tear down the split-levels and build homes on those lots, and design something nice for Suzanne and Grant. Why did he have to make such a stink about everything? If he wanted the new house to sell more quickly, he ought to fix it up, put in floors and fixtures so the buyers saw a home instead of a work in progress.

Kaye had told him so herself not long ago. He didn't immediately quash the idea. She'd been so excited she went over to the new house the next day with a paint-sample fan, a notebook, and some decorating magazines. She imagined yellow walls in the kitchen— Amber Waves, perhaps—and Palladian Blue in the living room. Blond wood floors were popular now; she'd scatter some thick area rugs around to make it cozy. She went up the unfinished steps to the second floor gingerly. One of the rooms smelled surprisingly lemony. That room, too, would be yellow or even toward orange— possibly Sunflower! It would be a sunny house even on dark days. Even the basement had possibilities. You could put in a little kitchen and turn it into a mother-in-law suite or even an Airbnb.

She presented her ideas notebook to Nick that night when they were watching TV. "Maybe I could be your interior designer," she said. Her voice was teasing, but she meant it. "Cox and Cox we could call ourselves." He'd patted her thigh. "Let me deal with this, hon. You've got enough on your mind."

The notebook had sagged in her hand. He didn't mean to be unkind. He was just used to being the provider, that was all. She knew she ought to be grateful, having someone who wanted to take care of her and the kids. And she was. But she still thumbed through that notebook sometimes, daydreaming.

Kaye sank down in the water until just her eyes and nose were peeping out. Sometimes she felt worthless. Less than worthless. Her kids didn't need her anymore. Her husband didn't take her seriously. Her neighbors hated her. But who could she even talk to about it? She and her friends from Beaufort hardly even texted anymore. There wasn't much to say. Who cared if the auction theme at Lindy's old school was "Caribbean cruise" if you couldn't help blend the piña coladas? And what did it matter if the girl who'd bought your house "fit right in," down to organizing the annual block party? Were you supposed to congratulate her for stealing your old life?

She'd lost contact with all but one of the friends from the sea island where she'd grown up—Lynnette, a girl who'd gone away for years, then went back to write poetry. She sent Kaye a link to one of her poems from a literary magazine a year or so ago, a depressing thing about cancer that didn't even rhyme. If Kaye ever were to tell anyone about her mammography paintings, it would be Lynnette. But the truth was, it was too embarrassing to tell a soul. She felt the heat rise to her face at the thought of all those painted breasts. She ought to get rid of them before someone realized what a nutcase she was.

Kaye didn't talk to anyone anymore, not really. Not since Jillian stopped coming over. Jillian seemed to like her, really to like her, but then suddenly she was gone. Lindy went through friends like some people went through packs of gum, but it was Kaye who had ruined that friendship. That's what Lindy said. Lindy said Allison had been so upset about the ear piercing that she wouldn't let Jillian come over anymore. Kaye couldn't understand why that had upset her. Why tiny little girls—even infants!—had pierced ears. She would never have signed the form if it had occurred to her that Allison didn't want Jillian to get her ears pierced. Why hadn't it occurred to her? The world confused her. It really did. Maybe it was because she didn't have a mother to explain how things worked. Maybe her kids would be confused, too, since she didn't know how to guide them through it. It made her sad to think of them going through life the same way she had.

She sank her head in the water. Her hair floated around her like that girl in the Shakespeare movie. If only she could just lie here until she froze over, like a giant ice cube. How long till Nick and the kids would notice she was gone? Summer?

She had a panicky thought. What if she threw out her mammogram paintings and someone dumped the trash on the lawn, like someone did the town hall trash last week? The Millers and the Davenport-Gardners would find them in the morning when they went to walk the dog. She imagined them all laughing together. She imagined the whole town laughing, their sides splitting. They'd tack them up on Lucy's bulletin board as a joke. Talk about adding fuel to the Cox-hating flames.

She popped her head out of the water, into the cold air. She heard voices. Someone was talking practically right next to her, on the other side of the wooden lattice the Millers had put up between the yards.

". . . the bastard." That was Ted. No question who he was talking about.

"You both were acting like kids."

"I was shoveling. How was it my fault?"

"Let it go. You're going to have a coronary." Allison.

"Snow in the face, WTF?"

"OMG. You sound like Jillian."

"LOL," he said, but neither of them did.

"I hate that guy," he said.

"I know."

"He's trying to ruin my life. He is methodically trying to ruin my life."

"So he's taking the day off tomorrow?" Allison said.

"Who?"

"Terrance. I'm changing subjects."

"I guess."

"Was he suspended?"

"He had a couple leftover vacation days from last year. Dana said he had to 'use it or lose it.' Can you believe this? We have to go outside to get privacy around here anymore," Ted said.

Kaye lay perfectly still. She knew the rules of politeness said she ought to let them know she was there, but it was awkward because she was naked. Instead, she breathed as quietly as she could, hoping they would go back inside before her fingers and toes got too pruney.

"Who knew a 'night or two' would turn into ten days," Ted said.

"They don't have anywhere to go."

"Did they really think the insurance company was going to pay to put them up?"

"It still might. Mold's a health concern . . ."

"You can't just destroy your house," Ted said.

"Some people learn things the hard way," Allison said.

"Mind if I bang my head against the siding?" Ted said.

"Watch out for splinters."

Kaye laughed. She didn't mean to, but it was funny. Her mind was all a twirl. They'd just given her another idea about how to smooth the feathers. Funny the way He worked. How He sometimes dropped ideas right into your naked lap.

SOMEONE WAS OUT THERE. IN THE DARK. WAS IT NICK COX, COME TO mow down the rest of the Millers' trees?

"What?" Allison said.

Ted put his finger to his lips. He peered into Cox's yard,

through the latticework. Kaye was in the hot tub. He could see the outline of her face and hair and the rise of her breasts by the little runner lights that surrounded the tub. He turned away before he saw any more of her.

Had she heard them talking? He'd heard Kaye and Nick in there often enough. It was embarrassing, the things he'd heard. He shivered. "Colder than I thought out here."

"I told you," Allison said.

"Let's go back inside."

"I thought you needed to let off some steam."

"I feel better now." He held the back door for Allison, then locked it behind them. Better to be back inside stifling his anger than to expose their lives to Kaye Cox, direct conduit to Nick-the-Destroyer. The television was on, loud, down the hall. Ted felt his shoulders seize up.

"You're a pretty good sport about all this, you know?" Allison whispered.

Ted nodded. He was. He might have pitched a big fit about hosting the Davenport-Gardners for so long, but what was the use? He'd known about Allison's weakness for foundlings before he married her. He envisioned Adam growing from boy to man under their roof. A man with headaches. Did he still have headaches? He seemed active enough these days, jumping on Jillian's bed, banging on the piano.

Ted got a glass of orange juice as Allison headed to bed. Jillian and Grant burst into laughter.

Jillian? Ted looked into the living room. When he and Allison went outside, Grant had been alone in front of the TV, but now Jillian was on the couch, too, eating sweet potato chips and watching a cartoon. Candy sat at Grant's feet.

Grant had brought the television up from the basement: ostensibly to entertain Suzanne, who had been to the hospital for a pregnancy-related procedure. Suzanne hadn't watched it yet, but Grant was making excellent use of it despite lousy reception. He seemed to have nothing else to do now that *Annie Get Your Gun* rehearsals were on hold. "I think Jillian's right. We really should consider getting a smart TV," Grant said one evening. We? The guy had a lot of nerve. Terrance came over and watched with him most nights. He'd left not long ago, taking some enchilada leftovers with him.

"Time for bed, Jill," Ted said.

"It's nearly over," Jillian said.

Grant cracked up at something on the screen. Ted thought of Allison, in their bedroom on the other side of the wall, just past the bathroom. You could hear everything through that wall. Grant reached into the sweet potato chip bag, then Jillian grabbed a handful. Allison had a rule about eating outside the kitchen.

Ted sat down on the arm of the couch. "Is this *The Simpsons?*"

"Dad! No!" Jillian said.

Ted sniffed. It smelled smoky. "Move over, sweetie," he said, and Jillian moved over. Sometimes the fireplace smelled smoky, but it wasn't that. He slid closer to Jillian and sniffed.

"Stop it," Jillian said, nudging him away.

He leaned back, taking in a lungful of air without moving his nostrils. Not quite the smell of cigarettes. Was it that smoky tea she and Allison sometimes drank? Lapsang souchong?

"He's the dad on the show," Jillian said, pointing to the screen.

Ted nodded, nostrils open.

Pot, he thought. He smelled pot.

"And that's their dog. He talks," Jillian said.

Was Jillian smoking pot? He shifted his arm over the back of the couch and leaned toward her, to smell again.

"Daddy!" Jillian said. Ted got a whiff of her hair as she swooped to the floor to sit cross-legged. She smelled fruity. Like shampoo or lip balm or something. What a relief.

"He's a cop," Jillian told Ted. "The dad is. On the show. Are you even watching it? I'm going to quiz you."

Ted sniffed in Grant's direction.

It was Grant. Grant smelled like pot.

Ted frowned at the screen, feigning interest. Jillian was watching what appeared to be an R-rated cartoon with their stoner houseguest. "Time for bed, Jill."

"Dad—"

"It's late."

She must have heard something dangerous in his voice, because she left without further protest. Ted slid closer to Grant. There was no doubt about it. He definitely smelled like pot. Ted imagined the "citizen profile" in the town newsletter featuring Grant Davenport-Gardner: Job: lawyer. Pastimes: community theater, running, getting high. Then there was the bulletin board. He could put a note up himself: *Grant Davenport-Gardner is a stoner.*

Grant laughed again, a real gut buster.

No wonder he found TV so entertaining. Had he been high at *Annie Get Your Gun* rehearsals? Maybe that was the real reason the show had been postponed—indefinitely, according to Allison. There were other reasons too. Apparently Rainier thought it was absurd that the town had considered granting Suzanne and Grant an emergency exemption to the moratorium guidelines, an opinion he voiced at rehearsal. An opinion to which Grant took offense. Grant had done a nasty imitation of Rainier, making his Austrian accent Hitleresque, and Rainier had stormed out—for good, he said.

Ted wouldn't have cared that Grant smoked if he behaved like

an adult. A lot of people did now, often out in the open. In some
D.C. neighborhoods it was as common a smell as cigarette smoke,
and who cared if you didn't make a public nuisance of yourself?
But Grant was a houseguest. He was supposed to be a role model
for Jillian and Adam. Instead he broke the household rules and
lay around, letting everyone else pick up the slack. The more Ted
thought about it, the more furious he got.

Grant shook the sweet potato chips bag under Ted's nose.
"Better help yourself before I finish them off."

Ted punched the bag out of Grant's hand. Bits of orange chips
skittered across the coffee table and onto the rug.

Grant laughed. "Good one!"

Ted opened his mouth to tell him off. "They deserve better
than you're giving," he wanted to say, and, "No wonder Suzanne
doesn't confide in you." She didn't. Grant had been as surprised as
Ted to learn that Suzanne was going to the hospital for a procedure
the other day. What kind of clod didn't know his wife was having
difficulties with the pregnancy?

Grant looked at him with red, pleading eyes, waiting for Ted to
speak. He looked so pathetic. One of his eyes looked oddly puffy,
and he looked like he was starting to cry. Ted's anger shrank back
to pity. "Oops," he said, scooping up the chips. Grant helped him,
wiping down the crumbs on the coffee table with his sleeve.

"Well, good night," Ted said, taking the potato chips bag and
his admonishing words along with him.

His phone rang. Terrance, no doubt. Ted had had enough for
one day, but if he didn't pick up, Terrance would keep calling.

"I'm going to get an ice scraper," Terrance said.

"But you don't have a car."

"Tomorrow. On my day off. I'm going to go to the hardware
store."

"Okay."

"Willard Park Hardware is giving them away to the first fifty customers."

"Go for it. You can get me one too."

"It's going to be for you."

"Thanks."

"I'm going to take the bus."

Seniors and the disabled rode for free, a source of infinite delight to Terrance, who sometimes rode the bus around for hours, sightseeing.

Ted brushed his teeth after they hung up, looking at himself in the mirror above the sink. He was looking at a good man, a decent man. A man who was there for his less fortunate brother. A man who helped his down-on-his-luck neighbor. If that wasn't true charity, what was? He was surprised Grant had cried. He must trust Ted, to cry in front of him.

It was only later, when he woke up to the sound of laughter, that Ted realized it wasn't tears, but pot that had made Grant's eyes red. He felt like putting a pillow over Grant's face, smothering the laughter and the man along with it. Instead, he put a pillow over his own head and tried to get back to sleep.

SUZANNE SAT AT THE KITCHEN TABLE RECOUNTING HER RECENT MIS-fortunes by the light from the kitchen-range hood. It was nearly two in the morning, around the usual time she woke up each night, but it was restlessness rather than hunger that had roused her tonight. Her uterus had been roiling for hours, as if it had a life of its own, she thought—before remembering that it did. It was only Braxton-Hicks contractions, she told herself, false contractions, practice for the real thing. She'd had them with Adam too.

But what if they weren't false? It was a question she could

hardly bear to ask herself. She had taken Dr. Fielding's advice and had the cerclage, but it turned out that that wasn't the end of the matter. Hers was still a high-risk pregnancy. The doctor told her to "take it easy." No heavy lifting, plenty of naps. Naps? She hadn't taken a nap since she was four years old. She was trying her hardest to be good, but her efforts were complicated by the fact that they no longer had a home of their own.

She couldn't lose this baby. She felt so close to her. She toyed with names at night, French names—Claire, Francoise, Solange— soft names, floating names, the names of a child not tethered by gravity. She imagined rocking her, nursing her, holding her close. Adam had no use for Suzanne now that he had Jillian. That was misfortune number one: she'd lost Adam to a twelve-year-old girl.

Her second misfortune was that the insurance company was blowing them off. They had sent out a number of inspectors to examine the house but they had yet to make a decision about how much, if any, the policy would pay out. If any! That house was teeming with mold! Well, maybe it was. There might be a little mold. Most houses had at least a little mold, didn't they? She called the office daily, but it seemed as though a new agent, unfamiliar with the case, answered every time, forcing her to go over the story again and again like a recording. She threatened to come to the local insurance office and raise hell, but they were evasive about their location. Thus she, like Sisyphus, was condemned to push her boulder up the mountain—for eternity, she feared.

Misfortune number three: the town had turned down their request to rebuild the house before the moratorium expired. Were they complete idiots? Didn't they read the articles she gave them about the dangers of mold? They didn't know there wasn't any. Only she, Nick, and Grant knew that, and they were keeping their mouths shut. She'd forwarded dozens of links in addition to having her research spiral-bound at the copy center to make the information easier to read, a copy for the mayor and each town council member, as well as a stack for the insurance company, which they'd requested she send to their main office in Michigan, where they probably had a bonfire with them. She would have given them Adam's health file, but the latest results—either luckily, or unluckily, depending on how you looked at it—did not further her case.

The allergist's skin-prick tests showed that Adam had a slight sensitivity to eggplants and cashews, which might possibly have explained the headaches if he ate eggplant or cashews, but he didn't. "What about environmental allergies?" Suzanne had asked the doctor at the follow-up appointment.

"Nothing." He showed Suzanne the section on grasses and trees on Adam's results.

"What about mold?"

"Nope."

"Dust?"

"No."

"Lead paint?" Suzanne asked.

"That's not an allergy."

"But there might be some allergens you missed, some rare ones?"

"This is a pretty comprehensive list."

Suzanne had stood up, realization tumbling down on her. She yanked the test results from the doctor's hands. "Are there other copies of this?"

"That one's for you to keep."

"I want the file on the computer."

"We'd be glad to send a copy to his pediatrician."

"Don't you dare!" Suzanne said.

The doctor took a step backward, his eyes shifting uneasily toward the door. Rightly so. When Suzanne looked down at her hands, she saw that they were fists.

No one else must ever know about the test results. Not Grant. Not Allison. Not even Adam. Not ever. For the rest of his life Adam would have to write "mold" on forms that asked whether he had any allergies. All anyone needed to know was that his headaches were improving, and this, Suzanne must convince them, was because he no longer was being exposed to mold from their house in Willard Park.

So what was causing the headaches? Suzanne now had a probable answer thanks to the neurologist, who had received the results of the blood tests she'd ordered: Adam had Lyme disease.

Suzanne knew about Lyme disease, of course. A tick bite followed by a bull's-eye rash and flulike symptoms—none of which had happened to Adam, Suzanne argued, but lab results were lab results. Apparently not everyone who got Lyme had flulike symptoms or a bull's-eye rash. Who knew? The neurologist theorized that the headaches, neck ache, and joint pain were probably the result of Lyme meningitis, which was similar to aseptic meningitis, but caused by the Lyme bacteria. He'd probably gotten the bite when they went to Chincoteague Island at the end of the summer, home to myriad pastoral, tick-infested deer.

It was good to have a diagnosis at long last, even better to know that he didn't need further treatment. The Lyme titers showed that he had had Lyme, but no longer did, thanks to the double dose of antibiotics the pediatrician prescribed, which, coincidentally, worked to combat not only sinus infections, but Lyme disease. Symptoms could last a long time with Lyme, months or even years, but they had lessened somewhat and would continue to abate, Suzanne was told.

Suzanne wanted to feel relieved, and she did, of course. Adam was becoming himself again. He'd returned to school after winter break, and was catching up on what he'd missed. Suzanne would have begun to get her life back again had she not destroyed her house.

If only they were rich, they could rent a nice house until the insurance company came through with a big check. That was misfortune number four: their impoverished-ness. Suzanne was loath to take out a loan on top of the one they owed her mother. It didn't matter if the house was no longer habitable. They still owed her. They might have used their own stocks to pay the rent if they hadn't invested so much in Sweet Dreams. And so they were stuck living at the Millers' for the time being, stuck in a tiny cottage, all three of them sleeping in one attic room. Six of them sharing a bathroom, she and Grant sharing a futon.

Which brought her to misfortune number five: number five was a doozy. It was funny, nearly, until you realized it was tragic. At first Suzanne thought they had somehow brought the mold with them from their house, but—get this!—she now understood that the fuggy, weedy odor she'd so often smelled these past few months, the smell that she attributed to mold, the smell that had been a pivotal reason for bringing Nick Cox in to demolish their house, rendering her and her son homeless, well, that fuggy weedy smell was . . . weed. Grant reeked of it when he came to bed at night. She couldn't deny it anymore. His attempts to wash off his sins were a joke: he was permeated through and through.

And, well, weed was one thing, wasn't it? Even she had to admit smoking wasn't such a big deal anymore. If he could smoke socially, the way people drank socially, be successful at work, and be a good husband and father, she could, perhaps, learn to live with his occasionally getting high, but he was acting like the druggies she'd known in high school, off in a land where a sleepy "Peace, dude" sufficed as conversation. She and Grant had had a weird exchange the other night, when she told him about the cerclage. She caught him in a lie, but she suspected there was a deeper lie beneath that lie. She wondered if he'd been fired. Would he tell her if he had? That was the tragic aspect. He couldn't seem to learn from his mistakes.

She didn't trust him anymore, she thought with a shiver. Had she ever? He'd always been a chameleon, transforming himself from lawyer, to lover, to husband and father. He was an actor, much of his act designed to "get the girl." Well, he'd gotten her all right. He'd gotten her good.

She hadn't meant to complicate her life this way: the Life Plan was designed to prevent this sort of collapse! She was going to spend her life in high-rises, in pencil skirts and high heels, buying and selling businesses until she dropped. Instead she was trapped. As trapped as Cinderella, as Rapunzel in her tower, as Snow White in the dwarves' cottage—an analogy that continued to serve. Her uterus squeezed tight, painfully this time. Suzanne took a deep breath against the pressure.

Ted appeared at the kitchen door, his expression shifting from pleased to concerned. "Are you all right?"

"I'm fine," she said, forcing a smile.

He tossed a bag of Oreos on the table. "Contraband."

She nodded, trying to look appreciative, but afraid the pain made her look ghoulish.

"Can I be honest with you?" he said.

She nodded.

"You don't look so good."

"They're only Braxton-Hicks contractions. False alarms."

He poured two glasses of milk, toasting the baby's and her health, and sat across from her.

"Some snowball fight you had out there tonight," Suzanne said.

Ted set a cookie on a napkin. "This is Nick Cox," he said, and slammed his fist down on it. Bits of cookie crumbled under his hand, but the cream filling kept it mostly intact. He shrugged, popping what was left of the cookie in his mouth.

"Want me to kill him? I could blame it on raging hormones," Suzanne said.

Ted shook his head, serious. "Killing isn't—"

"I was kidding."

"Oh."

Ted was such a sincere fellow, someone you could depend on. She imagined that he'd been like a middle-aged man even when he was a child—sensible, organized, conscientious. "Did you collect stamps when you were a kid?" Suzanne said.

"Coins. Want to see them?"

"No," Suzanne said.

"Okay."

"Now, if I'd asked you if you wanted to see my coins, would you have said yes?" Suzanne said.

"I'm interested in coins."

"What if you weren't? What if I collected bugs? Would you say yes anyway?"

"I like collections."

Suzanne laughed. "What's the biggest lie you've ever told?"

He considered.

"There must be something."

"I couldn't watch Jillian being born. I told Allison I did, but I closed my eyes."

"Grant made a video of my delivery. I asked him not to."

The overhead light went on. In walked Allison in her bathrobe. "I thought I heard a party. Can I join?"

"We were complaining about our spouses. Well, one of us was," Suzanne said.

Ted took Allison's hand and kissed her palm.

Suzanne wanted that. The comfortableness they had between them. She would never have it with Grant. They approached life's demands so differently: She took action. He ran from it. It was becoming more and more obvious with time. She smiled at them, wistful.

Allison took a sip of Ted's milk and a bite of a cookie. "Mm. Chemicals."

Suzanne could feel a contraction starting up again. It solidified and seized hold. She held the mound of her belly with her hands, but she couldn't hold back the tide.

"Are you all right?" Allison said.

"Braxton-Hicks," Ted said. "False alarms."

Allison looked impressed. "Since when are you an obstetrician?"

Suzanne's midsection radiated pain. It crawled around to her back, making her cry out.

"You sure they're false alarms?" Allison said.

"No," Suzanne cried, her mouth becoming a tiny *O*.

18

Grant practically ran down the hospital hallways toward the exit, his breath hard, his throat and jaw tight from a night full of stress and absent of sleep. He'd been wanting to leave all night, to call Marie—the texts weren't enough. He needed to hear the voice of someone sane, someone who was not caught up in this nightmare, but every time he tried to slip away to call her, Suzanne called for him to come back. "Hold my hand," she said, fear stamped on her face. He couldn't remember ever seeing her afraid before. Furious, excited, frustrated, desperate—yes, but never afraid. He was afraid too.

She'd gone into premature labor and the cerclage hadn't held. She'd dilated too much to be stitched up again. She would be on bed rest for the next several months, on medication to keep the contractions under control. The doctors would do all they could.

We're going to lose the baby, he thought, even as he thought, *Don't think that!* What would happen if they lost the baby? The world would fly off its axis. It was spinning too fast as it was. He still could not really picture them with another child, but he couldn't imagine losing it. Losing *her*. Adam and Suzanne, already so serious, would grow even more serious, their sad house even sadder.

He was a jerk to leave the hospital after Suzanne finally fell asleep and he knew it, a jerk to tell Allison he had to get to a deposition when there was no deposition to get to. He'd left Allison with coffee and the newspaper, peace offerings. Well, he was just taking a break. He'd be back as soon as he rested up; he'd return restored and steady, able to be the husband his wife needed him to be.

It was a relief to see sunlight beyond the lobby doors. He slid his parking ticket into the machine to pay and was rewarded with the message: "Thank you! Come again soon!"

The revolving doors took him from the clammy warmth of illness to the cool of morning, the sun rising with incongruous beauty over the parking lot. He took a deep breath, his first real lungful since Ted woke him to tell him Suzanne needed to go to the hospital late last night.

He'd felt a similar breathlessness the other night, when Suzanne told him she needed a cerclage and that Allison could drop her off before the procedure, but that he would have to pick her up.

"A what?" he'd said.

She'd known she had an incompetent cervix for weeks, but she hadn't told him. Didn't he have a right to know? As the baby's father?

"My body, my choice," she said, and he didn't know what to say to that. It was as if she considered herself the only parent, the queen bee, with him a mere drone.

Instead of apologizing for withholding this crucial news from him, she'd wrinkled her brow as if she didn't quite recognize him and said, "Are you wearing makeup?"

"No," he said.

"Yes you are."

"No. Well. Maybe a little."

She frowned. "Why?"

"The . . . play."

She looked even more puzzled. "It's been canceled . . . Is there something you need to tell me?"

"Nope. It's for the play," he affirmed, nodding, and went downstairs to watch TV.

Amazingly, blessedly, she hadn't followed him. If they'd been in their own house, she would have interrogated him; there were some advantages to living in someone else's house after all.

To be fair, he wasn't being entirely honest with her, either, but it was for a good reason. He wasn't even really wearing makeup—not like mascara and eye shadow! Just a little cover-up. There was a good story behind it, one he'd shared with his friends in Richmond, who'd found it hilarious.

It went like this: A few nights ago, bored with no rehearsal to go to, he'd Googled "Where to buy weed Maryland," and came up with the expected information about dispensaries and medical marijuana cards—but he didn't want to wait for a doctor's note. He wanted it now. Then he looked up "Where to buy weed D.C." and *bingo*!

In D.C. the laws were looser. You could possess it and smoke it, but you could not buy it. There was a loophole though: You could "gift" it, and certain businesses were doing just that. It was brilliant, and apparently legal. All you had to do was buy their wildly expensive product, and you'd get a little cannabis "gift" in return. Grant reviewed the offerings online—T-shirts, mugs, pizza, blown glass, cookies, rolling papers, and brownies, among others—and chose the brownies. He walked the cold quarter mile to the D.C. line lest someone notice the car was missing. He found a random address on Stephenson Place and placed his order: six brownies for seventy-five dollars. The wait time was anywhere from fifteen minutes to an hour. An hour? Hatless, scarfless, gloveless, he walked up the street and back again several times; then he jogged it, then skipped. He ran in place and did jumping jacks, boxed the cold air, anything to warm up, and an hour and a half later, a little car pulled up. Grant had grape-vined halfway up the block by then, but he sprinted back down, catching the guy with the apron over his coat before he rang the doorbell at that address.

He was handed a little brown bag that contained six very small brownies, and three little edibles shaped like gummy bears.

"Hey, man. Are you kidding me? For seventy-five dollars?"

"It's a gift. Take it or leave it," the guy said, but when Grant said he wanted to leave it, the guy told him all sales were final.

So Grant, understandably angry, reached into the brownie mobile to grab what he felt was his due, and the brownie guy grabbed him by his jacket and punched him in the face. He was going to have a black eye. Crap!

"I'm a lawyer. You didn't know I was a lawyer, did you? Well, I am, and I am going to sue you!" Grant said.

"You're the one who tried to steal my wares, *man,*" the guy sneered. Then he got into the car and drove away, leaving Grant alone on the sidewalk with his little goody bag.

Feeling defeated, he ate the three edibles on the way home, and texted all of the tech guys on the *Annie Get Your Gun* contact list to see who had weed to sell. One guy came through. Carl, who did lights, told him to stop by in the morning. It turned out Carl's weed was organic, grown in his basement right there in Willard Park. Locally sourced! They smoked together so Grant could see what he was getting. He should have started with the techies.

Instead of heading straight to work, Grant went to a coffee shop in Georgetown to get a second breakfast and play Candy

Crush until he felt less stoned—who said he couldn't learn from his mistakes? He meant to go over the bridge and into work in the afternoon, but ended up having a couple more hits and going to the movies instead.

This had been his pattern for three days running. He woke up meaning to go to work, then ended up getting high and playing Candy Crush instead. Today he was finally going to break the pattern. He smoked a little now, in the parking lot—anyone would feel stressed after last night—but he was going back to the Millers' instead of to the coffee shop. It was a start.

He turned on the car, then called Marie, who answered after the first ring.

"Hey," he said.

"Is she okay?"

"Stable. They're stable."

"Thank God."

"I'm a wreck though."

"I'm coming up there," she said. "Don't try to stop me."

But it never occurred to him to stop her. It wasn't until he hung up that he noticed he was breathing normally again.

GRANT IMAGINED WALKING UPSTAIRS AT THE MILLERS', FALLING ONTO that lumpy futon and into the deepest sleep of his life. But Terrance was sitting in the living room watching a morning news program on TV. The crowd was waving to the cameras.

"Howdy, cowboy Frank," Terrance said.

"Howdy." Grant sat down beside him. The camera had switched to the two commentators, a dimpled redhead and a man who looked like Mr. Clean.

Terrance pointed at the screen. "She and I are going to New York City. We're going to stay at a hotel."

"Lucky you," Grant said.

Terrance smiled. "Lucky me."

The house was a train station. Nothing less than a train station. Some passengers got off; others got on. Not that he had any right to complain, as one of its longest-riding passengers. They were just supposed to have stayed there one night, but no one had said anything about their leaving. Wouldn't Ted or Allison tell them if they were tired of hosting? They seemed to like the company. But it was a small house. There was no denying that it was small. It would feel even smaller when Suzanne was lying in the attic full time on bed rest. Or would it have to be the ground floor? She'd need to be on the same floor as the bathroom. Would she be able to get up to go to the bathroom?

"Let's make eggs," Terrance said. "Want eggs?"

Grant did. He hadn't realized it, but yes, he absolutely did. "And bacon."

"And cheese," Terrance said, and they got to cooking.

Terrance plugged his phone into the dock by the sink. "What do you want to hear? I'm the DJ."

"Disco," Grant said, out of nowhere.

Terrance grinned. Soon the Bee Gees were filling the room with falsetto. Grant started to sing along, and Terrance, thrilled, joined in, too, his voice off-key, but his enthusiasm right on target.

They danced around, chopping and sautéing everything they could find that might match with eggs, from onions to spinach to avocado. They even threw in some suspect things: apples, frozen peas. Grant brewed up a pot of coffee and poured them both big mugs. Terrance filled his with milk to the brim, then added a spoonful of sugar and another. And another.

"How much sugar do you take, bud?" Grant said after a while.

Terrance kept spooning it in. He took a sip of what must have been more sugar than coffee. "That much." He tipped his head to the side, thinking, then added one more. Grant laughed.

"Do you like recipes?" Terrance said.

"No."

Terrance put up his hand for a high five. Grant's hand met his.

"Should we make French toast?" Grant said.

"Too much food."

"So?"

Terrance thought about that. "Let's make French toast!"

What was wrong with this guy? Nothing, it seemed to him. Nothing. This was a good guy. A guy who was more chill than anyone who was considered "normal" in Willard Park. There was such a range in the world, in the town alone. He lined up people in Willard Park on a spectrum from not chill to chill. Suzanne was at the top: serious and smart. Brilliant maybe. No sense of humor. Did she have a humor disability? Why wasn't that a thing? Nina Strauss soon followed on his chart—or wait, she was worse than Suzanne. Dead serious. Calculating. He kept peopling his chart until he landed at the bottom, where he and Terrance sat side by side, as they did now, eating eggs.

"What are you thinking about?" Terrance said.

"How you and I are alike."

Terrance toasted Grant with his orange juice.

Grant was eating a juicy piece of bacon when he saw the note from Ted. "I took Adam to school. Call if you need anything."

Adam. He had forgotten about his son. Actually forgotten.

"Are you taking a vacation day too?" Terrance said.

"Not quite. But I am going to take a rest."

"Me too," Terrance said. "Can I?"

"That's one of the benefits of being an adult. You get to do what you want."

Terrance lay down on the couch in front of the TV.

Grant went upstairs and found a nice bud to put in his pipe. He blew the smoke out through the window screen. He'd nearly drifted off when his phone rang. He panicked. What if it was someone from work? Should he pick up? Should he ignore it? Maybe it would be worse to ignore it. He saw it was Nick and laughed.

"Say, Davenport," Nick said.

Grant was too stoned to correct him.

"How about moving out of the little shack and into our house for a while?"

"Wow," Grant said, when he understood what Nick was offering. "Wow." He couldn't think of anything else to say. It was uncanny how Nick called at that moment, that he was able to intuit his and Suzanne's needs. Fate. Grant accepted on the spot. The Coxes' would be an excellent change of pace. "I love you, dude," he said, which made Nick laugh.

He awoke to the ding of a text. Marie was there, her text said, out in front of the house. When had he fallen asleep?

He crept outside—Terrance still on the couch, sleeping—and made his way to her red convertible.

"Did you drive with the top down? You're nuts."

"Just in the neighborhood. Cute neighborhood!" Her hair was tangled from the wind. She scooped it up, twirled it, and stuck a pen through the top of it, turning it into a loose bun. He loved how she did that. Presto change-o. "You okay, General?"

When had she started calling him that? Junior year of high school, maybe. He smiled, remembering.

She held up a white, redolent bag.

"Turkey subs?"

"Extra mayo, lettuce, cranberry, sweet and hot peppers, unless your tastes have changed."

"Not me," he said.

He got in the passenger seat. She hugged him, her hands tight around his neck, her face cold against his. He shut his eyes. He felt something drop within him, a thin but solid veneer. It slid down his neck and shoulders, through his legs and feet, and out through his toes. He wanted to sink against her, to let her absorb the weight of him. He pulled her closer, breathing in the turkey smell of her. He had a thought, and the thought was: *home.*

JILLIAN WAS IN ENGLISH CLASS THINKING ABOUT RUNNING AWAY. She'd had enough of her parents, enough of the Davenport-Gardners—of Adam especially, who stared at her when she was doing homework and got into her candy stash. She was sick of waking up at six to get into the bathroom before everyone else, and the sound of the TV across the hall from her room was annoying when you weren't allowed to watch it. Suzanne was pregnant and grumpy and Jillian's father was even grumpier. She was sick of trees, and moratoriums, and houses, and all their stupid grown-up blah blah. Maybe she would run away to her grandparents' assisted living place in New York state. She started writing a letter in her head. "Dear Mom Mom and Pop Pop, the situation at our house has become . . ." She tried to think of a good synonym for bad that wasn't "sucks." Terrible. Rotten. Miserable. Unbearable. That was it. It was unbearable.

She glanced up at the clock, wondering how she would survive the fifteen minutes till the bell rang for lunch, when someone knocked on the classroom door. Mrs. Peters read the proffered note, then shook her head at Jillian as though she had purposely caused the disruption.

Jillian scanned her brain for possible disasters. She came up with Suzanne, who had gone to the hospital in the middle of the night. She swallowed, braced to hear that something terrible had happened. *Suzanne died, the baby is deformed.*

"Your mother is waiting to take you to the orthodontist," Mrs. Peters said.

Jillian had just had her braces tightened the week before. It must be a trick. Maybe a kidnapper was waiting at the office. *Your mother's had an accident,* he'd say. She wouldn't go with him. The attendance secretary would protect her. Or maybe she was supposed to go to the dentist and the attendance secretary just wrote "orthodontist" by mistake. Jillian gathered her books and made her way out of the classroom.

Freedom, freedom, freedom, she thought as she walked down the quiet hallway, thinking about all the other kids, stuck behind desks. She opened her locker and got her coat.

"Gotcha!" Lindy said, coming up behind her.

"I'm going to the dentist."

"Thanks to me."

"What?"

"Come on," Lindy said, pulling Jillian down the hall and through the cafeteria doors, into the side parking lot. "We're blowing off the rest of the day."

"I have a math test after lunch," Jillian said.

"You're welcome," Lindy said.

Jillian, half afraid they would get caught before they left school property, half afraid they wouldn't, let herself be led to the thin patch of woods next to the school. It wasn't worth fighting back.

"Mark's sick. We're going to get him on the way," Lindy said when they were around the corner, out of sight of the school.

"On the way where?"

"You'll see."

"If he's sick he might want to stay in bed."

"That's what *she* said," Lindy said.

They'd never done this before, any of this. Ditching school. Going to round up Mark from home. The most they did was walk home with him sometimes, hanging out on the swings at the elementary school until he said he had to go. Jillian made excuses at that point, too, but Lindy inevitably forced Jillian to go with her to the market for candy before releasing her. It was turning out to be harder to drop Lindy than Jillian had thought—and she'd thought it would be pretty hard.

It was a cold walk to Mark's. It was cloudy and the air was damp. The wet remains of yesterday's snow wormed its way through the sides of Jillian's sneakers, soaking her socks. She had visions of going home and crawling into bed, telling her mother she was sick. Her mother would put her hand on Jillian's forehead and bring her soup, a nicer scenario than the other one that came to mind: that her mother would catch her and Lindy walking through town in the middle of the school day.

Her mother would kill her. She'd be mad about the skipping, but she'd be even madder that she was hanging out with Lindy. "Find some new friends, can't you, Jill?" her mother had said after Mr. Cox destroyed the Davenport-Gardners' house. Finally! It had taken her long enough to say something. Jillian yanked up the hood of her parka to disguise herself. *Jillian Miller cuts school.*

They went up the walkway to Mark's front door. No one answered when Lindy rang the bell. She picked up the brass knocker and tapped it over and over. The short rat-a-tat-tats sounded like gunfire. Still, no one came.

"Let's go," Jillian said.

Lindy went around back and rapped on the kitchen window

until Mark came to the door in his sweatshirt and striped pajama pants. He looked like a little kid, his hair tousled, fuzzy blue slippers on his feet. Jillian had the urge to comb his hair with her fingers.

"Get dressed," Lindy said when he opened the door. "We're kidnapping you."

"I'm sick."

"You're faking," Lindy said.

"I have a sore throat."

"Uh-huh—and the math project was due today. Are you going to let us in?"

It was warm to the point of stuffiness in Mark's kitchen. Jillian imagined the bacteria multiplying, a thought that would have nauseated her if they hadn't been Mark's bacteria.

"So get dressed," Lindy said.

"I'm sick. I told you."

"So?"

He sighed and disappeared down the hall. Lindy sat on the couch and crossed her legs, striking the pose Mark's mother had made in her Christmas card. Lindy obviously wanted Jillian to laugh, but she wouldn't. *Run while you still can,* she wanted to tell Mark. But where would he run? They'd invaded his house. *I'm not like her,* she told him, through ESP.

"So, you like horsies? Are you a girl?" Lindy said, when Mark reappeared in a T-shirt and jeans.

"What?"

She pointed to his shirt.

Mark pulled out the front of it and looked at it, as though he hadn't realized there was a horse on it.

"I used to ride over at Meadowland," Jillian said.

"Yeah?" Mark lit up. "I want to live on a ranch, you know? Out west. This shirt is from a ranch in Montana. I've never been, but I will. I'm going to move there."

"You are?" Jillian said. He couldn't move away!

"Well, yeah. Maybe. I want a lot of horses. Like, like a dude ranch."

"But you live here."

"I know," he said, and he kicked the chair. It wobbled. Jillian and he caught it at the same time. "I just have to convince my mom."

"She won't move."

"I know," he said, slouching.

Lindy jumped in: "What's this? The My Little Pony Club? How about lunch? A good host would offer us lunch."

"Want some fettucine Alfredo?" Mark said. "My mom was too tired to eat."

"Who cooked it if she was too tired?" Lindy opened the refrigerator and poked around.

"Me," Mark said.

"Wow," Jillian said.

"*Wow,*" Lindy aped.

They stuck the plastic container in the microwave. It came out lopsided and soft, the pasta steaming. They each dug a fork in and ate, the cream dripping off the long, thick noodles. Afterward, they stuck their mouths under the faucet to drink. Jillian thought with a thrill of the day a few days from now when she would wake up with Mark's sore throat.

"Let's vamoose," Lindy said, and they made their way down the street, Mark and Lindy walking in front as though they were the parents and she, Jillian, the child. They were laughing about something. "What?" she said, but they ignored her. Maybe he liked Lindy after all.

Something glinted near a clump of wet leaves by the curb. Jillian nudged it with her foot. A purple cigarette lighter. She picked it up carefully, as though she'd just unearthed a grenade. It sparked like a Fourth-of-July sparkler when she tried to light it. "Look, you guys."

"Cool," Lindy said, grabbing it. She flicked it on, making a smooth flame flicker in front of Jillian's face.

"Let's put it back," Jillian said, but Lindy touched the flame to some leaves. They were wet. She had to light it a few times to make them smoke. Mark offered to help, then stuck the lighter in his pocket. Lindy swooped and dove, to take it back, succeeding in grabbing it finally with a joyful "Wa-hoo!"

"Quiet," Jillian said, stomping out the smoke. Now she felt as though she were the parent and they the children. "Do you want everyone to notice we're skipping?"

"Lighten up, Miller," Lindy said.

They took a left on Pecan.

"It's so quiet," Jillian said. "It's like there's been a nuclear attack."

Lindy and Mark said nothing.

"It could happen," she said. "We're in Washington, D.C., right?"

No response. She wanted to kick them. "Maybe it already happened. Maybe they used a sort of gas. Maybe we escaped it because the school walls are thick, but maybe we're about to die from it too. Or maybe some people could be immune to it. What would you do if you were the only person in town to live?" she said.

"I'd move to the country," Mark said.

Jillian coughed dramatically. "I'm dying."

"You guys are so immature," Lindy said. She stopped in front of the Sawyers' old house, a split-level with a no-trespassing sign nailed to a tree. "We own this," she said.

"Sure," Mark said.

"We do. I go here all the time."

"No you don't," Jillian said.

"How do you know?"

"You would have said," Jillian said.

"I have a fort at the White Elephant, though. Don't I, Jill?"

"She does," Jillian said.

They walked around to the back. Lindy went down the steps that led to the basement door and tried the doorknob. It didn't turn.

"We're trespassing," Mark said.

"Want to bet?" Lindy stared at the door, as though she could open it with her eyes. When it remained locked, she went back up the little staircase and poked around the yard. She came back with a rock the size of a fist. She smacked it against one of the little panes of glass that ran along the side of the door, once, twice, until it burst open like an egg. She reached her hand in and fiddled with the knob. When she pulled her arm back out, her wrist was cut. Lindy sucked at the blood.

Jillian and Mark gave each other a look, a look that said, *She's crazy,* but they followed her into the basement nonetheless. He was on Jillian's side. She could tell. The thought made her happy despite the fact that she was walking into what she thought a crypt would feel like. It was cold and a strong smell rose up, like old things: old papers and dust. Nesting animals, maybe. Or dead ones. Where had the Sawyers gone? "This is a bad idea," Jillian said. "Let's go to the White Elephant. We can play Ouija."

They walked through the unfinished basement. Jillian had been here years before, when Vicky Sawyer had a clown come to her birthday party. Vicky, a year younger than Jillian, spent most of the party crying.

"Why doesn't anyone live here?" Mark said.

"Yuck. Would you live here?" Lindy said.

"It's my house," he said.

"Ha, ha," Lindy said.

"It is. The rooms are all in the same place." He rapped on a cinder-block wall. "The laundry room is over here." Sure enough, the laundry room was over there. Jillian laughed for the first time since they'd broken in.

They had broken in, hadn't they? The truth of it hit her. Lindy had been the one to do the actual window smashing, but she and Mark were accomplices. So far today, she'd ditched school, kidnapped a kid who was home sick, and broken into a house. Her stomach twisted. They'd go to jail, or to juvie at least. She'd have to sleep on a metal bed and she'd never get to see Candy again. "Let's get out of here," she said, following the others upstairs by the flame from the purple lighter. There was a pillow and a light blue blanket neatly folded on the floor of one of the bedrooms. "We have a blanket like that," Jillian said.

They made their way back to the kitchen. The refrigerator was gone. One of the cupboard doors dangled from a hinge. Mouse poops dotted the counter. Lindy opened the cabinets one by one. She found a box of animal crackers in the drawer by the stove. She poured some into her hand.

"Don't eat that," Jillian said.

"They're mine," Lindy said. "It's my house."

"Let's go," Mark said.

"Let's just warm up for a while," Lindy said.

"The heat isn't even on," Mark said.

Jillian flicked the light switch. Nothing. "This is creepy."

"I'm leaving," Mark said.

"Me too," Jillian said.

"You guys are chickens." Lindy flapped her elbows.

Mark unbolted the kitchen door. The venetian blinds, dusty, shivered when he opened the door. Jillian followed him outside. They looked at the ground.

Mark kicked the old snow. "I have a fever."

Lindy came out, glaring. "So where would the My Little Pony Club rather go? The playground?"

"He's sick," Jillian said.

"I know where," Lindy said. Blood trickled from her wrist.

Jillian and Mark exchanged looks again. They could stand up to her. There were two of them. They could tell her they weren't going to listen to her anymore, but they didn't. One bully was more powerful than two nice people, it turned out. They followed Lindy past the community garden, withered in the January chill, down to the woods. They ended up at the tire swing by the creek.

"This is a bad idea," Jillian said.

"Everything's a bad idea to you."

"We might run into my uncle. My dad said he was taking a vacation day, to get an ice scraper."

"An ice scraper? Like for a car?" Lindy laughed.

Jillian shrugged, smiling because she liked her uncle. He was quirky, but she liked him.

"Is he retarded, or what?" Lindy said.

"He's learning disabled."

"Same thing,"

"It is not," Jillian said. "He's smart about a lot of things."

"We'll tell him it's a snow day," Lindy said.

"He'd know if it's a snow day," Jillian said. "He calls to tell me when it's a snow day."

"We'll tell him a pipe broke at the school. That'll be our story if anyone stops us. A pipe broke."

"Where are the other kids then?" Jillian said.

"You think too much." Lindy swung her leg over the tire, hung from a rope on a tree branch. "Push me," she told Mark. She shrieked happily when he swung her out over the icy water.

"A kid died here once," Jillian said. It wasn't true, but it got Mark and Lindy's attention.

"When?" Mark said.

Jillian tossed a rock through the ice. "A really long time ago. Like when my dad was a kid. He fell off and died."

"Liar," Lindy said.

"He hit his head on a rock."

"Higher," Lindy told Mark.

"The town cut down the tire after that, but someone put up a new one in the same spot. No one knows who," Jillian said, picking up another rock.

"Why didn't they cut it down again?" Mark said.

"They did," Jillian said.

"What was his name?" Lindy said.

"The boy?" She thought of an old-fashioned name. "Billy. Billy Wheeler. The other kids called him Frookie. Billy Frookie." Details made things seem true.

"Why?"

"I never heard this. You ever hear this?" Lindy asked Mark.

Mark shrugged.

"It's true. My dad grew up here. He remembers it," Jillian said.

"Your dad," Lindy said, rolling her eyes.

"What about him?"

"Mr. Moratorium." Lindy raised her eyebrows at Mark.

"What?" Jillian said.

Lindy looked back at her, innocent. Mark wouldn't catch Jillian's eye. Sometimes Jillian wanted to hit him, to make him choose. She skimmed the rock across the ice. It stopped on a branch.

"Tell the story," Lindy said.

"They cut the swing down again, but the next day, another one was up in its place. They cut that one down too. They kept watch for a while, to keep a new one from going up, but whenever they stopped watching, someone put a new swing up. After a while, they just left it."

Lindy shrugged. "So what."

Jillian threw a big rock to see how thick the ice was in the middle. It fell in with a plonking sound, splashing water up onto Lindy's pants.

"Hey!" Lindy said.

"Sorry," Jillian said.

"I'm all wet."

"I didn't mean to."

"I'll get you back," Lindy said, meanness in her eyes.

"Give her a break," Mark said.

"What's it to you? Is she your *girl*friend?"

Mark grabbed the rope and eased the swing to a stop. He let it hover in midair, over the water. Lindy shifted her leg over from the other side of the tire and sat sideways. "Your turn," she told Jillian. "I'll push you."

Jillian shook her head.

"Afraid you'll end up like Billy Frookie?" Lindy said.

"No," Jillian said.

"Chicken! Chicken! Cluck, cluck!"

"I'm going home," Mark said. He let go of the swing, sending Lindy tumbling off. She landed with a thump and a splash. She screamed. "Help me!" Then, when they stood stone still, she cried, "You're going to pay for this, Jillian Miller!"

Mark and Jillian looked at each other—their faces like mirrors reflecting exhilaration and terror—and they ran.

GRANT, SITTING NEXT TO MARIE ON A PICNIC TABLE OVERLOOKING Willard Creek, watched a squirrel dash up a tree and crawl out to the end of a branch. The branch bobbed from its weight.

"Don't jump!" Marie cried.

"Think of the children! Think of your dear mother!" Grant said. He and Marie were so high. So, so high.

The squirrel jumped, landing with a scramble in the next tree. Marie and Grant hugged in mock relief.

"That is one skilled squirrel," she said.

"No doubt."

"Maybe I should have his kids. I'm not getting any younger. Have to settle down sometime."

"It's worth considering."

"My brains, his agility. I'm thinking Olympics. Scholarships to college at least."

"On the other hand, he might already be with someone—or even more than one," Grant said. "Probably. And he probably has a lot of kids. You want a lot of squirrel stepchildren? I don't think so. Squirrels are not known for monogamy. You want monogamous, stick with gibbons."

"Gibbons?"

"Gibbons, wolves, eagles, barn owls, beavers."

"Truly? Beavers are monogamous? Are you making this up?"

"Adam told me."

"Does he even know what monogamy is?"

"Probably. He probably does."

"Well, shit," Marie said, and her entire body shivered; she nestled in a little closer to Grant.

"Want to sit in the car?"

"No. Fresh air, my friend. After sitting in a hospital all night, you need fresh air." She closed her eyes, tipping her face toward the weak January sun.

Grant took another bite of his sub. It tasted so good. It was the best food he'd ever eaten. Ever. "Thank you," he said.

"For what?"

He held what was left of his sub over his head like Lady Liberty's torch. "For this." Then he lowered it and took an enormous bite. Marie took a similar bite of hers, and they laughed, turkey and bread threatening to either come out of their mouths or choke them. When he'd swallowed enough to be able to speak, he said, "I'm a bad husband."

He'd left the hospital hours ago. Suzanne would think he'd abandoned her. He shifted uncomfortably on the wooden table, still moist from the melted snow.

"You're not so bad . . . ," she said, and then the sound of kids running and laughing, leaves and sticks being trampled, interrupted them.

They watched through the branches as first a boy—Nina Strauss's kid?—then Jillian, ran past.

Grant sprang up, suddenly not high anymore. "What was that?" he said.

"Two kids."

"I know them. Do you think she saw us? Jesus. I mean, I'm sitting here at the park while my wife is in the hospital. She definitely did. I'm an idiot. Do you think she's okay?"

"Who? Suzanne?"

"Jillian. The girl."

"She was running and laughing. Sounds like the definition of okay." Marie put the remains of her sub in the bag and tossed it at the trash can, where it smacked against the metal and slid to the ground, dumping meat and bread in the snow. "See, told you. Zero athletic skill."

Another girl ran past. Cox's kid.

"They're supposed to be in school, I think. Right? I should go after them. We're staying at their house. Jillian's."

"They're just kids, Grant. They're doing what kids do. Skipping school. Hanging out. Don't you remember?"

"Jillian wouldn't do that."

"So run after her. I don't know."

"You think I should? I should. And I should go back to the hospital, right? I'm a jerk to leave her alone." He tapped his fitness tracker, idly.

"I thought she had a friend with her."

"I'm her husband, Mare."

Marie laughed, but there was no pleasure in it. "I'm such an idiot."

"What are you talking about?"

"I drive all the way up here, like an idiot."

"What do you mean?" Grant said.

"You should be with your *wife*, Grant."

Grant nodded. "You're right. I know."

Marie stood.

"Where are you going?" he said.

"What's up with us, General? Why did you even ask me to come?"

She was the one who'd offered to come, but it didn't seem the time to quibble. "Because you're my friend?"

"Your friend."

They stared at each other.

"Your fuck buddy," she said.

"You're not . . ."

"Your ex–fuck buddy."

"Stop it."

"Your ex–fuck buddy who you call and e-mail every day, and text about a million times a day. How often do you text Suzanne?" She started walking up the hill, toward the road.

"Where are you going?" He followed her.

"I love you. You know that, right? I'm such an idiot," she said, opening the car door.

"Don't say that."

"That I love you or that I'm an idiot?"

"We're pals, Mare. You're my BFF." And she *was* his best friend. His best friend whom he wanted to kiss.

"You've got a wife and one and a half kids, General. It's time to call it quits. Give me your phone."

He gave it to her.

She borrowed his thumb to unlock it, then started tapping on the screen.

"What are you doing?"

"Erasing my number."

"No!"

"We can't stay in touch. No more texts. No more calls."

"I memorized it, so ha."

She slapped him, hard, across the cheek. They stared at each other. "Oh my God!" she said. Her hand rushed to her mouth, hiding a laugh.

Grant touched his cheek.

"I can't believe I just did that."

"Me neither." He wiggled his jaw to see if it was broken.

"Wasn't it theatrical though? Wasn't it just right?" She laughed. "I'm sorry."

He laughed, too, despite the throbbing. "I guess. I guess it was."

She kissed his cheek gently. "I'm sorry. Your face is all hot. And red. Wow. That felt good. I should have done that a long time ago."

"The kiss or the slap?"

She laughed as she got in her car.

"Don't go," he said.

"I have to. It was the perfect ending. What could we possibly do to top that?"

He leaned down into the car and kissed her. She tasted like onions. She tasted like summer. She tasted like high school and freedom. They kissed for a long time.

KAYE CHEWED ON THE ARUGULA IN HER SALAD, FEELING LIKE A COW in a field, munching, munching, munching. She was trying to learn to like it. It was weedy and it was bitter and it was in all the salad bags they sold at the Willard Park Market. She poured on more ranch dressing, hoping it would take the edge off, but it didn't.

Carmen had taken off early to go to the doctor, which was fine. Kaye didn't need the housekeeper to babysit her or anything, but it made lunchtime a heck of a lot lonelier. No matter. She got out a notepad and pen. She had things to do.

Grant had accepted their offer to move in. Kaye thought she'd have a hard time convincing Nick, but he liked the idea. "It'll probably piss Ted off," he'd said, and Kaye didn't bother to correct him.

She made a list of things she'd have to do to get ready for their guests: make up beds for the three of them, put out fresh towels, do a grocery run. It felt good to have purposeful work. When she looked up, Lindy was outside the kitchen door, her face muddy. She fought with the doorknob, fury in her eyes.

"Honey, oh honey!" Kaye unlocked the door.

Lindy slipped as she came in, practically knocking both of them over. Her jacket and pants were soaked and she was gasping, as if she'd been running. "Are you okay, Lin? What happened? Why aren't you in school?"

"I'm hurt, okay?" Lindy snapped. She showed Kaye her wrist. It was bleeding.

"Oh, sweetheart! What happened?"

Lindy tossed her jacket on the floor. She opened the refrigerator and drank the Coke straight from the liter bottle. "Jerks," she said.

"Who?" Kaye said.

"Give me a minute, would you?"

"Why aren't you in school? What happened?"

"It's not my fault! Why do you always think it's my fault?" She slammed the bottle on the counter. Coke spurted out the top, foaming and splattering.

"What isn't your fault?"

"Close the door. Will you? Is he out there?" Lindy said.

Kaye locked the kitchen door. "There's no one out there. What is all this?"

"You don't even care."

"I care, hon. I do!"

"He kidnapped me from school," Lindy said.

"Kidnapped?" Kaye felt dizzy. "What happened? If anyone touched you, I'll . . ."

"You'll what?" Lindy challenged.

"I'll . . . tell Daddy!" she sputtered. "Who did this to you?"

Lindy hesitated, as if she was afraid to say. Then she looked at the Millers' house. "Him."

"Jillian's dad?"

"No! The uncle. The slow one."

Kaye nodded against her will. Of course it was him.

"You don't even believe me. Great. My own mom doesn't even believe me."

"I do so!"

"He had a weapon. An ice scraper."

"Oh, honey. Look at your face." She touched Lindy's grazed cheek. Lindy jerked away. "Did he do that to you, Lin?"

Lindy shrugged, but Kaye knew. She knew with a mother's instinct. Fear clotted in her chest, forcing her words and her thoughts down low. "Did he interfere with you?"

"What?"

"Did he . . . you know, touch you? You know, in your private place?"

"Oh my God, Mom. No! You are gross. I said he *kidnapped* me. He stole me from school and I got away and he chased me, and I fell, and I ran home." Lindy ran upstairs.

Kaye started to follow her up the stairs, then turned around and went back to the kitchen. She reached for her phone, then started up the stairs again, feeling like a bumper car at an amusement park being bumped from one direction to the other. Should she go upstairs, after her, to comfort her? Or outside, to hunt the devil down? Or should she call the police? Or Nick? She needed to stand up for her little girl, to show her she cared. So which of those things said that most clearly? Which should she do?

JILLIAN WASN'T SURPRISED WHEN THE POLICE CAR PULLED UP TO THE Coxes'. In fact, she'd been waiting for it in some weird way. Obviously someone had seen the three of them skipping school and had turned them in. Would she be suspended—or expelled, even? Would it go on her permanent record, a black mark that would wreck her chances of getting into the college of her choice?

She watched from her bedroom window as a policewoman

walked up to the Coxes' door. She had a gun in her holster. She was coming for Lindy, the ringleader, first. Jillian would have to sit next to Lindy in the police car, Lindy casting awful looks her way. It had been mean of her and Mark to run away when Lindy fell in the water, but Jillian had been scared. Who knew what Lindy might do if she was really mad? Better to let her calm down, and then apologize. Jillian and Mark had given each other significant looks before they ran their separate ways, home. Jillian wasn't sure what the looks signified, but clearly something important had happened between them.

The police officer stayed in the Coxes' house for dragging minutes, then came outside and started up the Millers' front path. She didn't look mad. She looked bored, as if she was sick of arresting juvenile delinquents for skipping school. That's what Jillian was now. A juvenile delinquent.

She wanted to hide. The policewoman couldn't arrest her if she hid. The trouble was that Uncle Terrance was sleeping on the couch in the living room. Jillian had been surprised to see him there, but not shocked; he often ended up at their house. Luckily he hadn't woken up when she came in. Not even Candy had, which was a total miracle.

If Jillian hid and Uncle Terrance opened the door to a police officer, it might scare him. Then again, if the officer said she was looking for Jillian, Terrance could honestly say he thought she was at school, and Jillian knew from TV that you had to have a warrant to search the house—but did Uncle Terrance know that? What should she do? The police officer started up the front porch steps. *Hide!* She closed her bedroom door just as the doorbell chimed. Candy barked.

"Coming," Uncle Terrance called, groggy, after it chimed a second time.

Jillian listened to their conversation through her closed door, unable to catch more than a word here and there. She felt bad for chickening out. Uncle Terrance must be confused and maybe even worried about her. She turned her doorknob, wanting to rescue him, then let it go again, afraid. She'd never talked to a police officer before. She could hear the front door open, and the sound of voices getting louder—clearly the policewoman was leaving. When their voices had faded, Jillian opened her door quietly. The living room was empty except for the dog. Her tail thumped when she saw Jillian.

"Uncle Terrance?" she called, but the house had an empty feeling to it.

Jillian looked out the window in time to see the police officer nudge Uncle Terrance, in handcuffs, into the back of the police car. Jillian bounced up and down on her toes. She had to do something. She ran out onto the porch to tell her that it had been a mistake, that it was her, Jillian, they were after, but it was too late. The police car was already driving away.

ALLISON ROLLED SUZANNE'S WHEELCHAIR DOWN THE HALL TO THE elevator, her brain numb after so many hours in the hospital. All she could see was white. White lights. White shiny floor. White coats.

"What's the matter with him?" Suzanne kept asking, and frankly, Allison didn't know how to answer. Grant had not returned to the hospital all day. Now Suzanne was being released to go home and he still wasn't there.

"The deposition must have gone on longer than he thought," Allison said, a lame excuse that even she didn't believe. Maybe he got hit by a car. That would be a legitimate reason, but then wouldn't he have come to the hospital with injuries?

Was he panicking because they'd had a scare with the baby, or over the thought that Suzanne would be on bed rest for months? In either case, you couldn't just abandon your pregnant wife. Allison's estimation of Grant, so high during those first weeks of *Annie Get Your Gun* rehearsals, had plummeted.

Men, she thought, thinking not just about Grant but about Nick and Ted. She still couldn't believe they had gone at it last night, two foolish middle-aged men wrestling in the snow. It was the duel she'd always hoped for, only it turned out to be idiotic instead of noble.

Breaking it off with Nick was arguably the smartest thing she had ever done in her life. As smart as it was stupid to have taken up with him. Sometimes she missed the excitement, and, frankly, the human contact, but she was firm in her resolve. Her desire was like the lingering effects of a cold, the last sniffles or coughs before you felt like you'd recovered—though she wondered how long it would take to really feel like herself again. Maybe she never would.

"Wait here," she told Suzanne, parking the wheelchair in the hospital lobby and heading out to the parking lot.

Allison plugged in her phone in the car. New-call messages popped onto the screen rapid fire, the same callers over and over: home, Ted, Jillian, Ted, Jillian. Allison felt bubbles of panic in her chest. She dialed her voice mail and listened. It was all so garbled. Jillian, crying, something about Terrance. Ted, weary, "the police station," and one from Grant, "mea culpa."

TED SCANNED THE POLICE STATION, LOOKING FOR TERRANCE. IT wasn't hard to find him. It was a quiet station, near the high-end shopping and restaurant district by the Metro, a place that probably only saw action on the weekends, when drunks and purse snatchers came out to play. Only one police officer seemed to be on duty, and she was on the phone.

Terrance was sitting on a bench by the window looking out at the street, calm. Ted sat down next to him. "Hey, pal."

"Seven people crossed at the intersection that time, Ted. The time before, it was only three."

Ted nodded.

"One lady ran across when the light was green for the cars, and everyone honked at her."

"How you doing, Terr?"

"Now it's the cars' turn."

They watched the cars go. Even Ted found it soothing.

"I did something bad," Terrance said after a while.

Ted nodded, wishing they could stay in this moment, the before moment, forever. The police officer had called him to explain.

"Six people that time, Ted," Terrance said. "Plus a dog."

"You didn't hurt her, did you, bro?"

Terrance said nothing.

"Just tell me you didn't hurt her."

"I didn't hurt her," he said.

Ted nodded, feeling relieved until he realized Terrance was just repeating his words. "Didn't hurt whom?" Ted said, testing him.

"Whom," Terrance said.

Sometimes he forgot just how disabled his brother was. He knew Terrance hadn't forgotten what had happened today—he remembered everything, from what he'd paid for a hamburger last week to the shirt he wore on their last birthday—but the order of the importance of things was shuffled in his mind. "Do you know why you're here?" Ted said. "At the police station?"

"I cut down the Christmas tree," Terrance said.

"What?"

"That was bad. The police lady came to the house."

"You cut down the Christmas tree?"

Terrance nodded.

"The town tree?"

"Yes."

"During the meeting?"

"Yes."

"What the heck, Terrance?" Ted felt for an instant, the first instant in his life, that he didn't know his brother. Until now he'd felt like they were the same person, a slight variation on the same soul. Maybe he'd been wrong in thinking he could never have hurt Lindy Cox. Maybe Terrance was capable of all kinds of things Ted couldn't fathom. "How could you, Terr? Did someone dare you? Or pay you? Did someone pay you?"

"It was Thomas."

"Thomas isn't real."

"I was just kidding, Ted."

"Don't kid."

"Ever?"

"Now. Don't kid now."

"I used Dad's saw."

"You got it out of the toolshed to *cut down the town Christmas tree*?"

"I'm a responsible carpenter, Ted. You are too. We're both responsible carpenters."

"That was not exactly being a responsible carpenter, Terrance! I don't think Dad would have been too happy about that! I think . . . I think he might have revoked your privileges."

It was a mean thing to say, a knife to the gut—but hadn't Terrance stabbed him in the back by cutting down the tree? Terrance had cut down the tree?!

"Why, Terr?" Ted's tone was harsh. He could hear it, but he couldn't help it.

Terrance's eyes brimmed. "Nick Cox decorated it, and you hate him. And trees grow, right, Ted? The town can plant a new one. Right? I did it for you. For brothers. Right, Ted?"

Ted put his head in his hands.

"Are you okay, Teddy?"

Ted reached out a hand and patted his brother's shoulder. Another well-meaning gesture gone wrong. It was the story of their lives. "Oh, Terrance."

"It's okay, right, Ted?"

"Yeah. It's okay. It's okay."

Terrance shuddered the way Jillian used to when she was little, when she'd just completed a long crying jag and was coming into herself again.

Ted would buy a new tree, and plant it, one that was already a good height, ten to twelve feet—make amends that way. The way Cox should have. It would be kind of embarrassing, but Ted could stand it for Terrance's sake. And it was just one tree. Cox was to blame for the bulk of the damage in town. He'd been the one to inspire Terrance. Terrance never would have thought of cutting down a tree if Cox hadn't been cutting down all the little ones. He was still the real culprit. Ted would catch him yet.

Meanwhile, there were more pressing matters at hand. "You didn't hurt anyone?"

He shook his head. "I was careful."

"I mean, that's all you did?"

Terrance shook his head no.

Ted sighed. "What else did you do?"

"I pulled up some little trees when I was mad," Terrance said.

Ted stood up, his arms flying in the air. "You've been cutting down the little trees too? Jeez, Terr. Why?"

"Was that bad? Trees grow, Ted."

"Yes. It's bad. It's very bad!"

Terrance tipped his head, the way Candy did sometimes, when she wanted to understand her human family. Ted softened. "It's not great, Terr, but it's not as bad as . . . did you hurt Lindy Cox?"

"Who?"

"The little girl. The Coxes' girl. The blond one who lives next door."

"Jillian's friend."

Ted frowned. "I suppose."

"When?"

"What do you mean, 'When'? Tell me everything you did today, Terr."

"I took the eight fifteen bus and then I transferred to the L-4 and I walked up Wisconsin Avenue and I came to the house and Grant made me eggs. Then I took a nap," he said. "A long one. That's because I stayed up till three. They had a *Beverly Hillbillies* marathon on TV. I watched till three o'clock in the morning."

"Then what?"

"When I woke up the police lady was there."

"That's all?" Ted wanted to laugh, to dance.

Terrance lowered his head. "I didn't get you an ice scraper. Want to go now and get one?"

"Soon," Ted said, hugging him. "We'll go get it soon."

KAYE MADE A BIG DINNER THAT NIGHT. A BIG, FABULOUS WELCOME dinner for the Davenport-Gardners, complete with jumbo shrimp and porterhouse steaks, an arugula-free salad and baked potatoes with sour cream and butter and fresh chives. She'd cooked it up in record time, chopping and marinating and broiling so fast it was a miracle nothing was frozen solid or burned. The food sat on the plates like a meal in a cooking magazine, beautiful and untouched by the people surrounding it. The only Davenport-Gardner in attendance was Adam.

Suzanne lay on the chaise in the den. She had an excuse not to be hungry, having just come back from the hospital. No one knew where Grant was. Nick had been the last person to talk to him early this morning, when he invited their family to stay with them. Grant seemed to have disappeared.

Adam put a big chunk of butter on his potato for the thrill of watching it melt, it looked like. Jakey never ate anything but mac and cheese, so it was no surprise that he didn't eat. He looked down, as though he was feeling sorry about something, but Kaye knew for a fact he just had a video game on his lap. Nick made up for his lack of eating by doing an extra amount of drinking. He might as well have put the bottle of wine to his lips and saved himself the bother of dirtying a glass, Kaye thought, holding out her glass for a refill.

Lindy's seat was empty. She was in her room. She was grounded for the rest of her life. That and whatever the police planned to do to her for lying to them. For a while she'd stomped around upstairs, screaming and making the dining room chandelier shake, but she was quiet now. She'd probably worn herself out and had fallen asleep, exhausted, like she used to when she was little.

Jillian, shivering and rattled looking, had come by the house earlier that day. Kaye had been so glad to see her—she'd missed her!—but Jillian wouldn't look her in the eye. She told Kaye the whole story, about skipping school, and how Mark let go of the tire swing too soon. Her uncle Terrance had spent the morning napping, not kidnapping. She and Mark had already told the police what had happened. Kaye, arguably more embarrassed than angry, dragged Lindy down to the police station where Lindy, cornered, told them she'd made the whole thing up. Kaye had done the wrong thing, turning Terrance in to the police. It had felt like the right thing at the time, but it had been wrong.

She tried to get the dinner conversation going. "How's school going, Adam? I hear you're back at school." "Anyone need salt?"— but her attempts fizzled. Nick poked at his meat tentatively, like maybe it wasn't dead yet.

Kaye, tears springing up in her eyes, loaded her plate and the kids' plates up her arm—she'd not been a waitress all those summers for nothing—and dumped them in the kitchen sink, hard. One plate split neatly down the middle. It made her feel like throwing them, really slamming them at the walls and windows, but it might scare little Adam. Instead she stuffed them in the trash can, plates, food, and all, pulling out a few good chunks of meat for Rex. She cleared the rest of the table, singing, "Don't get up, don't get up," as she removed forks and knives and water glasses, wineglasses and the butter and the sour cream and the extra potatoes and the salad bowl and the salt and pepper and threw them all into the trash. Then she tossed the broiling pan and the cocktail sauce jar in the trash too. The kitchen looked as good as it did after Carmen cleaned it.

Kaye went back out to the dining room, smiling a brittle smile. "He's free now, all charges dropped, so no harm done, right?"

The little boys and Nick looked at her, expressions blank.

Kaye wanted to pick up a chair and throw it, but you couldn't do that, could you? Throw $2,000 chairs? Oh, what was the use of it all? All the worry, all the buying and planning, and trying to be a good hostess and wife and mother. All that fuss for nothing. No one cared. She was like the maid. Undervalued. Replaceable.

She brought in dessert, a layer cake from the fancy bakery near the Metro, an oversize wonder of a cake, thick with chocolate frosting and huge, chocolate-covered strawberries on top. It said "Welcome home!" in red frosting.

"Terrance Miller is probably at home watching TV," Kaye said, trying to keep the tears out of her voice. "He's probably got his slippers on and his feet up and a bowl of popcorn on his lap. He probably doesn't even remember what happened to him. Because nothing happened to him! It was an honest mistake. That's all. We all make them." She smiled hard and went back to the kitchen. She ran the water so they wouldn't hear her sob.

So she'd screwed up. It wasn't like it was deliberate, though you'd have thought so from the black looks the Millers gave her at the police station. She hadn't lied or anything. She'd just tried to defend her daughter. It was Lindy who'd lied. Lindy who'd turned her into the neighborhood pariah, a laughingstock.

She wasn't going to give them any more to laugh about. She was going to get rid of her mammogram paintings before someone found them. She grabbed the purple lighter she'd found in Lindy's jeans pocket that afternoon when she went to do a load of wash— why did she have a lighter, the little sneak? Then she went downstairs and snatched the films off the light boxes, slid them out of drawers and into boxes, and heaved them into the back of the car. She dumped armload after armload of films, boxes of paints both used and untouched, brushes, cleaning solvents, you name it. Then she got behind the steering wheel and backed out.

Where was she going? She had no idea. She took a right on Wisconsin Avenue. The county dump was north, wasn't it? She typed "county dump" into Maps, but it didn't come up. There must be another name for it. County disposal heap or waste facility or something. She typed in everything she could think of, but there was nothing. She slammed the phone on the dashboard. Stupid thing. She pulled out into traffic again, and drove till she got on the highway. It felt good to be driving. She turned the music to something rhythmic that made the car thump. She got off in

Gaithersburg, where she thought the dump must be. That's where she'd have put it. She drove down Shady Grove Road, passing the hospital. Was it legal to put them in the hospital incinerator? Maybe she could burn them at a park.

She typed in "park," and drove to the nearest one, Seneca Creek. She drove past the trees that lined the long road into the park. A sign was up, but its lights were off. She could just make out the shape of the words: WINTER LIGHTS. The moon was out and surprisingly bright.

She didn't see anyone, but that didn't mean there weren't people here. Kids having a few beers, lovers in the woods. If someone saw her, they might report her as doing something suspicious. She drove slowly, watching for signs of life.

The displays were still up from the holidays but they weren't lit anymore. A teddy bear. A doll. A train. She imagined the signs all lit, all the beautiful colors, a wonderland of lights reflected in what was left of the snow.

She got out of the car at the playground. The swings cast long shadows in the moonlight. She sat on one, overlooking the lake down the hill. A lake, here, in the middle of nowhere. The reflection of the moon and the clouds played on the water's surface. She backed up on the swing and pumped her legs, like a kid. It was strange to be at a park at night. Cold and strange. She felt oddly awake. As though she'd been asleep for years.

The White Elephant, she thought, out of the blue. She could take the films to the new house and burn them out back. Silly of her to drive all this way when the answer was two houses away.

By the time she got back in the car, it was nearly ten o'clock. Had Nick and the kids wondered where she'd gone? Probably not. She rolled down the windows on the highway. "I'm here!" she shouted into the rushing air. She sped down the highway, hoping, in a way, to get caught, but no one seemed to notice she was doing eighty miles per hour. Ninety.

Before long she was back in Willard Park, bumping over the speed bumps. She parked in front of the White Elephant, and took a box of films to the backyard.

She held the lighter to the edge of a film, experimenting. The film curled and melted where the flame met the plastic. It smelled terrible. She hadn't expected that. She tamped the melting film against the dirt. She would have to do it inside or someone would notice the stench. They might report it. She tried the kitchen door-knob. It turned. She was in luck.

She lugged the films down to the basement. It took several trips to get everything in from the car. It was hot work, tiring. When she was done she sat beside them in the dark, the moon making shadows of her and her art supplies. She'd get rid of it all and make a new start. She and Lindy both would. The two of them would start over, together. Maybe she'd take her away for a mother-daughter weekend, something to recharge their batteries, a spa or the beach. She opened the windows before she opened the turpentine. She'd always hated the smell of turpentine, but it smelled like real art and she liked that about it. She opened the canister and doused the cardboard, breathing through her mouth, then she lit the lighter and set it to the edge of a film.

The flames crawled and jumped. They slid onto the cuff of her shirt, a pretty white blouse with wide sleeves she'd worn for the welcome dinner. She tried to beat it out, but that didn't help, so she tore her shirt off and threw it, scared. It was a fireball in the air. She threw down some of the films, hoping to stamp out the fire, but the flames, fueled by the turpentine, leaped and spread. Her heart knocked around, making it hard to breathe. She started coughing. She whacked the flames with a film but it only made things worse. The basement was bright with fire and smoke. What were you supposed to do in smoke? *Cover your face with a wet cloth and crawl down low.* But there wasn't any water. Her mother used to tell her to sing when she was afraid, but it was hard to think straight much less sing. She found the wall and followed it around with her hands till she got to the back door of the basement. She turned the knob, hot from the fire, and rushed out of the house and into the yard, into the cold, dark night.

ALLISON SAT ON HER YOGA MAT IN THE LIVING ROOM, LEGS CROSSED, eyes closed, listening to the quiet thrumming all around her. Oh, but it was magnificent. A return to the old days, before her home became a boardinghouse. They were all gone: Grant, Suzanne, Adam, and even Terrance. Ted had invited Terrance to stay overnight with them after his exhausting day at the police station, but he declined, opting to go home after dinner.

"Home?" Ted had said. "This is home."

"It's *your* home," Terrance said.

"But it's your home too," Ted said. "It'll always be your home."

Terrance tilted his head at him, thoughtful. "Can we stop and get a bag of chips at the Safeway on the way home, Ted?"

Terrance had moved on. He had a home of his own, a life of his own. All he wanted was to go back to his routine. It was hard for Ted to accept.

That was all Allison wanted too. To get back to her routine. Suzanne had been afraid Allison's feelings would be hurt if they moved to the Coxes'—especially after what happened with Terrance—but far from it. It was all Allison could do not to laugh when Suzanne apologized to her. Let Nick pay for their sins for a while! She was all for it!

Allison took a deep breath through her nose and breathed out through her mouth, sinking deeper into calmness. Ted was off reading the paper somewhere, Jillian doing her homework in the dining room. All was as it should be.

She pressed back to downward-facing dog. Her eyes landed on an envelope on the floor in the front hallway. How long had that been lying there? She went over to look. It was addressed to her. "For ALISON MILLER." Allison with one *L*. "TOP SECRET." Top secret? It had something to do with Nick, she just knew it. Her indiscretion would haunt her for the rest of her life.

She ripped open the envelope to find an eight-by-ten glossy photograph of a woman sitting on a red couch. She wore a pink bustier with black laces up the front, pushing large breasts skyward. Then came scanty black panties and a pair of high black patent leather boots. The picture had been folded and it was torn at the corner, as though someone had taken a bite out of it.

Allison turned it over, looking for an explanation, but there was nothing to explain this woman, whose hair was tousled about her head as though she'd been in a windstorm. She had a terrific figure, but her face was mannish, a little puffy, her hair a little too brightly hued to be natural. She wasn't exactly young, though younger, certainly, than Allison herself. Her lips were painted a garish red, and they were open slightly, revealing the lurid tip of her pink tongue.

Allison turned the envelope upside down and shook it for more clues. A scrap of purple paper slid out. The note read: "TEDS GOT A GIRLFRIEND."

Ted? Was this a joke? Who in the world had pushed this into their home? She opened the front door, but no one was out there.

She pressed back to downward dog again and tried to focus on her breath, but she couldn't stop seeing the face of the woman in the photo. Was it someone at the university who was trying to blackmail Ted? Some malcontent whose story hadn't run in the university magazine? She moved into plank, then all the way down to the mat, and slid up into cobra.

Maybe it wasn't a joke at all. Maybe he had a girlfriend. If so, it served her right. And it would explain his lack of interest in sex. She pressed back to downward dog, then jumped to the front of the mat.

Ted walked in the room. "Hi there."

"What the hell do you want?" Allison said.

He started. "I thought yoga was supposed to be relaxing."

"Who's this?" she said, picking up the photo.

"Playmate of the Month?"

She studied his face. "You have no idea?"

"Should I?"

She showed him the note.

"They forgot the apostrophe." He frowned at the photo, scrutinizing it.

"Enough already," Allison said, snatching it away.

"It's not very well done."

"What?"

"Look at it. It's completely fake." They took it into the kitchen, where the light was better.

"What's fake?" Jillian said from the dining room.

"Nothing," Ted and Allison said in unison.

The face really didn't match the rest of it. The face was crisp, the rest of the photo fuzzy, romantic boudoir photo–like.

"It's a joke," Ted said. "Photoshopped. And poorly, at that."

"What?" Jillian said.

"Never mind," Allison said.

The phone rang. Allison answered. It was Suzanne, apologizing for calling so late, apologizing, again, for moving out. "Let it go,"

Allison said. "You sound terrible. Want company? I'll come over. I'll bring something that'll make you laugh."

SUZANNE LAY IN THE DARK AT THE COXES', WAITING FOR ALLISON TO arrive. She tried to make out the shapes in the room that had been set up for her: the television, the stocked miniature refrigerator she couldn't reach, the women's magazines—packed with recipes and household tips. Kaye obviously had tried hard to make things nice. She popped in and out of the room all afternoon, trying to make her feel at home. "I'm just tired," Suzanne finally managed. "I need to sleep."

Kaye nodded. "Of course. I know what you mean. Sometimes I just like being alone, too, but it's hard, isn't it? When you have a family?" She'd gone on and on, maniacally, until the doorbell rang. Jillian had come by, rescuing her. After that there was talking, then yelling, mother and daughter yelling—was that what Suzanne had to look forward to?—and then Kaye and the girls had left, leaving the house quiet—a relief.

Suzanne didn't need a girls' dorm room and a sorority sister right now. She needed a husband who was willing to step up to the plate, a man she could count on. Instead she had absolutely no idea where he was. Grant had gone AWOL when their baby's life was at risk. Calls went unanswered, texts ignored.

How was she supposed to do it all? Take care of Adam, fight with the insurance company, make a baby, and work on her business—from a bed? Four months felt infinite. Impossible. She could hardly eke out an entire night.

She felt like calling her mother and crying. Instead she fell into a heavy sleep. She had a vague memory of Kaye bringing in a tray of food. Could that be right? Maybe she'd just wished for that. When she woke up again, her mouth was dry and it was night.

The house was quiet except for the sound of a television somewhere. "Grant," she called. But there was nothing. Desperate, she
had called Allison.

"Yoo-hoo," Allison called. "Yoo-hoo," Suzanne called back until Allison found her. Allison turned on the overhead light. "This
is nice."

"I want to go home," Suzanne said, blinking.

Allison held an envelope in front of her. "Check this out," she
said, shaking out a glossy photo.

Suzanne took the picture from the envelope and studied it.
What?

She scrambled to sit upright. It couldn't be. But it was. It was a
boudoir shot of Grant's friend Marie.

A door flew open somewhere, and someone was running into
the house and screaming. Kaye appeared in just her bra and pants,
her hair wild, her face red. "Fire!" she yelled. "Fire!"

JILLIAN WAS WASHING HER FACE AT THE BATHROOM SINK WHEN SHE
heard the sirens. She turned off the water to hear if they were getting closer or farther away. They were getting closer. "Mom?" she
called.

"Sounds nearby," her father said, from the kitchen.

Her mother ran into the house from somewhere—where?—
and grabbed her camera. "Fire!" she called.

"Where?" Jillian cried. "Here?"

"Next door!" she said, running out again.

Jillian and her dad put coats and boots over their pajamas, and
hooked Candy up to her leash. It was exciting. Jillian had always
wanted to see a fire up close—but next door? It was so near you
could feel the heat of it from the yard.

The White Elephant was burning.

The firefighters ordered everyone across the street, away from the flames, away from the fire hoses and spraying arcs of water. The trucks were loud and there were bright lights on the house, like it was a movie set. It felt like Halloween and the Fourth of July all at once, but with an air of unpredictability that neither of those holidays had.

People ran out from their houses to see. Mr. Cox was yelling, directing the firefighters. Jillian felt as though she'd been put under a spell. A terrible, gorgeous spell. "Is our house going to burn down?" she asked her father.

He put his arm around her shoulder. "No."

They stared at the wonder of it. The trucks and speakers were loud. Her mother was taking pictures. Jillian watched how the fire poured. It really did pour. And it stank. It wasn't like the smell of a fire in a fireplace.

Mark and his mother arrived. "Awesome," he said.

"Can you believe it?" she said.

"Think Lindy set it?"

"She must be loving it," Jillian said. She hated Lindy for what she'd done today. Accusing Uncle Terrance of kidnapping her? What a mean and selfish person she was to do that to someone so innocent and good. Jillian looked around for her, idly, cautiously.

"Good no one was living there," Jillian's father said.

People speculated about whether it was the wiring or if someone had set it deliberately or what. "The second house to be gutted in just a couple weeks," someone murmured.

"Where is she?" Jillian said.

"Who?" Mark said.

"Lindy."

Mark looked around.

Jillian's heart, beating a little quickly already, began to gallop. "Where is she?" She said it louder, her voice reedy.

"Who?" her father said.

"Lindy. Lindy!" she yelled.

"Lindy!" Mark called.

Jillian called her phone. Lindy's message was simply, "You know what to do"—but she didn't know what to do. She called the Coxes' landline. No one answered. "Lindy!" Jillian shouted. Flames were continuing to gather, to reach and climb into the night.

"Where's Lindy?" Other people picked up her cry. Where is she? People called for her. *Lindy, Lindy.*

"Where is she?" Lindy's dad yelled, sounding mad, Kaye next to him, a look of misery on her face, Jakey's hand in hers. They all looked at Jillian as if she knew the answer.

And she did. Or, she was afraid she did.

"I think she's in there," Jillian said. She said it quietly at first, then louder, screaming, "She's in the house!"

Kaye started shrieking, "No! No she's not! No!" She shook her head like she was trying to get it off her neck, then she let go of Jakey's hand and ran toward the burning house, crying out in anguish, a cry that was a plea to the far ends of the universe. It was the most desperate sound Jillian had ever heard.

Mr. Cox ran after her. One of the firefighters tackled him as he tried to get inside. The crowd was roaring along with the fire now, screaming and roaring.

Jillian, screaming, crying, pointed to where Lindy might be, in the house, in the fort. "There's someone in there! There's someone in there!" she kept yelling, till a ladder was set up to the second floor. A firefighter climbed up in mask and heavy gear, smashing the glass with an ax and climbing in.

What if she died? What if Lindy died? Tears blurred her eyes. She kept wiping them away so she could see clearly, to maybe see Lindy first, to help her, but they kept coming, flowing down as the fire flowed up. The firefighter was in the house for a long time. Jillian's parents were alongside her, their arms around her.

"Shhh," her mother said, patting her hair. "It's going to be all right."

"You don't know that!" Jillian yelled, wanting her mother to say, *Yes I do. I know that.* But she didn't.

Then, after forever, the firefighter was coming back out the window, something in his arms. Someone! Jillian wept with relief, until she realized that Lindy wasn't reaching her arms around the firefighter's neck, but was flopped back like a dead person. Then an ambulance siren broke through the other noise and Lindy was loaded into the back and taken away.

19

It was warm, springlike, even though the calendar claimed it was winter. It had been unseasonably balmy for the past few weeks. Instead of snow, there were thunderstorms. Instead of a winter sun that kept its distance, like an acquaintance trying to keep you at bay, it loomed and pulsated, sending mothers for sunscreen and hats—both of which Jillian declined with a sharp, "Mom! I'm thirteen!" She was now. A teenager at long last.

People were saying the thaw was because of global warming, but Jillian knew it had nothing to do with that. It was because of the fire. Everything had melted since then. The anger that had been churning up in the neighborhood since the Coxes had moved to town had gone up in flames along with the White Elephant. Warring neighbors were friends again. Well, most of them. Some. A few at least.

Furniture was spread out all over the Coxes' lawn in the shapes of rooms, like someone was playing a practical joke—only it wasn't a joke. The Coxes were selling their furniture, nearly all of it. The house they were moving to in South Carolina, the house Kaye had grown up in, only had three little bedrooms.

Lindy called it a miniature house. "Like yours," she told Jillian with a laugh that made her wince, the movement pulling at the burns around her mouth.

Lindy still looked red and raw, but better than she had a month ago, when Jillian visited her at the hospital. At that time she'd been on a ventilator and wrapped in bandages. Being on the burn unit was like being in a nightmare. You could hear children screaming, like they were being tortured. Which they kind of were. Being burned was pretty much the worst torture ever. Lindy had had some skin grafts where the burns were the worst, and would have more surgery, including plastic surgery, but she would likely always be scarred inside and out. She was on all kinds of medication for pain and itching.

Kaye was on medication too. She looked terrible these days, skinny and sad. Her hands shook and her eyes darted back and forth, as if she was constantly on the lookout for unknown dangers. "I almost lost you," she told Lindy all the time, patting her like a baby where she wasn't burned, and Lindy let her, without complaint. When she asked Lindy if she would ever forgive her, Lindy told her there was nothing to forgive. "It was my fault I was in the house. I snuck out. It was my own fault," she said, drawing on a maturity she seemed to have acquired during her weeks in the hospital.

"What's wrong with your face?" Rebecca Thompson asked. "Rebecca!" her father said, shushing her, and Lindy, being Lindy, said, "What's wrong with *yours*?" Then she gave Rebecca her pick of the American Girl dolls for fifteen dollars. The Odinga sisters hauled away her purple beanbag chair and Amanda Giannangeli held her pink chandelier over her head like a sparkly hat. Moms scooped up great armfuls of children's clothes from the piles spread out on blankets on the grass.

Jillian lay on Lindy's bed—too big for Lindy's room down on the island; Mark lay beside her, like they were an old married couple.

"Eight dollars," Lindy said to Nora McConnell, who wanted the flowered pillows Jillian and Mark were using to prop themselves up on the bed, their sketch pads resting on their legs.

"But I said ten dollars," Nora said. She was seven, and missing so many teeth it was hard to understand her. "I said I'd pay ten."

"Five dollars, and that's my final offer," Lindy said. Nora snatched the pillows from behind Mark's and Jillian's heads without another word. Their heads thumped down on the mattress. "Hey. You made me mess up," Mark said.

He and Jillian were drawing pictures of squirt guns. Well, squirt *creatures*. Suzanne had told them she'd pay them for any designs she turned into squirt guns for Squirts for Squirts, her company that she was working on while she was on bed rest, waiting for the baby to come. Mark was designing a dragon gun that spat water instead of fire, Jillian a spitting frog.

"You're not a very good businesswoman," Jillian told Lindy.

"It's more fun this way." Then, "You guys are going to visit me, promise?"

Mark and Jillian groaned. "We already told you." Jillian wanted to. She liked the sound of the words "sea isle." She imagined sand and palm trees and misty, salty air. She pictured the three of them making sandcastles and biking to the market for ice cream once Lindy was well enough. She'd saved Lindy's life, and that gave them a bond that might last their whole lives.

Uncle Terrance forgave Lindy when she apologized after she got out of the hospital, and probably would have even if she hadn't given him homemade chocolate chip cookies. They were perfect: big and chewy and packed with chocolate chips. "You totally did

not make these," Jillian said, and Lindy admitted that she hadn't.
"My dad did," she said, which was probably a lie, too, but who
cared? They tasted better than Lucy's.

Lindy was going to see a psychiatrist in South Carolina. Her
dad had worked this out to keep her out of juvie for lying to the
police. "It's not like I need it, but maybe my mom does. Maybe if
I go, my mom'll go," she said, again drawing on that newfound
wisdom. She and her father were going to paint her new room in
the new house together. Not one of his workers, she pointed out,
but her actual father. She kept showing Jillian the deep blue paint
swatch, like it was a diamond ring.

Adam leaped onto the bed like a baby bird falling from the
sky, landing between Jillian and Mark with a bounce.

"Hey," Mark said.

Jillian tickled Adam, who shook with laughter.

"What do you want, Adam?" Lindy said. "You can have anything you want for one dollar."

"This bed!" he said. "Can I, Grammy?"

"I think that's a wonderful idea! But Mommy makes the decisions," she said. She was so nice. She was living with Adam and his
mom now. They were staying on at the Coxes', their furniture—
which had filled their old house—looking a little lost in just a few
of the Coxes' enormous rooms.

"He can have it," Lindy said. "But he has to jump on it first, to
see if it's springy enough."

Adam started jumping, bouncing Mark and Jillian onto the
grass.

"Special sale!" Lindy yelled. "Anything purple is free for the
next ten minutes." A band of little girls came running over.

"I wish I were moving too," Mark said as he and Jillian headed
toward another furniture grouping.

They sat down on an L-shaped leather couch and put their feet up on the glass coffee table.

"But it's never going to happen. I will never move out west and I will never have a horse. Nothing will ever change."

"You're going to a dude ranch for vacation this summer," Jillian reminded him. "That's new. That's, like, amazing."

He shrugged as if it wasn't that big a deal, but his expression betrayed him. "In Montana. For a week. Just me and my mom . . . and her cell phone," he said, glum again.

"Maybe you could bribe a horse to step on it."

"I'll bring extra carrots."

"There's always college."

"What?"

"You could go away to college," she said, but it was a lame suggestion. College was years away. An endless stretch of time.

"What about you?"

"We're not going anywhere," Jillian said.

"What if terrorists attack Washington? What if there are dirty bombs and smallpox spores? You'd go then," Mark said.

"That's not going to happen."

"The countryside would be safer."

"We're safe," Jillian said, and in that moment, she felt as though they were.

"Instead of knocking down trees, I should have made bomb threats," Mark said.

"That was you?"

"Your uncle too. We ran into each other a couple of times. He's cool."

"Uncle Terrance?" The idea of the two of them in the park, pulling up trees, made Jillian laugh. "Why?"

"Something my mother said."

"What?"

He shrugged. "Never mind."

"What?"

"How the trees were half the charm, and we'd have to move if people cut them down."

"So you thought you'd yank them all up? That's so stupid."

He shrugged. "Yeah. I guess."

She swatted him with her sketch pad. "It's not so bad here."

"Some things are okay," he said, swatting her back, and Jillian had a feeling that one of those things might just be her.

TED SAT ON THE PORCH, LOOKING UP FROM HIS BOOK NOW AND THEN to see the progression of the Coxes' yard sale. Ed Zyck loaded an easy chair into his trunk. Margaret Chen admired a TV. He'd imagined this scenario when the Davenport-Gardners' house was demolished on New Year's Day, and here it was, really happening.

He turned the page of the book on his lap, *Trees of North America*. He was in his element. He ought to have become a botanist or a historian, some kind of a researcher, instead of a hack writer who churned out stories about Foggy Bottom University bores. Then the thought struck him: he was finally going to write a class note for the alumni magazine. He had a new position in town and he was proud of it.

Ted had been appointed the official steward of White Elephant Park, the new town park that was to rise from the ashes of the house which—for now—still occupied the quarter-acre plot in charred chunks. Cox had sold the land back to the town at a bargain-basement price, with the understanding that the town would be responsible for cleanup. Ted's job was to choose the trees and plants, to put out bids and coordinate the planting. Kids would get student-service-learning hours for planting and tending to the park after all of the toxic material had been professionally removed.

There was going to be a theatrical fund-raiser for the park in the spring. The cast of *Annie Get Your Gun* had reunited and was back in rehearsals. Well, most of it had reunited. The role of Frank was going to be played by Phil who, along with Valeria and Sofia, was coming home for a visit. He was learning the songs on his own and would be taught simple blocking when he got back. Allison had offered the role of Annie to Valeria, but Valeria said something in Spanish that clearly meant "no chance, sucker," so Allison walked around the house mumbling her lines to herself and practicing song-and-dance routines. Ted had even joined the cast as a cowboy.

What would Thomas think? he asked himself. The answer was, *Awesome*. Thomas would think, *Fucking awesome*. He was channeling Thomas now. Thinking in words not he, but Thomas, would have used. And he'd have said it about Terrance, too. The twins might be able to do away with the big guy before long if things kept going in this direction.

The mail truck pulled up to the house. Ted retrieved the mail and sifted through it, looking for a promised postcard from Terrance, who was in New York with Free to Be Me. It was the social group's first excursion farther than mini golf in Rockville. So far he had texted Ted nearly hourly, and sent multiple photos, including one of himself in a Statue of Liberty hat and another of him wearing a Godzilla T-shirt that said I ATE NEW YORK. I hope you don't have indigestion, Ted texted back. It's just a joke, Ted, Terrance wrote. New York is too big to eat.

The postcard was at the bottom of today's mail, a picture of the Empire State Building. Terrance had drawn a little stick-figure man, waving from the top of the building. On the other side it said, "Looking out for you, bro." Ted had to smile.

Ted looked up to see Nick Cox heading up the walkway with his now infamous snowblower. Ted could feel his stomach tighten.

"A little gift for you, Miller," he said.

"Thanks. I guess," Ted said. "You can have my shovel."

"But it doesn't snow in the sunny south."

"Not for snow. For sand. Or to get yourself out of the next hole you dig yourself into."

Cox laughed. "No need. I got big plans."

"Mansions?"

"A water-treatment plant," he said. "Or cotton. I'm considering growing cotton."

"Cotton?"

"It's worked before."

Ted was about to say something about how well that had worked before, but thought better of it. They shook hands and Ted watched him retreat down the walkway toward his yard, rapidly clearing of oversize televisions and overstuffed couches.

ALLISON WALKED AMID THE COXES' OUTDOOR ROOMS TRYING OUT chairs like Goldilocks, imagining herself into the kind of woman who would want the furniture that was set out here: a lamp that was more valuable than the contents of her entire first floor, a chair so big and cushioned you had to put up a good fight with it to get up again. But her heart wasn't in it. She couldn't stop looking at Kaye, sitting on the porch with her hand in Jakey's. She looked so small and beaten down, a ghost of the bubbly blonde she had been before the fire. She rarely left the house these days.

Allison felt to blame, knowing the feeling was irrational. Obviously nearly killing her daughter had sent Kaye over the edge—but she still couldn't rid herself of a feeling of culpability. Her lust for Nick had turned to wonder at her own folly in the nearly two months since their fling had ended, but her feelings of guilt and shame held fast. Did what she did make her a bad person? Did it erase forty-plus years of trying to be reasonably good? Could she make up for it by being extra mindful for the rest of her life? She didn't know. She just knew that she had hurt Kaye Cox, even if Kaye didn't know it. And she hoped she never would know. Kaye had suffered enough.

She and Nick had met at the Sawyers' one last time after the fire, not to be intimate in their old way—Allison had made it very clear that was never going to happen again—but for a different kind of intimacy. Nick had cried about Lindy, and Allison had patted his back, let him release feelings that, she told him, he should start sharing with Kaye. He could start anew, she told him, be a better person. And if he could, maybe she could. Maybe redemption was a possibility.

She bought a tree-shaped cookie at Lucy's table, along with a cup of hazelnut tea and a lemon bar to take to Suzanne. Lucy had put up the old bulletin board on an easel and had tacked quotes to it: *Character is like a tree and reputation like a shadow. The shadow is what we think of it; the tree is the real thing*, and *Love is flowerlike; friendship is like a sheltering tree*, among a bunch of others.

"So you're WP Tree Poet?" Allison said.

Lucy raised and lowered her eyebrows, neither admitting nor denying it, but definitely capitalizing on it. Now people were only allowed to post beautiful things on the big bulletin board in back of the café. "I'm reversing its karma," she said, offering Allison an index card upon which to write her own sentiment.

Allison wrote, "And the tree was happy," and tacked it up with a blue-tipped thumbtack.

She poked amid the open boxes of plates and glasses, place mats, and flatware, old DVDs, computer games, and bed linens. When she spied a flat white box under one of the couches, she pulled it out, opening it to find poster-sized black plastic sheets like photo negatives on steroids.

She took one out and held it up to the sun. What she saw was both beautiful and strange. It was a negative of some sort, amorphous, yet familiar. It was painted in fantastic colors, like a haunted sunrise, with yellows, oranges, and green amid the gray and black. She set it aside, and pulled out another. This one was a melee of blues and greens, more like an ocean than the sky. There were dozens of similar negatives. She was about to take out another, when she heard a shrill "Noooooooooo" from across the lawn.

Allison looked up to see Kaye running toward her, a wild expression on her face. What in the world? Allison moved out of the way just as Kaye skidded onto the box, belly down.

"This is all trash. It shouldn't be out here. I missed a few boxes, that's all." Kaye sat on the box, then grabbed the two films Allison had and held them to her chest.

"They don't look like trash," Allison said.

"Well, they are."

"What are they?"

"Nothing. They're nothing."

"They're beautiful."

"Please don't make fun of me," Kaye said.

"Make fun . . . ?"

"Just forget you ever saw them. Promise me." She looked ashamed.

"But they're incredible. They ought to be in a gallery or something. Where did you get them?"

Kaye whispered something.

"What?"

"I made them," she said, her voice just audible now.

"You made these?"

"Hush!" she said. "Please?"

"They're amazing, Kaye."

Kaye looked at Allison with skeptical eyes.

"I didn't know you were an artist."

Kaye frowned. "I am?" She blinked back tears.

Allison bought two of Kaye's pieces for far more money than she would ever admit to Ted. She had insisted on the price, and Kaye had thrown in a light box as a bonus, for being the first person ever to buy a Kaye Cox original "mammographic." Kaye smiled, showing a welcome glimmer of her old self. Others came over to see what the fuss was about, and she sold several more, rapid fire, everyone afraid they were going to miss out on Something Big. And maybe they were right. Only time would tell.

Maybe Allison could sell her work, too, she thought. Not just the family portraits, but her town photos—of Willard Park at its most perfect and at its less-than-perfect. One of her shots of the White Elephant fire had been printed in the *Post*'s Metro section, and another in the county *Journal*. Maybe Lucy would hang them at the café. Maybe Allison didn't need to publish a book to feel like she had "made" it. It might not be the Venice Biennale, or her own company, but it was something. Just finding moments of beauty in life was something. Just living and appreciating was something. Maybe it was enough.

Allison passed the Coxes' stone lions on her way into the house—well, one lion, the other, apparently, had sold—and called for Suzanne. No one answered, but Allison ventured in anyway, knowing there was nowhere else Suzanne could be. Allison could hear her talking in her professional voice from deep inside the house.

She found Suzanne propped up in her bed, her belly a growing mound, surrounded by myriad papers and her laptop. She was on the phone, but she waved to Allison.

"By Monday," Suzanne said. "I'll expect to hear from you then."

Suzanne was working frantically these days, hoping to have a few un-squirt guns, as she was calling them, ready for the summer season—now only a few months away.

Allison gave her the lemon bar. Suzanne hung up the phone and smiled. "Bless you, Allison Miller. How's Adam doing?"

"Jumping on a bed, last I saw. With Grammy at his side."

Suzanne crossed herself. "My dear, sainted mother."

Grammy had gotten Adam to promise to come to her for help with *everything* during the next few months, so Mommy could rest, and Adam promised he would. Sometimes it got lonely, Suzanne admitted, but she was getting some work done for a change.

"It's just temporary. Remind me that it's just temporary." Suzanne called Allison several times a day to ask for reassurance.

"It's just temporary," Allison said. "Everything is."

Temporary, ephemeral, fleeting. Nothing lasted. Maybe that was good. The fight over the future of Willard Park had loomed so large for a while, until, suddenly, it didn't. After the fire, the town council unanimously agreed to adopt the building regulations of another similar town nearby, thereby ending the threat of mass mansionization. Problem solved.

But there were other, less solvable, problems. Like Grant. He'd shown up at the Coxes' two days after the fire. He wouldn't say where he had been. "It doesn't matter," he'd said, but it did to Suzanne. He'd tried to explain away the boudoir shot as a joke, but Suzanne wasn't having it. She told him to leave and never come back—and so far, he hadn't. The longer he was gone, the better her case for abandonment, Suzanne said, having consulted a lawyer. It seemed clear which way that marriage was going.

Her and Ted's was less certain. Valeria, who never called, made a video call in the middle of the night, Paris time, to offer her best-friend opinion after Allison finally told her about Ted's holiday from sex. "No sex? Are you kidding me?"

They'd done regular video chats since then, and one audio chat, during which Allison told her about Nick. She'd been afraid to do it face-to-face, not wanting to see disappointment, or even disgust, on Valeria's face, but Valeria surprised her by telling her about rumblings in her own marriage. Ted would have to agree to go to therapy with Allison. She would do her part if he did his. If he forgave her when she told him what she'd done. There were a lot of "ifs." There were no guarantees.

Allison went back home, to find Ted on the porch. He showed her the snowblower and she showed him Kaye's artwork.

"I'm going to miss those guys," Ted said.

Allison laughed. "You are?"

"No," he admitted.

She sat beside him, joining him in watching the goings-on next door. A pickup truck pulled up. A man stepped out of the driver's side, and got a sign out of the back. He hammered it into the ground in front of the Coxes' house.

FOR SALE, the sign said, and there was Nina's smiling face, in a photo Allison had taken.

The hammering stopped. And there was silence. The neighborhood had, for now, returned to silence.

Acknowledgments

So many people helped bring this book into the world! White-elephant-size thanks to one and all.

First, special thanks to my amazing agent, Suzanne Gluck, who somehow was unfazed by the fact that I inadvertently named all of my characters after members of her family and fulfilled thirty years' worth of dreams. Equally special thanks to Megan Lynch, my fantastic editor, whose editing brilliance gave the book the extra shimmer it needed. You are my dream team. I could not be more grateful.

Sincere thanks as well to all of the talented, dedicated, and kind people I've worked with at Ecco and WME, including but not limited to Dan Halpern, Sonya Cheuse, Meghan Deans, Miriam Parker, Nyamekye Waliyaya, Dale Rohrbaugh, Victoria Mathews, Sara Birmingham, and Renata De Oliveira at Ecco; and Tracy Fisher, Sylvie Rabineau, Matilda Forbes Watson, Alina Flint, Andrea Blatt, and Jamie Carr at WME.

Thank you to Allison Saltzman for the pitch-perfect cover and to Roger Ycaza for the little houses; thank you to Ilsa Brink, website designer extraordinaire.

Thank you to my family:

To my mother, Isabel, who is always there for me.

To Ethan and Sylvie, who watched me write for years without ever suggesting I give it up already—offering love, encouragement, and understanding all the while. Extra thanks to you, Sylvie, for all of your original art.

To my brother Kenny, the wise model for Terrance, who reminds me every day that kindness is what it's all about.

To my brother Stephen and my sister-in-law Jeanne, my niece Natasha, and my nephew Austin. To my cousins Robin and Holly—an extra shout-out to Robin for providing me with a New York home and the glam author photo. Canine thanks to Ginger, who made sure I got out for walks and offered a belly to rub during the long writing process.

Thank you to Jeannie Zusy—BFF, sister, writing twin—for love and friendship and unparalleled support since we were two years old. May we forever meet each other halfway.

To dear friends who helped in countless ways, supporting me at every turn: D.C. sister Cari Shane, California sister Ann Shulman, Spiderwoman Mary Koles, peace-loving Cheryl Dodwell, and best-ever-neighbor Audrey Singer. To the lovely and ever-gracious Susan Coll, who took me by the hand and led me over the wall. Grazie mille to Diana Meyer-Buchanan for a room of my own in Besacio, Switzerland, and to the rest of the Baum-Hackenberg crew. In special memory of Sylvie Hackenberg. Thanks to Cackalacky Michael Durbin, aesthetic magician Anna Kahoe, and my beloved yogi tribe: David Zyck, Susan Fensterheim, Cecile Giannangeli, Michaela Genitheim, Shannon Sharma, and the rest of the One Aum crew. Thank you to Lauren Cerand. Thank you to Siri, who heard "Happy Halloween" as "Gary Holloway" and therein named Allison's ex; look for another appearance in Jeannie Zusy's next book. Thank you to all of the more seasoned writers and bookish folks in D.C., New York, and beyond who so generously took me under their wings and to the debut writers who flapped along beside me—newfound friends all. Thank you to my yoga students and to everyone else who has been there for me in ways big and small throughout this long journey.